D0505754

STANDING TALL

James Wigfall

PAGE PUBLISHING, INC.
Conneaut Lake, PA

First originally published by Page Publishing 2021

ISBN 978-1-6624-3486-0 (pbk)
ISBN 978-1-6624-3487-7 (digital)

Printed in the United States of America

III

CHAPTER I

One Night—Father

"The war changed him, I heard." Like summer thunderstorms, rumors roll up and down the avenues of my Charleston suburb, West Ashley. Gossip become fact even if it is the furthest thing from the truth. There's nothing that I dislike more than gossip.

That day, the presence of Sergeant Arthur Wiggins seemed to precede his physical return. Everyone murmured, whispered, and gossiped. Bizarre occurrences punctuated the morning and afternoon—an old cat perished in our backyard, the tea kettle boiled in half the time, our foyer was filled with a ring of a dozen cicadas.

Every ten seconds or so, the call of a big, fat cicada overlapped a small one's, the sound curling its way into the depths of our house like a well-tossed fishing line. I peered outside at the hidden insects. They were tucked away behind leaves of the Spanish moss-covered magnolias, old oaks, and palmettos that lined our block.

Daylight begins to falter while we sit in the living room. My sisters and I are on an off-white couch facing the front windows. Fresh flowers rest in a pot on the table, and a large reading chair sits in one corner of the room. It hasn't been used in quite some time.

I look over at the mantle. The same pictures that I've seen for the past few years are there—a wedding picture of my parents, Loretta and Arthur Wiggins, a picture of me and my sisters during the holidays, and one of my youngest sister posing in a tutu. A particular picture, however, one of my father, always captures my imagination more than the others.

3

It's him in his military uniform, looking straight at the camera. To me, nothing about the picture is out of the ordinary, but the contrast between the wedding photo, his smile with his two front teeth popping out, and the depth of his severe expression in his uniform catches me, taps me on the shoulder like a sneaky kid in cops and robbers.

It was as if he was forcing a presence in one picture and concealing it in the other. There was less life or less of something of a human nature in this picture. Anyway, both of these Arthurs were unlike any father I had known. Each time he left the household for the war, he changed upon return. This was true, as gossip said. It was just, this time, he wasn't returning from war.

Day finally gave in to night, and suddenly, headlights swelled on the front windows. "He's here, darlings. He's here." My mother scurried to the front door, turned the handle, and opened it. We knew he would return today, but we didn't know it would be as late as dusk.

My father, Mr. Arthur Wiggins, with the porch light illuminating his face from behind, walks through the door, engulfed in shadow. Rather than a man returning home from his station, he looks immortal like a deity or a demigod of lost mythology. It has been a long time—two years to be exact—since he last lumbered through our foyer.

"Welcome home, Arthur," Loretta says. She leans in, and I assume they hug and kiss on the cheek. I can't see from my position.

Then I see his hand behind mother's head, and he says, "I'll be one moment, Loretta." He stomps upstairs with his large boots still on, his duffle bags in hand. Each step on the hardwood floors cracks and sends a quake down my back. It's as if something large is approaching but for the moment is still invisible.

The clock above the hearth clicks, and my sister Maisy begins swinging her feet to the rhythm. *Thump. Thump. Thump.* Well-groomed as we are, Maisy gets away with fidgeting, chatting, and laughing at inappropriate times because she is the youngest. And because she is the youngest, she has the loudest personality of the three of us. My mother pats her on the head as she passes us, and she makes her way to the kitchen.

"You need some help, ma'am?" I ask. My sister Lorna motions to stand up as well.

"You all stay put and wait for your father. I'm sure he'll want to see you all when he comes down."

"Yes, ma'am," my sister and I say, and then we smile at each other because of our synchronized timing.

Maisy's feet double in tempo, creating muffled thuds against the side of the couch, 120 paces per minute. Like the march of military cadets, 120 paces per minute, heavy thuds increasing in nearness. At the end of every school year, their muffled footsteps flood Charleston's streets on their way to Marion Square. I can still hear them, swelling as they approach the end of King Street.

My father, Arthur Wiggins, used to bring me to the square when I was a child. Though only a small patch of grass, the square carried heavy historical significance for being the center of Citadel's old campus. Each year, they marched here as a rite of passage, or so I was told.

Arthur forced me to admire the cadets, to strive to be like them, to make this march one day. He forced me to learn their rules and walk their way, to respond as they do, to follow command as they do, to greet a person, fold the corners of my bed, and polish my shoes as they do.

In my childhood, there was little time to be a child. When I learned how to walk, Arthur Wiggins bought me my first pair of shoes. They were uncomfortable and jet-black, and they were to be polished every day. I remember Arthur unrolling one of his navy-blue socks. "Heels down." He slipped it on.

"Take your shoe. Make sure it shines like a corvette on a sunny day. Take a damp rag, not too wet. Give it one wipe over, and then brush it with this here. Gently take out the tree, slide the shoe on, and tie it with both laces perpendicular. Symmetry is everything."

"But why? Why do we do this, sir?" I asked. Vitriol spilled from his eyes. His arm launched. The brush in his hand crossed my face, leaving shreds of the sharp bristles imprinted on my skin. I never asked again.

"Head straight, chin tucked, shoulders back, hup." Every Saturday and Sunday morning at dawn, he would bring me out to the sidewalk and clap 120 paces per minute. Towering over me, his shadow stretched long and wide. In front of me, the cookie-cutter suburban houses spread outward—brick chimneys, tiled roofs, and two-car driveways.

I marched until the soles of these shoes wore thin, until my feet outgrew them, until my form grew into a quick instinct, like "Fetch" at the snap of two fingers. Harking back on this, I instinctively corrected my posture on the couch.

"Please, Maisy," I said, referring to her kicks.

"What's on your mind, Steve?" she said.

"You kicking the couch is on my mind, you know? It's just bringing me back to my decision about school. I'm just anxious, that's all."

"It's going to be all right, Steve. Don't worry," Lorna said. "We'll be there for support."

"You don't have to worry. Daddy is going to be happy about you doing that," Maisy said.

"Thanks, you two," I said. "You can never tell with him, though. One minute, he's normal, and then, well, you know how he gets sometimes."

His footsteps near the top of the stairs, and he begins clunking downward. He reaches the bottom, and suddenly, I realize that I'd forgotten my father's stature. He must be a head taller and two bodies thicker than me. His neck resembles something of an old oak trunk, and he stands with his chest out, assuming more space than his already massive frame needs. Large is an understatement for his size. It's threatening, domineering.

"Daddy." Maisy runs to him, and he lifts her in the air with both arms and a smile on his face.

"Hi, Father." Lorna stands up and hugs him.

"Hello, girls," he says.

I hesitate. "Sir," I say, standing up.

He glances at me for a moment, and after that moment passes, we shake hands. Then he moves to the dining room table, and we follow. Laid out on the large six-person table is a spread of Loretta's cooking. The smell is inviting and dank. Fried chicken, mac and cheese, pork shoulder with greens, and sweet potato hash are all laid out on the table. I see my father close his eyes and take it in. *Who are you now, Father?* I think.

"Loretta, you've outdone yourself," he said.

"I'm just so happy to have you back, baby. We're all together as a family again. And I… I know it'll be a big change for you, but I just want you to be comfortable and to adjust easy, okay?"

"Yes, ma'am," he boomed.

"Me too, Daddy. I can't wait to…," Maisy starts. I watch as my father sends a stern look her way. *Still domineering.* "Never mind. I'm sorry," she says.

"Sorry, sir," he corrects her. "I can smell you used the cayenne pepper mix. You know how to make your man happy."

Everyone laughs. *Yet still charming in his own way.*

"I wanted to try out something special for your return. It's a new twist on an old classic, let's say," Loretta says.

"How so?"

"Not only did I put a little Cayenne but I also put some cumin and saffron in the batter. Flash-fry and then put it in the oven, it makes it less greasy than something you'd buy from the store."

"Well, all right, I'll take your word for it." He paused, and we sat. He looked around the table. "Steve, you still playing football?"

"Yes, sir."

"How'd you end up doing this year?"

"Fairly well, sir."

"Don't be modest, Steve. Your team went to State for the first time in a decade," Loretta said.

"The boy can tell me himself," Arthur said.

"Thank you for advocating for me, ma'am," I said in her defense.

"He also made first team in State, ain't that right?" Loretta said.

"First team?" he said.

"First team defense," I said.

"What position?"

"Cornerback, sir."

"Makes sense at your size," he said. "You haven't grown much since I last saw you."

"Well, sir, I held my opponents to the fewest—"

"Still got a jump on them?"

"Yes, sir. Fewest yards per game in my conference, sir."

"That's good." He paused. "Doesn't matter how good you are at something, though. You're going to have to work extra hard for everything in life, Steve."

"That goes to you too—" Loretta added.

"Okay, everyone," Arthur interrupted and held out his hands. "Oh, sorry, were you saying something?"

"No worries," Loretta said.

"Dear God, we are thankful for this meal you have provided us and blessed to once again be able to share it with one another. There are few things in this world more important than the fulfillment of duty and the fullness of a complete family. Our freedoms are not wholly free because we are grateful and indebted to you, always indebted to you. Amen," he said.

"Amen," we joined.

This is new. My father has a different tone in his voice than he used to have—grateful yet at the same time cynical and dark, very dark.

"Lorna joined the choir this year," Loretta said.

"Is that right?" Arthur said.

"Yes. They're having a solstice concert soon. She tried out as an alto, but because of lack of sopranos, they placed her in that section." After Arthur failed to comment, she continued. "It's a beautiful choir. They are composed mostly of adults from around the neighborhood, but the new leader runs a very nice service."

"Very nice," he echoed. "Anyone we know?"

"Uh-huh, the Thompsons and the Browns, but it has probably been awhile since you've seen them, huh?"

"Hmm," he grunted.

Sedated or maybe just tired, my father lounged. "Sir, what are you going to be doing with all this time on your hands?" I said.

He sets his fork down and looks over in my direction. A scowl forms. Have I said something wrong? When his eyes contact me, they look like a blind man's that cannot see you but intently looks toward you. I see the darkness again, slipping out, like a bank robber slowly removing a ski mask.

"What did I teach you about prying into others' business?" he said. "What did I teach you about that, huh?"

"Dad, you're being unfair," Lorna said. "We all want to know."

He took a bite as if reevaluating his approach. "I'm not sure. I guess I want to get back to work with my hands, but on the other hand, I like teaching people. Maybe I'll start a business," he grunted. "Or maybe I'll start a business that teaches people how to start businesses."

"A business that starts businesses?" Loretta said.

"That's goofy, Daddy," Maisy said.

"Oh, I think it's a great idea," Loretta said. "I support you in whatever endeavor you choose."

"Well, it's just a hunch. I've only returned home today, so it's pretty early for me to tell. While I was overseas, I got a knack for teaching the younger recruits certain commands and tactics."

"That's great, dear," Loretta said. "You most certainly started that at home too."

During the Marion Square years, the years my father was home, he aptly named these ways of a soldier daily objectives. If I succeeded, well, nothing would happen except achieving the reward of my own learning; but when I failed, he introduced me to a little thing drill sergeants called a racking.

Rackings normally consisted of extra training, such as push-ups or sit-ups. But one time, he went a lot further. It still hurt to think of, because now in his presence again, I felt a resurgence of these anxieties. When I really messed up, he pinned me against the back wall of my closet.

With his shadow draped over me, he yelled and began repeatedly punching the walls. *Thump, thump, thump.* He slammed the door of my closet and left. I sat on the ground that entire night, thinking about what I had done, coming up with strategies of how I could do this thing called life in a better, more efficient way.

Extra work stemmed from mechanical errors in my form. The night in the closet, however, stemmed from me choosing to voice my opinion. My choice did not lie in whether I wanted the life of a cadet, for that was thrust on me. It lay in whether I would continue to live that way. And I've decided I will.

*****

Maybe this is the ideal time to tell them about my acceptance letter, I thought. How would it go? I would start by staring at my father. "Sir."

And he would respond, "What is it, Steve?"

"I want to let you know that I'll be enrolling in the South Carolina Military Academy."

For a moment, there would be silence. I could do anything, but it would be best to wait, to let it soak in. Father would set his fork down and look over at me square in the eye for the first time since he had been home.

"Have you started your applications yet?"

"Sir, I'll be starting in fall. I've already been accepted."

"Well, congratulations, son. I guess this is also a celebration for you rather than just my return home."

"Thank you, sir, though I thought of you when applying."

"That's impressive, Steve." He would smile.

From here, it could go downhill. On the other side of the table, Mom would spring a look of concern. She would say, "And you chose now to tell all of us, Steve?"

I would reply in earnest, "Sorry, ma'am. I just wanted to break the news when we were all here as a family."

The percentage of that going over well was about fifty-fifty. She could get angry. "Steve, first off, what are you doing in my house clinging to secrets like that? Second, your father just came home, and

I can't believe that you'd make this moment about yourself. We raised you better than that."

"Ma'am, I'm sorry. I promise, there were no wrong intentions. I just wanted you both to know at the same time."

She would stand up and walk into the kitchen to escape the situation. Then my father would step in. "Now, Loretta, calm down. This is a good thing. The boy is finally going to be someone. You know, I was afraid you had a lazy bone, Steve. There ain't nothing worse than a man without an objective."

She would come back. Lorna would shift or do something as a show of guilt. It wouldn't go unnoticed. "Lorna, Maisy, did you know about this?" Loretta would say.

"No, ma'am, I swear to God I didn't know anything," Maisy would lie. She lied sometimes.

Lorna would stay silent, a confession in itself. "Miss, you knew?" She would nod.

"I'm sorry, but I'm going to have to ask you to go to your room. You too, Maisy. Steve, I need to speak with you alone."

*****

The strategy breaks down, lessening the approval from Father and magnifying the disapproval from Mother. I know she won't approve of this decision, but someday, regardless, she'll find out. Using both hands, Arthur devours the fried chicken. Loretta quietly eats greens, cutting small bites with the side of her fork.

"Sir," I said.

"Yes, Steve," he said.

"Did you have a chance to see the Ali-Spinks fight?"

"Hmm, I did. I couldn't believe my eyes. Ali, possibly the greatest fighter in his weight class, is finished, and by whom, a young hoodlum?"

"You think he's done, sir?"

"Definitely. The man's old. You reach a certain age and you can't do what you were built to do. I know from personal experience."

11

"Sir, yes, sir, but about him being the greatest fighter in his weight class?"

"Certainly. The way he throws that counterpunch is unparalleled. Of course, before him was Sugar Ray Robinson, and he was the best counterpuncher of the modern era."

"Who was Sugar Ray Robinson?" I said.

"He was before you were born. Possibly the best fighter of the fifties," he said.

"And he was a counterpuncher?" I said.

"Yes. The way he took a punch and then exploded back with strength, accuracy, and form, that's a prime example of what humanity is capable of. You see, strength requires training, sure. But you can have any guy hit the weights and be consistent. But to be able to counterpunch, well, that requires training and unrequited focus. Rather than practicing shooting a gun, you're practicing hitting the bull's-eye every time.

"When a boxer loads up his punch, he loads a certain potential energy in his arm." My father began to simulate it with his own arms. "This energy is a result of the strength training. Slowly, this potential transforms to kinetic energy as he delivers it, reaching the fastest point at the end of the punch, which then follows through during contact with his opponent's body. Boom.

"A counterpuncher, however, they have the skill to take all this kinetic energy and reverse it on the strongman. The kinetic energy is released and has nowhere to go except back to the sender. That's how someone of any size, color, or creed can batter their enemy until the strongman's strength wears out. David kills Goliath."

Out of the corner of my eye, my mother, Loretta Wiggins, who was tapping her fork on the table, had enough. I was so absorbed by my father's analysis that I had blotted her out. "This isn't appropriate talk for the dinner table," Loretta said. "Steve, why don't you help yourself to some more greens?"

"Yes, ma'am," I said.

"What are my girls up to now?" Arthur asked.

"I'm going into fifth grade, and I'm really excited because Steve tells me it was his favorite year of school," Maisy said.

"Oh, really? Why is that, Steve?" Loretta said as she finished her greens.

"Because you learn about outer space," I said.

"Hmm," Loretta said.

"And I bet they'll teach you about the Voyager mission," I told her.

"Oh, you mean the one from last year?" Loretta said.

"Yes, ma'am," I said.

"Why don't you tell your father what you were thinking about, Lorna?" Loretta said.

"Well, I'm starting to think about what I want to do after high school, and I might have a good chance of getting into a state school, but my advisor thinks that I can make it to an out-of-state school," Lorna said and looked over at me.

"Like where out of state?" Arthur asked.

"To, um, like Brown or Dartmouth," Lorna said.

"To Ivy Leagues. And I tell her she should reach for the stars," Loretta said.

"Yes, but you have to be realistic," Arthur said.

This statement landed awkwardly. Lorna looked down at her plate, losing the courage she once had to speak. Maisy, who had been silent pretty much the whole meal, felt absent from the conversation, and now Arthur had hushed Lorna too. My mother began picking up plates and bringing them to the kitchen. Something mean and cruel was boiling beneath the surface of this man's skin.

"What about you, Steve?" Arthur grunted. "Are you going to try and read me all night, or are you going to speak with all of us like a normal person?"

Wow, he had noticed. I thought that enough questions had come from my direction to be considered natural, but my strategy had been seen through. "Sir, ma'am," I said. They both looked my way. *Now is the time.* "I need to inform you both that starting this fall, I'll be attending the South Carolina Military Academy."

Great delivery. In a swift transition, Arthur's eyes opened wide, and a look of astonishment covered his face. He sat up in his chair, no longer absent, and said, "Steve, that's big news."

My mother, who was halfway into the kitchen at the time, dropped the plates on the counter with a crash. I had miscalculated. Her gentle temperament from dinner gave out, and she began to weep and weep and, worse, curse. I couldn't have seen this coming. Life would be hard not having me at home, at least for her.

Over the years, I had had the inkling that my father's military career was tough on her, but it was impossible for me to foresee, to know, that this would affect her in such a profound and devastating way.

"Mommy, don't cry," Maisy said.

"Mom, I'm sorry. I really didn't mean to—"

"It's okay, Steve," Arthur said. "I guess you already know how to counterpunch, except it landed on the wrong target."

I covered my face in despair. *Shit, shit, shit.* Loretta continued weeping in the kitchen, and I saw Maisy stand up to comfort her. There was nothing to do. I botched it. My mother took it much harder than I anticipated. I had betrayed her, betrayed her trust, betrayed my only mother.

"And just when I thought you were going to run along and master bagging groceries," he boomed. He was being a bully once again.

"Dad, can't you see he feels bad enough already?" Lorna said. "He obviously made this decision for you and not himself, so why do you have to rub it in like that?"

The room froze. I looked through my hands at her. Arthur also gave Lorna a stern look, but then his disposition changed, and he said, "Now calm down, everyone. Loretta, Maisy, come in here. This is a good thing. This can be, is still, a good night."

Loretta walked in covered by a dark, remorseful air. "This was a good night, Steve," she said. "The world that you're entering only leads to two outcomes: harming yourself and harming others. If I were younger, I would've said nothing. I stood side by side with your father as he tried to get over the most brutal acts that man can commit."

"Loretta, please," Arthur said.

"But I cannot stand by and accept that my child is putting himself in harm's way like this."

"I'm sorry, ma'am, but it's final. I start in September." She couldn't look me in the eyes.

"Kids, let me talk to your mom in private," Arthur said.

"Yes, sir," we said.

We leave the room and hobble upstairs. The tension escapes from under us through the cracks in our walls and through the mail slot in the front of the house. I go into my room and lie on my bed. Shortly after, my sisters wander into my room.

"Hey, Steve. Can we come in?" Lorna asked.

"Yeah, sure, but, Maisy, could you let just me and Lorna talk?" I said.

"No, please, I don't want to be alone in my room," she said.

"You're right," I said. "Sorry about that. And I'm sorry about turning tonight bad."

"Don't worry about it," Lorna said. "You had reason to be worried about telling him after all." We all laughed.

"I'm going to miss you, Steve," Maisy said.

"Yeah. I won't see y'all except on holidays. It's going to be a lot different with Pa back and me gone. You know, I might come back a changed man."

"Do you think that Mom could be right about it being so dangerous?"

"I'm sure she's drawing from Pa's experience in war even though it sounds like all he did was lead people around like he used to lead us when we were little."

"I just want it to be normal here," Maisy said.

"I don't think it's fair how he picks on you," Lorna said.

"Thanks, Lorna. Yeah, things are going to be changing all right."

At that moment, Loretta knocked on the door and opened it. "Girls, can I have a moment alone with my boy?" They both crawled out of the room. "Steve," Loretta said.

"Yes, ma'am?" I said.

"Were you ever told exactly what your father did overseas?"

"The only things that I remember, ma'am, are what were mentioned at dinners when I was younger or what you told me. I know that he went to Vietnam and then to Germany after that."

"That's right, to train other soldiers."

"But it all blurs together. It just feels like he ain't been around."

"Well, I'd like to tell you why I'm so concerned, Steve. Is that all right? You're an adult now, so we need to treat you as such. I've been with your father since he began his military career, and Lord knows I love the man. I love him, and I keep loving him, but something happens when you're at war. Something happens to everyone who is at war. Your father, he…he saw things that you can't unsee." My mom started whimpering.

I had never seen her like this in my life. I put my hand on her shoulder to console her as she wept. All my thoughts leading up to this decision didn't consider her. She was always there, of course, through my football games and boxing tournaments. She had always supported me—bringing me lunches and keeping a plate for me if I got home late at night. I was selfish, focusing only on my legacy and escaping the shadow that my father, Arthur Wiggins, had left for me. Contrary to how I felt just hours before this incident, I was still a child.

She said, "I'm all right. I promise I'm all right, baby. Anyway, on your father's first tour, which was toward the beginning of Vietnam involvement, before you were born, he saw considerable action."

"Yes, of course."

"And on his first tour, his troop came face-to-face with the enemy. In the defense of his troop, he did what he had to do to survive."

"He pulled the trigger on 'em?"

"Yes, and this is something that everyone does at war. But your father, after that, he was tied to the idea of serving his country. It became a part of him. He believed serving was a part of duty." She paused. "To go to war, it's courageous, and it is admirable. Well, to him, it was not a choice. But as a father of three young kids, it should have been unacceptable to choose to leave you at home for all the years he did. He placed his country over his family.

"When he came home the first time, I guess you were too young to remember, but he reintegrated into civilian life. He received his praise from everyone at church and even became a bit of an icon.

Then as soon as you were old enough, he taught you what he'd learned. I'd watch you out on the street, so proud of what a disciplined boy you were becoming.

"He pushed it on you and got you and even Lorna to practice his methods. I thought, and I still do think, that was a good thing. Then I remember the night like any other. Nixon announced to the United States on the television that we were going to invade Cambodia, that they were going to cease the Vietnamization where soldiers were able to go home to their families.

"This hit me in the gut because I knew that some poor mothers out there had to watch this when they thought their boys were safe, to see their boys get drafted, get drafted and prolong this war. Your father, even though he's a very pragmatic man, can make impulsive choices involving home and the country. He told me that with you and Lorna able to help out around the house and Maisy old enough, he had done his duty at home. So he volunteered to return to Asia."

"I didn't know he went for a second time." I paused. "But he already did his time?"

"Yes, he did. But the job in Vietnam wasn't done. That's what Nixon said. And I don't remember voicing an opinion against this position, or if I did, it fell on deaf ears. I can't remember really. We got by without him. It was difficult, but we got by.

"You and Lorna helped around the house and with Maisy. You kept up with your studies and grew up. So when your father came home the next time, do you remember? You were starting high school at this point. He was different, had a darker approach to things. He used to laugh at certain things in life, and it's like he stopped all of the sudden. He wouldn't open up to me, tell me what happened in Cambodia. So what am I supposed to think?

"I wanted to be quiet. All we knew over here was the news and how horrifying the war became during the end. He kept saying that he can't talk about it. And then what do you know? About a year later, the army invited him to train soldiers stationed in Germany. He was courteous about it as were all the officers who showed up at our house over the next few months, but I never had a voice in the conversation.

"I'm grateful that this time, it wasn't war, and I'm grateful that you and Lorna discovered yourselves in spite of this. You stuck to sports, and she stuck to singing. We made it this far." She paused. "I promised myself that if an opportunity like this ever arose, I'd give my conditions. I need to give you my conditions before you go to the academy."

"Yes, ma'am. What is it?"

"That you think of us."

"Ma'am, but I'm sure Father thought of us quite a bit."

"He definitely did. I'm sure that was all he thought about, our safety and well-being. But I need you to promise me that you will also think of your own, because I couldn't live with myself knowing that I allowed you to do this and you get hurt. Think of how we'd feel if you were hurt. Don't put yourself in harm's way for duty! Please, Steve."

"Okay, ma'am."

"I have a second condition, Steve," she said.

"Yes, ma'am."

"You need to be able to talk with me about whatever it is they put you through." She put her hand on my cheek. It was cold, but it came from a place of warmth and strength. I didn't respond. "I don't want you to close up. When I had that call, I thanked my lucky stars that your father was coming back to be with us again." She smiled. "Even if, admittedly, he has some social norms to adjust to, this time, it's for good." As quick as she had arrived, she left the room.

I sit on my bed, shrouded in thought. The wall in front of me warps, curves inward, along with these conditions. But am I up to the challenge? Since childhood, I had adored puzzles of logic. If you input A, then it leads to output A. If my father yells command B, then I execute action B, and so on. So it only makes sense to turn my mother's requests into puzzles.

Her conditions were mammoth and far too ambiguous, so I needed to narrow them to solve this puzzle before I could move on. *If they pop into my head, they could serve as an alarm*, I thought. Alarm was the effect, but what was the catalyst? How would the alarm trigger? Should I picture a holiday photo from our mantle or the photo of my parents' marriage? Should I conjure a memory? No, that wouldn't work.

To me, memories belong with gossip. They are unreliable. Memories come and go, illusions laced with inflated emotion. It would be too difficult in a time of peril to think up some random memory, to ground myself on a memory. No, that won't do either.

I look around my room at the closet and at my desk, which has a photo of me and my prom date. Across from me, there is a dark-blue drawer that has always been across from my bed. It has six shelves, each that open by putting two fingers through a hole and pulling. I stand up, and I pace over. My hand runs across the smooth wood. Then I begin shuffling through my drawers. Someone is playing "Just My Imagination" by The Temptations the radio downstairs, probably my father.

This drawer is perfect. It's the perfect effect to the cause. If I can memorize the specific items inside each compartment, I'll have enough tangible detail to hold on to. The top left holds some magazines. *Sports Illustrated* is on top, and then tucked under are some nudie mags. The next drawer has some rolled black and gray socks, nine pairs, then the next has a leather-bound Bible, a gift from my grandma, and two fake diamond studs, a brush, shoe oil, and other miscellaneous items.

Bottom left had folded T-shirts, the middle had dress shirts, and the right had pants. I stepped back and went over the order of the drawers once again. This would be my trump card, the solution to my problems. The radio switched songs to Blondie and broke my concentration.

I left my room and went downstairs. Arthur was sitting on the armchair that hadn't been used since he left. I hesitated, played a scenario in my head, and then joined him.

"Hello, Steve," he said.

"Sir, mind if I join you?" I said.

"Why not? Though, you know, I heard you up there, hovering on the top of the stairwell." He scanned me with a scornful judgment.

"Sorry, sir."

"Is this something that we taught you? To be overly tactful like this?"

"Sir, I just developed the habit, sir."

"Hmm." He looked at me. "And what purpose does this chess-like mentality serve you? Does it give you some sort of bird's-eye advantage?"

"Sir, I couldn't say. I got in the habit, and it allows me to see possible outcomes before they happen. It helped me in football, it helped me in boxing, and I'm hoping that it'll help me at the academy."

He snarled at this answer. "That's interesting, but it's backward, son. The academy will help you. It'll develop you and take you to new heights."

"Yes, sir."

"Sit."

"Yes, sir," I said and sat at the foot of his armchair while we listen to music. This would be the last time. I was leaving childhood behind to search for a semblance of adulthood, to prove to myself and my mother that I could enter this world of war and brutality and return back home unscathed. I believed in myself, and I believed in my trump card. I was ready for the academy.

I lie awake in bed, reviewing what occurred over the past few hours. The window leaks light from the streetlamps. Shadows of tree branches reach across the room. I have to live up to Arthur without letting down Loretta. I have to wait for my moment and then strike, like in boxing, but retreat when things get heavy.

I recalled the sound of punching bags fluttering, a sound vibrating throughout an airy gym. I stayed late in high school, later than others. Preparing for what, I did not know. And with one final thwack, I fell asleep under the weighty summer night.

CHAPTER 2

One Day—Idiot Bag

Day 1 at the South Carolina Military Academy is filled with the academy's trademarks—the Guidon, the five basic commands, and a knob haircut. But the first thing we receive is the idiot bag. Held up to the Charleston sun, an idiot bag is translucent, a plastic sleeve with a string attached to the top two corners. Having one means you attend the South Carolina Military Academy, no exceptions. Officers hang them over a fourth year cadet's neck like a cowbell, swinging in the breeze while he waits in a single file line outside the barracks.

The boys are anxious to be processed. They're anxious to be wrangled and tugged into the slaughterhouse. Inside the idiot bag, the contents are simple: nine by eleven sheets of paper, one for uniforms, a rifle, and a bedding and one to register into the system of the academy.

The Guidon, the official manual of the academy, holds no definition for this packet of papers. In the dictionary, however, an idiot is concisely defined as a stupid person. A bag is defined as a container made for carrying things. So we can learn that an idiot bag is either a container for a stupid person or a container for carrying a stupid person through their first day at the academy.

The difficult part begins when describing the actual experience of the steel gates at the entrance of the academy. Gravity swells and forces asunder your coordination. On entering, the focal point is a large, shiny ring, emblematic of the achievement of each soldier upon graduation. From there, your view spreads into a wide courtyard. Cannons line the near side of the field. Trees and flowers dot the campus. The barracks surround your periphery.

The barracks look pristine yet hollow like a skeletal palace. The off-white stone structures have columns in front of a dark doorway enclosed by metal bars. Each houses different companies. On the pathways ahead, one can see the optical trick of trickling water on the cement. In the center of the barracks lies the red-and-white checkerboard, aka the quadrangle.

A guard stands watch in the distance. Frankie Valli plays on the radio in my father's car as we crawl toward the entrance. It's bright, heavy, and tropical, a typical Charleston day. Arthur lowers the volume and then stops in front of the gates.

"May I have your full name?" the guard boomed.

"Steven J. Wiggins, sir," I said.

"Let's see, K Company, barrack number three. Report there right away," the guard replied.

My father thanks the guard, and we drive in. The car creeps along the road through campus. A strong gust blows into my window, and I turn into it, soothing some of the sweat droplets on my brow. Masses of people cluster together in long, messy lines stemming from each barrack.

I can't believe it. I'm here. This is it. The campus is surreal, beyond imagination, a serene place of distinct order—the grass is trim and uniform, shrubbery opens toward the Ashley River, and no litter is in sight. On the other hand, it resembles a place of war—uniformed soldiers with rifles stand guard and two cannons lie on the grassy field, facing the eastern barracks at the other end of the center field.

"This place is somethin' else," I said. Arthur confirmed with a head nod.

"Wow, groovy car, man." We both turned to see a group of kids my age heading toward the barracks.

"Thank you, gentlemen!" Arthur replied.

It was an orange Dodge Charger with blue accents and a vanilla leather interior. In his spare time since he had been back, he had fixed it up himself. I had never seen my dad like this. His normal demeanor was hardly containing the joy that it brought him to be on this campus.

He never had the opportunity himself. In fact, it had only been twelve years since the academy admitted James Conrad, the first black cadet. At that time, my father had already completed his first tour. But now he was driving with one hand, windows down, and sunglasses, a white T-shirt, and jeans on like a ballplayer returning to his hometown.

"Why don't you go along with them?" he said to me.

"All right, sir. Take care of everyone at home, and I'll see you soon."

Crawling to a stop, my father popped the trunk and put a firm hand on my shoulder. "Steven, there's something I have to tell you." He paused and looked as the kids walked ahead. "All my life, I've never quit at anything. If I had ever given up, I would've never accomplished anything. Commit to yourself."

We exchange a long, dramatic stare, his eyes direct and unclouded. Until I can no longer hang on to the eye contact, I stare. As I break my gaze, I say, "Yes, sir." I grab my bag, and he speeds off.

I watch him exit the school grounds. *It felt as if, for the first time, he noticed me.* Jogging to catch up with the other cadets, I notice a sudden lack of coordination. The bounce in my step is off. Heat waves rise from the ground.

"My name's Steve," I said. "How's it going, fellas?"

"Day 1 boys!"

"Steve, what's going on? Which company are you?"

"Uh, Kilo Company, I think," I said.

"Oh, you're over that way, then," one of them says. "Watch out, Steve. I've heard horror stories about K Company."

"You might not make it out with your head."

"Relax. I've heard horror stories about the whole campus," I said. "I can tell you cupcakes aren't going to last a week," I say. We all laugh, releasing pent up nerves. "I'll catch you all later, then."

I jog off toward the Smith Barracks and see a sign that reads "K Company Registrar." I've made it. Looking up at the barracks, it resembles a medieval castle, except it has a certain anonymity, a featureless exterior. Ashen, massive, and looming, it blocks out the sun as I walk toward the gates.

A cadet with a high and tight haircut and a clean-shaven smirk sits at a table with a list of names. Behind him is a blackboard scribbled with the daily duties and the registration process in a litany of bullets.

"Name?" the officer asks.

"Steve Wiggins, sir," I say.

"I'm going to be the first and last to tell you this politely. Preface everything you say with *sir*. It can be taken as offense." He stands. It isn't necessary, but he props himself into a large, threatening stance. His arms are large, and he crosses them while his face scrunches into a scowl.

"Sir, yes, sir."

"All right, boy, you're up on the fifth floor in the western quadrant. Drop your bag off upstairs and be back down in five minutes," the upperclassmen said.

"Sir, yes, sir."

The quadrangle spreads large and wide. Blood-red and off-white tiles line the entire proximity of the outdoor area. Several cadets fill the quad—chatting with their parents, saying goodbye to loved ones, and heading to other stations. I walk in the doors of the western wing. As I enter, conversations quiet, and the officers look at me.

I beeline for the stairs, ascend, and enter a clean, empty hallway. The hallway is empty yet well-documented, having thousands of footsteps come and then erased with tile cleaner. I approach my room, and I knock. I hear some shuffling on the other side of the door, and it opens. A short, freckled kid with shaggy brown hair answers.

"What's up?" he says.

"Hey, I'm Steve. I'm one of the roommates here."

"Steve, huh? I'm Clyde, Clyde Akron. Distinct pleasure."

"Good to meet you, man," I said.

"If you don't mind, I took the desk in the corner. I like looking at things while I work. I figured, first come, first dibs, am I right?"

"Sure, no problem."

"You're kind of a passive, calm type, huh? Peace and love."

"You could say so." I laughed. "Let me choose my bunk, then."

"That's fair. Which one?"

"The top, of course." I threw my bag.

"Top bunk, huh? Ain't you worried about busting your skull? Well, maybe you don't have anything valuable to lose in there."

"Oh-ho, respect, man. I'm going to come up with a word, all right? And when I say this word, you're going to have to chill out. I can tell you ain't from the South, that's for sure."

"Affirmative, Steve. I'll try to tone it down. I'm from Pennsylvania. You?"

"Charleston, born and raised."

"A hometown hero." He laughed.

"Clyde, great to meet you," I said, louder this time and through my bag on the bed. "The other guy was already here? Wait, are we a four- or three-person dorm?"

"Three. When I checked in, Commando Eagle downstairs told me we were the only three-person room on the floor."

"Damn, I don't like that."

"How come? It'll be fun. Who needs a fourth?"

"Are you out of your mind?"

"What? Why?"

"First off, as far as I can tell, I'm the only black cadet on campus. And on top of that, we're the only three-person room in the entire wing. Talk about a target."

"No, really? I didn't even think of that. So what about you being black? They don't care, do they?" I gave him a look. "The race divide just isn't as big up where I'm from, I guess."

"Certainly, I'm thankful for that, at least."

"Well, what now? Let's go do the rest of the check-in."

Shit. I forgot. Five minutes, I had five minutes to drop my bags and get back to the officer. It's been at least ten now with this talker. "Clyde, we've got to run, man. I had five minutes to drop my bags."

"What? We don't have time limits."

"I'll see you later, then."

"No, wait up. I'll come with." He drops his bag on the floor. We burst through the door and speed-walk through the halls. I begin skipping stairs to increase my pace. Then I hear, "Cadets!" We both freeze.

"Sir, yes, sir," I say. Clyde is silent.

"What the hell do you think you are doing running down these stairs?"

If I tell him the truth, will he let me off? Or should I run for it? No, I'm easy to recognize. What can I lie about? That I forgot something from my father? But that would leave Clyde open to questioning. He wouldn't have a reason to be running along with me.

"Sir, s-sir," I said as I watched him descend the stairs.

"You maggot, spit it out. Wait, are you trying to lie to me? Is that what this st-st-stuttering is about?"

"S-s-sir." I couldn't make words leave.

"Sir, we didn't know the rules yet, sir. We were just on our way to continue check-in duties, sir. We're sorry, sir, very, very sorry, like 'It won't happen again' sorry, sir. And I know that if you let us off the hook this one time, we'll be very quiet and thankful and resume with our dut—" Clyde apparently couldn't stop talking.

"Shut the fuck up, scumbag. I don't care if you didn't know," the large officer said. He looked annoyed by Clyde's plea. "On the landing, drop down, feet up, feet up on the stairs here."

Both Clyde and I dropped to the floor to assume what was to be our first official punishment. I couldn't believe my strategies within the first hour had already let me down.

"Twenty push-ups."

We start huffing out twenty push-ups. My arms are strong because of football, but I notice that Clyde is starting to shake.

"Twenty more," he said.

I exhale and think of the bureau back home. *This isn't too bad,* I think as I start the second set. And then suddenly, I feel a splat on the back of my neck. Wet gunk starts dripping off and sliding onto the floor behind me. It's mucus, a yellow-and-white glob that came from the officer. He spat on the back of my neck. Already, he was punishing us with push-ups, and he spits on the back of my neck.

"Off with you," he said.

"Sir, yes, sir."

As we continue walking down the stairwell, I can feel the remnants of the spit slide down my spine toward my lower back. A small droplet heads toward my waist. We reach the common area and bullet toward the door. Outside, we cross the quad. Our feet clack against the red and off-white tiles. It's quieter this time. The families have left for the most part, and the other first dayers have moved stations. The officer at the front entrance of the barracks is standing.

"Wiggins," he screams.

"Sir, yes, sir."

"I told you five minutes, and you, you get back here in, what, fifteen? Where in God's name do you think you are, day care, summer camp?"

"Sir, no, sir."

"Drop down and give me twenty."

You've got to be kidding me, I think as I drop down into a push-up position once again. This time, as I begin, I feel heavier, more cramped, than the first set. Once again, I think of my bureau back home and begin counting its contents. Clyde watches.

"You weak already, Wiggins? Can't finish them? Thirteen, fourteen, fifteen."

"Sir, no, sir," I said.

Suddenly, I feel an extra weight on my back, his boot. He presses down a bit. "Back straight, boy." He taps me with his foot. "Up."

"Sir, yes, sir."

"Here." He hands me a packet full of papers. "It's your idiot bag. Now do I make myself clear? This is not high school orientation."

"Sir, yes, sir."

After briefly scanning the checklist, I tuck the packet underneath my arm, and Clyde and I head to the company barber. Trekking around the center field, I take another deep breath and exhale. The officers are far enough that I stop bracing.

"You all right there, Wiggs? These guys are taking a liking to you, huh?"

"I'm all right. It just takes some getting used to. My pops, he used to…" I begin to say, and then I stop.

"He what? He gave you a whipping too?"

"Never mind. I don't want to bring up the past like that. To me, that's…that's the most useless thing."

"I can understand that. For some, it heals. But for others, it's like, why even bother?"

"Is your pops a good guy? What did he do?"

"Um, yeah. He's a good guy," Clyde said.

Then silence drops between us. It's the first time in our brief history as friends that I hear him fall into silence. For a moment, we walk in silence until we reach the end of a long line. Then he jolts back into his old form.

"This the line for the barber shop?" Clyde asked.

"Sure is," said the cadet in front.

"All they have to do is shave our hair off. How is it possible that there's this long a line? Up in the Northeast, we know something about lines. Yes, waiting in line is a sort of art form," he said.

The cadet in front of us turned. "Where you from?"

"Philly. You?"

"Augusta."

"Which company ya a part of?"

"K Company," he said.

"Hey, look at that, same company. Steve, same company."

"Yeah, I think we're all Ks. They staggered when the different companies arrived," he said.

While these two talked, I watched up ahead. It seemed there was a commotion in the front, a reason for why it was taking so long.

"I can't do it. I don't want to go here anymore," someone yelled.

"Dammit, cadet, just get in the chair. This is the easy part."

We turn to see a cadet scampering across the street into the center field, and two officers run after him. Each of us moves one place up in line. The officers close in on the cadet. He breaks right, and they track him. He breaks left, but they gain another few steps on him.

An officer dives and snags him by the legs, pulling him to the ground. The other pins him and subdues his arms. They push his face into the trim green grass. He lets out a scream that I kid you not could have been heard across campus.

"Wow, I know who I wouldn't pick for a football team," I say. Clyde and the other cadet laugh.

"What's so funny back here, cadets?" says an officer scanning the line.

"Sir, nothing, sir," we reply.

"Are you sure?" he yells.

"Sir, yes, sir," we said.

"Blackie," he said.

"Yes, sir," I said.

"Twenty push-ups," he said.

I inhale. It feels as if a weight falls on my shoulders. "Sir, but why, sir?"

He laughs. "First day, I guess you don't understand things here yet." He puts his hand on my chest and clenches my shirt. "You better do those push-ups." After he lets go, I drop down to once again huff out twenty push-ups. He leaves, I stand, and we continue in the line without a word.

As we near the front, the sound of the electric razor becomes more and more audible, and we could peek inside the barbershop like foolish kids peering at a beehive in his garage. The cadet getting his head shaved looks tough, stoic even. His features are rock hard on his face, his eyes piercing. Big locks of blond hair falls from his scalp to the checkered floor. He catches my eye because even though his hair has vanished from his head, he never changed his demeanor.

When the officer was done, he had a large smirk on his face. "Voila, cadet, there's your haircut for prom."

"Thank you kindly, sir." And with his deadpan face and a deep Southern drawl, he said, "Can you shave my ass while you're at it too?"

As he said this, the look on everyone's face in that proximity must've been the same—total shock—as a first-day knob had just called out a full-fledged officer. The officer nearly dropped his razor, and along with it, his jaw dropped quicker than the hair to the floor.

"What, maggot?" he said as he recovered. "Hey, come back here when I'm talking to you!" But by that time, the mysterious knob with the Louisiana drawl had a foot out the door. The officer stood dumbstruck. "Well, who's next? Who the fuck is next?"

The rest of the group cowers. Even Clyde looks reticent. So I stand forth and walk toward the front. "I'll go," I say.

"All right. Get in here." Then he began to shave. I saw tufts of hair drop. It wasn't bad. He pressed the razor hard against my scalp, but it couldn't have lasted more than ten minutes. And then he said, "All right, boy, you're all done. Next?"

I look up and hardly recognized myself. My head is smooth, tender but smooth. It's a fresh start, and I have to admit, I don't look half bad with a shaved head. I walk toward the door and sit on the steps to wait for Clyde. The Louisiana cadet is also standing there, pacing back and forth. I look up at him. In the sunshine, he seems shrouded by thought, his hand on his newly shaven scalp and his eyes staring off in the bright, murky atmosphere.

Above the field, heat waves emanate. It must be around ninety-five or one hundred degrees. A squadron marches, training it seems, with rifles in hand and uniforms on. When the rest of the guys are done, we wait outside for our corporal and basic training. We are mostly quiet, except for a couple who haven't shrugged off summer vacation yet. An officer walks toward us, beaming with a look of pride on his face. He seems friendly, informal even.

"K Company," he said.

"Sir, yes, sir," some us said.

"*Hola*, cadets," he said. "First off, your response should be, 'Sir, yes, sir.' Got it?"

"Sir, yes, sir," we all said this time.

"Are you boys ready for basic training?"

"Sir, yes, sir," we said.

"All right. Get in rows. Six of you to a row."

"Sir, yes, sir."

"Follow me to the field."

We cross the street in a somewhat orderly fashion. Our steps are out of sync, but for the most part, we're in rows. There is a large man in uniform waiting for us in the field. He has a sunken face like a crescent moon with the stature and looks of a Nordic wrestler. His eyes scour across us. On first glance, I feel afraid of this man, terri-fied. It is as if he holds great power while the officer leading us has a lower rank.

"Hello, cadets. I'd like to introduce you to the silent giant Squad Sergeant Edwards. And, ladies and gentlemen, if he talks, you better follow his word like Scripture. Do not—and I repeat, do not, ladies and gentlemen—take his word lightly. And do not—I repeat, do not—make the man repeat himself. See what I did there?"

Several cadets smile, including Clyde. I spot the Louisiana cadet, and he is staring straight ahead with the same look of intent that he had in the barber chair.

"And yours truly, I am Squad Corporal MacConough. I'm here, dragged from my comfy life at home to teach you your ten command-ments. Look around for a moment. These fellow cadets, your fellow soldiers, will be your compadres, your boyfriend, your therapist, your lifeline for the next year. We do not care who you were before.

"You may have been a jock or a prom king or you have banged half the girls across your home county, but we do not care here. Do I make myself clear? Do not dare to come to us with your stories about Sally tell-all. She will get over you, and when you graduate, you can go back to her and get her back. Do I make myself clear?"

Several cadets laughed, and one even whooped. Immediately, he must've regretted the decision because a heavy blanket of ten-sion fell on the situation. That was the wrong response. Corporal MacConough's face contorted as he walked toward us and did a per-fect corner around the group.

Just a moment before, he had the look of a true Southern gen-tleman, a catamaran-owning, cup-of-sweet-tea-on-a-long-veranda-in-the-afternoon type. Tan skin, a narrow chin, and despite a nose that looked like it had been broken a couple of times, he was a rela-tively good-looking guy.

He stops, then he turns, and out of the periphery of my eyes, I catch the most frightening glance. It's like an old portrait at Grandma's house that you see in your nightmares when you're a child.

"Cadet," he said coolly. "You're in for the ride of your life, maggot. You're going to be pulp when we finish with you. What's your name?" He paused. I couldn't look, but I heard a cadet whimper. "You heard me?" he yelled. He nudged the cadet's chin to face his own. "Do you fucking hear me, cadet? What's your name?" He paused again. "I don't hear you, cadet! I don't hear you!"

He had gone berserk. The cadet couldn't hold it in any longer. He started blubbering out loud. "Now I hear you. Now I hear you, cadet," he said. "All right. Pull yourself together. You're embarrassing yourself. You tell me your name afterward, all right? If you can stay quiet, speak when spoken to, and learn with the rest of your cadets, then you might be able to last here. If you cannot, I'd think about leaving if I were you."

The cadet stays but suffers from tremors in his legs and arms. All throughout the group, the tension can be felt. The group surprised me, however, as no one left.

"I'm going to teach you some basic commands."

"Sir, yes, sir," we all said. Summertime was over.

"Repeat after me. The five basic commands are: 'Sir, yes, sir.'"

"'Sir, yes, sir.'"

"'Sir, no, sir.'"

"'Sir, no, sir.'"

"'Sir, no excuse, sir. Sir, request better judgment, sir. Sir, request permission to make a statement, sir.'"

We repeat these lines and then begin the marches.

"Forward hup!"

At 120 paces, he leads us forward and back. Several of the cadets are sloppy in their footwork, easily out of place, and the cadre moves. In the squad, I notice the cadet with the Louisiana accent has perfect form. Clyde also quickly gets the hang of it. But MacConough doesn't look amused.

"Stop, stop, stop," MacConough say. "Let's try this again."

We start over. Footsteps thump in the green grass. After minutes, hours, the thumps become clear and synchronized with time. The sun rises high in the south, and then it curves along, its bulk present, arching over the field for hours and well into the afternoon.

Out of the corner of my eye, I notice Squad Sergeant Edwards staring at us, at me. There is something to fear from this stare. His arms are crossed, eyes barely visible underneath the brim of his hat. I don't know what to think of this man of power or the power structure that is so blatantly obvious, like a food chain in a small lake where the small fish must stick together to survive.

All of a sudden, our sightline connects, and I know that I've made a grave mistake. I try to recover and stare straight ahead. The shadows of my squad stretch in the afternoon. His motionless stare breaks, and he begins walking, nearing the squad.

As he approaches, I implode with terror from the impending minutes. However, I keep my breath and my pace, 120 per minute. He nears the squad. Sweat pours down my forehead from tension. MacConough yells commands, but all I hear are his soft footsteps approaching our group.

"All right, cadets, let's break and get to the mess room," MacConough yells.

Suddenly, gushing like a waterfall, each of the cadets breaks and runs to the mess room. I use this flow to escape Sergeant Edwards. Back in the barracks, we walk through the halls to a spacious room filled with picnic-style tables. At the entrance, two officers scan a list and show the knobs their assignment.

"Sir, Clyde Akron, sir."

"Sir, Steve Wiggins, sir."

"Table 7," the officer said.

"This way, Wig," Clyde said, and I follow him to the table. There was one cadet at the head of our table controlling the conversation. He pointed at some of the officers and whispered.

"Howdy," Clyde said as we sat.

"Steve Wiggins, K Company."

"Me too. I'm Randall Stevens. I was just telling the boys some of the faces around here." The boy had light eyes and a cluster of freckles surrounding his nose.

"Oh yeah? Like who?"

Randall scanned us and then said, "First time's free, but this kind of information is expensive. You gotta pay me back next time." The table fell silent.

"I like your game, kid," Clyde said. "You think you can come in here charging us for some information that you probably got from a cousin who went here last year?"

"So what if that's the case? I said this time is free. I'm just trying to let you guys know, if you need something, ask me, okay?"

"Now that I think about it, how do we even know what you're telling us isn't made up, huh? How do we know? You could be bluffing to all of us at this very instant."

Trying to dissolve the heat, I said, "All right, so what can you tell us about this guy here?" I pointed at MacConough.

"That's Corporal Colin MacConough. He's a fourth year, top of his class. He's an easygoing guy, a charmer, one of those guys who gets handed everything on a platter and decides to share. Apparently, he was offered to be a sergeant but decided against it."

"How do you know this stuff?" Clyde said. "Tell me, kid."

"Look, don't blow my cover," Randall said. "My brother offered to help. He's an upperclassman and gave me the list to help me survive at this place. I studied that shit just like I studied the Guidon. If I'm going to be a commanding officer, I need to know everything, know my superiors, know the ins and outs. Can you guys just trust me?"

Randall was impressive. Through his connections, he had been granted a high ceiling, and his determination would enable him to reach it. Clyde, however, didn't back down.

"What's the list? Where is this list?" Clyde asked.

"It has the bios of each of the ranking officers. It's something they publish every year."

"So just like that, you give up all the info, huh? You don't think like a businessman. You know what you ought to do? Reprint this list, change it with more personal info and gossip, like their weaknesses and maybe their birthdays, and charge all the knobs for a copy."

"That ain't a bad idea." Randall looked at me. "I like this guy. Clyde you said your name was? And—"

"We can trust him, Steve. He ain't smart enough to make a scam."

"This fucker," he said, laughing and pointing at Clyde.

34

"I trust him too," I said and turned to him. "I'm Steve, Steve Wiggins. We're roommates." I paused. "Incoming."

Within seconds, MacConough guns for the table, slams both fists on the head, and plops down. "This, my young knobs, is the zoo, and here, you can't pet the animals. As you hopefully have read in your Guidon, at all times, you must have your backs straight, shoulders back, and chin braced. You must sit on the front six inches of the bench. You must be silent."

He snapped his fingers, and we realized he meant for us to adjust to the Guidon rules now. We scrambled for a few as he continued. "You will be subject to questions at all times, so you must eat with small bites. Careful, K company knobs, or you will be eaten. Now hup, hup. Go get your grub."

Each of the characters in this drama is impressive, I thought. *MacConough is an utter wild card, Randall a prince, and even Clyde is a hotshot at times, especially when he challenged Randall for no reason earlier, no reason but good reasoning, I guess. Not only did he give Randall a better business idea but he also figured his angle out in seconds.*

We stand in line as our trays fill with green peas, sweet potato mush, chicken in some kind of white sauce, and a burned biscuit. It's nothing like mom's cooking. She would be shaking her head if she knows what garbage they are feeding us. I better eat, though, for the energy. It could be the only sustenance they give us the rest of the day. They also place a carton of milk and a small stick of butter.

As I near the table, several seated officers scan me. I carry my tray, and I walk with my shoulders back and head braced. One of them sticks his foot out and trips me. Several solutions run through my mind as I topple to the floor. One, I could accept the fall, toss the food, and use my elbows to quell the tumble and protect my head. Then it would fly and hit possibly one or several people. This, in turn, would cause several people to be mad at me, sweet potatoes everywhere, but at least I would be intact.

Two, I could make myself a laughing stock by falling with the tray, milk on my uniform, and at least I would have a face full of my meal. But this would label me as prey, and on the first day, that is something I don't want to do. Three, I could use my boxing footwork and hop over the leg. This, however, could mark me as a target. Four, I could try something that I'm not sure I can do. Arthur told me to commit to myself.

The leg hits my left ankle and sweeps under me. I begin to fall forward, and as I do, I shift the tray to my left hand only, gripping the edge. My right hand spreads wide and far from my body to brace for the ground. As I near the tiled floor, I slowly contract my arm to lessen the impact of the fall and manage a one-armed push-up stance. With a swift movement, I place the tray on the floor, unscathed. Then off my knees, I stand and pick up the meal. I begin once again to walk toward the table.

"Cadet, what the hell was that?" The officer stood.

I turned and braced. "Sir, no excuse, sir."

A moment of tension arises between us. He gives me one look over. He really wants me to be on the floor with the meal in my face. Everyone in the vicinity watches.

"Get outta here."

"Sir, yes, sir."

I turn, continue toward my table, and sit. Out of my periphery, I see that most of the bracing cadets are looking at me. MacConough gives me an inquisitive look, his eyes wide. *What is MacConough thinking? Is he analyzing me as I am him?*

"All right, cadets," he said.

"Sir, yes, sir." We sit in our eating positions, shoulders up and back, looking ahead, and positioned on the first six inches of the bench.

"Well, just to start, let's see how you did on your Guidon prep work. No pressure."

"Sir, yes, sir."

"Negro with the fancy moves, what is discipline?"

"Discipline is, um." *Shit, I haven't memorized the full definition yet.*

"Strike one, Jr.?" MacConough said.

"Sir, request permission to speak, sir," I said.

"Permission granted," he said.

"Sir, I thought you said no pressure, sir."

36

"You complaining? Strike two, Jr.?" MacConough continued.

"Sir, yes, sir," Clyde said.

"What is discipline?" MacConough repeated.

"Sir, request better judgment sir," Clyde said.

MacConough laughed. "Okay, we're going to have to work on that one. Wiggins."

Back to me already? "Sir, yes, sir."

"What is the honor code?"

I know this one. "A cadet does not lie, cheat, or steal or tolerate those who do," I replied.

"Bravo!" MacConough clapped. "Stevens." He took a glass of milk from a tray passing him and opened it. "How is the cow?"

"Sir, she walks, she talks, she's full of chalk."

As Randall continues, I take a small bite and glance around. I need to work harder. I need to take every single moment seriously. Earlier was a brutal entrance into the four years ahead. The feeling of spit down my spine is still there. To be a leader, I have to figure it out and think several steps ahead.

Randall had an incredible leap gifted to him, but I had also been gifted by association. I had been gifted a challenging, fiery roommate like Clyde, someone I could learn from, to learn to act as an aggressor from, pushing for the best rather than preparing for the worst.

When Randall had finished how the cow was, an odd question, MacConough looked back at me. I braced. "Don't worry, Wiggins. I'm not going back to you yet." He winked.

I tensed from embarrassment. So easily he rattled me. It was true, he had already gotten to me. He had infected my confidence, venom from a spider, a wound ballooning scarlet from the initial bite. I had narrowly escaped Edwards earlier and gotten first day mercy from several upperclassmen. Rather than worrying about measuring up to Randall or Clyde, maybe I should first worry about survival. I needed to reexamine this puzzle and find more solutions.

After our meal, we leave for the quadrangle. By now the sun sinks low, and the entirety of the inner barracks is dwarfed in shadow. The tiles look black and white, black and white. Several other squads have corporals commanding them, and I hardly had a look before

MacConough begins commanding us once more, drilling each of the five basic commands into our skull. The grand cement beams stretch upward to the ceiling. Six sources of bright stadium lighting illuminate the barracks. Until 8:00 p.m.—or at least that is what we are told—we march.

When we finally break, I find Clyde. "What a day, man," I say.

"Definitely. I am beat. Ready for showers and bed."

"Who do you think our last roommate is?" I say.

"With my luck, it'll be another black guy." He laughs.

"Something wrong with that?" I say.

"Just that you draw more attention than Nixon in the red-light district. Chill, man."

I laugh. "I appreciate that."

"I feel like an appetizer." He laughs. "They beat me up before they get to the main course."

"Some buffalo wings."

"No, like a fancy appetizer, like an antipasti. I'm your antipasti."

"If you're the antipasti, this poor sap here is the dessert," I said and pointed at an overweight kid who was red in the face. He was getting racked by a corporal whom I didn't know. The corporal had square glasses like a scientist but a high and tight cut and a deep tan. He tapped his foot as the fat cadet barely got through a set of sit-ups. *Not all my competition is bellicose, I guess.*

We walk upstairs and begin getting our schedules together and things assembled in the manner that the Guidon instructs us—personal belongings on the right, military on the left—when our third roommate scrambles in the door and clambers onto his bed.

"Wattaya doing, man?" Clyde said.

"Just give me a moment," he said.

"I think you have the right idea." I laughed as I walked over to him. "What's your name?"

"Harry Bolstrom."

"Steve Wiggins and Clyde Akron," I said. He rolled over. Sure enough, it was the fat cadet from the quad. The poor guy could hardly catch his breath and at times whimpered. "Hey, you gotta calm down," I said.

"I just had no idea what I was in for," he said.

"It's going to be all right, Harry. We have to hang in there together. Just unpack and you can pass right out. The finish line is there."

"Who thought that the first day would be like this? What the hell did I do to deserve this kind of treatment?" he said.

"Come on, it's not that bad," I said.

"Honestly, I want to go home. I don't need this."

"Would you shut up?" Clyde yelled.

To this, he started whimpering again and at an increased pace. I looked over at Clyde. "It'll get easier, okay, Harry? Give him a break, Clyde."

"Look, sorry, Harry, but you gotta realize, even if they're picking on you and messing round with you, it's for a reason, okay?"

"In the end, it'll be good for you."

At this, he stops whimpering, and I realize he has passed out. Clyde and I move into a silence that comes before realizing it, a silence of fatigue. Taps follow this silence. The ominous horn swells over campus. "That means lights out, knobs," yells someone in our hallway.

Harry had already fallen asleep, and Clyde was sketching something in his notebook. I had everything stowed away and properly ready for tomorrow. Poor Harry was starting out behind everyone. "Lights out!" They banged on our door.

"Damn, they're not playing around with anything here," I said as I hopped into bed.

"You got that right, Steve," Clyde said as he put his things away.

"What were you writing?"

"Oh, I was journaling some details to write home."

"That's nice of you," I said, and silence rose between us again.

CHAPTER 3

One Week—The Zoo

"Time to wake up, maggots! PT time! Up, up, up!" an upperclassmen yells as he storms down the hallways. They are clanging trash cans together. *Where am I?* My eyes open as if I haven't slept. I check the clock on the wall. Red numbers emanate through the darkness: 5:30. Outside, a faint blue on the horizon signals the sun.

I hop up and shuffle through my drawers to put on my PT uniform. Harry is already up and dressed in the dark-blue shirt and shorts. He's panting. His forehead shines like a mirror, and dark spots seep through where the academy's name is on his chest. He looks like a wreck, but still, he's the first to be prepared.

"Harry, have you been up doing some push-ups or something already?" Clyde said, still on his bed.

"No. It's just too damn hot in here. I can't get used to this." He grabbed the collar of his shirt and shook it to cool himself.

"Where are you from, Harry?" I asked and then shook Clyde's bunk. "Come on. Get up, Clyde. Last thing we want is to be late on the first real day."

"All right, all right," Clyde said and descended the ladder.

"A small town in Illinois. The breeze comes off of Lake Michigan, so we don't have to worry about heat like this. I mean, it gets warm, but even the nights here seem unbearable," he responded.

"That's really cute, bud. Small town Harry. Small town, big dreams," Clyde added.

"So I guess I'm the local. Well, you'll get used to it, at least by the time winter comes around." I laughed.

On the quad, the officers organize us into several squadrons and begin calisthenics. The first day of training sink in as it doesn't take as long to fall in formation. Clyde, Harry, and I stand next to one another. The brisk morning air is delicious.

MacConough paces around the group, but Edwards is nowhere to be seen. Next to their squadron are the eight other squads from K Company. Their corporals seem as brutal as MacConough, though there's something that makes him stand apart. Three squads merge to create a platoon, the platoons merge to create a company, and the companies come together to create the entire battalion.

Together, the company exits through the barrack's gate, and we start our run through campus. MacConough leads the pack, so I tail him. *The corporal doesn't have a limp when he runs.* After about ten minutes, I notice Harry falling behind; and as I search for him, the Louisiana chap comes into my periphery.

The air is moist, refreshing. Bird calls glide over the sounds of the cadets' pace, *thump, thump, thump* through the sodden grass. The sun's first rays brush us in gold, and the warmth rises like pot of boiling tea as we reach the far end of our run and turn back. I find myself not quite awake yet as I stare at the Louisiana cadet. He jogs over.

"What's your deal?" he said in his drawl.

"What're you talking about?"

"You some kinda queer or something? I notice you keep looking in my direction."

Shocked, I responded, "No, well, I…" It was an opportunity. I couldn't let him talk like that to me. "You'd get yourself smacked with a mouth like that if you were where I am from."

As if absorbing the hit, Louisiana paused and then said, "You'd have a lot worse happen to you if you talked back like that in my town, boy." He did a choking motion around his neck.

"Hey, lay the fuck off, man." Clyde had overheard. He shoved the guy, who proceeded to lower his shoulder toward Clyde to try and ram him. I countered by pressing his shoulder downward, and he nosedived into the mud.

"Fuck you, guys."

Clyde and I stand over him while he brushes the dirt off his uniform. Clyde is laughing. "How you like us now?"

All of a sudden, MacConough stopped and turned toward us. "You two nincompoops." He grabbed us by our uniforms. "Report to me before breakfast." Out of the corner of my eye, I saw Louisiana act as if he took no part in the exchange and began to run again.

"Sir, yes, sir," we reply, out of breath. We slowly start again, now at the back of the group with Harry.

"God, that guy is a worm," Clyde said.

"I know, but after that exchange, I get the feeling that I shouldn't speak out of turn like that. Some people can get away with that, but I sure ain't one of them."

When we returned to the barracks, an uproar filled the quad. "K's the best. The hell with the rest!" The entire barracks, everyone from my squad, joined in, yelling in cacophony. The shouts climbed up the walls and onto the different echelons of terraces, announcing the arrival of the K Company.

Then something magical occurs. What started as an uproar slowly transforms to a unified chant. For a moment, euphoria sweeps over me. I swallow it and exhale laughs and chants with the rest of them. Each of us stands on the quadrangle, jumping and shouting and chanting with pride. The corporals are on the precipice, kicking around and joking. We cadets are now in full cohesion. Echo bounces off the walls with the clarity of a stone skipping off a limpid lake.

Finally, when it begins to die down, people taper off into the mess hall, but I have to report to MacConough. Clyde and I both walk toward him and begin bracing. MacConough is joking with some of the other corporals when we arrive.

They scan me. McConough points at Clyde. "Steve Wiggins, Clyde Acorn, Akron?" he says. "Acorn, get outta here. Go on, get the hell outta here." Confused, Clyde looks at me and then runs toward the mess hall. Each of the other corporals are taller than six feet, taller than me, and now I'm alone.

The corporal to MacConough's right has huge biceps and a square jaw. The one to MacConough's left side has dark hair and a narrow face. I don't get much of an opportunity to look their way before MacConough gets in my face.

"Well, howdy," MacConough said. "You may ask yourself how I know your name. You may ask yourself, 'Why am I the only person here? How did I get myself into this situation?' And I'm sorry that I have to tell you, it's not because you're different. No, it's not because of the color of your skin even if it is true that my comrades might see you as a little easier to target.

"It's because you view yourself as different. That's why you're over here. And I'm sorry to tell you that you are, in fact, going to have to learn the painful truth that you are no more or less ordinary than anyone else. You have strong individual character. I applaud you for that. Shoving a comrade into the dirt first day, great move."

The other corporals give me a sarcastic applause, and the one with the square jaw whispers something to the one with the narrow face. Their gaze is unbearable. I look at my feet.

"You see, that's not what the academy is about, this individual thinking. How you brought your friend into the dilemma with you is beyond me. We are a collective, which means we need to brush off all these little differences to become a better unit. It doesn't matter what your code is back home. Survival of the fittest, no. Here, we band together. Here, you are the same."

"Colin, you're touching my heart," said the corporal with the slim face.

"Anyway, that doesn't quite answer the first question. How do I know your names? Well, I pride myself on getting to know those around me. Don't you? I don't like judging people off of first glance, which equates to me letting you off easy today."

"Sir, yes, sir," I replied. *Though I must admit, I'm having a hard time following him. My legs feel weak and my stomach as well.*

"So," MacConough continued. *It doesn't make any sense. Why am I being punished, and why are Louisiana and Clyde getting off the hook?* "Drop down and give me fifteen."

The corporals are still laughing at me and joking around. *I can't let them get to me.* I huff through the fifteen, and then suddenly, I feel the weight of a foot on my back. It gets heavier. My arms are having difficulty keeping me up.

"We got a fighter!" he said.

An immense amount of weight shoots through my back, but I can't give up. My breath escapes me, and the scenery turns blurry. *Wait, the shelves, the shelves in my room at home. How many were there again? Six, there were six. What was inside the top right again?* I feel the weight of his shoes. *Sports Illustrated magazine, Muhammad Ali on the cover knocking out Liston.* At a standstill for what must've been fifteen seconds, the corporal struggles to literally crush me underneath his foot. Finally, he lets his foot off. I look up. It's the square-jawed corporal. He smirks and walks away.

"He doesn't quit, just like a roach," the square-jawed corporal said.

"Do you think you're better than the other cadets?" MacConough asked.

"Sir, no, sir!"

"Do you think you're different than other cadets?"

"Sir, no, sir."

"Good responses. Up, up, up." MacConough clapped.

I stand and start doing more high knees while MacConough stands right in front of me and the other two go behind me. The high knees aren't difficult. I try to picture the shelves once again, but with his eyes staring at me, my focus wavers. Staring into MacConough's menacing green eyes is painful. It's as if they are hypnotic. *Who is this guy?* He feels different, like he is hiding something demonic, menacing.

The other two tap me on the side of the head while yelling in my ears. *Smack, smack, smack.* "Where do you think you are, boy? You don't belong here." *Six shelves,* I think. *Thwack.* The upperclassmen hit me in the head.

"All right, that's enough. You're a good kid, Wiggins. Get some food in you. You're dismissed," MacConough said. The two upperclassmen seemed unimpressed.

"Sir, yes, sir," I replied and then left.

I return to the mess hall and find a seat next to Clyde and Harry, who are across from Randall. There is a lone empty space on the bench. It's for MacConough, who, after my rack session, goes directly back to kicking around and joking with other corporals. Randall leans in across the table. Dissonance floods the mess hall.

"You see next to MacConough, those are the other squad corporals," Randall said.

"Yeah. Some of them were in my rack session just now. MacConough seems all right, at least, but the other ones like him, total nutjob." I point to the large corporal with the square jaw.

"That's Petersson."

"What does your list say about him?"

"Stay away from that guy." He laughed.

"Why? What about him?"

"This guy is trouble. He's been picking fights with people since he knew how to talk. We're lucky they didn't give him any more power than he already has."

"Yeah, but I'm sure some of the sergeants are like that as well," Harry said.

"From what my brother told me, they're usually more conservative with their power. They have too many people under their domain to target specific cadets."

"Really? I can't shake the feeling that Edwards has it out for me," I said.

"Why do you say that?" Harry asked.

"No reason in particular. It's just the way he scours the squad," I said.

"I understand it's intimidating, but don't play the victim. These guys smell fear," Randall said.

"All right, who else should we know?" Clyde asked.

"Well, these four are notorious. Petersson is the muscle. Nicky—it's what everyone calls him—he's the one with the tan skin and dark hair. My brother says he's kind of the personality of the group. MacConough is the storyteller and the ringleader. And then over there is Warren. He's quiet and calmer with cadets." Randall pointed at a guy with a high and tight haircut and square-framed glasses.

"He was the one racking me yesterday," Harry said. "I don't know if I'd say he goes easy."

"Well, he didn't go against protocol, did he? Lean in, guys. Apparently, he has a dark side where he gets carried away with things." Randall paused as if he was letting our fears build. "Do you remember the death of the black cadet last year?" he said.

"No. What happened?" Harry said.

"Theo Waters, he was a black knob who went missing in the second semester of last year, and weeks later, they found his body drifting in the reeds. He couldn't swim, so they marked it as a suicide even though his mother said that couldn't be possible. It was all over the news here. I couldn't tell my mom about my enrollment until that died down," I said.

"They're saying that Warren was behind it," Randall said.

"No way."

"That's what my brother says and a lot of their classmates."

"How would they even go about accusing someone for something like that?" I said.

"He was just close with the guy, or he, like, took him under his wing, I suppose," Randall said. "So make sure none of these four take an interest in you, Steve, or else you might be next." Randall laughed.

I looked from MacConough to Petersson to Warren, then over to Edwards, who was already seated and eating. "Are we in a shark tank or something?" I said.

"I guess that's why it's called the zoo," Clyde said.

"Imagine when all of the upperclassmen get back. It's going to be so hard," Harry said.

"You better get rid of some blubber before then," Randall said. Harry shut up after that.

We learned more about marching every day. Practice began in the early hours. First, the basic commands—rotating, stopping, and starting—all with signals from MacConough. Then we started arm functions, pretending like we held rifles. Slackers would do push-ups, and quick learners would also do push-ups. Edwards stood in the background like an eagle on his perch.

Well into the afternoon we would march. The bright orb struck the backs of our necks, and the grass lit up in a golden sheen. When it was dark, we would find ourselves back in the barracks, sweaty and broken down. Poor Harry seemed to have every misfortune there was—a sunburn, dehydration, and athlete's foot.

The days opened before us in the same way—the clang of trash cans down our hallway, a bright-blue line on the horizon, and then our PT run. The regimen was arduous, but I felt accomplished one day after the next. My calves ached, the muscles tore and healed, and slowly, I became buried in fatigue and, worse, anxiety.

At night, we were told how to prepare for an inspection. They told us again that personals were to be stored on the right and school supplies on the left. They taught us to polish our shoes, iron our uniforms, brush our hats, sweep our floors, and take out waste.

Even though we were exhausted, we kept watch over Harry. His hands would fumble through each task, which was not a good look when officers came around. So I taught and retaught him how to do all these medial tasks. Clyde and I would huddle closer to him when an officer walked by to camouflage his poor dexterity.

Midway through the first week, we heard a knock on the door. "All in!"

We lined up in the way we were taught. "Sir, yes, sir."

MacConough and Petersson stood at the door. Petersson walked in with his hands out front. "Is anyone there?"

"Sir, yes, sir."

"Are you sure? I can't see a damn thing. There's just this black shadow where someone's supposed to be." He started laughing as he put his hands on my face. "What is this, a pig?" he said.

MacConough looks fed up with Petersson's behavior and begins walking around the room. He stops every so often to inspect more closely. He turns to look at us and walks back toward the door. "Everything looks proper. Good work, Wiggins, Acorn, and, uh, Bolstrom," he said in a blasé tone. Then he leaves the room, but Petersson stays. He stands there without saying a word.

We all continued to brace, waiting for any sign that he was going to leave. Next to me, Harry began huffing. "What was that?" Petersson said. None of us answered out of fear. "Hello? I'm talking to you," he yelled. "You know what I love about knobs? It's that they're tender like baby cows." He grabbed Harry's cheek.

Then two other officers hopped into the room. "Surprise! Rack party!"

"You thought you could pass your inspection unharmed? Get down. Thirty push-ups!"

So the process commenced. Each day, it seemed, Petersson had a different racking for us. It looked fun for him. He would come in nonchalant with a gimmick, such as a bad news, like one of our relatives passed away or that upon review, our admittance to the academy was declined, and then he would turn abrasive and tell us to submit to push-ups or sit-ups. He had no reason, it seemed.

In the meantime, I searched for solutions. I would watch my roommates' faces when the officers entered and how they carried themselves afterward. My bureau, my trump card, had already failed me. The week wore us down, and apart from the ten minutes of time for free talk in the mess hall, even this area became a warzone, the zoo. Officers would trip other knobs, push them to the floor. Once, MacConough swiped someone's tray from their grasp and demanded them to clean up after walking the incorrect way.

The atmosphere was insidious. We couldn't watch our backs because we were in a constant state of bracing. We transitioned from fear of the officers picking us out to fatigue from training, then back to fear of having our own rooms invaded. And after three nights straight, on Friday, I found Harry sobbing in his bunk again. Clyde was also steaming.

"Who the hell does this guy think he is racking us every day? I mean, how are we supposed to focus on learning with him preying behind our back?"

After a long silence, I said, "You guys may not see it now, but it'll be good for us. You can think of it as extra training."

"That's real good, Steve. Bonus points for us, just what I've always wanted," Clyde said.

Harry began huffing again, like he was having a panic attack. I went over to him and put my hand on his shoulder. "Harry, you've got to calm down. This is what they want," I said.

"Well, it's working, Steve. I don't know if I can do this anymore," he said.

"You fucking can, man," I said. "I'm going to tell you guys a story, all right?" I cleared my throat.

"When I was nine years old, my father came back from Vietnam. You know the old colloquial, 'The war changed the man'? They used to say this all the time back in my neighborhood about soldiers that served their time and came back to their families a different person. Before he came back, they prayed he hadn't changed, and then they said he did once he returned. He did change. He laughed less, showed emotion less. But I think this talk hurt him. People would act like they were talking to a cactus or something.

"He became introverted, more in the past and less in the present, and he took it out on me more. He wanted me to be prepared for the horrors of what the world had to offer. When I questioned his methods, they just became worse. He did things much worse than push-ups and burpees. It was a fucking trial. And it's going to help us down the road." I paused. "I've thought about it, and it seems like this guy Petersson relishes in agony. You can't give him what he wants. Next time he shows up, I'll show you how to proceed, all right?"

"Damn, Steve. You should have a TV show or something," Harry said.

"I don't know if I buy your father's methods. It's a bizarre way of showing your kid the world. But who am I to judge what happened to you, I guess," Clyde said.

This comment angered me. "Yeah, who are you to judge, Clyde?" *No, not this time. Let this one go.* I take a deep breath and exhale.

"Thanks, Steve," Clyde said.

Instantly, I'm relieved to have let that one slide. A new air of calm sweeps over our room. Under the drifting taps, we turn out our lights, hop in bed, and go to sleep.

It was 0520 a.m., ten minutes before the trash cans, my first new solution. I awaken early this morning and will every morning henceforth. This way, I will get ahead of the day. The faint blue creeps over the horizon. The stadium lighting twinkles, shines, and bounces off Clyde's desk in the corner area of our room. The air is silent, mysterious, a homage to morning. My head is clear for the moment. And then I hear it.

The trash cans rise, storming through the hallway with the malicious voices of the officers. I hear my roommates stirring. Harry hops out of bed and stumbles to put his gear on. I wonder if this is a strategy he has or an instinct. Outside, we stretch and practice our calisthenics. MacConough calls our squad, and we head out on our run.

The grass is green and moist. Fresh air funnels inward, and I exhale in large puffs. Steam rises to the dark-blue sky. I look over at Clyde, who gives me a nod of confirmation. We see other squads on their runs and other commanders breaking in other knobs, some of whom we have yet to meet and others whom we never will but are, in the academy's theory, the same as us.

Back in the mess hall, we sit in our normal group—me, Randall, Clyde, and Harry plus some of the guys from the rooms near us. It seems as if all the knobs are getting along despite our limited interactions. Randall sits in the middle, relishing his place as the arbiter of information. He passes on gossip and tips about how to survive the first year at the academy—that is, until MacConough sits down. We begin to brace.

Saturday passes as normal. One noteworthy incident, however, is the registration for classes. Each of us spends about an hour walking around the center field to a counselor where we choose the freshman block of classes for the first semester. Back in the dorm, I compare schedules with my roommates; and unfortunately, I don't have classes with either of them. *Damn.*

Instead of waiting around for Petersson to show up, I decide to take a shower before bed. The halls are different at night. I can hear passing voices, laughter, and arguments. For a moment, they register, then they vanish like dust in a vacuum. Overhead lights reflect off the tiled floors. Cadets pass me with their toiletry bags, and finally, I arrive.

Another one of the dreaded experiences at the academy is the bathroom. The showers are laid out in an open space, and there is no division between toilets. The tiles are white, which are frequently cleaned but also often made messy. Tonight is no such exception.

I begin to remove my clothes and turn on the shower. The scalding-hot water warms one quickly from the cold linoleum floor. Then I hear, "Uh-oh, we caught a Wiggy in here."

This time, an image of the word *mother* flashes before my eyes. I had discarded my image of the bureau. I grab my towel and my things, but there isn't enough time. I see them enter the shower area, and I begin to brace. *Need to focus on my strategy and breathe.*

"You know what we call where you're standing?" Petersson said.

"Sir, no, sir."

"We call this the fish bowl. And you know why?"

"Sir, no, sir."

"Because every so often, we get lucky and catch a little minnow in here who needs a cleansing. And guess what? Today is that day."

"Sir, yes, sir," I said. *Focus on the strategy.* Each of them brings out pillowcases stuffed with hard objects, soap bars, I would say. *Focus. Breathe.*

"Do you want to quit the academy?"

"Sir, no, sir," I said.

His arm slashes forth, and the object slams down across my shoulder, the hard object whipping on my shoulder blade. It hurts, but I can't focus on the pain long before another comes from my periphery and slams on my ribs. *Ack! This is going to be harder than I thought. Breathe. Focus.*

Another slams my chest and another on my lower back. Then all of a sudden, a large figure appears. Another hits me. A large being appears behind them. Am I hallucinating? Has my father come to save me? I start howling with laughter.

"What the hell are you laughing at?" I point behind them. They turn and look. "Oh, uh, sir," Petersson says.

"Sir." The rest of them brace.

I'm on the floor, body naked and shaking. The pain still shoots through me, but all the while, I'm howling with laughter. The violence was brutal yet shallow and insignificant to me. Behind them stands Sergeant Edwards, the silent giant.

"Petersson," he said.

"Sir, yes, sir," Petersson said.

"This is against protocol. It can even warrant a demerit."

"Sir, if I may, he needs to learn his lesson, and we were prepared to stop before it got out of hand, sir."

"I'm not so sure. He looks pretty beat up," he said. Edwards looked from Petersson and his weapon to me, sprawled on the floor, half naked and still trembling. "Wiggins, can you speak?"

"Sir, yes, sir," I said, masking the pain, and then I hopped to my feet and retied my towel around my waist.

"Are you okay?"

"Sir, yes, sir," I said.

"All right. I'm going to let this slide with a tacit warning, Petersson. Please clean up your act, and only rack according to code. You all may leave."

Surprised by the benevolence of Sergeant Edwards, I leave and head straight to my dorm. "It's nothing," I tell myself. The harm sustained from those blows are minor, and a few nights of sleep and icing will lessen the bruising. I decide not to tell my roommates about it and fall asleep.

My new strategy of enjoying Petersson's racking hadn't worked. But for the moment, I was happy that something or someone had stopped Petersson's barrage.

My eyes close and open again. It's 0520 a.m. My roommates' heavy breathing undulates across the dark room. This time, I get up. I get up and look outside. For the first time, I really look out the windows, concentrating on the details that I had skipped over the previous days.

Below, a walking path separates our barracks and another—it takes a moment to remember—Stevens's barracks. With the lights off, the barracks look desolate, dead. The road takes you to a tree-lined path, which passes another barrack, and then Indian Hill, a large, grassy field with a water tower jutting out at the top. A faint blue line streaks across the horizon. Then I hear the trash cans.

I hear them. My roommates stir once again. The beds creak and sheets shift. We get dressed and leave. As I close the door, I notice a note on the floor. "Only I get the last laugh." It was signed by Firos.

In the mess hall, I ask Randall what he thinks of the letter in exchange for my breakfast sandwich. "Beats me," he said nonchalantly as he took a bite. *Fucking guy.* The rest of the knobs at my table look around like pigeons at a park, wondering if this meant that something would be in store for them as well.

Sure enough, MacConough came to the table and said, "All right, K Company, tonight's a big one for all you knobs. It's called Hell Night. I'm sure you've heard the rumors. Am I correct?"

Then it struck me what the note meant. "Sir, yes, sir," the cadets said.

"The first of many stand-out memories that we'll have together." He put on a sardonic smile, and we brace. *I guess it isn't over with Petersson.*

*****

The reality of Hell Night swept over us like hurricane winds. We felt as if we were standing in line for the electric chair. It started with our doors bursting open, being yanked and forced down the hallway, and then being led in and organized at the gates.

Lieutenant Dorchester, a commissioned officer who must've been a vigorous fifty-year-old, erected himself in the middle of the quad. There was an uproar from all echelons, all angles. Four stone walls blocked out the moon, and fluorescent lights shone down. We stood on the quad with bitter anticipation flowing through our veins. "Welcome to Hell Night!" we heard from the balconies. "Rack the shit out of them!"

I braced. I was alongside others in a block formation at the center of the blood-red and white tiles of the quadrangle. "Go home!" Lieutenant Dorchester flexed his thick forearm muscles and curled his hand into a fist to give a signal. Suddenly, one by one, we were snagged by upperclassmen. "You miserable night crawlers don't belong here!"

I make out Petersson from about fifty yards. Someone gets in my face. "What are you doing here? You're weak!" Petersson stomps toward me with his large jaw in a grin, chin protruding further than his nose. Sure enough, that man keeps his promises. He shoves the other upperclassmen out of the way and blocks my view of anything else, and his face changed from bombast to furor.

Next thing I know, my face kisses the pavement. It is peaceful on the ground, if only for a moment. From my view, I can only see the academy jumpers, blue and white, and then Petersson's upside-down smug returns to my line of sight. Petersson crouches, twisting his head upside down like an anaconda, and smirks at me.

"Twenty-five push-ups, go!" Petersson yells.

Nothing submerges below my breath. It brushes the ground. I huff through each of the twenty-five push-ups and then quickly switch into a squatting position.

"Duck walk!" Peterson walks next to me. "Go, go, go!" I press my hands together to create a center of gravity and increase speed while the upperclassman sidesteps along. "Get up!" High knees are next. Petersson places his hands where I am supposed to reach. I thrust my knees into them as fast as I could go, then push-ups again.

"Down! Once again, twenty-five push-ups! Go, go, go!" This set drains every ounce of my determination. Petersson laughs, his hands on his hips. With no reservations, he is clearly enjoying himself. "Is that it, cadet? I thought you had more fight in you than that, you little bitch!"

MacConough is professional, if somewhat methodical, about his racking, but Petersson is an unrelenting maniac. "On your back! Sit-ups. Go until I say time!" I follow. After about three minutes, my abs and back start cramping, so I slow. Petersson grimaces as if he is bored by me.

"Have you had a chance to look around at your fellow cadets?"

"Sir, no, sir!" I reply.

"Well, look around. Your class is a bunch of silver spoon bitches. Stop. Look around for a second."

Several of the cadets look as if they are shattered. Other corporals and upperclassmen are screaming at the knobs while some knobs are complaining and crying. I see Harry lurching over and then throwing up. It certainly is a scene from hell.

"Do you want to be like them?"

Earlier that week, they racked me for thinking that I was different, or at least that was what MaConough said, but now Petersson was asking me if I wanted to be a silver spoon bitch. "Sir, yes, sir!" I said.

"Seriously? Okay, then."

He comes next to me mid sit-up, and in one swift motion, Petersson kicks me right between my ribs and my hips. A surge of pain jolts through me, and I roll onto my side, clutching my torso. I don't make any noise, just writhe in pain. *The drawers in my room at home, I need to focus on them.* I see my hand reaching for the blue drawers. *How many of them were there? Two rows of three? Six.*

"You want to be like them? Keep going! Vomit, asshole!"

I recover and begin doing sit-ups again, each one a triumph in resisting defeat. "Sir, yes, sir."

"Then why don't you cry, Wiggins?"

"Sir, no excuse, sir!" He kicks me again. "Sir!" I screech.

"There we go!" Petersson yells.

What color was it again? Gray? No, blue. Thump. Then everything goes black.

There are patterns of commands being yelled across the blank dark sky, constellations of sound. They have no owner or receiver, and to me, every command is lost. *Where am I?* I look around. The other cadets are still being racked, but Petersson is nowhere to be seen. Squad Sergeant Edwards moseys out of the shadows and over to me with his hands behind his back. Petersson follows him with a sunken look on his face. Edwards gets down on one knee next to me.

"Do you need medical assistance?" Edwards asks.

For a brief moment, I think about giving in. "Sir, no, sir," I reply, but my voice is dead.

Edwards stands up and brushes his knee off twice. "I think that's it for you tonight." Then he walks back toward the corporal. I stare up at him. He is a portrait of discipline with each movement—practiced, almost robotic. He leans in and whispers to the corporal. An austere look descends over Petersson as if a switch has been flipped. Edwards retreats into the shadows of the barracks.

"All right, finish your sit-ups," Petersson says.

I start again, and Petersson walks off without a word. He leaves mid set, and I decide to finish anyway. After the officers complete racking us, we stand, shaking and withered. Dirt and sweat stains blotch our uniforms. The sergeants gather the cadets like dirty pennies on the floor and take us inside. We follow them in silence down a corridor.

Shouts can be heard through the barrack's walls. The upperclassmen who have returned tonight want more. We enter a bright room. The air is sticky, and it lacks oxygen. First Lieutenant Dorchester stands at the front. He is a relatively small man but has a powerful posture and is especially thick. His neck, arms, and even fingers seem twice the size of a normal man.

Composed in comparison with the other officers, he begins his speech. Randall seems to be correct in saying that the higher-ups are more conservative with their power. They have more power but impose less of it on individuals. Suddenly, the lights are rotated toward the cadets. It was like sitting under an interrogation lamp.

"Hello, cadets. I am K Company First Lieutenant Dorchester. Congratulations. The fourth class system is officially in effect! The first week is training, but now all rules apply. This means no more complaining, whining, toddling, lollygagging, and what have you after this point, or you'll wish you never had. No excuses from here on out. Is that understood?"

"Sir, yes, sir," the cadets replied.

The upperclassmen wear menacing grins while the shaking cadets attempt to stand still. I feel MacConough's presence but see only the sergeants who stand directly adjacent to Dorchester. Dorchester, as first lieutenant, is second in command of the entire company. The only man above him is the company commander, but he is nowhere to be seen.

Beside Dorchester was First Sergeant Rodham, who was a right-hand man and the senior officer of the students. Behind the first lieutenant were several squad sergeants, those of Edwards's ranking, and then in the shadows of the room were the corporals, the seniors who had direct contact and responsibility for training the squadron of cadets.

"Now here are some ground rules. Okay. First off, you are now required to square corners. Squaring a corner means that you make a ninety-degree angle whenever you take a turn on campus. Such as…" An upperclassman demonstrated by quickly rotating ninety degrees. "This is so we don't have you hooligans littering our sidewalks with your nonsense. We need to keep you in order.

"Each class walks in through these doors and receives the same treatment. They receive the same commands, which may seem unnecessary at times, but I promise you, it's all for an end cause." He paused. "If you don't feel up to the task, you may leave now, and you won't hear a word about it. But from here on, there is no turning back!"

Dorchester continues covering the canons of the institute. He explains shirt tucks, which can only be performed by a pair of cadets. He explains how we should walk while we are outside of campus and the events that are off-limits and how we should act at ones we could attend, including sporting events, school dances called hops, and school-wide ceremonies. After Dorchester finishes, he dismisses us, and we flee for our rooms.

The steps are full of upperclassmen, and at each level of stairs, the fourth class cadets are racked. "Want to get back to your room?" They start and then quiz us on what we had just learned. If we get something wrong, the upperclassmen force us to do push-ups.

Into the room we clamber. Harry looks exhausted and on the brink of surrender, snorting like a beaten hog. Clyde merely looks angry. He sits at his desk, looking out of the window at the moonlit grass across the campus. A communal silence descends on the room. I am too tired to be angry. We're all supposed to have similar experiences, but I feel that Petersson is the worst person from whom to receive the experience. My head and my sides are still throbbing, and my heart weighs heavily. But it's over now as I fall onto my mattress.

CHAPTER 4

One Month—
Indoctrination

Every morning during each PT, we run to an invisible destination, a vanishing point somewhere on the horizon, where supposedly we'll reach our goal; and just when we think we'll reach it, we're instructed to turn back and enter our barracks. Then they close the gates, and they lock us inside.

Amid a bog, I awaken. The stench of sweat and dirty clothes emanates through the room. The desks are clean and the floor polished, so the stench could only be us. Sun filters in through our window. I hop up and crack it open to get some air. A northern wind blows gusts, but as I look down toward the road below, I can tell it's scorching outside.

"Let's go, boys," I said. My voice felt as if it came from somewhere outside my body. Harry rocked on his bed and nearly fell off, jolting himself awake. Today was the day the upperclassmen returned. Because of the dreadful night before, Hell Night, the academy allowed the knobs to sleep in today, and boy did we ever.

I look over at the clock. It reads 9:41 a.m. In contrast to matriculation week, which culminates in Hell Night, this week, the upperclassmen finally focus on their own lives and getting ready for their own school year rather than making sure ours is damned.

I stand from my chair. My head rolls. I clench it with my hand, but then my sides ache. I lift my white shirt to see dark bruises covering my midsection. Walking toward my bed, I look at the sheets. Spatters of blood and dirt stains remain from the night before.

"How you feel? How you feeling, Harry?" I said with strength mustered from some far-off place.

"Like a squashed sack of grapes," he said. "You know like when you make wine and you have to make sure you step on every single grape? Well, yeah, that's how I feel."

"That's disgusting, Harry," Clyde said. "How about you, Steve? I heard there was some misconduct against you. We had to stop action for a minute because they said you were out cold."

"Yeah, that was rough, but to be honest, I don't want to talk about it. Just wanted to make sure you're all right."

"I think it's fucked up how that guy Petersson seems to keep going after you."

"He wants to break the tough guy. At least that's what he said."

"So you don't think it has to do with you being black? It's not a…not a…what do you call them, a hate crime?"

"I think maybe it started out because I'm black," I said. Then I saw a portrait of my father staring at me, disappointed for speaking where I shouldn't. "Actually, forget I said that, guys. I think he's just competitive, that's all."

In the mess hall, Randall is waiting for us. I see MacConough kicking around and joking with some other corporals. He's always directing conversation, always kicking around jokes, while Nicky feeds off him with goofy gestures. They look at me as I pass, and then I notice Petersson isn't there.

We sit with Randall and look over at the corporals. *Did he get suspended?* I think and turn to my friends. Suddenly, Petersson enters the room. I'm shocked. *Some kind of deferral or punishment should have been in the works. The corporals are impervious to the rules, I guess. A slap on the wrist and they continue their assaults.* We all make sure to eat quickly and then head to our next activities before the sophomores and juniors arrive.

The day culminates in a large arena normally designated for basketball and other events. The general is to make his commencement speech. Only fourth years attend as the audience, yet several upperclassmen oversee the room from the sides. I jump on the first set of seats that I come across.

A few minutes later, Harry, Clyde, and Randall squeeze past people to join me. We chat for a moment, talking about the difference in the atmosphere with the upperclassmen here. Drills are much faster, and even though we now have to walk in a strange, robotic manner, living is easier.

Suddenly, the doors open. General Larousse enters and moves to the front of the arena like a large wave in the ocean, which nullifies the clamor as he passes. He is a well-groomed man—heavy tan, slicked salt-and-pepper hair, dimples, and excellent posture. He seems approachable in appearance, avuncular in demeanor. When he reaches the podium, several other high-ranked alumni or members of the academy's board stand and shake hands with him.

"Hello, class of 1982. We welcome you, for you have chosen to pursue a career here at the academy, which means we are one, a united force. Our history spans back for over a century. Here, as you well already know"—he chuckles—"we believe in instilling certain ideals, and discipline is a part of this process.

"Discipline, in fact, is paramount in this process. It has been ceremony since our inception, and we are proud to have you become the next class of cadets to go through this ceremony. This is my tenth year as general, one that I will cherish as much as the last. This year, we're running things a bit differently. In an attempt to make some changes while still keeping the original system intact…"

A composure and a quality of leadership is present in him that I have never seen before. The general uses dynamic hand gestures, emphasizing each point he makes. It's captivating. His phrases cut like knives and reiterate the main point of the academy over and over without feeling redundant. "The individual parts of a body must work in cohesion for the body to be a strong one"—it seems simple in phrasing but complex in practice. How does one become a leader, a hero, if he must assimilate with others? And then he says it.

"We no longer tolerate hazing. If you are found hazing, it can be punishable by suspension and even expulsion. We want an atmosphere of fairness and equity among all students, so I've assembled a group of the university's top students to regulate and carry out the rule of law." *That must be it. That must be who Edwards is.*

"I assure you that we will prevent another incident like the one last year. On Wednesday, courses commence, and the academics that we instill you with will capture a large amount of your time. Walk away from this experience as a positive one, a difficult but fair one.

"Stay inside of the lines and you will make it through. Step outside and there will be dire consequences indeed. This year will be grueling, and it will push you, but I assure you, if you stay a straight line, you won't be in danger. Trust me."

"This guy speaks in platitudes," Harry whispered.

"What do you mean?" I said.

"He isn't saying anything of value, just these sweeping statements of how we're going to be okay as long as we have faith. It's like a preacher."

"Welcome to the South." Clyde laughed.

"Thank you. I'm glad to be able to speak with you today. If you have any concerns, my doors are always open," the general finished.

While at first it seemed assuring to have the general speak up on the issue, Harry was right. How could I trust him when he made such sweeping statements? Edwards helped me, but he was late each time, coming in right as Petersson was to issue a blow beyond repair.

The next day, I awaken to a blue tinge crossing the horizon, loud as a rooster, as bright as bombs. At 0530, the crescendo of trash cans storm through the hallways. PT, our morning jog, and then breakfast is at 0615 hours. Knob clean-up duty is at 0645 hours. English is at 0800 hours. Calculus is at 0915. At 1030 hours, knobs learn about the world of the cadet in Army Reserve Officer Training Corps, a mandatory class that introduces them to the fundamental skills that they'll need for the rest of their career. Then lunch.

Breathe.

In the afternoon, I have biology and American history. Dinner is at 1815 hours, and 1915 hours to 2230 hours is ESP, study period. Nothing is permitted except study—no music, laughter, or conversation. And finally, we have knob duties, which we fulfill until taps when the eerie horn floats across campus, after which all the lights dim. Sleep and the day begins again. The knob's life is a difficult one, and to make it worse, this is a life lived under the watchful eyes of others. An upperclassman can force you to sit, stay, walk in the gutter, or prance like a dandy.

I quickly adjusted to patterns, which meant I caught up to this routine. By the Friday of matriculation week, I had already begun waking up at 0520. This strategy paid off. When the clatter of trash cans commenced, my eyes opened. The upperclassmen's abrupt wake-up was a surprise, a psychological tactic, a sneak attack. But my 0520 wake-up unlocked time to calculate, to plan ahead from the start.

After the speech that the general gave, I felt as if I had a new sheen on my suit of armor. The upperclassmen backed off me since the middle of the first week, the routines were gelling in PT.

"Let's get this groove thang," I say to my roommates, and we start laughing as we exit the room in the morning. At breakfast, I brace, move around the mess hall with prudence, sit with my required posture, and eat in small bites. For knob duty, the academy assigned me to clean up after the first meal, wipe down, and sanitize tables. There is always leftover gunk on the tables and splatters of milk on the floor from some poor cadet being leveled. It's tedious but necessary work.

After knob duty that first Wednesday, I grab my school supplies and head to my first class. It is bright on the main lawn, still summer. Out of the corner of my eye, I see two figures approaching. Petersson and Nicky walk up with wide smirks and looks of malicious intent.

"Uh-oh, you've done it now, knob!" Petersson comes over.

"This is the one, isn't he, Petey? What're you going to do to the poor kid, huh? It's just his first day let out of the doghouse."

"Sorry, Wiggins, but as much protection as you hire in the barracks, it's free-for-all out here. Drop down and give me twenty." My nose is forced to the cement, and I start sweating through my school clothes as I push through a set of twenty.

"He's not so tough," Nicky says. "Hey, we have to get to class."

"Wiggins," Petersson says.

"Sir, yes, sir?"

"Get down into a plank position and hold it until the bell tolls at 0800 hours." Petersson laughs.

I realize this would make me late for my first class. "Sir, may I have permission to speak, sir?"

"No. You better do as you're commanded. And don't think about leaving just because we're gone. We have eyes everywhere, you little maggot."

They walk off in a swift manner while I remain motionless. I look up from my plank position. Planted in front me is the sign for Duckett Hall. My strategy of enjoying the racking does nothing if he isn't there for it. Edwards's domain stops at the exit of the barracks.

Chance was all Petersson needed to attack. Like a game of cards, he was one move ahead. It wasn't painful, but I decided once again to picture my bureau at home. It helped pass the time until the bell rang. Sweat gathered and created dark splotches on my white shirt. The heat continued to ravage my senses. Charleston summers were unforgiving. I started trembling. A few footsteps shuffled by, then minutes later, quicker ones.

Finally, after about five minutes, the bell rings. I jump up, grab my belongings, and run toward class. Slipping down the empty hallway, I start to panic for the first time. Being racked is one thing, but my mother's reaction to a tardy on the first day of class is another. In front of the door, I take a deep breath, my shirt drenched in sweat.

I open the door. The teacher is still taking roll. "Name?"

"Sir, Arthur Wiggins—I mean, Steve Wiggins, sir!" *My father's name. I had really said my father's name.*

"You look like a mess, kid. Take a seat. Can you do that for me?"

Ashamed, I scour the room for any open seat; and sure enough, there is only one. As I walk toward the seat, the neighbor looks at me in resentment. It was Louisiana. He scans me, and I return the sentiment, shocked that I am being forced to sit next to him. I shake my head. *Enough*, I think. *This is petty.* I sit and watch the teacher as he begins.

"So the course will be divided…"

It seems as if he has already done an introduction. The man is lean and tanned with long, dark hair. He wears a button-down shirt with squares and a vest. On first impression, he looks like a bit of a nerd, and his speech pattern reinforces that.

"The first unit I've named creating dialogue. It's a little something that I've developed over the years. As a commissioned officer, you'll need great deal of communication, so this class will hone not only your ability to write a thesis and support it but also develop your ability to convey it to someone else. So as a warm-up, you're going to introduce yourself to the person next to you and talk about yourself for five minutes, then switch off."

I look around in a nonchalant manner. I know that means Louisiana. I turn to him.

"Sup?" he said.

"Hi," I replied.

"So what's your name?"

"Steve, and yours?"

"We're supposed to start with you, Steve. Now where are you from?"

"Charleston."

"Born and raised?"

"Yes, sir."

"Why are you at the academy?"

"To learn to be a better citizen to my community."

"Is someone holding a gun to your head?"

Shocked, I take a second to recover. "What do you mean? What are you talking about?"

"It's my turn to ask the questions. Why are you at the academy?"

"You heard me the first time."

"And I say that because that's what you sound like when you speak, like some invisible person from your past is holding a gun to your head and forcing you to answer in that manner."

I looked at him. That was a different viewpoint of things, that was for sure. It seemed as if he had been reading me as I read him. It reminded me of when my father stopped the conversation that night and asked, "Are you going to join the conversation or just analyze us all night?" The teacher surveyed how the students were doing, and he stopped at me and Louisiana.

"I'm hearing a bit of animus coming from you two. Now what might be the problem?"

"Can I switch partners?" I asked.

"No, you may not. What's the problem?"

"There's no problem, sir," Louisiana said and looked over at me.

"That's what I like to hear. All right now, everyone, it's the others' turn."

"What's your name?" I asked.

"Simon."

"Where are you from?"

"Dallas, Texas."

"What are you doing here?"

"I want to learn how to fight for my country."

"What's up with your attitude? Why are you so pugnacious?"

"Pugnacious, what's that mean?"

"Combative. You act like you want to fight."

"Let me give you something, Steve. What I believe is, this world is full of thieves and crooks. If you can provoke them into being who they are, then you can have an upper hand in life. They can't deceive you into thinking that they're something else. You get me?

"Like plenty of these power-hungry fools walking around like they own the place. You call their bluff and they deflate like hot air balloon. But you, I can tell you're not a bad guy. There's something going on in your head, that's for sure. You overthink things, go around like a victim, wondering if everyone's out to get you. This why you respond with force.

"But you have people who defend you, and you accept the consequences of your actions and lead without words. Oh, I saw. You know what that's called, a victim who should be a leader? That's called a martyr. Not a bad guy to know."

I smiled. "And you say I overthink things, Louisiana?"

"I think things through. There's a difference. Wait, what do you mean Louisiana?"

"Yeah, I always thought you were from Louisiana because of your Southern twang. So have you been to a Dallas Cowboys game?"

"A huge fan. My dad has season tickets."

"That's great. I've always wanted to go to an NFL game. It doesn't hurt that they won the Super Bowl last year either."

"They're looking to repeat. Did you see how they demolished the Colts last week?"

"It was 38–0. Crazy, man."

"You like some football?"

"Yes, sir."

The teacher ends discussions and gives us a list of books for the semester. I grab my belongings and leave. Outside the classroom, I watch Louisiana, or Simon, walk down the hallway. This is the first good surprise of the year, that we seem to get along so well, especially in contrast to that first confrontation.

The other classes pass in a blur. They are full of bulletin points, lesson plans, and a syllabus, except ROTC where, instead, we begin learning the faces of several commanders. In history, I notice Randall in the class, so I grab a seat near him. I quickly learn what it means to have a friend in the same class. Randall feel the need to comment on everything.

We are to learn about great military strategies, which sounds interesting, but the professor is an antique of a man. Long, thin hair covers the top of his head, and he is hunched over from the weight of aging, and his short-sleeve button-up has pens in the pocket. Though old, he doesn't seem to command respect and instead resembles a tome—full of information but often disregarded as still relevant. With Randall chattering above his melancholic voice, I can't focus. About an hour in, I ask him to stop just as the class is dismissed.

The next few days pass in similar fashion. I wake up at five twenty, taking time to analyze my day, then the trash cans pass, and I witness blue grace the horizon. Petersson cuts me off each day, racking in uncreative ways. He forces me to do high knees, burpees, and push-ups, and each morning, I would be late for class and in a terrible state. Simon once commented that I wasn't a morning person. I told him, "Sure, I'm having troubles in the morning, but the morning wasn't the trouble."

On Thursday, my first period teacher pulls me outside and asks me if I could try to be on time to his class. "A week of tardy classes is a fast-track to failure," he says. I have no excuse. Ratting out a corporal only puts me in deeper water. Petersson has nullified both of my strategies of enjoying the rackings and visualizing a different place. I need a new solution.

That night, taps drift across campus, and Harry turns out the lights. I pretend to be asleep, but in reality, I begin to develop strategies. *I'll sneak out a different exit, increase my pace, and creep through the long shadows of the morning. That's phase 2. However, phase 1 requires that I make myself seen less. I'll enter a different door to the mess hall or, better yet, avoid it altogether. During our PT, I'll stand in the shadow of the barracks and run behind the large kids on our jog. The upperclassmen will forget me.*

The next morning, I enter the mess hall at a different time and a different door. Eyes turn toward me. Vibrant whispers carry over the loud chatter. Sharpened gazes pierce my bracing. I sit alone for a brief moment. I eat, toss my garbage, and commence my knob duty. It still accomplishes my goal.

No one dared to touch me in a crowded space, in PT, or on the quad. I was off-limits. During the time between, that was fair game. I braced the entire time—arms tucked in, shoulders back, preparing for the worst. It never came.

Dinner was a different set of circumstances as it was necessary for me to attend the meal with my squad. MacConough held the table as a regular live spirit. He and Nicky would joke around and hurl knob knowledge questions at us. "Who was the third general of the corps of cadets?" If someone got a question wrong, they would end up with milk all over them, wet and humiliated.

As time passes, I sink into this new regimen. I am a shadow of the day, only seen after the main part of it has passed. During ESP, my focus starts to wane. It quickly submerges into a large ethereal substance called doubt. I am choosing this life, and it works, but it certainly is not heroic.

Who is Petersson? An ego-driven oaf. Potentially, the rackings are an ego stroke. Randall says he's hard on people, and I've seen him blow up on a couple of people but never like he does on me. It's not out of anger when he punishes me. It's like a weird fetish, a morale booster for an easily bored child. He laughs manically. He feeds off it.

When Sergeant Edwards stopped him, he seemed defeated even if he wasn't punished. There's no way of outlasting someone who feeds on racking. I need to cut him off. Maybe if I stand up to him. But standing up to him can cause a stir. It can cause his nerves to tighten the next time he approaches me. It can cause him to not fully commit to his behavior. With the lights still on, I drift off, analyzing Petersson. In result, I wear a crown of restless sleep.

I awake in a haze. Too early I had fallen asleep. But now I hear a soft whimpering. "Harry, you okay, man?"

The whimpering continues. "No, man, I'm not good. I don't know how much more of this I can take. We're only one week into classes."

"What happened?"

"I'm on runner duty, and they racked me all night, calling me a fat fuck and piggy until they were bored and wanted me to run their stupid errands. It was humiliating."

"Harry, those are just names, though. You can't let that get to you. I mean, you're already slimmer than when you got here. You should be proud of that." I paused. "This ain't all that's bugging you. What'd they do?"

"I don't want to talk about it."

"All right, man, but we're all here for each other. You need to talk through that shit, let me know and I'll try to come up with a strategy. You see, it's a communal struggle, but it could be worse. They can beat up our physical, but we still have our brains to figure our way out of this mess. Petersson, he was making a fool out of me. He racked me so I was late every day of the first week. Teacher said I could fail."

"Shit. What'd you do about that?"

"I made myself less noticeable and slipped by them on campus. It worked. But I was thinking."

"Thinking what?"

"Is this who I want to be?"

"Well, you have to do what you have to do to survive, right? I mean, we all just have to survive."

"Yes, but just because we find a solution, do we block ourselves from all the other solutions?"

"Hmm, I guess I can see what you mean. What are you going to do, then, Steve?"

"Not sure, man. I'm still working that out. How about you? What's going on? You can tell me."

"I don't know, man. It's just hopeless."

"C'mon. Remember what MacConough said at the beginning of matriculation? We need to trust each other."

"Sorry, Steve. I'm sorry. I can't." *Man, Clyde and I really got this guy as a roommate. He's hopeless.* And then to my surprise, he starts. "Well, I was just doing what they asked, running notes to other corporals, then running them back, and I guess I messed up one too many times.

"All of a sudden, they had enough and told me to hang from a pole. So I got up on the pole, and they took out a sword, like one of their actual swords from marching, and stuck it underneath me, yelling, 'We're gonna pop you like a piñata!' They were swinging it around. It was insane. I don't know where they get these ideas."

"Wow."

"Yeah. I mean, they're always picking on me because of my weight. But you know, in the Midwest, most people are around my weight."

"Oh yeah? All the corn and cheese, huh?"

"And the cold winters."

"They got you looking like some bears." To this, Harry paused, and I could tell that he was smiling.

"Can you guys go to fucking sleep?" Clyde said.

"Sorry, Clyde. Look, Harry, this doesn't help you solve your problem, but maybe I can give you a new way to look at it. You have to stop worrying about things unless you can create solutions to them. Okay? It's that simple. Things are going to change for us anyway once we get a little breathing room."

The next morning, I see Harry awaken right as the trash cans reach us. I give him a head nod as Clyde stirs. After knob duty, I leave the barracks and head to English class. On my alternate route,

I see no sign of Petersson and Nicky. Engulfed by the shadows of the barracks, I look at my hands. Callouses bubble up on the inside of my palms. *Not today. I'm not stepping into the light today.* So I walk through the shadows to English. I sit down and enjoy the five minutes of peace before the bell rings. The teacher gives me a wink.

During classes, Simon and I were becoming chum; and between assignments, we chatted about forming an intramural football team for the K Company. Simon was a QB in high school, and while his high school was somewhat underfunded, they made it to State, though he admitted to having attitude problems when things weren't going their way.

We were supposed to keep a log of each other's responses on a panoply of topics. Each week, we had to type up what the person said and how they could say it in a more efficient manner. Simon and I were having such a good time that we ended up responding in a roundabout way, and our corrections looked like miracles on paper.

Class ended. Simon and I both left for our next classes. Throughout each period, I was completely tuned in. My math class turned out to be engaging and easy to learn. Then in history, the teacher taught us of some of the great military strategies. The first section was entitled envelopment. It consisted of psychological implications of a rear attack to complement a frontal assault, letting your forces cave in, disperse, and eventually surround the enemy forces.

That day, Randall had a toothpick, a bit of a bruise under his eye, and a brazen attitude. "So, man, I hear you're pretty badass over here. Corporals are loving you, making you do planks in the schoolyard. If I were you, I'd do something to get that noose up from around my neck, you know?" he said as he chewed his toothpick.

"I'd check your sources, you dig. That's old news, and the situation has changed."

"Oh yeah? Not what I hear. I hear everyone's coming at the little black guy in K Company."

"They haven't laid a finger on me in a week."

"The whole campus is figured out. Even if they're laying off you one day, at any time, that shit can change, you know? I wouldn't get too confident."

"Put down your little guidebook. I guess reading it before bed gave you a black eye."

"Ha! That's good, Wiggins. Maybe you should take notes on strategy instead of thinking that you have it all figured out. No one likes a nigger speaking out of place."

Asshole. "Yeah, let's listen to the lecture for once. I'm done talking about this."

"Okay. Just know you're getting a reputation, bud."

"What?" I said. "What do you mean a reputation?"

"They're saying how you act tough, but in reality, you only take the blows you can handle, how it's a front. It's not foolin' me, though. They want to talk about that, it's fine, but I know you're just a sensitive guy under that black skin."

"Where did you work up the nerve to talk to me like this?" I said.

Randall leaned back in his chair and looked me up and down. "You really ain't that bright, huh?"

I stood abruptly. Everyone's attention shifted to me. This outburst broke the veil of the whispers we had created. "Sorry, sir," I said.

"Wiggins, that's your name, right?" the teacher said.

"Sir, yes, sir," I said.

The venerable teacher took two feeble steps toward me. "'This is the only means of becoming a great captain, and acquiring the secret of the art of war.' Do you know what Napoleon was referring to when he said this line?"

"Sir, no, sir."

"He spoke of study and the importance of studying those before him."

"Sir, yes, sir."

"What do you think Napoleon's downfall was?"

"Sir, I request better judgment, sir."

Frustrated, I stared blankly at the professor. He wouldn't allow me to speak at ease, and he was pecking me with these inane questions just to establish authority. I thought of a response. Too late.

"Thinking he knew it all."

"Sir, I understand trying to make a point, sir. You needn't worry about me disturbing the class again."

I can't focus for the rest of the class period. I now know that people are talking behind my back. Randall did me a favor by revealing this fact. Still, his disrespect is unforgivable. At the end of class, he comes up to me.

"Look, I'm sorry about that. It slipped out," he said.

I looked around to see who was watching. Phrases like that didn't just slip out. I said, "It's okay. I have to get going."

"Hey." Randall held my arm and then looked me in the eye. He pointed at the bruise underneath his own. "No matter who has the upper hand, we're all in this," he said. He walked away.

"Piece of shit," I said in a hushed breath. Then I turned and saw the professor. He pointed at me.

"Mr. Wiggins, would you please walk with me to my office?"

"Sir, I would, sir, but I have class."

"Then come into the classroom just for a few minutes. You're not in trouble, but I'd like to make something clear to you." This was the second professor whom I had been asked to speak to after class. Frankly, the attention was unfair. "I don't need to address how you acted in class today. We both know that you were out of line," he said.

He must've noticed something on my face because he remarked, "We need to have a mutual respect, Steven, as teacher and student, and for you, you never know where advice will come from. Now you participate and keep quiet in class. So I'm going to assume something was the matter today, as is often with the stress of knob life."

He's more engaging one on one. I wonder who he is. "There you go again analyzing me."

"Sir, sorry, sir."

"Wiggins."

"Yes, sir."

"Do you enjoy war strategy?"

"Sir, yes, sir."

"I thought as much. You are excused."

That weekend, the gray-and-blue flag rose high above the white sun in the sky. The cadets marched from end zone to end zone toward the small amount of space reserved for them and then faced the home side of the academy's football field. An arena opened up with bleachers on both sides and two large brick walls at the end of the field that blocked any intruder from watching.

The flag waved in the distance. The cadets saluted, and then they turned about face and saluted the visiting fans, who reciprocated the respectful gesture. The true test of a Southern institution was not only how the institution played ball but also how the institution composed itself around its team. The players on each team were warming up, running routes, and tossing the ball around on the sidelines.

"C-O-U-G-A-R-S!" the cadets boomed. "Cougars! Cougars! Rah!"

I was ecstatic. I had never seen this level of football live before. Clyde and Harry were next to me, shouting at the top of their lungs. We wore short-sleeved foggy-gray uniforms with a black overseas cap and dark slacks. I tried to see if there were any cute girls in the stands, but another signal came, and the cadets quickly became one. A commander waved the flag again, and the cadets broke out into a chorus of Dixie.

"I wish I was in the land of cotton," everyone sang. The song of the South stung to sing. Immersed in prejudice and racism were these traditions. Only the glory days remembered.

> Old times there are not forgotten,
> Keeping it around felt as if the air was constricting, and tense.
> Look away, Look away,
> Look away Dixie land.

When the song was over, a gust wiped the stadium anew. I took a deep breath, trying to push all these negative thoughts away. Then it was kickoff. The cadets stood yelling at the top of their lungs and singing fight songs. The players' cleats ripped the fresh grass as the home team returned the ball to the thirty-yard line. The quarterback snapped and threw a shovel pass to the wide receiver, who broke past the initial defense and kept moving to get a ten-yard pickup.

By the end of the first half, the academy already had a lead over the Presbyterian college. Clyde offered to get them some food. Harry and I goofed around until he returned and out of the corner of our eye came MacConough. We all braced ourselves.

"Boys! You boys having a good time?"

"Sir, yes, sir," we responded.

"At ease," MacConough said. "So how about academy football, am I right?"

"It's the best thing I've seen live in person, sir," I said.

"Good. That's the right answer, Wiggins. Learn to love your troop," MacConough said. "Hey, Bolstrom."

"Sir, yes, sir," Harry said.

"I thought I said at ease. Man, you're a wet blanket. Look, something came up. You're off runner duty. The guys don't like you very much, too fat and, um, easy to make cry. Some wonder if you even belong here at the academy," he said with a sardonic grin. Then he scanned Harry as if looking at a discardable object. "For now, let's transfer you to janitorial. You'll like it there. Fit right in."

Harry was silent. "Say something, Harry." Clyde nudged him.

"Take some advice from big-mouth Acorn here. Answer me when I'm speaking to you. Otherwise, it seems like you're ignoring me—"

"Sir, I'll do better, sir," Harry blubbered.

MacConough struck Harry with the back of his fist. "I don't like doing it, but don't you ever interrupt me again. I was coming over here to break the news, not to cause a scene now. Boy, you guys are the crew."

Several knobs were looking in our direction, but when they saw MacConough return the gaze, they turned and acted as if they hadn't seen anything. "Sir, yes, sir," we all responded. Harry staggered a bit.

"Wiggins, you're the new runner," MacConough finished.

"Sir, yes, sir."

"Just so you know, Wiggins, we've been keeping tabs on all you freshmen. We're putting wagers to see who will last the longest before they break down. A lot of the guys are saying they'd love to crack you open like a pistachio. Only a few other freshmen fire them up like you. Hey, one of them is actually Randolph over there." MacConough pointed at the black receiver.

"Sir, he's a freshman, sir?"

"Yes, he is, and you wouldn't believe it, but you two are the ones these guys care about. So make them work for it, eh?"

"Sir?"

"Go ahead. Spit it out."

"Any idea why, sir?"

"Ever heard of racism, Wiggins? Some people don't think you or your tribe belong here. Anyway, that shouldn't be any surprise to you." He paused and then looked out. "You should meet him, relate over your bad decision to enroll here. Together, you could pull through."

"Sir, yes, sir," I said with a straight face.

This unnerved MacConough, and he scrunched his forehead together. "Lighten up, kid." He left. Harry seemed a bit shaken up by the encounter.

Clyde empathized with me. "Sorry about that, man."

Harry said, "What are you saying sorry to him for? MacConough likes him."

"Harry, you're not the one people are gunning after. You just got caught in the path of destruction. I can't believe the way he said that, like it's just okay that everyone's racist here."

"So what if people are racist? That's not going to stop me from living my life," I said. "It's the tradition here."

"You know they got to me," he said.

"They cracked you open? How'd they get to you?"

"Yeah. Hell Night was too much for me. From the beginning, I was expecting to be battered and bruised, but I had this guy, Corporal Firos. He started asking me all types of personal questions as he was racking me, so for every push-up, he knew a detail of my personal life. And then he turned everything I told him against me. He said that my father even, who abandoned my family, would be ashamed to come back and see the person I've turned into.

"It's such trickery, but I got caught up in the moment. He said that the upperclassmen would service my girl better than I could. He asked for her phone number so that he and the boys could call her up for a good time. I felt like exploding at him, ripping his head off, but I couldn't, and I just imploded. I felt so helpless."

"That's abusive. I can't believe he got away with that. What'd you say the corporal's name was again?"

"Firos."

"The same name as the note on our floor. What'd he look like?"

"Like a nightmare. He had on like a ski mask. I never got a clean look at the face underneath."

As Clyde finished, the game ended, 28–17, with roars from the crowd. Everyone was in a good mood, except for us. I was disturbed by Clyde's story and by Petersson, Nicky, and the rest of the corporals. They gave one another high fives and roared to go out. "Let's hit the town," Petersson said. "We better not see any of you faggot knobs in our path tonight."

"Look at the little guys cower. You can't do that to them. They won't be able to sleep tonight," I heard Nicky add as they passed.

We funneled out of the stadium in the same order in which we came, in formation and separated by company. It was lockdown, so we could only go to our rooms and go to sleep.

On the second floor near the stairs where light drops off as you look into the stairwell, I'm afraid again. It is a long corridor lined with doors equidistant from one another. Radiators stand by every other room. Three floors below us, the seniors' level looks identical to ours. I knock three times and say, "Sir, reporting for runner duty, sir." A bead of sweat rolls down my arm, and my palms are glowing. MacConough opens the door.

"C'mon in."

The room resembles mine, except that it is a two-person dorm with separate beds instead of bunks. The walls are unadorned, and desks have photos of families, but nothing is unfamiliar about the room. Corporal Warren sits at his desk, scribing something. He looks up with a blank stare from behind his glasses. I stand attentive in front of the door.

"I don't like you looking around. Go face the corner," MacConough says.

I walk over and face the corner of the room. I can only see the off-white wall paint. My breath bounces off the corner. Time passes as I stand. Footsteps echo in the near hallway. I hear the sound of a pencil on paper and turning pages. Every once and a while, Warren lets out a big gasp. My knees begin to hurt from standing in the same position.

"Oh, I forgot about you," MacConough says. "I don't have anything for you tonight."

"Sir, yes, sir." I meander back to my room, and the pent-up fear deflates from my body.

The next few nights passed the same way. He would have me enter the room and then stand in the corner. He would then completely ignore me. I had never felt like such an afterthought. Was he protecting me? Or was this torture? Several thoughts would pop into my head while I stood in the corner, but I strangled them and focused on my breathing.

One night, I hear the voice of Petersson in the hallway and of a door closing. Judging from the pace in which he walks and the time it takes to reach the door, he lives two doors down. It feels like avoiding a shark in small waters. On the other hand, now I know where his room is; and from this thought, I form a new strategy. *I'll create a map. This way, I can avoid Petersson and still roam campus in the daytime.*

MacConough's room was on the second floor, the second room on the left from the stairs. Petersson was the fourth door on the left. Each night that week, I continued mapping the campus, piecing together patterns of the day.

MacConough dismissed me after the second week and said I would be moving to janitorial. "I've been watching you," he said. "And so has Buzz over here." *Warren, the suspect in the Theodore Waters case.* "We like you. You're calculated—always taking the back seat in PT and staying away from us during the jog. A lot quieter than that old Theodore Waters from last year."

What the hell is this? They'd been luring me here for two weeks now without a word, and all of a sudden, he speaks about Theodore Waters, the most scarring name. A sneak attack? Envelopment?

"But we want to hear your voice. Talk to us. Maybe we'll listen."

"Um, I'm not certain about that, Colin. I'd say his demeanor is speaking loudly right now," Warren said as he shifted his glasses.

This was the first time I had heard Warren speak. The Theodore Waters suspect just spoke to me, and he sounded mighty guilty.

"You may go. Until next time," MacConough said. I exited the room and broke out into full sprint to the hallway and three flights up the stairs.

"I thought I couldn't stand runner duty, but janitorial is for the birds. It's disgusting, and there's no glory in it," Harry was venting to Clyde.

"Listen to yourself, man. You can't be so negative. The negativity has consequences. It has consequences. We all have to go through this, but the negativity isn't helping you out of it. In fact, it's probably making it worse for you," Clyde said.

"You should listen to Clyde, Harry. It follows you like a cloud, feeding on your energy," I added. I didn't feel like myself. In fact, it was the worst I had felt since I had been here. Shattered, I sat on the bed.

"Look, I'm just trying to let what's inside my head out, and one thing is that I regret coming here. I really do. I don't know what I thought it was going to be—"

"I'm not sure what you thought it was going to be either, Harry! Did you think there would be cookies? Did you, you maggot, you worthless piece of dog shit?"

Clasped in my right hand, I had Harry's shirt. I felt his huffing on my face. What had happened? I couldn't remember. Was it not just a thought? This paroxysm, of course, quieted the entire room.

"What the hell, man?" Clyde yelled.

"I'm sorry, Harry. I'm sorry. I just… I just blacked out." As I sent this apology to Harry, I saw his face change from a concerned look to a look of understanding.

"Runner duty," Harry said as he broke free and brushed himself off. "What'd they do to you?"

"Nothing. I mean, nothing at all for the first thirteen days. They made me stand and face the wall in the corner."

"What happened tonight?" Harry asked.

"Not much. Everything was normal, and then they started speaking about Theo Waters."

"Who?" Harry said.

"The dead cadet, the cadet whom Buzz Warren is suspected of killing."

Oxygen leaves the room. We stare at one another for a long stretch of time. Without another word, we start organizing our articles. Then we ready for bed and hear taps sound across campus. As the lights go off, Harry's voice comes through the room.

"Don't worry, buddy. They can't do anything like that to you," he says.

Silence fall again. A moment passes in the dark. "I wouldn't bet on it."

*****

Temperatures finally drop as September comes to a close. My classes ramp up the amount of work, and for the most part, my grades are strong. In math, I am a natural, so I score near-perfect marks on the first few quizzes. My ROTC and biology scores are also at the top of their class, and my history teacher keeps me under his wing, so naturally, I am in the upper crest of my peers.

We had gone beyond such concepts as envelopment to flanking, attrition, blitzkrieg, wait and bleed, and guerrilla warfare. The problem didn't lie in these concepts, as they were easy to remember, but the teacher had a subjective view crafted by age. He wanted us to explain which tactic applied to a said situation—basically, to read his mind. English, however, hadn't had one mark given, and instead, we had progress reports at the end of each month.

Each ESP I broke down into precise segments, allotting small amounts of time to cover the classes of lesser importance, and then ramping up to those of immediate pertinence. Like clockwork, I compartmentalized each class to achieve full focus on the next. When there were quizzes the following day, I would practice while I scraped gunk off toilets during knob duties, computing imaginary graphs on the stalls and monotonous hallways. I fell asleep with that as the last thing on my mind and woke up early to review.

I felt I was progressing into a meticulous person, the academy as the ideal blueprint to practice. Every Monday, an officer came to inspect uniforms, equipment, and tidiness of the room. They checked if we had organized the drawers in a four-tier system and that our desks were in academy order. I split my drawers into neat sections.

Each of them contained six pairs of socks in two columns of three, boxer briefs pressed and folded in half, and accessories laid out without touching anything else. Personal belongings were to the left. Military equipment were to the right. The uniforms were untouched, the boots sparkled, and the hats were brushed.

Clyde, Harry, and I decided to turn it into a game, and whenever we found something out of alignment, we would have to do push-ups. I hadn't received demerits when it came time for inspection. Harry and Clyde did at the beginning, but when we started our game, the room became notorious for the presentation.

The room across from us, a group of four, approached our room with curious envy one night. "How do you guys do it?" one of the other floor mates asked.

"Self-policing," I said.

"Seriously? That's it?" Lionel said.

"Yeah, but you have to read the whole white book first. Maybe that's why you guys are screwing up. Did you just scan it after you bought it or what?" Clyde added.

The truth is that my military upbringing had molded me. I already know most of these rules. While some of the academy's requests are a little more specific, I just add these to Arthur's laws, and it takes me next to no time to adapt. Thanks to him, it is second nature.

The self-policing rule maintained perfection between us. Clyde and I made an unspoken agreement that we would try to trick Harry into suffering through extra push-ups. But we were a month in and he hadn't made a mistake since. The room across from us was grateful that we had shared our secret, and Harry responded, "Of course. We're not in competition, guys. Don't let the walls separate us."

Harry's potluck-style attitude was the first change I had noticed. I decided to ask the four cadets and the four next to them if they wanted to start a K Company intramural football team, and they hopped on board.

*****

The two weeks of janitorial was up. After ESP, I made my way back to MacConough's room with a stiff walk. I knocked and announced myself. MacConough took a little extra time to answer. Today, there were three upperclassmen in the room—MacConough, Warren, and a third whom I didn't know. I didn't get a clean look before MacConough sent me to the corner. I heard pages turning and the three discussing terms of the book.

Tonight, I resumed my mental map and started listening to the sounds in the building while creating this map. I had gathered a lot of data for it in the past few weeks, and I had convinced myself that after this week, I would be ready to step into the daylight again.

Footsteps, closing doors, and shuffling of papers paint the landscape of the hallways. Commanding officers bark at squadrons on the center field. The clack of boots and cadets' salutes swell from campus. A collective of sounds unique to a military school gathers. Then MacConough speaks. "Wiggins."

"Sir, yes, sir," I replied.

"Have you seen Sergeant Edwards recently?"

I stopped breathing, and my fist trembled, but I continued to stare in the corner. *How should I respond? If I tell him I have seen Edwards, then they will know that I'm under surveillance. But if I...*

"Don't worry about answering. Your silence gave up enough. When do you usually see him?" MacConough said.

"Sir, permission to speak, sir," I gasped.

"Permission granted," MacConough responded in a ho-hum voice.

"Sir, he came to our room last Friday, but we assumed it was for inspection, sir."

"Okay, so it's safe to assume he's going to come every Friday?" the third voice said.

"I don't think we can assume anything with Edwards. He's a rather unpredictable man," Warren said.

"Well, I've waited long enough. If this campus wants to watch us like an eagle eye, so be it, but senior year only comes once."

"I would advise against this," Warren said.

"Wiggins," the third voice said.

"Sir, yes, sir."

"My name is General Firos, and I'd like to welcome you to my rack session." He started cackling.

They were waiting, wait and bleed tactic. That's why he was sending me to the corner, waiting for me to let my guard down, to find out information and then strike using this info.

"Don't worry, Wiggins. It won't be every night. Just enough to keep you guessing." MacConough laughed. "Like I said, everyone gets their turn."

Firos put his hand on my shoulder and turned me around. Covering his face, he had a red mask with large eyebrows and small holes for eyes. It was sheer terror. My mind flashed to Clyde's story of Hell Night and the death of Theodore Waters. I checked if Warren was there, unmasked. He was.

General Firos grabs a broomstick and then places it at the back of my knees. He forces me to squat down into a duck walk position. Immediately, the broomstick locks between my thigh and calf. No circulation. I can't feel my legs.

"Here are the rules. Get five questions correct and you may stand," he says. "Then you have to squat again. Three sets."

It is difficult to breathe. "Sir, yes, sir." My head begins throbbing, and my voice moves to the back of my throat. *Three fucking sets. Can I make it through one?* Firos begins questioning me. My tongue feels numb and swollen, like a large slug writhing into the back of my throat. The upperclassman bashes me with questions.

"What's that, cadet? I can't hear you, cadet," he said.

I finally voice the answer. "Sir, yes, sir." He continues to assault me with questions. Blood floods to my head. Things grow blurry, and he forces me to sing the alma mater. Firos walks toward me and crouches down.

"You may stand. That's set one."

"S-sir, yes, sir," I say as I stand. "Ack."

"What was that? Do you admit defeat?"

Think, Steve, think. What are my options? There are two, surrender or persevere, nothing else. On one hand, I let my mom down; and on the other, I let my father down. "Sir, no, sir."

"You want to keep going, Wiggins?"

"Sir, yes, sir."

Then Warren begins walking over. Warren bends over and gets next to my face. My heart throbs. He puts a finger to my neck. "Maybe you should remove the broom, Firos," Warren says. "He's going to lose consciousness, and we don't want a case on our hands."

"Well, how the fuck am I supposed to break the kid if he doesn't give up?"

Almost there. I've almost made it. My surroundings blur. Through the darkness, I see Arthur Wiggins. He's sitting in his chair, watching Muhammad Ali fight. Ali sways, almost losing consciousness. His guards are down, and he dodges defeat by pure instinct. On the ropes, the crowd roaring, they scream for him to continue. Arthur turns to look at me and stares deep into my eyes.

Firos removes the broom. I've done it. I spring up, attempting to show them that the trial hasn't fazed me whatsoever. Behind the red mask, a look of shock enters his eyes, and he, or it, looks like a demon incarnate about to be slain. Then something shifts.

Underneath me, I feel my feet, my foundation, slide and crumble. It's as if I'm on air. My legs fail. I topple to the floor. My arms instinctively brace for impact, but the side of my head cracks on the ground, and my neck snaps in a whiplash motion. Blood drips in small amounts and smears on the off-white tiles as my arms struggle. Warren takes immediate action, sitting me upright. He grabs a towel and applies pressure to the wound.

"Fucker," Firos said and grabbed paper to clean up the blood.

"Dammit, Anthony," MacConough said in a low voice. "All right, Warren, I'll get ice. Once it looks like it's stopped, let him stand and regain balance. When I return, we'll clean him up and send him up. You okay, Wiggins?"

"Sir, yes, sir," I croaked.

MacConough leaves the room. Warren continues to apply pressure and checks the wound. "It looks like the blood is coagulating," Warren says as he applies pressure. *He's the suspect in a manslaughter. That can't be true.*

"Damn, knob. I can't believe you had to go and fall like that," Firos said.

"C'mon! It's not the time for that," Warren shot at him.

My breath eventually steadies, and MacConough returns with ice. They wrap my wound in a paper towel and tell me to hold it to my head.

"Go take it easy the rest of the night. Report to me at the same time tomorrow," MacConough said.

"Sir, yes, sir."

I crawl back to my room, sneak behind the door, and clamber into bed. My head throbs. The cold compress is there but does nothing. I give in to fatigue and close my eyes, and once again, I see my father's face.

CHAPTER 5

One Month—It's All Funk and Games

Paxton Randolph is almost an entire head taller than me. His large lips and odd jaw structure gives him a permanent scowl, which he carries around campus just as he does on the football field. He has an unapproachable air, an air of someone with their guards up at all times.

Later, I found out that he was a 'Bama boy from an impoverished region. His size subjected him to torment growing up—rolling marshlands, heavy air, broken-down trucks, and sweat-stained clothes. And he was only a stone's toss away from this past.

I introduced myself to find someone hesitant to meet strangers. "Whatchu want, bub?" he replied.

"Could we talk? I want to ask you some questions as a fellow brother on campus."

"Look, man, I don't know what you're trying to sell, but I'm not that type of guy."

He closed up, both hands clasping his bag. He had no intentions of shaking my hand. "You cadets think that you can latch on to me because I get football privileges, because of my celebrity status around here."

"Uh-huh." I paused. *What is up with this guy?*

"So you gon' let me get to class or what, brother?"

"Didn't you attend the opening assembly?"

"Yeah, yeah."

"What, the general didn't convince you?"

"Ah, c'mon, you bought it? You buy anything of what the man says?"

"I'm not sure. That's what I wanted to ask you about."

"I ain't got time for this, man."

It's a warm October day, and the harsh sun beats down on the center field. Rifle squads march in the distance. Between our silence, I can hear the count of the sergeant. I am going to be late for my afternoon class, but right now, I don't care. I need to get to the bottom of it.

"Look, I have a cadet who comes to inspect me every Friday. He watches me when I'm on the field and shows up if I'm getting racked. If it weren't for him, some bad things could've happened."

"Like what?"

"I could have ended up in the infirmary, injured, or in the extreme, like Theo Waters."

He gave me a serious look. "Fine, man. You want to have this discussion, then? Steve, you said your name was Steve, right? I don't know what they did to you. Frankly, me, I'm just trying to keep my head down and get an education. I don't want to cause no drama or be a part of any conspiracies. I've seen some bad things, like real bad things, and nothing that they can do here will push me back toward that life, you dig? I'd love to play Watson, but frankly, I'm not that guy."

"I'm just telling you, man, keep them eyes peeled."

"Are you threatening me, man?"

"Nah, I'm giving you a friendly warning. What's your problem?"

"Hold it!" A couple of upperclassmen that I had seen before walked up. "Shouldn't you two be in class?"

"Sir, yes, sir."

"Then what are you boys doing congregating here?"

"Sir, permission to speak, sir," I replied.

"Cadet," he said.

"Sir, I was just on my way to class, sir, but I noticed a fellow cadet whom I've been recommended to meet, sir. I introduced myself because it's important as a fourth year to know your compadres, sir."

"Very well. What's your name, boy?"

"Sir, Paxton Randolph, sir."

"Don't you play on the football team or something?"

"Sir, yes, sir."

The upperclassmen made a noise of acknowledgement and then turned to me. "You are dismissed, Wiggins."

"Sir, yes, sir."

I depart for class. Over my shoulder, I see Paxton questioned and racked like a suspect at customs. He would hate me now, but I don't care. He's naive, and this makes me worry for him. I hope that they are just questioning and nothing further.

To history class, I am late and petrified. My history teacher takes notice as I meander in way past the bell and plop next to Randall. A pamphlet spreads on my desk. I sit and scan the front page: "How to Survive Knob Year Part 1." I look over to Randall. A grin widens on his face. "On the house." He winks.

The teacher is staring at me. "Mr. Wiggins," he says.

"Sir, yes, sir," I say.

"Have you finished your homework? You were supposed to turn it in when you enter class."

"Sir, yes, sir. Sir, sorry, sir," I say. I walk with my head down to the front of the class and turn in the assignment.

"Very good, then."

As he resumes his lecture, I take a look at the pamphlet. What Simon told me is true, info can be found on Petersson, Edwards, and a few of the other cadets. But after scanning the first page, something repulses me. I look up at Randall. The writing is drivel, tabloid gossip. Nothing here is analytical, just purely conditional. I can imagine that Randall has an ulterior motive just like he did on the first day. He wants to separate the pack into the weak and the strong and become the fucking ringleader. I can't believe that Clyde agrees to be a part of this nonsense.

I shifted my focus to the professor. He was covering tactics of World War II and the usage of false information. At Normandy, the Allies had created inflatable armies that drew Hitler's forces into combat only to create openings elsewhere. The tactics we learned I saw as useful to everyday life. Creating an inflatable punching doll for the seniors would save me a lot of trouble. I could walk where I pleased while they took out their anger on this diversion.

At the end of class, the teacher once again calls me to his side. I rise out of my seat with shock. My classmates exit the room. "Sir."

"Wiggins, it's not my place to talk about your personal life, but while your work and quiz scores have been exceptional, your behavior in class doesn't reflect it. You nearly missed half the class today. Something just doesn't add up to me."

"Sir, no excuse, sir."

"Tell me something, Wiggins."

"Sir, I've a duty to not speak out against my commanding officers. Gossip has and never will serve any purpose to me."

"Ah, there we have it, a soldier's silence. All right, well, Wiggins, I think you're a good student. I'm going to give you the benefit of the doubt," he said.

"Thank you, sir," I said. "I've really learned a lot from your lectures on tactics," I added.

"Is that so?" He scanned me. "You want to know how I became involved in the military? Mind if we sit?"

"Sir, yes, sir, of course," I said.

I look at him. Behind his spectacles, he has friendly gray eyes, the eyes of someone who has seen history unfold. It takes him a moment to shift his transition-frail frame to his large chair. Then he gazes up at me. "Well, I was just a kid from Connecticut when I volunteered—to go to Europe, that is. It wasn't on vacation, I'll tell you that, Wiggins." He chuckles.

"From the start, I was very lucky. I had a fantastic commander who was up for the task of training us whippersnappers. We used to call him Mr. Atlantic, a massive man who'd been across the ocean so many times he lost count. He was big into the psychology of warfare, and I'll never forget what he told us.

"He said, at some point on our first tour, it's going to be raining bullets, and it's our job to act like weathermen. When you predict that the storm is going to end, you go out and have a party. This meant counter them Nazis. Reprisal, Wiggins, reprisal, because the rain will stop, and you don't want to find yourself under an umbrella your whole life."

*****

That Saturday, Simon, Clyde, Harry, the others, and I all trudged out on the field in our sneakers. It was chilly with bursts of rain, but despite the slick terrain, Simon kept his promise of being a very good quarterback, and one of our floor mates, Larry, made a great receiver.

The offense quickly cohered. Running from one side of the field and back, the opponent's defense wore down. Meanwhile, on the defensive end, Harry surprised everyone off the jump with several sacks, and I had a pick six. Ending with 35–7, it was Kilo Company's victory. This win raised everyone's mood, and now we had a large group sitting at the mess hall. Harry sat at the middle, acknowledged as one of the MVPs of that game.

While I still dodged him on campus, I was no longer afraid of Petersson at the zoo. When MacConough sat to question us, he went easy, perhaps in retribution for them nearly cracking my head open. With my new strategy at hand and things gelling at the academy, I felt like instead of treading water, I was getting places. A sword could turn into a snake, however, and optimism could turn around to bite you, I had found out.

The week slowly rolled around into the first big event of the school year, Parents' Day. On Thursday, the annual ring ceremony took place. Each year, the academy inducted the seniors into their legacy by granting a ring studded with a palmetto, the state tree and symbol of the school. It was emblematic of the tenacity and discipline they experienced over the four years.

Naturally, this ego rub led to a visceral release, so the seniors had the tradition of going to Dino's, a large bar in the city, where they could do whatever they wanted. The night had become notorious to Charleston locals as one to turn off the lights, close shop, and roll down curtains. Late-night food places locked their doors, and knobs got to their rooms early to avoid confrontation with the raging seniors.

I'm walking down the hall to the bathroom when I hear footsteps clonking on the stairwell. "Wiggy, we're coming for you." It's Petersson's voice. Take it on the chin, roll with the punches, and other idioms don't express the rush of this tsunami wave headed in my direction. Along comes Nicky and Petersson. I stand and brace.

"Halt," Petersson yells.

"He wasn't moving, you dumbass," Nicky says.

"I know, asshole. Just making sure," he says. They walk up to me.

"Wiggins," Nicky says, "consider yourself lucky. It's a grand tradition we have, and anyone who has this on their face has good fortune going forward at the academy. It's like a little Chinese ritual or something. You get me? You'll be marked like a warrior bud."

"I don't know where you've been on campus, boy. I've been looking for you everywhere. Stand still, all right?" Petersson says.

"He's not moving, Petey. Jeez, sometimes…" Nicky says.

"Yeah, I'm telling him not to move, Nick, not that he needs to stop moving."

"Sirs," I say, and they both turn and smile at me in a malevolent gaze. Petersson grabs me by the shoulder and slowly presses the ring of the palmetto on my forehead. It feels like hours pass. The pressure increases until it becomes a searing sensation. It crawls through my body, affecting one inch after another.

Then when I think it can't get worse, a second one is added. Nicky presses on the other side of my forehead. I want to cry. I want to scream. But acting this way gives in to fear, and the only way to confront fear is to stay silent, to not let a tear form or drop.

A deep red crosses my forehead. At first, I feel it, and then it becomes the only thing I feel. It drips over my eyes, slowly falling to the floor. The blood drips in the deserted hallway. Both of the upperclassmen's expressions turn from gratified to astonished as they look down.

Below them, I sit with two imprints of the rings marking me on opposite sides of my forehead like devil horns. Petersson regains his composure and grabs Nicky by the shirt. They leave in a flurry, and I drudge, sullen, back to my room. Luckily, the lights are off when I enter. Without a word from my roommates, incapable of withstanding this glowing pain, I pass out.

We awake to clamor in the night, the upperclassmen, no doubt. I drift off, wondering how a civilian would react to a polished cadet from the academy entering, drinking, and commandeering a bar.

*****

The blood dries, and I awaken to two scabs surrounded by dark bruises on my forehead. The clanging of trash cans echoes through the hall as I shake the throbbing off. Today, I'm admitted into the regiment. The knobs officially become members of the K Company and the Corp of Cadets on Parents' Day. Most of the quitter cadets have left by now. I hop up, burnish my shoes, and make sure my uniform is in peak condition. I cover my blemish with the brim of my cap.

We wear these black caps, company blazers, and white slacks in the company area, shuffling around in buzz. The parents gather outside and peer into the barracks. Upperclassmen begin the performance, saluting one after another and marching with precise command movements. The seniors march four steps forward, then turn left and march eight steps forward, then backward three. The commander directs them through a flawless performance, the peak of human refinement. Finally, they run off, and parents applaud.

After the seniors finish, the knobs are called to the quadrangle. We stand in neat rows and spread all throughout the grounds. Sergeant Edwards stands at the front. A bugle sounds.

"Ladies and gentlemen, the class of 1982, six hundred and forty-two strong!" he shouts, the loudest I have ever heard him speak. The parade begins, an especially important one. Edwards leads us out of our company area to join the upperclassmen who had just dazzled the guests. The band plays, and parents watch from the sidelines.

Each company marches through the parade field, passing the review booth. Graded on our formation, discipline, and uniformity, we circle back and return to the battalion. The parade is acknowledged as a complete success, and while we know this, we need to contain our excitement just a bit longer.

"Get into your PT uniforms and meet back here stat!"

"Sir, yes, sir!"

The cadets chant the whole way up and down stairs: "K's the best. The hell with the rest!"

When I get back to the barracks, the quadrangle's checkered pattern is dizzying—red and white, red and white. The parents accumulate at the sally port, peering in at the cadets. I stride out onto a red square dressed in my PT uniform of blue shorts and a sweater separated by a red-and-white belt. As soon as everyone is here, we head out onto the campus for a five-mile run. When the gates open, we run.

The crowd spreads around us, blurred faces and various shouts of "There he is" and "Go, son, go." The trees rise and bend over the surface of the vast horizon, cascading down into the river at the precipice of campus. It is the same run that we complete each morning; however, with the parents here and the sun overhead, the importance multiplies.

Who switched on gravity? I see Harry beginning to slow, and I signal Clyde. We both lag back and grab Harry by the arms and push him beyond his limits. He regains pace and runs on his own. Snapshots of PT runs flash past us. They seem to dissolve with the warm winds as if they haven't happened at all. This run is proof of the others, proof of progress, I assure myself.

After about two miles, we cross an obstacle course. I duck and jump and proceed through it to continue my run. This time, we transition to an Indian run. Once I am at the back of the formation, I have to accelerate to the front. Gassed, I steady my breath and my pace at the front until the next row passes. I hear Harry grunt as he makes his way to the front. The third mile in, we finish the Indian run and go into a half sprint back toward the battalion. Simon leads the pack. As we near the battalion, we slow in case of stragglers and sing jodies as we arrive.

Open the gates and open them wide.
Mighty Kilo's coming inside.

Open the gates and open them wide.
Mighty Kilo's coming inside!

Once we enter the gates, they close, and an officer locks them. The cadets spread out on the floors of the quadrangle once again. The parents watch in anticipation. Sergeant Edwards walks around the cadets in full uniform and the emotionless mask upon his face. I clench my hand into a fist.

"Cadets!"

"Sir, yes, sir."

"Upperclassmen!"

"Sir, yes, sir."

The upperclassmen march out onto the quadrangle, much like an organized coup, and they each take a few cadets with them. Some stay on the quadrangle and are forced to duck-walk. I, however, am taken up the stairs by Warren this time.

"Push-up positions!"

"Sir, yes, sir"

"Drop down and give me twenty!"

Corporal Warren commands the knobs but with a less forceful approach than what I'm used to. Each of the cadets pounce through the twenty push-ups. Then Warren leads us to the next side of the barracks where we duck-walk to the end.

I figure that each length has a different exercise, so I begin conserving energy. We carry one another for the third length and then switch for the fourth. Many of the cadets seem wiped out by the fourth length of the battalion, and in turn, the parents grow worried. Warren tells us to run up one more flight of stairs in his direct but monotone voice.

The next flight up, Petersson is on this level. "Push-up positions!"

"Sir, yes, sir!"

"Drop down and give me thirty!"

A realization sweeps over us that we will have to do it again. On the third length, while carrying Clyde, someone next to me falls on his knees. A parent yells, "Not my baby!"

Others look tense. The smell of doubt coats some of the cadets, but our parents begin rallying. When I finish the fourth length, I see my father for the first time that day. Our eyes bridge the gap for a moment, and then I run down to the courtyard with my arms tucked in and elbows bent like a dinosaur.

"All right, class of '82, let's finish strong with one push-up per class year!"

Each of us cadets gets down in push-up position and start. Bouncing off the quadrangle, each has already shown progress from where we were before. After about fifty, my arms are throbbing, but I have to continue. At eighty-two, Sergeant Edwards says, "One for class '82 and one for K Company! And drop!"

A large exhale releases from the battalion, and all the knobs, without exception, are exhausted. After a couple seconds of recovery, Sergeant Edwards tells us to go kiss the academy's symbol, and then we can join our parents. The company, friends, and floor mates alike look around at one another in relief. I make eye contact with Simon and then turn to Harry, Clyde, and several others I have met so far. We made it.

I walked over to join my family. My mother was wearing an elegant orange dress with a red print on it. Sweat flowed down my face, so I held my hat with two hands. As I approached, her smile turned into a look of concern or worry. Arthur remained stoic, but my mom leaped forward and put her palm across my face. She took a close look at my forehead, at my two devil horns.

"What in the Lord's name did they do to you, Steven?" she yelled.

"It's nothing, ma'am, just a tumble I had during ROTC training." I smiled at her.

"What? Look at these things. I don't believe you, Steven. You tell me what happened this instant!" Loretta said.

"Please, ma'am, ignore these blemishes. I'm alive and vital, as good as I've ever been," I said. For a moment, the sound of other parents congratulating their children rose between us.

"No, no, that won't do at all, Steve. I'm sorry," Loretta said. "You remember? You promised me that you'd tell me what is going on. You'd let me know if something happened, that you'd think of us when putting yourself in these kinds of situations."

"I'm sorry, ma'am. This was unavoidable. Just an accident."

Infuriated, my mother put her face in her hands. The two blemishes on my face had grown into a deep purple, aligning almost exactly on the corners of my forehead. My sisters gave me two big hugs.

"I missed you, Steve," Maisy said.

"I missed you too," I said.

"The house really ain't the same without you," my big sister, Lorna, said.

I look over to my mother and father. He puts his hand on her shoulder to try and console her, but she turns away. We walk off campus and to Arthur's car. Dinner is terribly awkward. Arthur is quiet through the entire meal, which isn't out of the ordinary, but my mother is also silent.

My sisters pepper me with questions about cadet life and my schoolwork. I reply that I am doing well and have a 3.5 GPA. I look to my mom for some sort of acknowledgment. This behavior is isolating, to say the least. I want to relax at home, but it seems as if the academy has infiltrated my home life, ruining what stood before it. Suddenly, I catch the gaze of my father. His eyes either communicate a serious intent, an acknowledgement of progress, or a life raft.

One, I can apologize to my mother and tell her that I have been thinking about them very much and explain the situation. I mean, she's my mom. She'll forgive me. Two, I can apologize to my mother and tell her the truth about my forehead and explain the events that preceded, tell her that I was forcefully fed two steel rings into my forehead until I bled, tell her that...that I'm sorry but that this is what happens at the academy. Three, I can tell her that it'll never happen again.

Well, option 2 is definitely a no-go. I can see my father denouncing me for voicing what troubles I have been through. "You haven't done much growing, son," he would say. Fourth option, I can change the topic.

"Steve." My mom burst my thought. "I'll save you the trouble, all right? This is about your promise. You promised me that you'd let me know what was going on with you," she said softly.

"I'm sorry, Mom. I'm sorry. This is just part of it."

"What's 'this'? You can't say nothing and expect me to understand."

"This, not speaking about it. It's the whole thing."

"Not speaking about it? No, you can always speak about it. You always have the choice to speak about it."

"It's not optional to speak about it."

"What do you mean it's not optional?"

"It's like a code, Mom." She looked puzzled and frustrated. I glanced from my father to her and back.

"Let the boy eat in peace, Loretta," Arthur boomed.

The room went silent. I looked at my sisters, from Lorna to Maisy. Lorna had a look of deep sadness on her face. Her mouth was scrunched, emotionless, but her nostrils flared and her eyes, well, her eyes told the story. Maisy's head was lowered, her napkin tight in her hand.

I caused this. This dinner was for me, and I ruined it. I caused this pain for everyone just because of this stupid belief system that they had ingrained in me. They—who the hell were they to tell me who I was when I was in my house? Then I looked to my father. My father is "they," I guess.

"Sir," I said, "ma'am, I'll tell you. You promise that you won't do anything hasty. Please, Mom, please."

"Steven, do not wager with me like that."

"Please, Mom."

She set her napkin down. "All right, but you promise to tell me the truth and all the truth."

"Yes, ma'am. Two boys did it. They say it represents good fortune at the academy to press the ring on your forehead, so I agreed to it. See? There ain't no harm in that."

"There ain't no harm in that," Arthur echoed. Silently watching this scene play out, Arthur approved. Clearly, he had been in my situation before.

"Uh-huh. Your forehead looks like a war zone and you say there ain't no harm in it, huh?" She took a deep breath. "Well, thank you, Steve, for telling me." The tension dissipated, and my mother began speaking at a normal pace. We finished eating, then they took me back to campus for the night.

On Saturday, the academy allowed parents to enter the company area and rooms. When I took them upstairs, my mother and sisters were out of breath. I opened the door to a spotless room.

"Wow, Steve," Maisy said. "Are you sure this is your room?"

"For real," Loretta said, shocked, and everyone laughed.

Completely absorbed, Arthur checked the bunks and lockers, inspecting each inch of the room. "Very nice," he said when he was finished.

We march out to the quadrangle in a similar manner as the prior day. Sergeant Edwards and other staff sergeants present us with a golden *K* on our uniforms, replacing the number 4 from before. With our chests out and shoulders back, we march out to the football game. We head down the sideline, saluting once the flag is waved and then saluting the visitors. Being parents' weekend, it is one of the most important games of the season. We begin singing "Dixie" at the top of our lungs.

> In Dixie's Land, where I was born in, early on one frosty mornin'.
> Look away, look away, look away Dixie Land!

When the song finishes, the football players run out onto the field, and its kickoff. A short return by the home team up to the seventeen-yard line. The quarterback snaps, and they run the ball. We are as loud as we can manage between plays on offense to encourage this important win. The defense, however, forces them to punt after one set of downs. As the offense returns to the bench, I search for Paxton. One by one, they take off their helmets, and I see him.

A large red gash scars the top of his cheekbone, hooking underneath his eye. It spans from his eye to his ear and looks gory and severe. *I must be seeing things.* I try to look away and bury this image underneath my chants and jodies, though I keep thinking about it and asking what those upperclassmen did to him that day.

> I wish I was in Dixie. Hooray! Hooray!
> In Dixie's Land I'll take my stand,
> to live and die in Dixie.

The cadets continue yelling at the top of their lungs, but the game slowly slips away. The coach takes Paxton out and sends him to the bench. I decide to leave the cadet area and run over to the fenced area behind the bench.

"Pax. Yo, Pax!" I yelled.

"What? What is it, Steve?" Paxton yelled back in anger.

The roar of the crowd filled my ears as something muffled was yelled over the microphone. "Come here, man," I said and took a closer look. "What the hell happened?" Tears of anger welled in my eyes.

"Nothing, man. What happened to you?" he said in reference to my blemishes.

"Did those guys do something to you when I left?"

"They ain't do nothing. Look, before I met you, all I cared about was practice and sleep. Now I just want to make it outta here alive," he said. "Please stop talking to me." He was shivering, scared.

"Yo, don't turn me into the enemy here. We're suffering the same, man. If we can't talk to each other, then who can we talk to about this?" I said.

"I think that's the point. We shouldn't be talking. We shouldn't be snooping. I think it's a trap."

"That's not what I'm saying. I think that we'd be better off as a team, that's all. Paxton, I'm going to find a solution, I promise."

"No. Stop searching for answers, Steve. You're just in denial that we're in a bad situation. There's nothing you or I can do about it." Paxton wagged his finger, and he left. *What if it is a trap?*

The academy loses, 24–38, to Western Carolina. The cadets are crestfallen. Despite the loss, we are given an overnight pass to sleep outside of campus for the night. I don't know what to think. On one hand, I get to sleep at home; and on the other, I've just figured out that there is a race-based target on me and Paxton and that because of that target, Paxton doesn't want any association. This is fubar.

Anguish from that encounter hangs over my head like smog. Everyone I talk to assumes it's because of the game. Toward the end of the afternoon, Harry sheepishly asks if he can sleep over. His parents couldn't make it from Michigan, and he didn't want to sleep at the academy by himself. I accept. Maybe this goof will put me in a better mood, I think.

From the curbside, the front windows are illuminated by a full home, my home. Seeing this flips my perspective on things. A warmth quickly overtakes this steely feeling that I have acquired from the empty hallways of the academy. Not only would I be able to sleep in my bed but also Randall tells us that there is a party being thrown that night. This is a part of the college experience I haven't yet known and that I have dearly missed.

Across the street, "One of These Nights" by Eagles emanates from the house. Trucks fill the nearby spaces. People spill onto the dark-green grass. Two perfectly maintained ovoid bushes stand on each side of the entrance. October brings chilly evenings, even in this Southern town.

Lights of all different colors wink in and out from different windows of the one-story house. Harry and I drive up in my parents' Oldsmobile. We had split a twelve-pack beer, but we haven't finished it yet, so we decide to bring the rest inside.

We walk through the front and quickly perk up when women pass. Harry carries the beer but let's his arm drop at the sight. A beer rolls out onto the floor. The house is packed, noisy, and smoky, so at least no one notices. "Be cool, man," I say.

Out in the open living room, I spot Nicky, MacConough, and a third person whom I didn't know chatting away. After a moment, MacConough and the other person burst out laughing. Avoiding eye contact, I walk into the secluded kitchen where a couple is having an intimate conversation.

I check the fridge, but there isn't any place to put the beer. That's when I turn back to see Harry giving the upperclassmen a deer-in-headlights look. Harry takes the crate of beer and cradles it like a football. He motions like he is going to leave the house. In an instant, Nicky jumps over the couch and grabs Harry.

"Where you going, piggy?" Nicky says. "It's my house, and I say you stay. C'mon, little guy, stay and hang with us." Harry freezes. The other upperclassmen walk up behind Nicky and peer around his shoulders with fake scowls like satirical bullies. I decide to help.

"Wiggins!" Nicky and MacConough exclaim.

"Sir." I salute them.

"What the hell are you two goofballs doing here?" MacConough says.

"Would you like a beer?" I offer, and Harry holds up the crate.

Nicky and the third upperclassman take one, but MacConough declines and says he isn't drinking that night. He is wearing a lavender-patterned shirt and light khakis like a never-ending summer. Nicky has on a navy polo with a white stripe through the collar and brown pants.

"Hey, MacConough," Nicky said.

"What is it?" MacConough asked.

"You never told us the one about the two freshmen who walked into the party." He snorted with laughter and looked around. "Look, you two, this is my house. You somehow just became my guests. We have a band coming on in a little bit, so relax, get situated, and grab a view," Nicky said. He tapped me on the chest.

"Stay out of trouble, all right?" MacConough said.

"Sir, yes, sir," we both replied and walked away.

Harry whispered, "That's weird that MacConough doesn't drink, huh?"

"Maybe he's driving," I said.

"I guess you're right." He laughed.

We exit the living room to a capacious yard. A band is setting up their drum set, mics, and amps, and people crowd around, socializing with beer cans and red cups in their hand. I recognize some other faces from the dorms but no one with whom I have had an extensive conversation. And then I see Mr. Annoying, Randall himself. He is surrounded by a large group of people our age.

"Hey, man," I say.

Randall looks at me. "Steve, Harry, you guys made it. Steve, this is Miranda, and you said your name was Claire?" Randall says.

"How do you do?" I say. "We're classmates of Randall."

"Hardly." Randall laughs, "These guys are some of the lowlifes that wait around the academy to get kicked out. Just kidding. Harry, c'mon, you know I'm just kidding, right?"

"Thanks for the introduction, buddy," Harry says.

"Why don't you all get to know each other? I'm needed in other places. Good seeing you guys," Randall says and leaves.

Miranda was wearing a patterned shirt with strawberries on it and light-washed bell-bottom jeans. Through a friendly smile and a few well-placed quips, all four of us were dancing to "Evil Woman" by Electric Light Orchestra.

"C'mon, Steve, show us what you've got!" Miranda said to me.

I move both hands, ready to snap my fingers to the beat. Then I break my knees and do a fancy wave motion with my body. I have to admit, I'm a bit stiff, especially with the prospect that upperclassmen may be watching. The girls start giggling at my moves. I motion to have one of them take my hands, and Miranda accepts, so I twirl her once, two times, and bring her closer.

I look at the scenery. MacConough is staring directly at me. When he sees me looking, he takes a sip of water and glances in another direction. *What the hell does he want?* I break my gaze and see Harry standing awkwardly, so I bend in to Miranda and whisper a plan. She takes his hand and connects it with her friend's. Then I introduce Harry to both of them.

"We're both roommates at the academy!" I yell over the music.

"Wow, nothing better than men in uniform. He's a big boy too!" She laughs.

Harry blushes, and she grabs him by his cheek. Perfect. A wide smile forms on my face as I look over to Miranda. She's smiling as well. I have never seen such a sheepish reaction garner affection. The band comes on, and Claire takes Harry's hand, and they thread through the crowd.

"We make a pretty decent team," I say and immediately think it sounds lame.

"We do." She laughs.

"Where are you at school?"

"Charleston College."

"What do you study?"

"Education and Spanish."

"That's cool. Why Spanish?"

"To travel. I want to teach English in South America." Silence. "How about you?"

"I'm still in my knob year, uh, my freshman year, so we don't have a major yet."

"Oh, okay," she says. Then the music divides us. *How come all of a sudden it's awkward?*

"Do you like Charleston?"

"Yeah, for the most part."

"Yeah, summers get a little too hot."

"Yeah."

I stop speaking. This conversation is going nowhere. I look around. MacConough is still looking at me. Maybe he's playing head games. I need to block him out.

"So how do you know Randall?"

"I went to high school with him and his brother. He's always been like a little brother to me. He's so cute."

"Yeah, he is," I respond without listening to her. *MacConough, stop!* I think. *He's still looking at me. Why?*

"What?"

I look at her. "Nothing, nothing. Look, to be honest, he's not so cute. To me, he's a complete asshole."

"Excuse me?" She looks offended.

"Let me explain to you. He's a total douchebag, a spoiled brat. He takes everything his brother has done and rides that as far as it takes him. He cheats his way through things. He gets help cheating his way through things. He calls me racist epithets—nigger, darkie—and always adds comments on my skin color, so frankly, I don't like the guy. He acts like he's the center of the solar system, so he moseys by with his smug looks and his supercilious gestures.

"I wake up early and go to bed late. I eat at twice the speed and walk through the shadows of campus, and still, they want to kill me. But a guy…a guy like that will never understand what it feels like because he was literally given a guidebook to the school that helps him troubleshoot everything, and then he's given the idea to sell it, which, in turn, gives him more influence.

"He's not sweet or cute or whatever you thought of him as a child. He's manipulative and deceitful, and I don't think a beautiful girl like you should be interested in someone like him."

At this point, I am rambling, hurtling everything I could without regard for thought or rationale or repercussions, and she looks at me with her big blue eyes. I feel embarrassed at releasing all this onto her, but then she closes her eyes and leans in and kisses me.

I don't know what I did to deserve that, but boy did it happen, and I tingle from my lips down through the rest of my body, undoing everything that the two bludgeons on my forehead have originally caused. It feels as if she has healed me. Right then, I am back.

"Let's dance, right?" she said and took my hand. "And I'm not a fan of him anyway. I just thought you two were friends."

This was a different kind of moment from those I usually experienced. For once, letting go, letting my real thoughts, how I was feeling at the moment stand, granted me a win. The rest of the night, I had a very hard time staying in the moment. I thought of my father. He had told me to commit to myself and my strategies. Maybe for the first time, that was happening. We danced together for a few songs. I looked over to see Nicky dancing like a maniac and surrounded by several beautiful women.

At the end of the set, I take down Miranda's number as did Harry with Claire, and we split ways. I look out over the garden with beer cans sprawled out and lights dangling above no one. The night is over, and MacConough is gone, nowhere to be seen. Harry and I walk home, laughing and joking about Harry's first kiss.

*****

Janitorial didn't have quite the stink that I put up with. I would empty trash bags, clean up gunk, and the worst of it, wash toilets and urinals of my fellow classmates. At the academy, the presiding commanders scheduled each cadet's duty for the week on their little board at the inside of the barracks. The cadets would pass it when they went upstairs to their rooms. I knew that it was suspicious for MacConough to have me as a runner for more than a few weeks at a time, so he switched me for a different knob.

Each night, I cleaned feces and disgusting leftovers, and I treated it as a way to see areas of the campus that I had never seen before. I figured, most of the barracks were of similar layouts—seven levels with four long white corridors that swing around at ninety-degree angles and rooms equidistant from one another. The stairwells were at the end of the hallway, and the bathrooms were in the center of the hall furthest away from them. The exceptions were the first and third levels, which had recreational rooms for the cadets, one for upperclassmen and one for knobs.

I learn the layout of the barracks much quicker than expected. When it is time to give up janitorial and shift back to runner duty, my map is almost complete. I know Indian Hill. I know the marshes from the Ashley River to the boathouses. I know all the halls, all the pathways, and now all the barracks. If I want, I can avoid human contact on my way to classes. I begin to share some of this knowledge with my roommates, but I never fully expose my map.

My return to runner duty is my first personal interaction with MacConough since the party. Immediately, MacConough puts me back into the corner. This time, however, he pulls up a chair and sits behind me.

"How're classes going, Wiggins?"

The end of October is coming, and my grades have slouched a bit, but I still maintain above a 3.0. "Sir, I have a 3.1, sir," I say.

"That's okay, but you're going to have to do better, Wiggins, if you want to stand out at this school, at least," MacConough said. This was the most gentle voice that I had ever heard from him. "You know what I like about you, Wiggins?"

"Sir, no, sir."

"It seems as if your instincts are smart. I've never met someone like that before. It's like your actions and answers are always thought out carefully even if your response is your natural response. You weren't like that when I first met you, and I'm assuming it's because you were nervous, but now I feel you have what it takes to do well here."

"Sir, thank you, sir."

"Just don't get ahead of yourself, all right? And try a little harder in academics. If you need something, you can always come talk to me. Don't hesitate to ask your fellow cadets for help as well."

"Sir, thank you, sir."

Silence descends over us. Corporal Warren isn't there, and his absence swells. *Where is he?* This meeting with MacConough turns from routine to bizarre. Did he want to lure me in like last time, or does he want to help? Does he want to unsettle me, or is he trying to communicate in tacit speech? MacConough is playing weird mind games, and these tactics are destructive.

"Did you end up meeting the other black cadet like I recommended?"

You didn't recommend. You said they were all out to get us. "Sir, yes, sir."

"So I take it you saw what they did to his face," MacConough says. I freeze. "It's a shame the events that transpired after that. A man shouldn't be punished for something that he didn't do."

MacConough stands and begins pacing. "You see, Wiggins, there's a whole side of this academy that you probably aren't aware of. There are a lot of politics and bullshit that become order without due process. And now that we're at the end of our last year, everyone is trying to do what it takes to make it out of here"—at this point, he is practically yelling—"with the best reputation or even just their reputation intact.

"And when you're not at the top, things get nasty. People do what it takes to pull you back down. They devolve into scum. That's why it's so important to get a good start like I'm telling you. At first, when I saw you, I felt sorry. Everyone wanted to pound you. You got knocked out by Petey." He laughs. "He got carried away, for sure. Then that bloody head.

"You and whatever his name got it the worst. Why? Because you stand out. But you, you seem to get by. I've never heard you complain or pout or anything. I see the lengths that people go to teach someone else a lesson or instill them with some kind of modesty, and I wondered to myself, is that right? It sure doesn't seem like it. I don't know, but that's just what I've been thinking about. So I want to back up my statement that you can come talk to me if there are things bugging you."

"Sir, yes, sir."

"I talked your ear off enough, I guess. Get back to your room."

I walk back to my room plagued with these riddles. My other two roommates are present. "Yo, Steve!" Harry says as he walks through the door.

"What is it?" I laugh.

"Halloween's coming up. Round 2. We were just discussing plans."

"I still can't believe I missed this guy's first kiss," Clyde says. "That must've been so-so awkward. Did she start screaming and running away, Harry?" We all laugh.

"No, we're actually planning on hanging out one of these nights."

"You better follow up on that, Harry."

"How am I supposed to?" he says.

"Next time we get off campus, give her a call," I say.

"Speaking of which," Clyde says.

"What's going down?" I say.

"I know of a party," Clyde says. "Some of the upperclassmen are teaming with a sister school and creating a huge thing."

"Damn. Here we go," I shout.

"Yeah, the only problem is that we don't have the night away from campus, so we're going to have to sneak out."

"Clyde, you maniac, I'm not sure if I like that idea," I say.

"Let's hear him out, Steve," Harry says.

106

"I've been coming up with a plan, a big, grand plan. Remember that map you said you've been creating when you're on runner duty? Well, we need your skill, Steve. We need you to use your goddamn talent to break us out of here and have the time of our lives! Can you do that, Steve?"

"Um."

"Look, it's laid out. We sneak outta here, go to the boating area, and raft down to the marina where the friend of Randall's brother is. He takes us to the party. He has the alcohol and everything else we need, and then we just have to get back right in the morning." He paused and then turned. "And, Harry, unfortunately, we're going to need someone to cover."

"What do you mean?"

"You can't come. We need someone here to prevent us from being AWOL."

"Really? There's no other way?" Harry said.

"Look, I really don't think it's worth it," I said. "We should just wait until next year when we're given actual nights away instead of this ludicrous plan." This landed awkwardly as we fell into silence. Taps hovered over campus. "I'll think about it," I said in the darkness.

The next day, motivated by MacConough's words, whatever their intent may be, I focused throughout each of the periods. In my ROTC course, we were preparing for a retreat in two weeks where we would do field training. In history, Randall and I had not spoken to each other in days, but I mentioned Halloween and that I was going.

We study some of the tactics used in the Vietnam War, such as scorched earth and guerrilla warfare. The former is a method for destroying resources so the enemy can't use them, and the latter are small surprise attacks to gain psychological advantage. That is the real tactic the upperclassmen use. Still, I am enthralled.

Math was my strongest class, as the formulas came quite naturally in my head. I frequently participated but only when I was positive of the answer. The math teacher didn't have much patience for wrong answers, and several students would shrink into their notebooks while he searched for a volunteer.

In ESP, I knew that before long, my 3.1 would be irreversible, so I created a study guide with sharp patterns to help me remember more abstract concepts from class. Formulas were intrinsic to me, but the abstractions learned in class left too vast a room for the same perfection and too vast a room to quantify. By the end of the day, I was exhausted, and a small push by Clyde convinced me to commit to their Halloween plans. Harry was disappointed.

After taps, I think of how I didn't construct the map for this purpose. It's supposed to liberate me and my friends from rackings.

*****

With the moonlight suspended above the academy's fields, the grass highlights each of our footsteps with the absence of light. There are no stars from under the fluorescents, and when we swing into the shadow of the barracks, there are only a few from the shade. We meet Randall at the base of the water tower behind the barracks and continue to the outskirts of campus.

We haven't seen anyone. This is partly due to my navigation and partly due to the campus, which seems subdued on Halloween with only the exception of a few upperclassmen dressing up in costumes in the mess hall, racking knobs. The three of us sneak through the darkness with the midnight mist and make our way to the boating channel where during the day cadets and members learn nautical apparatuses. The channel connects to the Ashley River. The river leads to the meeting point.

A large kayak hides among the reeds. Randall and Clyde hop in while I hold steady, and then I jump in the raft. Slowly, we untie the boat and begin paddling from the channel into the Ashley.

"Hey, Randall?"

"What is it, Steve?"

"Just one question. Did you come up with this idea yourself?"

"Obviously, you have to have the means to do it. It's not like everyone sneaks off of campus for Halloween. That's definitely one of the perks of having an upperclassman brother."

"So you're saying it wasn't your idea."

Randall turned around. "Why are you so threatened by me, Steve?"

"I'm not threatened by you. I just had one question, and you evaded it."

"Stop it. Stop it, guys. Let's just have fun tonight," Clyde says.

The river is languid and wide. There hasn't been much rainfall this year. Once we make it to the edge of the Ashley, we start the small motor in the boat, figuring we are no longer within earshot. We cruise through the smooth waters, ripples severing the moonlight in twos and threes. Brush cover the banks as abstract black figures, and in the distance, the bridge stands with car lights dancing over the river's surface.

"You know, Steve," Randall said, "these are the same waters that Theo Waters was found drifting in."

"Yeah," I said remorsefully.

"Did you ever hear the story of how it happened?" he said.

"What story? There's no story. I don't want to her that anyway."

"C'mon, Wiggs, it's in the holiday spirit! Where's your passion for Halloween?" When we dock, Randall's friend waits in a black Jeep in the gravel parking lot. The two round headlights shine. "What's up, man?" Randall shouts.

"Randall! How're you doing, bud?"

"Good. That was just like they said, no problem at all. Do you have everything?" Clyde and I sit awkwardly, half in the conversation. "It's all here, alcohol and costumes. This party's going to be crazy."

We climb into the back of his Jeep, and I speak up. "Hey, man, I'm Steve."

"Hey, Steve. Here, these are for you guys. It's a haunted house theme, so I figured we'd all go as ghosts."

We drive off into the night and down a bumpy road back into town. I look out of the window as the radio plays. A groovy song that I haven't heard before plays. It goes, "Freak out," and then the bass skips out a groove line and then, "Ah!"

"This is the jam!" Randall says. He opens a bottle of liquor, and we begin taking swigs. We remove the costumes from the bag and try them on, white bedsheets with holes for eyes.

I look around at them. "I can't wear this," I say.

"What do you mean?" Randall asks from the front.

"They look like KKK uniforms," I say.

"What? C'mon, Steve, are you kidding me?" Clyde says.

"No, I'm not kidding you. Look, it's the exact same, just without the point at the top."

"It's Halloween. Be something scary. KKK members are pretty damn scary." Randall laughs. This is infuriating. I take a deep breath to calm myself. "I can't believe you, Steve. You always have to make it a race thing," Randall says.

"Hey, c'mon, guys, let's just focus on the night ahead," Randall's friend says.

"You ain't ruining my fun, buddy." Randall points at me. "Maybe we should dump beer on you. You could be a wet blanket. Huh, you like that better, Steve? I can't believe you convinced me to bring this guy, Akron. Fuck you, Steve."

"Hey, lay off him, man."

"I'll lay off of who I feel like lay-y-ying off of."

"What's the matter, stu-stu-stutter boy? Do you need your brother here to back you up? You don't scare anyone," I say, and then to the song, I add, "Freak out." Clyde's staring over at me and covers up his mouth with a fist. I guess he is surprised by my retort. He shrugs his shoulders to say sorry.

Through the back streets of an upscale Charleston suburb we went. Cookie-cutter mansions, basketball hoops, and large cars told this was an upper-class area of nonlegacies, one-generation Charlestonians who moved here when the city went downhill.

We pull up to a large cookie-cutter mansion that has a massive six-car driveway that cascades down to the street. Looming hedges and white pillars decorate the entrance of the house. We put our ghost costumes and walk up to the door. A large brick fireplace rests at the hearth of the living room. It's dressed for Halloween with cobwebs from the stairwells and ghouls from the ceiling. People chat in bunches.

Randall's friend greets the host and moves through the crowd. With his ghost costume on, Clyde gives me a look, signaling that there are women about. I take the whiskey and beer to the kitchen and place them among the many other bottles on a large island. I scour the room.

"Look, it's a black Klan member," I overheard someone say.

"They call that the unholy ghost," someone else said.

"Lawd, save me," a third yelled.

I try to move throughout the house unseen like the ghost I am. Outside, people dance the boogie. I see another ghost at the far side and maneuver through the crowd. Someone spills a glass of wine on me. The red spreads over the white sheet like someone who has been gravely injured. People in the crowd start laughing. I take the costume off, and then in return, they start booing, both like ghosts and critics. I plop down on the grass and put my head in my hands. A girl joins me, but I'm overwhelmed with negative energy.

"I saw what happened, you poor thing," she says. I look at her but don't reply. "Are you okay?"

"I will be," I finally respond.

This hits her in a bad way, the way I intend it. I mean, she's nice to look at, but I am not in the mood. We both turn to the crowd for a moment, and then she leaves. After a moment by myself on the grass, I stand and walk back inside to find Clyde. He is in the kitchen, talking to someone I don't know.

I pull him aside. "Hey, man. I'm really not feeling comfortable at the party in this costume."

"No one's making fun of you, Steve. Just have fun, all right? Don't worry about all the bullshit. I can't remember. Are you still in touch with that chick? Is that what this is about?"

"No, not at all. People keep saying I'm a black Klansman. I don't like that."

"You've got to take it easy. Stop taking what people say so seriously."

"C'mon, man," I say.

"Look." He points to the other person and then to me. "What does he look like to you?"

"A ghost."

"A mother-loving ghost! That's what I'm telling you, Steve. You gotta lighten up. Enjoy things," he says, but I don't hear him. I leave and walk to the front of the house where a winding set of stairs leads to the next floor. Upstairs, it seems quiet. I walk up, checking to see that nobody witnesses me. The hallway is black and filled with closed doors, except for one.

There is a light emanating from the room and the distant whir of a fan. Inching closer, I peer around the corner. It's the bathroom. The door shuts. I find myself inside the bathroom and looking at my reflection in the mirror. There's nothing wrong with me, but somehow, I've changed. The rings on my forehead have healed.

It's one thing with upperclassmen, but it's another with my own supposed friends. I can't stand this school. I'm at my wit's end. There's a large bathtub with a cushioned seat inside. It looks comfortable, better than being with all of those people. I step in and look at the bottle, and then I begin taking swigs of whiskey.

"Freak out!" I sing.

CHAPTER 6

One Night—The Mask
of a Soldier

In the beginning of November, autumn is only a gateway to winter. Each morning, the morning itself pushes further away from us; and after each run, I feel further from grasping the blue string on the edge of the horizon. When we awaken, suddenly, it's beyond brisk. It's downright chilly. Cadets mellow and are less combative, less interested on imposing themselves on others. Rack parties aren't as often—once a week, if that.

Tonight, my hallway is bare. Radiators hiss and blow hot air throughout the barracks. Fifteen-minute cycles they run through. I've measured once. You notice when they stop. It's subtle yet abrupt, replaced by an eerie silence in the hallways, and then suddenly, they begin again.

They line each hallway, equidistant from one another, such as everything at the academy. I imagine that they speak to one another, that they know of and whisper of the secrets that lay beyond the closed doors of the academy. I've seen these doors. In the underground, below the mess hall and student lounges, the hallways snake and divert into a maze. There are doors upon doors that lead to rooms upon rooms full of drawers of files, documents, and artifacts.

The academy was founded in the early nineteenth century and had a compendium of historical significance. One could argue that the Civil War began here. An institution steeped in the dark side of history buries its past selves in its fields, underground, or perhaps river.

After dinner, I tromp down this barren hallway to my dorm room. Anger from Halloween still eats at me, gnaws at my insides like bacterium. I'm beyond tired and overly sensitive. Physically, I'm worn down from the party last night only to wake an hour later for PT. The hallways sparkle with an extra sheen of fluorescent lighting, vivid and harsher than usual. It's blinding. Tonight, I'm in my head, true, when I should be focused on my studies. I can't believe my comrades turned on me on Halloween.

I try to batter away these negative thoughts. It's crazy how I can't follow the advice that I gave to Harry. I push my door ajar. As I enter the room, something feels off. The room is familiar, but it's not my own. The truth creeps over like shadow. *Shit, I know whose room this is.* I turn and look as my superior lurches backward into the center as if he is controlled by a puppeteer. There is another cadet, one whom I have never seen before, leaning on the desk, facing MacConough.

The room goes silent. Both upperclassmen stand still and eventually turn to me. I am so out of it that I must've instinctively gone to MacConough's room. *Wait, what did I just see?* My two superiors glare at me like raccoons under a newly illuminated porch light. Heat emanates throughout the room, and a bead of sweat forms on my temple. I can feel it hanging there. MacConough takes a deep breath, adjusts his clothes, and speaks.

"Wiggins, come inside and look at the corner," he said. His voice carried a fabricated calm to it.

"Sir, yes, sir," I said and walked to the corner. I braced. "Sir, if I may, sir." The bead of sweat strolled down my face.

"No, you may not, Wiggins. Stand there and listen to what I have to say to you." Then MacConough said, "You gotta get out of here." He told his companion to leave. I heard ruffling, and then the door creaked and closed. "What in God's name are you doing here?" he burst.

"Sir, it slipped my mind that I didn't have runner duty today, and I, um, sir," I replied.

"But it's ESP right now, cadet. It's ESP. You wouldn't be going here anyway. That story doesn't make any sense. Why would you just enter the room? That's not how runner duty works, and you know that. I mean, what slipped in your mind? Obviously, you couldn't have been spying because you just moseyed right in. Plus, you look like you done seen a ghost. But still, this is unwarranted."

My breath quickens, but it can hardly be heard over MacConough's huffing. He is pacing behind me in a furious manner, at a loss for words. We both are, but the panic in MacConough's voice strike me. I have seen the corporal with a razor-like demeanor, and I have watched him from afar joking with the other commanders, but never have I heard exasperation in his voice. What did I walk in on? Suddenly, it dawns on me. Forsaken in the South and forbidden at the academy, my commander is gay, and I've just discovered his secret.

My mind began racing at the prospect of this situation. Options came out of thin air. Swallow my pride, accept that I would be in trouble, live a life on the run, or confess. I could tell on MacConough. Everything surged over me like waves onto a mighty steamship. No, I needed to calm myself, trust myself, and react on intuition.

"So what am I going to do with you, Wiggins?" MacConough said.

"Nothing, sir," I said. With this answer, MacConough stopped pacing. I could tell it caught him aback. It might've even come off as a brazen answer. Nothing. Nothing. It replayed through my head.

"What's that supposed to mean, nothing?" MacConough yelled.

"Nothing, sir."

"Nothing is supposed to mean nothing? You better reason with me real quick about what you meant."

"Sorry, sir. It's just, I mean to say I've seen nothing because I don't know what I've seen, and trust me, I won't tell a soul about it. Nothing happened. I won't do anything, so you shouldn't do anything. Don't worry. Don't doubt in my abilities. You have my word, sir. It just caught me off guard because I realized too late that it was the wrong room." I paused. "We both know that I saw nothing, so if you do nothing, nobody will have to know."

"Fuck, Wiggins," MacConough yelled. Then I heard a large clatter behind me. "Look at me."

I turned and saw one of the wooden chairs flipped. MacConough seemed to have regained some calm. "Sir, may I say something, sir?"

"Yes, Wiggins, what is it?"

"Have others seen nothing?" My question buzzes around the room like a mosquito in the dark. MacConough takes a moment to respond. I can't tell if this is because he is still taken aback by what just happened or if he just doesn't want to disclose his answer.

"If anyone found out about me, I'd be crucified like Christ, hung like Turner, finished."

"Sir, you might as well go out as an icon like those two instead of sinking into mediocrity."

"How naive you are," he says. "Watch carefully, because whether you like it or not, we're going to be in each other's encampment from now on. You need to watch what I do here. This is the reality of the situation." MacConough closes his eyes for a moment. Slowly, his grimace changes to a smirk, his furrowed brow relaxes, and his eyes that only moments ago were full of despair transform into the normal piercing gaze. His physiology changes back to normal, chest out, no longer fazed by anything.

"I haven't told anyone. I can't tell anyone. I'm sure you know what the consequences would be—barred from the school, publicly humiliated. I wouldn't make it outta here alive." He pointed to his face. "This is what they call the mask of the soldier. It's the same mask that we wear when we endure tragedy or hardship. We put it on in the morning during PT run, and we wear it when someone is in your face, barking at you at work.

"Everyone wears this, but a little secret, this place will teach you how to put it on whenever it's necessary. It teaches you that to survive, you can never let anyone know who you truly are, because at the academy, everyone is the same. Your classmates are going to find this out eventually, but now you know, and you're paces ahead. Being a knob is like being at the bottom of the food chain. You're all worthless and, therefore, equal.

"Now I remember you used to take things very personal during the first month, but it doesn't seem to be the case anymore, so perhaps you are already learning the ways of the mask. Well, when you master it, no one is able to read you, because nothing gets in or out." He paused again. "But now, now that you've seen behind my mask, either I have you destroyed or choose to trust you."

"Sir, yes, sir," I said. I maintained my demeanor.

"And judging by what I've seen of you…" He paused for a third time. From what I could tell, he knew how to create pressure using his mask, similar to Sergeant Edwards, similar to Arthur Wiggins. Those few seconds clicked longer than the PT runs in the morning, longer than the taps at night. He drew out his answer, not out of reflection but to increase pressure at the conclusion.

"I'm going to trust you, Wiggins. I know you have sense of what's right in this situation."

MacConough's delicate speech, this long scene of candor, caused an instant relief. His choice to confide in me meant that he would carry it out, and at the same time, it validated the severity of what I had discovered. There were certain sides of people that you never see, similar to how the moon was never fully exposed. But right then, I had caught a glimpse of the dark side beneath the soldier's mask, as he had put it earlier.

"About this incident, I'm not asking you to forget. I'm not going to play your game of pretending you've seen nothing."

I was frothing at the mouth to say something, to ask questions. There were so many variables to consider. Homosexuality was forbidden. He was my direct superior. He was at the top of his class. With my own status, would anyone believe me even if I told? Not to mention the target that I had somehow avoided for the past few months. Also, the mask of a soldier—who else wore this mask?

"Sir, once again, I apologize about my absentmindedness. It will never happen again, sir."

"All things are meant to be, Wiggins. I guess we just have to accept it and move forward, though I appreciate you being frank," MacConough responded.

"Sir, one more question, sir."

"Yes?"

"What happened to Corporal Warren, sir?"

This question is brazen. It seems as if it left my lips in a failure to arrange my strategy. In response, MacConough looks around the room as if there are rules written in invisible ink, then he turns to me. "He's suspended, found guilty for excessive racking of a fourth year."

What? Does this have anything to do with Paxton, or is it the Theo Waters case reopening? What the hell is going on in this place? "Is there anything more that I can know about the case?"

MacConough looks frustrated. "He'll be back soon. Anyway, go back to your room, Wiggins. Let's not speak of this again until it's time to."

"Sir, yes, sir," I say and walk off.

I'm relieved to arrive at my door. "Hey, guys," I say as I step in.

"Edwards was looking for you," Harry says.

"No way. Did he say anything?"

"Nothing really, but it seemed urgent," Harry says.

"Really?" I says. This is news to me, but I honestly have bigger trout to catch at the moment, meaning I don't know what I will do with this MacConough situation.

You see, in my church growing up, we didn't speak about homosexuality much, but the two things that I was really taught were that it was a choice and that it was an unholy choice. I learned that my whole childhood. Boys from around West Ashley area would make fun of one another by saying they were gay. They used it as a slur.

I didn't have any other reference other than that it was a bad thing. My parents never talked about it. Then in high school, there was a boy named Luke who acted all weird. I didn't dislike the guy. He didn't do anything to harm me, but I decided to remain indifferent toward him.

Over the years, I saw him around school. He became less outward about things, but the other kids, they knew, and they were relentless. Luke would constantly be ridiculed if he spoke up during class. Once, I saw my football teammates beat Luke up after practice for watching us. They claimed he was pleasuring himself to them even after he said that he just liked the sport. They offered me to get a hit in on him, and I passed. In response, they said that I must be gay. I didn't want them thinking that about me, but I quickly got that worry out of my head.

Truthfully, it hurt to watch them. I had to ask why someone would choose this. Why would someone subject themselves to this kind of torment? The kid had to live in the shadows of the halls. I guess now that I thought about it, it was similar to how I had been at the academy.

I don't have the courage to step out and confront my pursuers. There is no other way to get by is what I reason. I can't hide who I am, so I have to hide my body. MacConough, however, shatter all these preconceptions. He thrives at the academy and stands at the top of his class while hiding himself from the eye. To do that, he must be a genius or know the right people.

Maybe he's the key for me to be able to step out of the shadows. At the same time, I don't want to get too close to him. That could render dangerous because of what's going on with Warren. Maybe this could be a way to utilize what he calls the mask of a soldier.

"Hey, guys, I'll be right back."

"Steve, man, it's almost time for lights out."

"I'll just be a minute."

I leave and walk back into the barren, brightly lit hallways. The hiss of radiators covers my quickened footsteps. Chatter from surrounding rooms drifts in the hallways, and each conversation blends with the last until I reach the bathroom. My toothbrush is in hand for facade.

Staring into the mirror, I look deep into my own face, at my eyes, cheeks, lips, and chin. I notice how each muscle in my face feels and reacts to the other when I stress them. I put on an expression that satisfies the way one should look, and I hold it. As I'm doing this, imprinting this expression, suddenly, my father pops into my head.

My father wore this same expression, and this continuous expression—or demeanor, I should say—was behind each of the other expressions, like someone behind the scenes who directed how all other emotions would be shown. When he smiled, frowned, scowled, or grinned, this demeanor became transcendent both beneath the expression and flowing fluidly through them. It would only make sense to call this the mask of a soldier.

CHAPTER 7

One Day—Space Invaders

On the second Saturday of November, the general spoke to us for the second time that year. It was a snap assembly, which meant it wasn't planned and it was urgent, and because of this, it was all the more important. The nipping cold contrasted sharply with the stuffy air as we entered the arena. A sense of anxiety cushioned our seats. Same as on commencement day, the cadets packed into the basketball arena. I sat next to Harry, Clyde, Simon, and the rest of our football team.

We were to play the championship game later that afternoon. The room buzzed with anticipation. What would this be regarding? I saw MacConough, Petersson, and Nicky all standing watch in their uniforms and their caps snug tight around their heads.

When the general walks in, we silence. The clack of his boots deaden the rest of the noise as he crosses the floor to the podium. He removes his hat and tucks it under his arm. With practiced movements, he snags the microphone and clears his throat. I stare forward, though out of my periphery, I watch the upperclassmen. They stand statuesque, like gargoyles lining an old building.

He begins. "Hello, class of 1982. Happy to see you are all still here." He laughs. "I'm going to get right into it. Due to recent incidents regarding the welfare of all students, I want to make sure that I reinforce my support of you. One will have a few hiccups with the implementation of any new agenda, but I believe that this one has been a smooth transition so far."

I wince. *Is he referring to Paxton as a hiccup?*

"I want to make it clear that race-related hazing will not be tolerated on or off campus. Anyone who is found guilty of these acts will be suspended and could face withdrawal of classes and loss of credits." Several of my teammates look at me, surprised by this news.

"In an attempt to crack down on hazing, I ask that you all play your part and enforce these new regulations. We have laid out new formations of each squadron. There are two squad sergeants, as you know. If you see something odd, hear of an incident, or witness something that you believe qualifies as hazing, tell your squad sergeant. He will report to us, and we will eliminate the use of excessive force"— *Blitzkrieg*—"or whatever fear tactics"—*guerrilla warfare*—"are used. Those who try to hide these perpetrators will be held accountable to."

I guess that would be considered, uh, scorched earth. Hopefully, my quiz yesterday went well. The bad thing about this speech was that if these policies didn't work, I would only be racked harder.

The general took an emphatic pause. "Any questions?" To my surprise, Simon raised his hand. "Yes."

"Sir, how do you distinguish racking from hazing, and could you categorize them for us, sir?"

"Yes, good question, and it will be addressed on a pamphlet that you will see spread around campus. But the answer will have to wait until then. You see, it is a rather complicated distinction, especially to categorize without the use of intention. So let's leave it for written words."

"Sir, when will these new policies be put into effect, sir?"

"As of now, we are practicing them. Any others questions? Perhaps from someone who is particularly affected."

I raised my hand. "Sir, what do you intend to accomplish with these new policies, sir?"

"We hope to eliminate hazing, of course. What was once thought of as an important part of training a cadet psychologically is now being seen as detrimental to your growth. For your kind and for all, I hope that we will be able to accomplish this." As he finished speaking, the team looked at us. I could tell they were impressed by my and Simon's courage to speak in front of our entire class.

"I wish you all the best for the rest of the semester. Keep an eye out for these new policies." He left in the same air that he arrived in.

Riled up from our questions, the team got behind us as we marched to the field. I cleared the thirty, twenty, ten. I turned my head to the opponent's line of sight. Always stay two steps ahead, and always react before they react—when the pace changes, when there is a difference in their breathing, when there is a difference in arm movement.

The quarterback decides to go the other way. It drizzles with bursts of wind. The quarterback steps back and hurls one, but it sails over the reach of the wide receiver, fourth down. The Kilo Company knobs are up in the finals and need to hold Charlie Company knobs. Paxton is on the sidelines as are other cadets. Even some of the corporals gather to see which knobs will reign supreme.

C Company decides to kick it off. Larry, our star receiver, returns it, but his flags are ripped pretty easily. Simon leads the offense on the field.

"All right, boys, you heard the general. We can't let nothing happen to little Wiggy over here. So we're going to rip these racist C Company knobs to shreds. Ride for the man. For Wiggy on three," he said as he smirked at me.

"Dammit, man," I said under my breath.

"One, two, three," he said.

"For Wiggy," they all yelled.

They get on the field, and from the sideline, I hear Simon talking smack to the defense. He snaps and pitches the ball to Clyde, who breaks left and goes for a twenty-yard gain.

"Great run. We got 'em on the ropes."

Simon steps back, looking for a receiver downfield. One of the C Company knobs breaks through the defense and starts running toward him. Simon spins and drifts toward the left sideline, then he fakes like he is going to throw it, which catches the defense off guard, and picks up eight yards.

"Woo-hoo! You little shits ain't got nothing on K Company!" Simon yells at them.

"C'mon, man, stay composed until we get the win," I yell from the sideline.

The guys huddle and break into formation. The ball snaps to Simon. He steps back and tosses a pass over the middle to a K Company knob, who catches it and runs to the side. I run with him. A defender flanks us from both sides—envelopment—but we outpace them, and I block the closest. Touchdown! Our team has a two-score lead, and there is only a little more than a minute left on the clock. The team kicks it off, and the C Company kneels and admits defeat.

The K Company knobs are exuberant, jumping and hugging one another like they have won the actual Super Bowl. I walk over to Paxton Randolph. He looks amused. His gangly body is arched over into a thinking man's stance. The scar on his face is still healing.

"So I come to find out that you play too," he says.

I laugh and walk up to him. "You good, man?"

"Yeah, and yourself? That was quite a showing!"

"I hear Carolina Panthers scouts were out there in the audience," I joke.

"It's too bad that God only made you five nine."

"I'm five eleven," I correct him, and we both laugh.

"Well, hey, Steve, I wanted to tell you that I appreciate you trying to look out for me. Sorry for being so hard on you. I'm probably going to be changing schools, and I don't want to leave on bad terms." He paused. "I thought it'd be a good opportunity to play at a small but known school like this, and now that seems to be backfiring on me."

"Really?" I said and looked down. "Does this have anything to do with that?" I pointed at the scar. "Has enough time passed? I'm just concerned, you know. I stopped searching like you asked."

Paxton looked around with circumspection. "I shouldn't talk about it here."

Simon strolled up. "Steve, who's the giant?"

"This is Paxton Randolph."

"Hey, man, nice to meet you," Paxton said in his low voice.

"You too," Simon echoed. "Steve, you missed it. Lieutenant granted us the night off, so we're all talking 'bout going into town for some drinks."

"All right. I'm in, Simon. Thanks for letting me know."

"Are you in too, big guy?" Simon asked.

"I'm not part of K Company," Pax said.

"That's too bad. When Simon's in a crew, women always accrue." Simon laughed.

"All right, Louisiana, and that's not even catchy," I said to him as he walked off.

"Louisiana?" Paxton said.

"Yeah, I call him that because of his accent." I paused. "You know I'm from Alabama."

"Oh yeah? No, I didn't know that."

"I can tell just from that conversation that he's not from Louisiana. More like Texas, if you ask me."

"Really? How could you tell?"

"He speaks too fast. He must be from a city, I'm thinking. All the white boys I knew in 'Bama were slow and big. This guy's the exact opposite."

I laughed. "Damn, boy, you got it spot on."

"I had all types of recruits coming after me since high school even, most of the big names. Trying to rescue me from home, take me back with them to Texas."

"Ah, I see," I said. "What'd you think of the general's speech earlier?"

"Ah, man, I told you, I don't really want to talk about shit like that on campus. It's just, I feel trapped here. Everyone knows who I am. That burden is heavy. You can understand, right?"

"I feel similarly, that's for sure."

"And that's good enough, you know? That's enough for me to know that someone else feels the same way, you feel me?"

"Huh? I never thought of it that way." I paused. "But it's not enough for me. I don't want to merely survive here. I'm convinced this is the most difficult terrain to take, but that's the kind of terrain you need to become strong."

"Ain't you a brave one."

"Don't get it twisted. I am not trying to talk myself up here. I'm just saying how I feel about the situation."

"All right, Steve, well, I bid you adieu, mister."

I give him a strange look, wondering where his attitude comes from, and he leaves. Something about Paxton gets under my skin. It's as if he doesn't accept help when it's available.

The team of knobs are thrilled to get the night off. We take hot showers and mess around—whipping with towels and hooting and hollering as we get dressed in our freshest uniforms. Clyde stares in the mirror and amps himself up. I'm right next to him, feeling in my freshest skin. The upperclassmen no longer pose a threat to us.

It feels oh so sweet to walk out through those gates, our night passes proudly hanging over our necks like sheriff badges. We head to King Street and go straight to Dino's, a local tavern where cadets have discounted drinks. It's a spacious bar with clay-colored floor tiles, a sweeping red counter, and several booths. Near the back, there are all types of bar games—billiards, darts, and even the new Space Invaders festooned in lights. The cadets disperse. A couple of them order pitchers of beer, and others sit at a table.

"Harry," I said.

"What's up, Steve?"

"Call the girl."

"There we go, good idea number 1 from Wiggins," Clyde said.

"Aw, c'mon, you really want me to?"

"What other opportunities are you going to get? Tell her to bring her friend too. I mean, that's assuming they're hanging tonight," I said.

"Get it, Harry! Mr. Bolstrom is in the building! No more little Harry. It's Mr. Bolstrom now."

"Dang, boys, why you making all this fuss over a phone call?" Simon said.

"Why are you not minding your damn business, Louisiana? This is roommate confidentiality."

"Pshaw. You guys are a bunch of fools. C'mon. Rack them up."

We start a game of cutthroat billiards, a game where we each have to defend our third of the balls and knock in the others. Harry goes to the back to place this phone call. I take a sip of beer between shots and hit one in, then another, but finally, I miss.

"That was quite a boondoggle, Steve. Means that it didn't lead anywhere," Simon said as he lined up and hit a shot. "You like that big word, Mr. Pugnacious?" Then he hit another and another.

"Jesus, this guy doesn't play around, huh?" Clyde said. "It's like all y'all do from the South is drink and play bar games."

"What do you up North city slickers do?" Simon said as he continued his roll.

"We meet women and take them home, warm them up."

"You don't know how to romanticize women like us Southerners," Simon said as he finally missed.

"I think you mean romance. Yeah, we also have English courses in the North."

"Do they teach you how to kiss it in the North too?" Simon said with a playful look on his face.

"Kiss what?" I said.

"Kiss my black ass." Simon mooned Clyde as he tried to take a shot and hooted.

"Someone cut this QB off. I think he suffered from a concussion today," Clyde said.

Harry trudged over to us. "She's on her way!"

"Attaboy," Clyde said.

"Sorry for you, Steve. Miranda ain't coming tonight."

"Ah, really? Any word on why?"

"Nothing, but to be honest, Claire did act kind of weird when I asked her that."

"Huh," I said.

One of the guys goes over to the Space Invaders game and put in a couple of nickels. He starts yelling as a couple more cadets join him. Clyde, Simon, and I hold our pool sticks and see what all of the hubbub is about. Apparently, Larry sets the high score. He yelps and laughs, attracting the attention of the entire establishment.

"What is this?" I asked.

"It's called a video game, Steve. You play the game off of the screen. I forgot black people probably don't have this, huh?" Larry said.

"Cut it out, man. It's called Space Invaders. Look, you just try to keep your little ship alive and mess up some UFOs."

"Did you beat it?" I said.

"No. It's next to impossible to win."

"So last year, we start shooting messages into space. And this year, the aliens are back to terminate us all," I said. They all laughed.

"That's right, Steve," Simon said.

We all drink beer and take turns playing, making bets on who could beat Larry's high score. Then someone walks through the door.

"Uh-oh," Clyde said. "Is this the lucky lady?"

"Yes, sir," Harry said and walked up to her.

"Hey, Steve, you want another beer?" Simon said.

"Yeah, sure."

"Come on."

So we walk up to the bar. The bartender is a grizzly man with a thick light-brown mustache and a large rose tattoo covering his neck.

"What'll it be, boys?" he said.

"Give me two Jacks, neat," Simon said.

"So what's up?" I said.

"What's up? The general's speech today. What the hell do you make of it?"

"Like a more powerful statement than the one at the beginning of the year, almost like he is on the offense."

"Right? It's like he fucked up and he's trying to pounce on his mess, to clean it up before anyone sees it. Something doesn't feel right to me."

"Any ideas on what that could be?"

"I'm guessing it has something to do with you, right, Wiggs?"

I laugh while he downs some of his drink. "I do know what incident he's referring to."

"Of course. What is it?"

"You know how I feel about gossip."

"C'mon, Wiggins. Don't do that to me, buddy."

I look around. Harry and Clyde are chatting with Claire. She smiles and looks back and forth the two of them. The others are still at the back, playing Space Invaders.

"Corporal Warren, the one with glasses, is suspended, apparently for excessive racking. His roommate told me."

"His roommate? You mean Squad Corporal MacConough? Why are you referring to him as his roommate? Are you in cahoots with the guy or something?"

"What does that mean, in cahoots?" I said.

To this, Simon finished his first and ordered another round for us. "Friends, buddies. Drink up," he said.

"No, no way. I was his runner, and all of a sudden, Warren is missing one day, so I asked," I said.

"You asked him?"

"I asked him. I stood up, and I said, 'Where the hell did your roommate go, the same guy who is a suspect of murdering Theodore Waters?'"

"You asked him, did you? Just like that?"

"I asked him," I said.

"You asked him?" he boomed, and he gave me a suspicious look. "You ain't lying to me, are you, Wiggins?"

Dammit, Simon. You're going to blow everything, you lunatic. His outburst broke the veil of our conversation. The barmen and even Clyde looked over at us. Harry focused on Claire, though.

"Jesus, man, slow down on that Jack, would you? Plus, you're missing the main point I was going to make," I said to distract him. He leaned in. I could smell the whiskey on him. "Warren got suspended just after the scar shows up on Paxton's face."

"Too easy! He did it!"

"Maybe, but MacConough was complaining about how Warren is innocent and saying that they charge people with acts before they have proof. Warren might even have to extend to next year because of this. He also said that there are a lot of politics at this school that we don't see."

"I could've told you that, Steve! I could've... I could've told you that."

Simon had finished his whiskey and was on his way to ordering a third when Harry walked up with Claire. "Hey, Steve," she said.

"Hey, Claire," I said and paused. "So, uh, Miranda didn't want to come, huh?"

"You told me he wouldn't pry, Harry," she said.

"Yeah, that's not like you, Steve. What's the matter? Is it the liquor? He's drunk," Harry said.

"It's talking with old Baton Rouge over here. He's got me all revved up on a couple of whiskey drinks."

"Who's this nigger talking about?" Simon said, drunk off his ass, and then all of a sudden, he burst with laughter.

"Whoa, hold your horses, buddy," I said.

To this, Simon cheered me and downed most of the double shot of whiskey, and I finished the second. Claire looked angry now.

"She didn't want to be seen with you, that's what it was, Steve," she said.

"What? What's that supposed to mean?" I said. Simon leaned on my shoulder, looking at Claire.

"Her family wouldn't be okay with her dating a black guy, that's all. Don't take it personally. But you know they're that super conservative, good family type," she said.

"Ah, really?" I said. It was disheartening to hear.

"What? Are you kidding me?" Simon yelled. "No person, n-no person, should ever be treated that way. This is outrageous. Good family? That doesn't sound like any family you want to be involved with, Steve!"

"Hey, calm down, Louisiana. It's okay. Believe it or not, this is a relatively normal thing. So I take it she's not the rebellious type, huh?"

Claire's expression softens when she hears my response. "She had a really nice time with you at the party. Anyway, I'm sorry about that, Steve."

"You can't treat my chum like that, Claire." Harry and Claire walk away.

"That's such horse dung. That's the bottom of the barrel. I've never heard of something so foul," Simon carried on.

"It's too bad. I really liked her friend too," I said.

Clyde walked up. "What's this kid saying?"

"Apparently, her friend is too good for Steve here."

Clyde got a foul look across his face and turned toward Harry. "Hey, Harry! What's the matter with you? You can't stand up for your friend?"

"What are you talking about?" he said.

"I'm talking about you, Claire. Why is your friend afraid of being seen with Steve?" Clyde said.

"Let it go, Clyde," I said.

"No, I'm serious. You have to step up to that kind of behavior, or else it'll exist forever. I mean, c'mon, we're almost in 1980! Surely things have changed here since the Jim Crow era."

"I agree with you," Claire said. "But what are we supposed to do about it?"

"Tell your roommate that she needs to step up to her racist father or whoever is in charge and tell him that things are changing."

"Yeah, we can't have things like that going on here!" Simon yelled.

"I'm sorry, but I can't get in between her and her family like that, Clyde," she said.

"What's the matter with you?" Clyde yelled. "Don't you know that by doing nothing, you're just perpetuating the problem?"

"I just can't do that."

"Hey, huh? Hey, huh?" Clyde said as he prodded her with his hand.

"Hey, hey! You lay off her!" Harry responded and shoved Clyde.

This outburst quiets the bar. I have never seen Harry act like that before in my life. His face is red, and his breath turns into a kind of wheezing; his chest sticks out with his arms wide, like a bear on hind legs. Bending over, wheezing, he places his hands on his knees. His face is turned toward the tiled floor.

"Whoa there, Harry. You all right?" Clyde said.

"Can't we just enjoy this night, guys? C'mon," Harry said.

It was a desperate plea, and the statement blew like a strong wind, whistling through branches. It felt true to all of us not because of what he said but because of what it meant. Did it really matter who was right? I mean, of course, that mattered, but were we all going to hold on to our viewpoints so tightly that we couldn't see anyone else's? *That's not right,* I thought.

In the scheme of things, we were different people with different ideologies forming. Harry, a passive knight, was ready to fight for chivalry. Clyde, an idealist provocateur, was ready to challenge the common opinion. Simon, an aggressive rebel, had zero cares to give. We all stood in a shootout, but at the end of the day, we were comrades, cadets, and students of the academy.

A couple of cadets come over and sit Harry down. Claire joins him in a booth. I order two beers, one for the both of them, as Harry sulks, head in hands, after this outburst of energy. Claire thanks me and apologizes for Miranda. She adds that she'll relay what a good guy I am to her. I say that's not necessary, but she insists. Interesting. Larry challenges me to a game of Space Invaders. I sit and get peppered by insults from Larry while I ultimately break his high score.

When we arrive home that night, each of us carry a newfound pride and respect for our comrades. But I fall asleep outlining the schedule coming up.

1. Return home
2. Thanksgiving
3. Dead Week
4. Finals

CHAPTER 8

One Week—Mother

It feels cathartic to look back and see the bone-white barracks diminish in the distance as if my problems diminish along with them. We merge onto the highway and cross the languid river to West Ashley. The Charleston peninsula once again becomes the other side of life.

Through the streets, we drive; and around 7:00 p.m. on Wednesday, Arthur's vintage Charger pulls into the driveway, headlights beaming. I step out and look ahead at our house. The light inside illuminates the front blinds, but it's quiet like a landscape. I yank the duffle bag out of the trunk and stride toward the front door.

"Do the honors, son. It's a great feeling," Arthur booms.

I ring the bell and hear someone shift around inside. Then the door opens. It's my mother. The porch light surrounds my portrait and is framed by the doorway. The dark sky coats the background. I am home. Arthur walks up behind me, dwarfing me in shadow.

I hug Mom, and then I grab Maisy and swing her around. Up the stairs, I take my duffle bag to the room and unpack. My sisters follow and hang around the doorway.

"I made it," Maisy said, referring to the bed.

"Thank you, Maisy," I said.

"So you don't look too banged up this time," Lorna said. "Mom will be happy about that. Hopefully, it'll be less awkward than last time."

"Yeah, you look well too," I said and chuckled.

"Do you have any stories for us this time?" Maisy said.

"No, not really. We've just been doing a lot of training, regimental stuff. It's going to be weird taking days off without someone telling me what to do." I laughed. "Lorna, Maisy, could I have some time to myself?"

I unpack my bag, starting with rolled socks, then underwear, three T-shirts, two pairs of pants, miscellaneous items, notebooks, pens, scraps of paper, and the Guidon. Then I drop onto my bed and stare up at the ceiling. Finally, I can unwind, or maybe I can't.

Immediately, I start thinking about how the guys are doing, if they are able to unwind at home and let it all go. The regimen still feels implanted within me. I tense and feel my brow contract as if at any moment someone can burst in and rack me. I try to turn my focus on each inch of the ceiling, examining the same ceiling that I've had since I was a child, but my mind still drifts back to the red-and-white tiles of the quadrangle, to the fluorescent stadium lights at night, to taps, and to darkness.

Then I realize: the dresser, my dark-blue dresser. I sit up and look at it. *You haven't been much use to me, huh? Why did I even bother?* The academy is too strenuous, too irrefutable, for such mental exercises. Besides, every time that I strain to envision my dresser to redirect pain, I instead see my father walking into the room. It is a strange phenomenon, but for some reason, I feel as if he is always watching and always judging the sins of others and the reactions of myself.

Through the darkness of the house, downstairs, past the foyer and the living room, Arthur is sitting in light. A spread of food lies on the table—fried chicken, green beans, biscuits, and casserole—and everyone else gathers around it.

I sit, reflecting on the meal in front of me. Arthur says a prayer as we bow our heads. I eat slowly and methodically, taking small bites, and sitting on the front of my chair with my back straight. The food is tremendous, exponentially better than the cafeteria slop that I've gotten used to. I don't talk. Each bite warrants a small inhale to savor the taste.

Across the table, my mother tells us about the plan for Thanksgiving tomorrow. First is the local food drive, an event that she spearheads this year. Afterward, we're driving to Mount Pleasant, another suburb of Charleston, to visit her extended family per tradition. It's a tradition that I've grown up with and known to love.

My mother seems pleased at my reaction to the food. She doesn't mention the absence of blemishes on my face. My mechanical way of eating doesn't fall under scrutiny. My silence isn't overbearing; it's natural. Arthur seems impressed or maybe just content with a chip off the old block. Finally, as we finish the meal, I feel myself relax. The ooze of pressure slides off me. My mother's cooking is all I need to feel at home.

The next morning, I'm awakened by Maisy creeping into my bedroom. She climbs on my bed and starts jumping on it. It is worse than the trash cans at the academy. "Dang, Maisy, stop. Wait, what time is it?" I ask. It is late.

"11:00 a.m.," she says.

I get up. We stop by Lorna's room, and all three of us then head downstairs. Loretta has a vibrant red-and-orange headband wrapped around her as she finishes up a Thanksgiving dish for the family dinner. The kitchen is somehow simultaneously clean at the same time as she cooks. She says there are flapjacks and adds that we need to eat quickly so that we can get a move on.

"Get dressed. We'll leave within the hour."

Arthur sits in his chair, reading the post. He glances up at me. "Steve, you got up late, boy." This statement is meant to be critical.

We pile into the van and head to the food drive at church. People are setting up as we get out. It is bright but nippy. There is an unloading area and a large white tent for volunteers to sign in. Then there is a drop-off point where trucks would come to pick up food to bring to the food shelter. I help bring materials out of the truck. Cans of beans, diced pineapples, and loaves of bread emerge from the trunk. Throughout the hour or so, members of the church show up and leave. Many say hi to Loretta, who reciprocates with a dazzling smile.

My mother is in control. She organizes and filters those through the supply chain. On the other side of the volunteer tent, she has set up a gallery of local artwork, sweetgrass baskets, and pottery for auction, charity for the homeless. My eyes swell at the amount of work

Loretta has put into this event. Then a big van shows up. Out hops the Robinsons, a friend of my mother at church.

Theodore Robinson, a portly man with a mustache plopped on a friendly face, gets out of the driver's seat and signals to me. "Boy, Steve, you've sure grown."

"Yes, sir," I affirm. "How are you?"

"Not too bad. Not too bad," he says as he looks me up and down. "There's something different about you now. What're you up to in life?"

"Enrolled at the academy, sir. Anything I can help get out the back?"

"Oh, most definitely. Alyssa can show you."

He points to a dazzling woman—straightened dark hair, skin darker and finer than mine. Her flowing black jacket absorbs the sunlight, emphasizing a beauty mark on her left cheek. I've known her for years, but apparently, I haven't known her at all. As we approach, I notice that her lips, full and pink, contrast with her skin and create a heart shape. She has heart-shaped lips. She smiles as she sees me. Without thought, I smile too. I near almost faint, but luckily, my instincts are tough, so I fight off the fluttering feeling.

Arthur breaks the moment. "Theo," he says.

"Good to see you, Art," Theo responds.

With my head back in the present, I walk over to her. "Alyssa, how's it going? What can I help out with?"

"Hey, Steve. We just have a lot of stuff in the trunk that could use your help taking out," she says.

"No problem. Just let me know which things."

"Pretty much everything, to be honest," she says.

"All right." I laugh, and I start wishing our conversation have been more lengthy. Cans of peaches, water bottles, chili, potatoes, and onions—I fix them in my arms and transport them from the van to the large area where a truck is going to collect them. I see my mother directing incoming cars.

"Ma'am, you've done organized the Super Bowl," I say, and she laughs.

I put the sacks of onions at the drop-off spot and decide to take a small break. Despite all my training, this is still hurting my back, and my arms are swelling. I walk over to the area dedicated to local artwork. Sun shines on the canvases and brightens the colors. It's impressive that my mom has put all of this together.

A figure is painted in black, and then water colors are splotched in seemingly random colors. *Never mind. Honestly, art is not really my thing.* Sometimes, I try to act interested in it, but it doesn't do anything for me. My mother walks over.

"Sorry, ma'am. I'll get right back to work."

"Steve, it's okay. Don't worry about it. What do you think of the paintings?"

"They're nice," I replied.

"Aren't they? I especially like that one," she said, pointing at the one with the color splotches and black figure.

"Uh-huh? Why do you like it, ma'am?"

"The juxtaposition of colors. There are no edges. All the colors blend into the black figure. You know, it's as if saying we're all composed of these different colors and experiences. With no order to them, they still compose us. To me, that's a beautiful outlook on life."

"Huh, yeah, I guess I can see that. Very interesting," I said. "Which ones are yours?"

She pointed to these two vivid, old-fashioned scenes with women making sweetgrass baskets and backgrounds of rice patties and brick plantations. In contrast, these had definitive lines separating one color from another. The picture contained a lot of yellows, light blues, and greens. One thing was definite: it was emblematic of our ancestors' lives. Barriers were everywhere.

"I like yours better, Mom," I said. She laughed. "All right, well, we better get back to it," I added.

"Thank you so much, Steven."

I stand and look at them for a moment longer. The sun has moved, sliding further across the sky. I walk back toward the Robinson car. Alyssa is talking to my mom.

"The law never hurt anyone, only wrong interpretations of it. That's why I intend on serving it the right way, ma'am."

"Wow, aren't those grand visions that you have of the world. What a time it is."

"Yes, I'd certainly love to go into politics and create a better place here, especially considering how bad things are getting on the peninsula."

"Oh my, I hope you're staying safe. Now you are staying safe, aren't you?"

"Yes, ma'am, I promise," she said.

"Who are you, and what have you done with the Alyssa I knew back in the day?" I said. She laughed, finally.

"My, Steve, isn't that an entrance," Loretta said.

"I'm just coming back to help out some more," I said.

"Thank you, Steve," she said and walked away.

"What are you doing nowadays?" I ask Alyssa, and we begin talking, talking and laughing. She tells me all about the updates in Charleston, things that I have missed out on since I have been at the academy. Nothing gets in or out of those white stone walls. She works for the mayor, who, apparently, is a real progressive type.

When she smiled, I felt an immediate comfort with her, as if I could open up or say nothing and both would be fine. My eyes connected with my father's, who gave me scowl like, "Get to work, boy!" We exchanged numbers, and I continued unloading her truck. After a couple more trips, Theodore Robinson stopped me.

"Boy, you know your father has made quite a name for himself."

"Uh-huh," I said, unsure how to respond.

"He's got the Midas touch when it comes to business. Started an old body shop just a couple of months ago, and he's already breaking even on things he tells me. Does vintage convertibles, so rich folks get them towed all the way across the river and pay a small fortune. What I'd do if I had hands like that. God gave me all thumbs."

"Yes, sir," I said. I couldn't stand gossip, but if I hadn't heard this, I wouldn't have known that my father opened his own business.

"Arthur acts as quite the capital too. Everyone comes around his body shop to have a beer or shoot the breeze. Sometimes, you got folks rolling dice out back. He doesn't mind. That's to say the big man doesn't participate either, but sometimes, it helps to just have a silent ear. Last time I went, my car didn't even have damage. He was working on this beauty of a Camaro. He had a couple of people lining up to admire it, some beauties of the human kind as well.

"I'll tell you, I feel like he gives us big dreams when he works on those cars—the shine, the smells, and the curves. Hey, uh, speaking of curves, maybe I'll meet me a new girlfriend there. Last time, we put on some slow jams. Stayed late if you know what I'm saying, Steve. I have a feeling they like to watch your father work. How're the ladies treating you?" he said.

"Fine," I said.

"Boy, they make you believe that women just like younger men, but if you get to my age, we have an upper hand on a little thing called experience—"

"Sir, you'll have to excuse me," I said.

The exact reason I don't like gossip is, it turns from something useful into something you wish you haven't heard at all. Then you waste all this time trying to get it out of your head. I leave him mid-sentence and get back to work.

After the hour passes, my mother decides that it's time the Wigginses call it a day. We pile into the van, head home, and then back out to the relatives' house in Mount Pleasant.

In a rickety old house that could use a paint job and maybe a new deck, the whole family gathers. Loretta's mother greets us at the door with the warmth of the sun on the equinox. Inside are Uncle Duff, Aunt Hally, Great Aunt Martha, Grandma Ritsy, Cousin Albert, Aunt Rawlins, Uncle Jeremiah, A. Floherty, the four brothers—Ron, Rob, Job, and Joe—Sarafina, Glorianne, Hope, Faith, Dawn, Saul, Paul, and little Dolly.

We bring in the dishes that my mom have prepared—big glass containers with tinfoil—and place them on the buffet table. After a prayer, everyone helps themselves to a piece of turkey, gravy, dressing, mac and cheese, and greens. I laugh as I see Maisy stuff two biscuits in her pockets for later. The girls and I sit on the floor, plates, plastic forks, knives, and a mess of food in our laps.

"Lorna, how is the choir going, dear?" Great Aunt Martha asked.

"It's great, ma'am. We are actually going to perform at one of the mayor's ceremonies coming up."

"Well, is that so?"

"Oh yeah?" I said.

"Yes. The mayor has been doing a lot lately to incorporate everyone into the mix," Loretta added.

"That's what I heard. Things are changing around here," Cousin Albert said.

"Not too fast, I hope," Aunt Rawlins pitched in.

"Here, here. Times are changing, but family does not!"

"Don't you go around making promises for others with my old bones here."

"Oh, nah. Lord'll give you another thirty years!" Everyone started laughing. At this get-together, it was impossible for such a family to stay on one topic for more than long.

"Just don't take her to the beach. We don't want Jaws to snatch her up."

"Mama could take down a whale. Ain't no silly shark going to eat her."

"Let me atter," Mama yelled. We all started laughing louder.

"Have you seen the original, Cousin Steve?"

"No, I must've missed it," I said.

"So what's the academy like dear? How is school going for you?"

"Yes, ma'am, it's going well. It's definitely, um, tough. We have very rigorous training and schoolwork on top of that, but it's nothing I can't handle," I said.

"Big Steve, just like his father."

"No, Cousin Steve, we want to hear some descriptions, not just the general stuff."

"Yes, it must be changing too. When your father was enrolled in duty, they didn't allow students of color at the academy."

I couldn't reveal too much, but my description needed to seem honest.

"What's it like, Steve?" Maisy asked.

"Well, every morning, we wake up at five thirty. Then we go for a long run through the darkness. The birds chirp as we pass them." I paused. "Then we eat breakfast with our squadron. We have briefings by superiors. Go to class, study, and go to sleep. That's a fairly standard schedule for most days."

"That sounds boring," Maisy replied. Everyone started laughing.

"Have you learned anything about yourself?"

"You know, ma'am, I haven't really thought that one through. I'll get back to you on that."

"And what about being a brother on campus, Cousin Steve? How has that been?"

To this question, I look over at my father. His face focusses on his plate and a yam casserole. He seems disengaged from the entire conversation. *No gossip,* I think.

"It gets difficult sometimes, but to tell the truth, it doesn't stray far from any cadet's experience. You see, at the beginning, they teach you that as a cadet, we're all the same, and that's how I feel when I'm there."

All of a sudden, my mother speaks up. "Really? Steve, it's true you haven't said one negative word about the troop, but do you really expect us to believe that they treat you the same as everyone else?"

What is up with her interrogation? I look from my father, who still nonchalantly chews his food, to Lorna, who gives me a sympathetic look. My mother has had her say in the matter.

"Mom, please," I say. I shrink back into myself, my head down in my food. How could she put me on the spot?

"So then how is it really?" Grandma says.

"I'll let him tell you," she says.

I look up. "I don't condone gossip. Maybe someday I'll tell everyone what's really going on in there. I promise, I'll have stories. But for right now, I'm just focused on getting through to the end of the semester, so please."

A dramatic change occurs in my mother's expression. She softens. Without words, she must have understood how difficult it is for me to attend the academy; and while the omnipresent worries of me becoming detached like my father swarm her, she can also tell that this conflict in the house makes things harder on me. My grandma and great aunt also give me looks of love in a different way. Life isn't as hard now as it was for them, but there are still borders to be crossed, castle walls to be overthrown.

"What is the mayor doing?" I ask.

"Oh, he's been trying to clean up crime a bit. He's working with a lot of church groups to try and create support houses. He knows how important these churches are to the civilians of Charleston."

"Guess what, Steve?"

"What's that?"

"He went to the academy."

"Oh, did he?"

"Yes, so maybe we have another mayor in our midst."

"I believe so, but I hope you aren't thinking of me," I say.

"What do you mean?"

I turn to my sister. "I think, if anyone could be mayor or future president, it'd be Ms. Lorna Wiggins."

She smiles. "Thank you, Steve."

Back at home that night, I find myself looking out of the window. The tree's limbs stretch and contract from the force of the wind. They fragment the clear night sky. MacConough crosses my mind. Is he hiding his identity from his parents and family just as at the academy?

Today, I have done so fairly well, relying just on my learned instincts. It seems easy to do so but hard on your conscience. The truth sets you free, makes you light on your feet, like Ali, but lies, they hold you down. MacConough probably doesn't consider it an option.

If I had relinquished any of the things that had happened to me, my mother would've indulged. She would've served me a portion of lessons with extra portion of teachings. Considering, I think I played the situation well. But what of MacConough? Did he ever used to bring a girl to the meal? I did last year, but it felt it natural, like I didn't have to think about it.

The branches outside my window scratched the walls of the house. From my bed, I saw the blue dresser in front of me, shut and clean. I knew all the contents in the drawer, but at the moment, they were not visible. Then someone knocked on my door.

"Yes," I said.

"It's your mother," Loretta said.

"C'mon in," I said.

"Steve," she said.

"Yes, ma'am?"

"I want you to know that I'm proud of you and that I'm sorry for putting you on the spot like that earlier today."

"It's quite all right, ma'am," I said.

"Also, there's something you should know," she said. Thoughts ran through my mind about what it could be. *Could it be regarding Arthur? No, no, it must have to do with earlier.* "About a month back, after I saw the shape you were in at Parents' Day, I decided that I needed to take matters into my own hands.

"So I wrote a letter to the general of the academy. I told him that I'm a worried mom of an African American child at the academy and that I didn't think that there was enough being done about hazing, especially after the suicide on his hands last year." *She knew about Theo Waters?*

"I was aghast that something bad could happen to you. Not only that, but look, something did happen, and you wouldn't tell me about it at first. You have to understand, Steve, with your father, it was different. But to see my baby go through this..." She huffed and quickly calmed herself. "To be honest, I hoped it'd do something, but I didn't expect it to."

"What do you mean you didn't expect it to? Did something happen?"

"Yes, Steve. About a week and a half later, I received a response from his office."

"What?"

"Yes, the general wrote me back. He said that they were in the process of implementing a new plan of action but that he would take further action because of my note. It was incredibly encouraging."

There's no way! Was she the reason for our snap assembly? That seemed highly unlikely, but if word ever got out, it could be dangerous. If I had ever been safe, I certainly wasn't safe again. I mean, I couldn't blame her, but by her doing this, I was one piece of gossip away from a death sentence.

"Anyway, I just wanted you to know. Has anything happened since Parents' Day?"

"Yes. There was an assembly, and they said that they'd issue pamphlets with the new rules on them soon."

"Well, that's good. I hope you know that you can always count on me."

"That makes a lot of sense. Thank you, Mom, for sticking up for me," I said.

"Good night, Steve. I love you."

"Love you too, Mom," I said.

After she leaves, I turn the lights off and stare at the ceiling. A profound despair creeps into my room. The moon shines resolute and brilliant onto the wall. Over time, the shadows of tree branches swell and writhe. At least for now, I am safe. These new agendas have saved me before. But could any agenda stop a bounty on my head? Edwards certainly did stop Petersson from injuring me.

Why does someone like Petersson exist? What drives a person to become addicted to violence like him? The feeling of the academy engulfs me, and I wake up in alarm. The next day, groggy and slow, I go for a walk with my mom around downtown Charleston and the piers.

Off the waterfront, construction signs pollute the avenues near Broad and Market. Historic houses slowly shift into dilapidated shacks as you head north. Stones roads crack in decay. Businessmen and lawyers abandon the city to drifters and fiends. At this time of year, the air is crisp; and while sunny, there is a stark glare that stems from the angle of the sun off the marina.

"Whoa, I guess they were telling the truth when they said a lot was going on," I said. We stared down the boulevard.

"It's crazy."

"How's pops doing?" I said.

"Oh, you know. He's doing well. He started a body shop right when you went to school, so he's there a lot of the time. It seems to make him happy to be at work with his hands, to be fixing something."

"He used to work on army vehicles, right?"

"Yes, he did, so I guess it satisfies him for now. Sometimes, I wonder if his head is drifting back off to those times."

"He must think of it. I mean, three days out of the academy and I can't put it aside."

"I don't think he wants to," she said.

"I don't think it's a choice, Mom," I replied.

She looked at me with an austere face. My mom normally had a subtle style, but today, she wore a necklace with a gold plate around her neck.

"Well, at least we get him home for dinner. I've had plenty of freedom to volunteer, paint, and set up events." She paused. "Plus, I've been trying out all these new recipes—scallops in creams, red rice, and shrimp."

"Maybe you should open up a restaurant, ma'am." I laughed.

"Hey, now that's not a bad idea," she said. "I'll have to keep that in mind when Lorna heads out for college."

"That's so great that she's considering Ivy Leagues. It's almost unbelievable."

"Yeah. Your father doesn't think it's the smartest idea, and unfortunately, I think he's gotten in her head a bit. I understand where he's coming from. It's a big risk financially, but she could really do it!"

"I think she should go for it. That's just his 'I built my own house' talk, you know? I can understand that now."

"What do you mean, baby?"

"Well, with PT every day and the regimens that we have as soldiers, they instill a sense that you can accomplish anything with hard work and repetition, so having an Ivy League title won't do anything different than hard work would."

"Fascinating. Steve, it sounds like you're taking some wisdom from your experience."

"Thank you, ma'am, though I do need advice on something." I approached the next sentence with prudence. "I have a friend who has a secret, a secret that he's trusting me to protect. I'm not entirely sure what to do because if I don't tell, it could hurt me. But if I do tell, it could potentially hurt both me and him."

"I think you shouldn't tell a soul, Steven. Do not put others in harm's way because of your actions. Do you understand me?"

We walk past the beautiful manors of Rainbow Road. The houses have large circular beams that rise to support the roof. A tall doorway in front leads to a veranda hidden behind it, closed from the public. Those are the single houses of Charleston. Blue, pink, green, and yellow—they each have a different color paint, all accentuated by the sea and sunshine.

After a quiet evening in the West Ashley house, our phone rang. I plucked it from its holder and put it toward my ear. "Wiggins's residence," I said.

"Hi. Steve? This is Miranda," she said.

"Miranda?" I replied. *Miranda, not Alyssa? The girl from Nicky's party?* "Hi, Miranda. Sorry about that. How's it going?"

"Not too bad. Hey, I was wondering if I could see you sometime?"

"Really? Um, well, I have to go back to school Sunday, so tomorrow is my only free day, I guess."

"What about tonight? Can you slip out of the house?"

"Yes, I think so. Why so urgent?" I said.

"There's no urgency. It's only if you want to."

"Why can't we just talk here?" I said.

"Okay, whatever," she said, and the silence unfolded. I thought about what I had said, and it was what I had wanted. She couldn't treat me, an academy cadet, just any old way. "I want you to know that I felt really weird about what happened. Claire told me everything about when she met up with you guys and how you seemed like a sweet guy. I just didn't want any controversy in my household."

"And I told her that if that's how you feel, it's okay. These things happen in life."

"Yes, but how can you be okay like that?" she said.

"It happens all the time—" I started.

"She told me you'd said that. But to just put it to the side, like, with no frustration or anything?"

"Yeah, that's life, and it doesn't affect me beyond the initial disappointment."

"So you were disappointed?"

"Sure," I said. "No, actually, *disappointed* isn't the right word. It was just another incidence."

"Steve, how can you? Do you think each relationship is a game of statistics or something?"

"I didn't mean to treat it that way. We'd only met once."

"Didn't you feel anything?"

"Sure, but why are you questioning me like this?" I said. She was cornering me.

"That night, before I'd gone to the party, I'd gotten into an argument with my parents. They don't want me going into law. They think that I should study early childhood so that I can be a teacher just as my mom is. My father says I'm too brash for law, and that's that. I was furious, frustrated, but in the end, I had to submit to them.

"All the time my dad threatens to take away his support for college if I take the law into my own hands, so I hold back how I truly feel. Every. Single. Time. Then at a stupid party that my friends forced me to go to, I meet this man who, without knowing me, tells me how he truly feels about inequality.

"He lets it all fly out of his mouth, and it's beautiful. And as he is telling me, I keep thinking how I have forever been told by my parents how to live and who to date, how I'm not adequate to study law but how I'm too good for certain people. It all kind of bubbled up in one moment."

"So you kissed me. You kissed me to get back at them?"

"No, no. Steve, please."

"I mean, it's okay. I'm okay with that."

"Well." She seemed taken aback. "I thought that at the time it was just to get back at them, but something inside of me formed, and I started thinking that it's not just revenge, that I liked you and that I could like you. It doesn't matter what my parents think."

"I have to admit, I'm a little overwhelmed right now," I said. "You're telling me a lot over the phone."

"Well, you told me to, silly," she said.

"I did, didn't I?" *I can't help but wonder if she wants to have dinner sometime.*

"Yes, of course," she said.

Wait, had I said that out loud? "Sorry?"

"You just asked if I wanted to go to dinner. Tomorrow, then?"

"I don't think I'll have time tomorrow. What about over the break?"

"In three weeks?" she said.

"Two and a half, yes."

"So you can't do tomorrow?"

"I don't think so."

"You don't know?"

"Miranda—"

"Steve, I just want to see you."

"Okay, okay," I said.

"I'll pick the place," she said.

"You know what? I really shouldn't," I said.

"What? Why?"

"Because it's my last evening with my family, and in the academy, we're so locked down that we don't get a lot to spend time with them."

"Aw," she said. "Okay. I'm going to go, then, Steve."

"I'll give you a call over break to see where things are at. Good night." I hung up.

On Sunday, I awaken at 5:20 a.m. and pack my duffle bag. Once finished, I walk downstairs, chug a glass of water, and brew a kettle. I sit and think in the wee hours of the morning. A limpid blue graces the sky above the long-limbed trees. I walk out front. The wind is gusting. I head back inside and pour a cup of tea.

I hear my father's footsteps. I offer half of the paper to Arthur as he comes downstairs. He takes the business section and the weather. On the front page of the news, it reads: "Harvey Milk was assassinated yesterday. Gay rights leader, political hero, and friend to many was slain in San Francisco on November 27, 1978."

The first person to cross my mind is MacConough. This news of assassination must be terrifying, flat out, to see someone advocating his people's rights killed on the front page. It's like MLK or Malcolm X, heroes who lived in a different time and are gone now.

My mother comes downstairs and joins us for some tea. "Morning, love," she said.

My father kisses her on the cheek. She smiles at me. This presence and this smile wipe away all thoughts. It pulls me back into the house, back to the table. She has the power to do that. Everyone is here, I think, and they will still be here when I'm gone. But when I leave and march through the iron gates and past the large white stone walls and walk down the cold, barren hallways, who will I become?

CHAPTER 9

One Month—
The Pamphlets

Upon my return, salmon-colored pamphlets lifted by the December winds blow across campus. One lands on the side of my foot as I cross the center field to my barrack. I push it into my pocket without care for its state. It's gray outside but still balmy. A thunderstorm brews from a warm front of weather.

As I near the barracks, I feel the first drops. I salute the guard, then enter the sally port. Heavy drops of rain bombard the quadrangle now. I rush across to the entrance. In the room, Clyde is looking outside at the rain while Harry is lying in bed. They turn to me as I close the door. I take off my shoes and shed my wet clothes. Then I slap the pamphlet on the table.

"Check this out, guys." I read. "'Due to recent incidents, new agendas are in effect immediately. Hazing and racking will be categorized based on severity and intent. Hazing: the use of vigorous exercises by upperclassmen to humiliate or harm knobs. Example: the broom handle punishment.

"'Racking: the use of appropriate exercises by upperclassmen to condition, strengthen, or teach knobs. Example: extra push-ups if a knob has spoken out of turn. One, no hazing is allowed on campus. Two, no racking during ESP. Three, all rack sessions must have an authoritative figure present Inspections will continue as scheduled.'"

As I finish, I turn to the boys to find them perked up and attentive. They look at me and the pamphlet. "That's freaking crazy," Clyde says.

"Wow. Yeah. So we don't have to worry during ESP anymore about these guys bursting in," Harry said, "I mean, for the rest of our knob year."

"Only halfway through and we're already in the clear, buddy. Here we go, Bolstrom," Clyde said.

"That's not a sure thing," I said. "Look, it says that inspections will continue according to schedule. How do they expect to stop hazing during ESP if inspections can still occur at any point?"

"Those are always off-the-book inspections, though. I don't think that they're meant to be during ESP anyway," Harry added.

"All I know is, thank you, idiotic upperclassmen, for pushing the button too hard and too many times. These numbskulls unknowingly changed the course of this school forever. Freaking idiots. Doofus Petersson probably read this and cried."

"Do you still think we'll become as polished as them, though?"

"What's the matter with you? You act like you're going to miss being racked."

"No, not at all. I'm just saying, all of the seniors were racked as hard as we were, and even though we experienced it a little, think of the next years to come!"

"You think they'll become soft?" Harry said.

"Yeah!"

"You're soft," Clyde said to me.

"Eff, you Acorn." I laughed.

"Speaking of soft, Harry, how was it being back home? You got some quality time alone with some cake and brownies?" Clyde said.

Harry laughed. "It was so cold but great. Ugh, sleeping in my bed, ten times more comfortable than this one. Though, I have to admit, the last few nights, I had trouble sleeping."

"Oh yeah?"

"Yeah. I think because I ate so much and didn't do a whole lot. Seriously, my energy was all outta whack. Oh, my mother told me that I looked slimmer."

"There we go, getting compliments from the ladies," Clyde said. "How about you, Steve?"

"Harry, that girl called me," I said.

"Which one?"

"Miranda," I said.

"What, really? Even after all of that at the bar about her family?" Harry said.

"You better not have agreed to meet up with her, Steve," Clyde said.

"Confirmed. Actually, I was going to because she insisted so much. I told her that I didn't have time for it, so I let her go."

"Whoa, that's crazy," Harry said.

"C'mon, man, backing up my soft theory. You can't see her after the way she treated you," Clyde said.

"She explained to me why she was behaving that way. Plus, I didn't hold it against her in the first place."

"Well, I also have some news," Harry said.

"Oh yeah?"

"I asked Claire to be my girlfriend."

"You what, Harry?" Clyde said. "I can't believe it! Am I going crazy, Steve, or did the man just say what I think he said?"

"I did. I decided, if not now, then when would I conquer my fear?"

"Harry, you're a beast!" I said.

I found myself the next morning telling Simon in English. We were prepping our notes to write a final presentation that we would give to the class instead of an exam, but we had a hard time getting our shit together, that was for sure. The teacher sat on the front of his desk and read the newspaper as all the other students deliberated and planned. Simon and I did the one thing I hated: gossip.

"Yeah, so I noticed that the way I responded to her was steely, and I couldn't break out of it. It was almost as if even though what she was telling me should've caused a celebration, I couldn't. And in the end, I think it really disappointed her."

"Huh. So you're saying it's like a coat of armor, basically."

"Metaphorically speaking, yes."

"I think that's normal, to be toughened emotionally after what we go through."

"Yeah, but to not be able to remove it?"

"Interesting. Anyway, she totally deserved it." He looked at me with a steely expression, eyes partially closed and mouth in a grimace. Then he started laughing. "I am Steve. Meet the robot. Steve Robot. Steve Robot." I started laughing too—that was until the teacher turned to our direction.

Our final assignment is to write a transcript of dialogue covering our differences and a report about the overall speaking with each other throughout the semester. The professor calls it condensed conversation. It's constructed as a way to communicate the necessary aspects of speech in the smallest amount of time possible. In the end, we will have to stand in front of the class and present.

With ease, I put English to the side and focus on my other courses, especially the ones that require memorization. With the new agenda in order, I walk down the halls with more assurance. During the stretch before finals, upperclassmen are supposed to ease up anyway. This agenda has been in place for decades, to let cadets grapple with their academics and fully focus.

Harry, Clyde, and I begin prepping. For the classes we have in common, we create a large box of flash cards and plan to quiz one another at random, similar to knob knowledge. During PT, in the mess hall, or before bed, we spring questions on one another until the knowledge becomes second nature. A parry of information is always being exchanged between us.

Dead Week commences, and the library becomes my terrain. After the brief respite of Thanksgiving, I feel prepared to demolish my finals. Whenever I offer to my roommates, however, they decline. Clyde prefers the solace of his corner desk, and Harry his bed.

Night after night, I trek from the library to the barracks. An inky blackness dwarfs the center field. A chill hovers. Even though it's late and cold, I can still hear a lone troop marching, their commander booming signals and dampened footsteps following. You are never truly alone at the academy. I still try to walk in a sly manner, but the new agendas ring clear in my mind that I'm going to be all right. Finals week is near and then the finish line.

I return to the halls. Radiators hiss, and the hallway is freshly polished with fluorescents lights beaming off it. It's quiet. I stop for a moment and embrace the silence. Breathe in, breathe out, and then I continue to my room. I open the door and see both of my roommates cozy in study positions.

"How's it going tonight, boys?" I whisper.

"Not too bad, Wiggs," Clyde says and turns back to his book.

I lie in bed envisioning the notes that I have just gone over again and again and again and again and again. Then I do as I do at home and try to picture the ceiling, studying each inch of it. Suddenly, knocks ring out like gunshots.

"Open up," we hear.

All three of us looked around at one another. A red alert must've gone off. Had something happened, another assembly? There were knocks again, this time at the door next to ours.

"Open up." Harry hops out of bed and walks toward the doors. He is stripped down to a tank and boxer shorts.

"Don't do it, man," Clyde says. Again, we hear them furiously pounding on our door.

Clyde and I hop up to join Harry at the door. He slowly opens it, and it's flung open by a long, muscled arm. Petersson. *Wait, Petersson with a mask on?* The stature of the upperclassman is unmistakable, but the mysterious cadet wears a Halloween mask.

"Get out here, you three. Wiggy, Acorn, piñata boy, c'mon," Petersson said calmly.

"Sir," we all said. Outside our room, our neighbors from down the hallway were standing in underwear and pajamas, forty or something faces, each sullen, worried, bleak. Surrounding them were several upperclassmen in masks. Upperclassmen stood behind Petersson. Upperclassmen stood, blocking the base of the hallway.

"Welcome to the semester one roundup. Since it sounds like a lot of you believe in the general's new laws, we'd just like to make something clear. You are never safe. We still rule these hallways. We

153

still own the campus. And you, poor knobs, will continue to tread the fine line of survival. So who wants it first?" Petersson proposed.

A fearful silence stampeded throughout the hallway, accompanied only by the radiators' whispers. I could hear several knobs breathing heavily. There were no whimpers. We were too far along in the school year for that. But an anxiety covered us, a bracing for what might happen.

I look down the outstretched hallway. The polished tiles shine with a lucid resonance. The light amplifies and spreads down it, eliminating my anxiety. At the end of the hallway, a dark figure appears. It's not Edwards. It's my father standing at the doorway to the stairwell, looking in like a deity, the exact way he had the night that he returned home.

"Sir, where have you been, sir?" I say to Arthur.

"What was that, Wiggins?" the masked man yells.

I raise my hand. "Sir, I'll go first, sir," I say.

Several cadets gasp as the man in the mask sizes me up. "We have a volunteer! All right, then, Wiggins, drop down in squat position! Everyone, clap with me. This is a fun game. Firos!" Eight upperclassmen with masks entrap me in a circle. I drop to a squat. The man in charge begins clapping and counting off.

"One little monkey, two little monkeys, three little monkeys." The rest follow suit. Trapped like a spider in a jar, I duck-walk from one side of the circle to another at the pace of the claps. He increases the pace each time I reach a side and have to turn. "Twelve monkeys, thirteen monkeys, fourteen monkeys, fifteen monkeys."

Then all of a sudden, he starts yelling, "Ape, ape, ape!" They start slamming the floor with their hands like gorillas. Then the masked man points at one, who stands up and starts at me. I hobble to try and get away but am no match for his pace. The upperclassman lays out and slams me with his shoulder.

"Ack!" I spill to the floor. The knobs gather in horror. I see Clyde lurch forward, but Harry holds him back.

"Get up, knob! Squats this time." The masked man grabs me by the collar and pulls me to my feet. "One little monkey, two little monkey."

What can I do? There are eight of them, all equal distance from one another, each bigger than me, each masked. Petersson, the man

I have been trying to slip by, beat in this awful game and is now orchestrating the rack of my life. Tears are welling up. *No, I can't give in like that.* I volunteered. I am the only reason that I'm here.

"Sir, what do you expect to accomplish, sir, defy the general? I know who you are," I say to distract him. The man in the mask looks at me.

"But where are your witnesses, Wiggins? None of the others knows it's me, and there is no visual proof that I am who you say I am." I can't find a strategy. I'm out of time. I blink. I hear yelling, hands thwacking the tile floor. "Ape, ape, ape, ape!"

My eyelids close. I feel my body leap upward, and my fist thrusts outward into my strongest uppercut, directed straight toward the mask. A second later, I find my arm clenched by a terrifying grip. He starts laughing. "What the hell do you think you're doing, cadet, trying to strike a superior?" one of them yells at me. "You could find your way in the academy courtroom for actions like that."

In one swift counterpunch that lasts but an instant yet feels like hours, I fail. This is my reprisal. It does nothing. He's far too powerful. Petersson throws a punch aimed at my stomach. I flex and try to absorb the hit, but it hurts. He's a lot stronger than anyone I've been hit by before. It lands square in my stomach. I can't breathe. My dinner feels on its way up. I bend over. Hacking like I'm going to puke, he still holds one of my arms in his grip. Half of my body bends over like a tree weakened from wind.

"You, Wiggy, up, up, up." He tugs my arm, forcing me to stand. "As punishment, you see that pipe over there? You have to do fifteen pull-ups, all right?"

"Who's next to go in the circle? Let's see."

Some cadets cower while others attempt to stand tall in his wake of fear. I hobble over to the pipe and hop up to it. The pipe is scalding. It was the hot water for showers in the winter. I can't hold on. I complete three and feel the need to drop to the floor.

"Wiggins, what the hell are you doing over there? You can't do fifteen?"

"Sir, the pipe," I say.

"Yes, we know. Jump back up and do fifteen."

This nightmare can't go on. What the hell is happening? My forearm is bulging, I can't do fifteen. "The pipe, it's burning!" I yell and do two more. I topple to the floor, losing all coordination.

"Oh, you're in for it, Wiggy," Petersson says.

The upperclassmen swarm me and start kicking. I put my arms up to defend my head, but they begin kicking my body all over, loud stomps, heavy, loud stomps. I can't see. I can no longer feel.

"We're one semester through knob year and you still can't get it right, huh?" Petersson said.

"Pull your dogs off of him!" Clyde screamed.

"You, up on the pole!"

"You must have some kind of testosterone problem, man! What the hell is wrong with you?" Clyde yelled.

"What was that?" He struck Clyde across the face, causing him to stumble backward into the other knobs. Several knobs grabbed Clyde and propped him up. The masked man picked Clyde by his shirt and pulled him off his feet. In the knobs' faces, the fear started transforming into anger as a disgruntled murmur formed. "Enough!" the man in the mask yelled.

The upperclassmen stop kicking me. Shaking, I lift my hands to touch my face. My eyes are swollen. Bludgeons cross my body. Blood smears on the floor once again. I'm not dead, but my mother is going to kill me.

"Stay in your lane, maggots," Petersson says. "Stay in your lane. No matter what agenda is passed or what area of life you may find yourself in, know that you are not safe. I will catch you, and I will eat you up like the fucking dinner rolls that you are."

He drops Clyde and starts down the hall. The upperclassmen follow Petersson as he nears the stairs, and finally, he exits the floor. The rest of the knobs watch. I manage to stand, hobble over to Clyde, and pull him. My body aches as I lurch him up.

"Nothing more to see here!" Harry yells. The knobs reticently disperse, talking only as they enter their respective rooms. "Steve. Steve." Harry shakes his head. "Why'd you have to volunteer, man? Why?"

"I had to answer his challenge," I answer. "I'm not afraid of him anymore. There's nothing else he can do except hurt me. If I hadn't volunteered, he would've picked me, that's guaranteed. But he also might've picked others as well as me."

Harry stares at me with wide eyes. I see him fade, fade into sadness. He starts huffing and cries. "I can't believe you, Harry. Stop being such a coward, man. We're one semester in already and you're still crying. Fuck crying. Fuck being the victim. You have to stand up for your people," Clyde says.

"I wanted to, but I couldn't. I just froze. I-I dunno, man. I'm sorry. I wanted to help you, Steve," Harry stammers. He looks sick and frail.

I lift my hand and put it on his shoulder. "Don't be so hard on him, Clyde. I appreciate you backing me up, but there's nothing anyone could do. Petersson planned this whole ambush. He sealed off the exits and wore those masks so that no one could prove it was him. He's smart."

"Smart?"

"Yeah, smart."

"You think that bozo is smart? Only way he gets an A is by picking on the teachers in the bathroom."

Something comes over me, a landslide of emotion. I start laughing, cackling like a madman. I fall onto my bed laughing, writhing in pain.

"Poor guy," Clyde said.

Blood begins to gather underneath Clyde's eye. I feel both of my swollen lids close just for a moment, and for that moment, I see my parents gathered at the dinner table. I bounce up. I leave the room and glide down the hallway and move to the shower. The knob squeaks and water steams and pats the tiled floor. I step in.

The hot water sears my bruises, and pain quivers throughout my body. They got me good. Only moments before had I been laughing but purely from nerves. I break down, weeping, bawling, the salt of my tears mixing with the hot shower water and swiveling down the drain. Saliva and splotches of red exit my mouth and follow the tears.

The water stings my hands, causing tremors throughout my entire body. They are burned, badly. I switch the water to the coldest it can go and face the showerhead. For as long as I can, I face this direction, then I exit. In the mirror, the bruises aren't fully visible. Twitching each time I need to use my hands, I open my eyes wide. It is time for runner duty.

I am to report to MacConough. I have dreaded the day since November when I found out his secret. It has been over half a month since I've talked to him, and I have buried and uncovered his secret several times, unsure of what to do with it. Now that I am going to see him, everything will surface once again.

I double-check that it is the right door and knock twice. MacConough opens it. "Jesus, what happened to you?" MacConough says.

"Sir, nothing, sir."

MacConough began laughing and came closer to me, and I instinctively flinched. "Whoa there. Are you afraid of me? I was just trying to take a look," MacConough said.

"Sir, I apologize, sir. It's the nerves, sir."

"Well, I don't really care much right now. Just ice your face. It should decrease the swelling in a couple of days. How are your course finals? Are you going to pass?"

"Sir, I believe I'll achieve a 3.5, sir," I said.

"Very good, Wiggins." He paused and then said, "I have to bring up that no one has mentioned anything to me about our little encounter, and I attribute that to you keeping quiet on your end. Thank you. So what do you say we have ourselves a little deal?"

"Sir, no thank you, sir," I said.

"Excuse me? What's that supposed to mean?"

"Sir, if I may," I said.

"At ease, cadet."

"Sir, it's part of my duty to keep your business to you. I have not and will not disclose this to anyone even if they threaten to beat it out of me."

"It looks like they're going to beat it out of you no matter what. I think I have a solution to this problem."

"Sir, a solution?"

"Well, I know you've probably got your mind on Christmas, but don't be surprised if you find some Easter eggs, incentives for keeping everything a secret."

"Sir, that's really not necessary, sir."

"Ah, don't mind it. You're a good cadet, Wiggins. From what I've seen, the other knobs respect you, like a martyr almost. It's too bad about Petersson's penchant for singling you out. Someone like him doesn't understand that just because your skin color's different or who you love is different, you're not any different of a soldier. We're all still part of the corps of the cadets," MacConough said.

"Sir, but I don't understand. What is this solution that you're speaking of?"

"You'll find out next semester."

*****

English is the first class that I finish. Simon and I bobble a mediocre presentation and oversell the amount of work that we did. But our synchronicity is there, and when one of us fumbles a point, the other saves it. This surpasses the expectations of the professor.

When we finish, he applauds our authenticity of friendship. He says that especially considering the first day, we have come the furthest one can possibly come. We receive an A. After class, Simon puts my head in a headlock and gives me a noogie.

"We did it, ya son of a bitch."

"Cut it out!" I yell and explain that my head is still tender from the racking. He then proceeds to put my head in a headlock once again.

By finals week, the swelling on my face subsides a bit. I make sure to ice and check in the mirror. Similar to the organization of my books on the shelf and my belongings in the drawers, I filed each of my finals, allotting the proper time and consideration to the individual class.

As they arrive, I pull last-minute cram sessions with my roommates and some of the other cadets down the hall. We would pack up our things and bring them to the freshman lounge. Over the night, we would snack on chips from the vending machines, mess around, and create notes to crumple them up and play paper basketball with the garbage can. We stay up until 0200, trudge upstairs, and wake up again at 0600 to continue studying until our exams at 0800.

On Monday, I walk out of history unsure of my score but feeling accomplished. These are sunny, crisp days of December. I mosey around the center field, eat, head back to the library, and then study. The week crawls sluggish, but since the racking, we don't hear from the upperclassmen. Harry wakes chipper, and Clyde complains, but we each push one another through the days.

Wednesday, I walk out of math sure of an A. Then two hours later, I walk out of biology feeling the same way. With my head high, I march across campus to the mess hall and lunch. I see Clyde sitting with Randall. They wave me over.

"Steve, bud, how's it going?" Randall said.

"Not bad at all. I see the finish line, that's for sure."

"Nice, nice. I agree with you there. Can't wait to get back to the Southern Peninsula. How do you feel about that history exam? Pretty tough, huh?"

"Definitely. For some reason, I keep thinking that he's going to have more on the terms, but it's always stupid essay answers. You can never know how well you do on them."

"That's true." Randall began laughing.

"What?" I said.

"He was just telling me how he had answers to the test," Clyde said.

"What?" I boomed.

"Clyde, you bitch, c'mon." Randall laughed. "It's true, Steve. I got all the answers from a friend of mine"

"That's great. Good for you," I said.

"Yeah, it serves our professor right. The way he grades, everyone should be able to cheat in class."

"I don't agree. But you know what, you found what works for you, Randall."

"Oh, c'mon, Steve, don't pretend like you wouldn't utilize them if you had them."

"That's a good point but completely hypothetical. I didn't have them. You did. You used them, not me. But congrats. They mustn't have been easy to come by."

"I mean, I couldn't write the essay answers word for word, so I had to switch things around a bit."

"Sounds extremely difficult," I said.

Randall seemed bothered by this response. He really wanted to play me. "I like what you've done there. Is that a new eye shadow you're wearing?" he said, referring to the bruises on my face.

"Thanks. Why don't you ask Clyde? He has the same."

"Steve, cut it out, man," Clyde said.

As he said this, the chain of events streamed past me—Paxton's scar underneath his eye, Halloween, a promise made by the general shattered within the month, and getting tortured by Petersson. The promise to my mother hadn't been broken but smashed to a thousand pieces. No matter what happened, what new agendas or strategy I implemented, I couldn't win. There were too many variables, too many foes. I just had to accept it.

"Fine. Look, it's been a rough week." I paused and took a bite. "I'm not in the mood for pussyfooting with you, Randall." I took another bite.

"Fuck did you say?" Randall said.

"Chill, you guys," Clyde said.

I had no idea why Clyde told us both to chill. I was as cool as a glass of sweet tea. I took another bite.

"Whatever, Steve," Randall said. He walked off.

"You guys can't seem to be in the same room, huh?" Clyde said.

I laughed. "Hey, I have no problem with him. When are you heading home?"

"Tomorrow, Steve, tomorrow."

"Cool. Well, I'll see you later, then."

"Later, Steve."

*****

On Thursday, I had my last final exam in ROTC. It was a fitness exam where we tested our stamina through several different tests of pull-ups, push-ups, wind sprints, etc. I pushed through and broke into the top ten in the knob class. Afterward, on that cold December day, I saw Paxton making his way across campus. I thought about our last few interactions and how he hadn't been warm to me and also how this could be my last opportunity to talk with him.

Paxton speaks with apprehension and wears large bags underneath his eyes. When he motions, he's slower than usual, and then he reveals. "I'm transferring, man, University of South Carolina."

We measured each other up. He seemed to be shivering, his scar fully healed into a long black hook. A cold wind blew passed us, but I stood motionless. He noticed my swollen face, forehead gash, and cheek bludgeon.

"Will you at least help me out?" I ask. "Let me know what happened to you."

"Yeah, okay, Steve. I got nothing to lose now, I guess. So one night after football, they invite me out to get some drinks, being especially pushy. Now I don't drink alcohol. I've always been so focused on my athletics, so I haven't had time for partying and stuff, but I figured, why not? We're just celebrating a win.

"I went out with some football guys, and all of a sudden, we joined a bunch of others who weren't even on the football team. We moved to one of the guys' house. They had a whole plan of debauchery—to drink some whiskey, play some poker, and then drive out and do some cow tipping at one of the farms outside the city.

"We get to the guy's house and are having a good old time, and then one of them—his name was Firos, I think—starts upping the ante. They start making wagers of who would do what to me. To me! So I get up, and I try to leave, but I have no idea where we are.

"One of the guys blocks my path, so I figured, sit down, cool off. Maybe it's just some dark humor and they're joking. But I'll tell you, Steve, the ante gets so high." Paxton took a deep breath, and my eyes grew as I focused on the story.

"Well, Firos wins the hand, and as a bet, he says, 'This boy is so dark you can't see the regular eye black when he's on the field.' You know, the stuff you put under your eyes. 'We need to give him a permanent eye black or something like that.' He's all drunk and shit, places his knife on the table, and points to one of my teammates.

"There was no way out, so one of my teammates took the knife, and they just slashed me with no remorse." He made a motion below

162

his eye. The trees across campus rustled from the wind. A silence rose between us that faltered only as we heard the rumble of cars across campus. We turned to see parents arriving to pick up their kids and upperclassmen saying good bye to one another.

"I'm sorry, man. That's horrible."

"Now you see why I'm leaving. A team member did that to me. There is no way I can ever trust these guys."

"You know Firos is a fake name, right?"

"What? Seriously?"

"Yeah. Petersson, one of our corporals, used the same name when he racked me and gave me these bruises. I think they use it as an identity protection. Have you ever seen this guy before?"

"Nah."

"This might seem like a random question, but did the guy have glasses?"

Paxton gave me a strange look and said, "Look, I understand that you think you're on to something, Steve, but you should just steer clear. There ain't no mystery, ain't no one person in charge. They all just want to hurt us."

"I don't think that there's a mystery either, Paxton. I know that with the way things are, no matter what, bad things are going to happen, but you can change the way they affect you instead of running away from them."

With this, I walk away. Paxton Randolph, the black football-playing freshman, is gone. Knobs have left before him and will leave after him. That's the nature of the academy. *Time to go home,* I think. One last time, I enter my dorm room, sparkling from a recent clean. Clyde is there. We hug and wish each other good breaks. Harry already left for Michigan. I am going to miss them.

When my father arrives, he doesn't say a word about the bruises on my face. I can tell, however, that he notices them. The bass line of an O'Jays song coats the car. Once again, we coast away from the academy. The road stretches behind us, and we cross the river once more.

Along the banks, light flickers on as the sun drops behind the tree-filled horizon. The further we inch away, the more it dwells heavily on my mind—the academy, the looming bone-white barracks, the blood-red and slate-gray quadrangle, the cannons on the center field, the roaming troops at night, Paxton's story, and MacConough's promise.

My father and I pull into the driveway. The night is quiet but laced with restlessness. Winter spreads over the neighborhood, muting the traffic like stars in a dense fog. I grab my duffle bag. This time, it's heavier—my textbooks, notebooks, and tokens from the academy that hold symbolic value. I need to hold them during the break.

I brace before opening the door. I brace because I know my mother will be shocked. My father stands behind me. "What's wrong, Steve?" he says and passes me.

"Nothing, sir."

Arthur begins to open the door. The light from inside the house exposes my face. Regrets flicker past. *I shouldn't have confronted Petersson*, I think. *I should have taken my return home seriously.* Regrets engorge and swell until they engulf my sightline. I take a deep breath.

"I'm home," I say.

I attempt to creep up the stairwell before seeing anyone, but my mother catches me first step. Her hand on my shoulder, she ushers me to turn and face the blunt truth. I turn. My eyes close. They open once more. A smile crumbles. I see a cascade, a joy plunging into sorrow.

"Oh, Steve," she says and covers her mouth.

"Hi, ma'am," I respond. I hug her and then continue upstairs. She looks too shocked to say a word. I feel embarrassed, disappointed, fleeing upstairs like a squirrel back to its nest. I need sanctuary. I need my room.

*****

When I descend the stairs maybe twenty minutes later, I come with my soldier's mask on, armed and ready. The table is set. My sisters, however, sit on the couch. Arthur is in his armchair, and my mother is in the kitchen. One shouldn't have to feel like they need to put on a suit of armor to be home, but I need it. Otherwise, I will be the one who is hurt.

"Hey, Steve," Lorna said.

"Hey, how're you doing? Oh yeah, how are school applications going?" I said.

"They're good. I submitted to South Carolina and Charleston College. I also applied for North Carolina, but Dad wouldn't be too happy about me going there."

"Oh yeah?" *She should be able to apply there if she wants.*

"Well, good for you for applying. So did you decide against the Ivy League schools?"

"Yeah. We decided it'd probably be for the best to save me some sanity, you know?"

"That's probably a smart idea," I said, then paused. "Well, I'm happy to be home.

At the dinner table, Mom was noticeably upset by my appearance. She wouldn't look at me square in the eyes and fidgeted to make sure all the seats were set with serving utensils. I watched as she meticulously set everything. She took a deep breath and exhaled, and her face changed.

She looked toward Arthur. "Can you please lead us in prayer?" I closed my eyes.

"We are grateful to once again be together, joined as a family. Thank you, Lord, for this meal…"

Had she been able to shake it off that easily? Maybe the initial shock of my face isn't as deep as our interaction over Thanksgiving. "Amen."

I remember my soldier's mask as I begin to serve myself. I take small bites and sit in the Guidon's written posture. The front six inches of the chair are my friend, and my elbows are tucked in and held tightly to my body. The meal passes, delicious, but I don't smile. The smell of wonderful Southern cooking rises and disappears as the plates empty.

All is fine on the surface, but underneath, something has changed. It is no longer a genuine experience but an echo, imitating our past family meals rather than being the real thing. I ask if I can be excused and head to my room. The night is young, but I feel exhaustion settling over me.

Upstairs after dinner, I decide to figure out what I'll do outside the household. Running and PT, of course, but I really need to hang out with people. I need to be surrounded to get sucked out of my own psyche. Old schoolmates could be a solution, I think.

Then I come across a thought. *What about Miranda?* So I give her a phone. We talk for maybe twenty minutes. She seems happy to hear from me. Chatting leads to plans, and plans lead to commitment.

We finally meet midway through the following week. She wears a breezy white shirt, a long denim jacket draped over her slender frame, three-inch leather boots, and a bead bracelet, accentuating a rebellious style. I have a rather pedestrian outfit—white T-shirt, my high school letterman, and blue bell-bottom jeans. She has convinced me to come back over the river to King Street Charleston, a bar strip that is normally flooded with students from Charleston College.

We enter the bar with neon lights flooding the walls. A large mosaic lamp hangs from the middle of the ceiling, delicately lighting the bar in multicolored hues. It's crowded and noisy. From the jukebox, "Miss You" by the Rolling Stones rolls over the hubbub.

"So you gave me a shot, huh?" she said.

"I did, but only because you did so earlier. Your roommate said I was out like it was set in stone."

"It was, but like I told you, I thought about it, and it's wrong," she said.

"So would your parents really cut off your college funding if they saw you here with me?"

She laughed. "I don't know, but we're here, so who cares now, Steve?"

"I care. I just want to know what I'm getting myself into. Are they full on 'You can't date a black guy,' or are they 'I can do what she wants' type of parents?"

"I guess we'll just have to find out, won't we? All I know is that you're the first black guy I've kissed."

"Huh. Okay," I said.

She studied my face. "Oh, did that upset you?"

"It's not that I disliked it. I'm just not sure how to respond. Sometimes, I wish race didn't have to come up in everything I do, you know?"

"I'm sorry," she said.

I paused. "Don't worry about it. I'm just thinking out loud."

"What's up with your bald head look, though? Didn't you ever think of growing it out?"

"I used to have it all big and puffy, but the academy made us shave it on the first day."

"That must've been so cute." She laughed, and I laughed too. "So who is Steve Wiggins the cadet, and who is Steve Wiggins the man?" The crowd babbled in the background.

"You know what, let's order," I said.

"Vodka soda for me," she said.

I grabbed the bartender's attention. "Jack and Coke and gin and tonic for the lady."

"Why'd you order me a gin and tonic?"

"Vodka is a communist liquor."

"Oh, next time, allow me, then." She laughed. "Well, I guess you and my father would agree on that."

"What does he do?"

"He's a lawyer."

"Is he strict?"

"He can be, but I don't know if that has to do with him being a lawyer. More about his upbringing."

"Huh," I said.

"So how about you? You aren't going to worm your way out of this one. You even seem different than last time we spoke."

I study her. She doesn't have an ounce of hesitance, a complete change from last time. She sips her drink, waiting for an answer. I never give it.

*****

The next morning, I go on a run. The streets are gray and quiet. Low clouds hang over the tops of the bare old oaks. The air is smooth.

I walk out toward the middle of the street, and there's no traffic, no sign of anything alive. I turn back, and there's the paper boy, tossing the post into front yards. I wave. He nods. We go our ways.

When I return home, I grab the paper off the dew-laden lawn and walk inside. Warm air engulfs me. Our house feels hollow, like a low-burning candle inside a glass. My mother and I haven't been talking this break. My father rotates between home and work, but we haven't had much to talk about either.

There is a strict yet tacit code between us of not speaking on matters of the academy. With my mother, however, it feels like a large elephant is sitting in my father's armchair. This emptiness requires action, not passivity, to fill it.

After my father leaves for work, I hear footsteps on the floor above. They register as my mother's walking pattern. She exits the hallway and enters the stairwell. I have made biscuits. The smell of butter churns with the morning air, adding much needed life to the blotted gray indoors.

"Good morning," I said.

"Hello, Steven," she said.

"How're you feeling this morning?"

"Oh, I'm all right," she said and put a kettle on a burner. "Brr, it's cold in here." She was wearing a dark-blue head wrap and a large cloak-like robe.

"Sure is."

"Why're you wearing just a T-shirt and shorts, then?"

"Oh, I just haven't changed from my run this morning."

"You're running in the morning. That's good."

"Yeah, I gotta keep in shape. Don't want to lag behind all the other cadets."

"Hmm," she said.

"You want a biscuit? I made some fresh for you and the girls."

"Thank you, Steven, but I don't eat heavy things in the morning."

"Oh, I didn't know." There is a silence, and then the water starts glugging in the kettle. She shuffles over to turn the heat down. "Ma'am, do you have something you'd like to say to me?"

"Not in the morning, dear. Not in the afternoon, and not in the evening. I think you should know that all these scars you have, they are all manifestations of what I feared they were doing to you, what I feared that you were somehow covering up and keeping secret from me, and I was right. There is no accident or ritual that could've happened to cause this much harm. But I don't want to have this discussion. It's morning, okay?"

I sink into myself. "Yes, ma'am. Sorry I brought it up." Nothing I could say would repair the situation, so I retreat with a biscuit and the newspaper.

After a shower and a shave, I decide that instead of staying home, I need to leave. I want to see my father's workshop. So without goodbyes, I hop on my bike and tread through the streets of West Ashley. House after house, front yard after front yard, you can notice a pattern—two-car driveways, trimmed hedges, and white brick two-story houses with chimneys. The streets droop into the gutter. They are wide and languid, replicated and jaded.

Merging onto a boulevard, I glance both ways, but traffic is still few and far between. I see the body shop. Big Art's it's called, a wide garage with a big new sign and his name in cursive. I take a left and swoop onto the driveway and hop off.

Big Art, aka my father, is working on a vintage T-Bird in the shop. For a moment, I want to be informal with him, but my instincts save me.

"Hi, sir," I said.

"Steve," he said, "what are you doing here?"

"I wanted to see your shop, sir," I said.

"You should've asked," he said. A gust of wind enters through the garage door. A radio plays a tune that I can't quite make out in the background. "Since you're here, I suppose I can give you a tour."

He walks me through the lounge area where people can wait it out over a coke. It's also probably where all the slick talkers like Mr. Robinson come to hang out. Then we see his office, as spick-and-span as I expect. Finally, we exit to the garage, and he illuminates me on the different models in the shop.

"Now do you want to help out? If you do, you gotta be ready to get dirty and learn your different tools. Do you know your different tools, Steve?"

"No, sir. Can't I just hang round here for the day?"

"No, you're just going to slow me down, son."

"All right, sir. Tell me the tools, and I'll memorize them," I said.

"Socket wrench, pliers, torque wrench, screwdriver. Everything else you should know. One-fourth, three-eighth, one-half inches. You got that? Need me to repeat?"

"Sir, no, sir," I said.

He looked at me suspiciously as I chirped this automatic response. "Pliers," he said.

"Sir, yes, sir," I said. I handed him the pliers and watched attentively as he used them to contort the wires. "Socket wrench," he said.

"Sir, yes, sir," I said. I ran to take the pliers and replaced it with a socket wrench. After a few hours, I still stood attentively.

"Water," he said.

"Sir, yes, sir," I said. I smiled and ran to get him water.

"Grab some for yourself too. Not bad, Steve. They trained you well."

This was the biggest compliment that I could receive from him—"Not bad, Steve. They trained you well." It was another validation of my furious work ethic and tenacity. For a moment, I lost modesty, but I let it pass and ground myself once again. I ran back with two little paper cups of water from the cooler.

"It's been a long day. What do you say we take this car for a ride and go get something to eat?"

"Sir, yes, sir," he said.

Spinning out of the driveway, his off-white Dodge Charger looks like lightning down the lonely street. Trees droop down toward the road. A mixed backdrop of lush greenery and bare trees swamp the car. We come to a clearing. A small shack sits adjacent to the river. Dilapidated wood weighed down by the wet air, the shack is open for business. We drive up and meet the nicest darn woman in the whole world, leave with a hot plate, and eat it right on the curb. A perfect afternoon is simplicity.

My father needn't talk to be warm. This had always been a mystifying quality of his. He needn't smile to show acceptance. I felt, for the first time, that I could forgive him for what he did to us. But part of that forgiveness must've started with empathy. I now knew what he had known all this time.

Ironically, as I feel this warmth, I feel distant from my mother. There must be another way, I think. There must be more than two sides to this story. After a few bites, I take a large breath, making sure, as Louisiana said, not to overthink it.

On Christmas Eve, I receive a call from Miranda, who is radiantly warm to talk to on the phone. We chat a bit about how break has been and how home is with our families. We make plans to see each other again, once before New Year's and on New Year's. When I hang up, I hear laughter in the hallway.

"All right, you can come out."

"It was her idea," Maisy said.

"Who was it, Steve?" Lorna said.

"Just a girl," I said.

"A friend?" Lorna said.

"Yes," I said.

"Ooh, a girlfriend," Maisy said. "And you're going to kiss her on New Year's, aren't you?"

"Well, I'm not going to kiss a stuffed animal."

"Hey, leave Pumpkin out of this," Maisy said. We all laughed.

"If I hear you two spreading gossip, I swear," I said.

"What? You swear what?" Maisy said.

"We both know how much you don't like gossip, Steve, but sometimes, it just happens. It's inevitable," Lorna said and raised her arms.

"It's wrong to gossip, you two," I said.

"Well, then can you just tell us what's going on with you?"

"What do you mean?"

"You're either away or up here in your room. We haven't seen you at all this break. And on top of that, why are you and Mom in such disagreement?" Lorna said.

I sighed. "I don't know what I can say."

"Just tell the truth," she said.

"I have never lied about anything," I said. I was just standing on neutral territory. "I don't mean to cause a rift in the household, girls, but what happens at the academy is private."

"Why?" Maisy yelled. All of a sudden, there were no more smiles, no more laughter. Maisy was downright almost in tears.

"It's just the way it is," I said. "But I'll make more of an effort."

On December 29, I receive a letter from the academy. I rip it open. My grades. I look down and see four As and a B+, a cumulative score of 3.84. The results for PT we will receive upon return to school. This GPA places me comfortably on the general's list and, according to statistics, on the top of my class. I am overjoyed and can't put it down. I spring into the kitchen to my mom, who's writing in her planner.

"Mom, look, 3.85. I did it, general's list."

For the first time since I have been home, she looks up at me and smiles genuinely. "Good job, Steve. Maybe we can do something as a family to celebrate," she says.

"Not necessary, ma'am. The reward is in the achievement." Elated by this surprise, I float upstairs into my bedroom and prepare for the day.

The next few days are full of surprises—cheese grits with fatty bacon, shrimp gumbo and fried tomatoes, and sweet monkey bread, all left with a little note that said, "Congrats, Steve." Loretta is looking out for me even if she is still disappointed by my secrets. It's as if she is cheering inwardly, too emboldened by her principles to forgive me. Maybe she has forgiven me, and instead, she is telling me that this is how it will be until I let her in. All I know is that I can't tell her or anyone about what happens at the academy. It is part of my duty.

New Year's Eve crept up quickly as did the entire winter break, it seemed. Over two weeks had passed, and I didn't feel any further from the white walls and fluorescent hallways of the academy. Each morning, I ran, read the paper, and moped around, unsure of how to spend my day. Relaxation was no longer enough.

I had seen friends from high school, but they only reminded me of how much I had experienced at the academy and of how different we had become. They felt stagnant, frozen. The academy life was one of agitated circles. It was one of fidgeting, of "Wake up!" "Pay attention," "Get down, maggots," a writhing anxiety. Whether it was routines during PT, training in ROTC, funneling in and out of class periods, or the bustle of a moving mess hall, we had order.

On the peninsula, for the youth's yacht association New Year's party, I am required to wear a suit. Miranda giggles as I show up. She's wearing a subtle black dress, which accentuates her glowing light-brown hair. I'm wearing a dark-brown suit that's a bit too large for me and a white shirt.

"What?" I ask.

"You are such a dork," she says. "Look at the way you walk."

"This is the way you're supposed to walk. What do you mean the way I walk?"

"You're like this," she says, and she begins to imitate me.

"Watch this," I say and then furrow my brow in a model pose. Then I switch to a disco move.

"Wow, like John Travolta." She laughs. "Are you ready to groove tonight?"

"Is there anything else on the menu?" I say.

"Let's see, there's an entrée of introducing yourself to some people followed up with the next course of dancing and a little dessert of walking along the docks. What do you say?"

"Sounds pretty good to me."

"Wonderful!" she says, cheery as ever.

We walk into the large room on the side of the water. "So your entire family are members of this association?"

"Yes, but like I explained to you, they're out of town, so it's just us tonight." She smiles.

We enter through the front into a lavish ballroom full of well-dressed people and circular tables covered with white cloth. The walls are festooned in white balloons, and colorful streamers cover the tables. Two bars stand on opposite sides, and a large buffet of food stretches from one bar to the other side of the room. It is going to be difficult for me to restrain myself from taking one too many trips.

"So you attend this party every year?" I said.

173

"Yes, since I was a little girl," she said.

"I see, and you are sure that it doesn't worry you that a family friend will relay information back to your parents?"

"It's true. I thought about it." *Whoa, she's honest.* "But let them find out. We're coming up on 1980, and there ain't nothing wrong with a little change."

"That's not a bad attitude to have. Hey, why don't I get us some drinks?"

"What do you want me to do?"

"Wrangle up some people to introduce me to," I said.

"Aren't you the brave one. See you soon, love," she said.

I must've floated across the room after she had said that because I didn't remember the journey. Suddenly, I was at the bar. The barman, who was quite busy, gave me a "One moment" finger. He had three or four customers to take care of at the moment. So I glanced over to the other bar, which seemed better controlled.

I begin traversing the room again, wearing a friendly, nonthreatening smile. It's not that people are looking at me. Most seem thoroughly engaged in their own conversations. However, I admittedly feel out of place. Self-consciousness leads you to only think of yourself.

Maybe it is time to break out the mask. I pull my shoulders back and march like we do at the academy. Within moments, I arrive at the other bar. He has two patrons to tend to and seems to be conversing with them as he crafts their drinks. I scan over toward Miranda. She has caught the attention of an older couple.

I look back toward the barman and try to get his attention with my gaze. No effect. I raise my finger. He continues his conversation. My patience runs thin. Obviously, he should notice me by now; and by forcing me to announce myself, I seem like the villain. What can I do?

"Sir, I've been waiting quite some time. Do you intend on serving me or not?" This slips out, and as it registers in his ear, I wonder if it's even me.

"Oh, sorry, sir. I didn't see you there," he said.

"That's quite all right. Two gin and tonics please."

"Two, huh? We have a strict one at a time policy. That's why these vultures over here hover around the bar."

"It's the most efficient," one of them said, raising his glass.

I let out a fake laugh. "Well, I'm sure you can make an exception if I'm just the courier." He studied me. "No tricks. She's right over there." I pointed to Miranda.

"Oh, the Clayton's girl."

"Yes, sir."

"What are you, her help?" one of the drunk gentlemen said.

"No, sir, but I'd be lucky to be."

A few moments later, I joined Miranda with two gin and tonics.

"Hello, sir, ma'am," I said.

"Mr. and Mrs. Flemming, this is Steve."

"Pleasure," Mr. Flemming said.

"Charmed," Mrs. Flemming said.

We chat for a few minutes and excuse ourselves. After the conversation, Miranda introduces me to many others as we drift around the association. We bounce from conversation to conversation, none digging beneath to anything genuine. It is easy for me. It feels as if this sort of soldier's mask, the stoic way, allows me to blockade information that would be too personal. A few hours later and a couple more drinks in, I decide that I, too, want to belong to associations of this sort.

"Miranda, this is fun," I said.

"Oh, you like shaking hands. Well, I'll tell you, they certainly are talking. When I went to the ladies' room, I overheard someone speaking about you."

"Really?" I said. Torn. I was torn between indulging in gossip and minding my own business. *But why would they speak about me?* I wondered.

"Yes, very biased stuff about you, and they don't even know you. Steve, you've really opened my eyes about a lot of things."

"What do you mean?"

"Our circumstances are very different, but I feel genuinely similar to you. I don't know how to describe it."

"Did you think the opposite before?"

"No, it's not that. But you have to understand, my father, he is a scary man. You have to be in criminal law. He was very harsh, strict on us, when we were growing up."

"I can relate to that. My dad was in the military."

"Is he why you're at the academy?"

"I'd like to think that it's for my growth, but I know that he played a large role. It's like there's always a shadow. And we were taught a certain way to approach everything."

"See? Totally alike. But I think despite how we were raised, people have similarities. We all love certain things like coincidence, Italian food, and lazy Sundays." I began laughing. "When we were young, we went to Italy during the summers," she said.

"That must've been amazing, you and your parents," I asked and then realized the only possibility.

"No, not with my parents."

"Oh, so you went by yourself, wow."

"Well, no, I went with my sister."

"I didn't know you have a sister. I have two younger sisters." Her demeanor changes.

What's happening? She tears up and says, "Ah, shit. You know, um, maybe we can go for a walk. I think I need to clear my head." She takes deep breaths to try and control her tears, but they keep flowing.

"Hey now," I say. I take off my suit jacket and wrap it around her shoulders. As we walk off, I notice eyes and glances directed toward us. Of course. Her tears, it appears, the onlookers fault me for them.

We exit out of the back of the main room into a small corridor that leads to a large dock. A bone-chilling breeze carries off the bay, striking me in the buttons of my shirt. A dense black hovers across the marina. Boats clank against the docks, creating an eerie chime. She clenches my jacket.

"Maybe it's too cold to be out here," she says and takes my hand to reel me back inside.

"Are you feeling better?"

"Yes, Steve," she says and forces a smile.

When we enter the ballroom again, people turn back to stare at us, the shivering couple, partly wet from the spray.

"Almost midnight," I said, attempting to act casual, then I leaned in. "They're all looking."

"I know," she said and kissed me. I was shocked, and I leaned back. "They wanted something to watch."

I feel my blood boil. Discreet and polite is my aim. Because of her, I am accomplishing neither. "Are you crazy?" I say.

"Steve, are you angry at me?"

"This isn't a game or a show or whatever. I feel like if I make a slight mistake here, it'll follow me around like a shadow."

"It isn't for me either," she says. "I'm already taking a big risk having you here."

This statement could've been another match for the flame. I take a deep breath. "Well, okay," I say. "It is a big risk," I agree. It is a big risk for her. "I don't like gossip, okay? And I really don't like subjecting myself to gossip. My aim is to accompany you and make you happy while being discreet."

She looks at me as a child looks when she's in trouble. "I'm sorry. I didn't mean to act imprudently. Sometimes, I feel like I've processed losing my sister, and then a wave comes over me. It's very daunting."

"Losing your sister?" I say and pause. "I'm very sorry about that." I embrace her.

"I'm all right, I promise," she says. "I don't want this night to be remembered like that. I just wanted good company."

"Me too. Look, one thing to know about me, I'm not good at emotion. In fact, at the academy, it has become a habit for me to block emotion." I pause. "What you are going through in life, I'm very sorry, but I'm not going to ask about it. You're going to have to tell me about it when you think it's right."

She smiled. "Oh my." She looked at the clock.

"Ten, nine, eight, seven," everyone chanted.

She wraps herself in my arms. The tension dissolves, and at the count of one, we kiss. Balloons drop from the sky. Moments later, on the cold dock, colorful azaleas bloom in the night sky.

"Steve, you're a little odd, you know that?" she says, staring in my eyes.

Chapter 10

One Month—Second Semester Begins

I find myself following MacConough and Corporal Warren in the night down a dark street near campus. Through the streetlights, I can see my breath rise. The clunk of our shoes follow one another. They speak, joke as normal, but none of it is audible to me. I can't relax.

Off campus, you pass the football arena before you reach college houses and then King Street. The giant bulldog appears demonic at night. The streets are empty except us. Suddenly, a car takes a slow turn. Its headlights sweep past us, and the car itself zooms by. Trees reach overhead and seem to strangle what's left of the sky.

We reach a small white house. I hear the jingle of Warren's keys, and then he opens the door, but perhaps I should start at the beginning.

A rejuvenating breath enters the academy along with 1979. Clyde, Harry, and I are now labelled the dream dorm because of our abstaining from demerits and our arising chipper while the clang of the trash cans funnel through the barracks at 0530. No longer is it a problem but rather a mechanical function at the academy.

A distant frozen blue breaches the horizon like cracked ice. My arms feel heavy and sluggish as we line up for PT. But after some breathing and stretches, I feel back to normal form. Jodies ring out as we exit the barracks: "When I go to bars, the girls they will say, How'd you earn your living, How'd you earn your pay, And I replied with a cold kind of nod, I kill commies for my God! Sound off 1, 2 Sound off 3, 4."

Weather-wise, it is damp, brisk, a hostile start to the year. In the clearing of the center field, no longer are birds chirping or the sun humming above the trees. The mood is austere, downtrodden even. I glance around for familiar faces. MacConough is up front with a somber mug. I recall our pact at the end of last semester. I dreamed of it and feared the day when we sit face-to-face again.

I spot Simon and run up to give him a dap. We turn and head back toward the barracks. At the barracks, I see MacConough, Nicky, Petersson, and Warren, who was back from his suspension. They are standing in silence, hands behind their backs, as Lieutenant Dorchester surges forth. "Listen up. Vacation's over. Let me give you a brief rundown of what will occur over this semester, because this semester will determine where you belong in the academy.

"Either you get on a fast track to becoming an officer or you become a nobody. Depending on your grades and ROTC scores from last semester, you will be sorted into different squadrons. We didn't notify you of this system before because we didn't want to incentivize you. Your personal growth should have been enough motivation on its own. During field training every other week, these selected squadrons will face off in combat."

In the distance, I saw Sergeant Edwards. Where was he when Petersson felt like assaulting us? That attack by Petersson was so orchestrated, so vile. Thinking about it now crushed my spirits.

"Do not worry, knobs, these squadrons will be equal. The top of the class will be paired with the bottom of the class and so forth. After this PT, the lists will be inside on the mess hall bulletin board. So get on your A game. Now drop down!"

"Sir, yes, sir."

After PT, we congregate in the mess hall. The knobs huddle around the bulletin board, trying to get a glimpse of where they are placed. I see Clyde, Harry, and my other floor mates in the crowd. The corporals and upperclassmen laugh at us clawing our way to view our fate. After about five minutes of intense pushing, I emerge. Randall is speaking to Clyde with Harry listening in.

"Fuck yeah, rank no. 5. Everything's going as planned, Akron. I got a bunch of new copies of the cheat sheet printed." I look at Clyde and Harry. Randall sees me and shoots a condescending look.

"Remember to stay black and stay humble, Randall," I say. Clyde and Harry laugh, but Randall seems pissed.

"You ain't going to ruin my momentum, Wiggins," Randall says and leaves.

"So how'd you boys do?" Clyde said.

"No. 78," Harry said.

"Not bad, Harry," he said. "Out of four hundred of us, that's not bad at all. It'll put you at, what, fourth in the squadron?"

"Yeah, I think so. Couldn't have done it without you guys, though. You really pushed me to commit there. We did a good job supporting each other."

"How about you, Clyde?" I said like a card player holding his hand close.

"No. 22"

"Damn, Acorn, you're the king," I said.

"Wiggins, Bolstrom, Acorn, quit messing around," MacConough said. "Sit, boys."

We sit at the table with a battery of other cadets and wait for MacConough to allow us to grab our food. Then we stand and silently file in order to grab some grub. We're back into the food chain of the academy. When we return to the table, MacConough starts to pepper us with questions.

With a large grin, he verifies that we haven't forgotten our knob knowledge. It seems that the zoo is open, and several cadets get their trays swiped from their hands. Clangs from trays and knobs falling over surround our meal, but we remain untouched.

Afterward, we sign up for classes. In the registrar, Simon has just gotten out. We chat, and I find out that he hasn't gone home and instead visited some family in Louisiana. I get a kick out of that.

The next morning, we awaken and chase the endless horizon once again. It seems so far now, barely registering on the surface of the earth as we draw nearer. Our footsteps thud through the sodden grass toward the precipice of academy grounds, but then we turn, and as we reach the barracks, once again we sing.

When I go home
The hippies they will say
How'd you earn your living
How'd you earn your pay
And I replied as I pulled out my knife
Get out of my way before I take yo' life

After morning duties, I head to class with a new semester in front of me. It's disappointing to no longer have English with Simon to start the day. Now my days start with psychology. The only course that carries over from last semester is ROTC. We'll be learning during the week, and this weekend, we will convene for the first time in our squadrons. Class after class I attend, the teacher reads their syllabus, they introduce themselves, and then they dismiss the students.

"What do you guys think'll be different about this quarter?" I asked my roommates.

"I'm not expecting much. More racking," Harry said.

"Yeah, they have to step it up another notch, right? I think I saw Petersson drawing up a plan like a football coach with x's and o's attacking from all sides," Clyde said.

"Well, I don't think the academy's philosophy is to ease us in," I replied, "so it can't be much harder than last semester."

"That's true. Maybe he was just trying to draw up a plan to get his first girlfriend," Clyde said. We all started laughing.

"Speaking of girlfriend, did you guys get any action over break?" Clyde asked. Harry giggled. "What?" Clyde yelled.

"Harry!" I said. Both Clyde and I jumped and started pummeling Harry as he hid under his covers and pillow.

"Stop, guys, stop!" Harry said. We both paused.

"How'd it go, big guy?" I said.

"What do you mean how'd it go, Steve? Do you think it went well? Honestly," Clyde said.

"Well, look at his face." Harry had a million-yard smile.

"What'd I tell you?" I said. "So what are the details? Did this happen back home? What about Claire?"

"I actually flew in a few days before I was required to, and we spent some time together."

"Really?" I said.

"Yeah. I had to ask permission to stay on campus as an out-of-towner, but they understood. Well, so Claire and I hung out every day. We went to some restaurants, parks, bars, and each night, I'd come back dreaming about her."

"Whoa, lover boy," Clyde said. "Harry, Harry, you're going to make me cry if you keep this story up, Harry."

"By the way, I like Charleston a lot, Steve. I got to explore it more, and there's some pretty cool history here," Harry said. "So finally, the night before everyone was supposed to get back, well, she invited me over."

"Oh my god, Harry." Clyde laughed. "Oh my god."

"Settle down, Clyde," I said.

"It's just, look what we have on our hands, Steve. We have Romeo, Steve. Romeo is in the barracks." I laughed. "I'm proud of you, Harry," Clyde said.

"Me too, Romeo," I said.

"Thanks, guys."

"Well, me too, Harry, me too," I said.

"So are you dating now?"

"Yes, sir," I said.

Suddenly, taps float across campus. We turn off the lights and hop in bed, though we all feel an energy throughout the room.

"By the way, Steve, you never told us what your ranking is in the academy." A silence dropped in the room.

"No. 4," I said.

*****

Late in the week, I notice that I haven't been racked once. No whispers arise on campus when I pass. No shifty eyes scour me during class. I can tell that both Harry and Clyde have been racked when they arrive in the dorm room and plop into bed.

Late that week, there is a rack party. I hear it occurring down the hall, and I'm not invited. The upperclassmen actually tells me to go for a walk. I decide to put on my mask and act accordingly, though I couldn't conceal my intuition. *Could this be MacConough?*

2 by 2 and 4 by 4
K knob company at your door
Iran ain't no friend of mine
Reza Shah is out of time. Sound off:

*****

For the first week of ROTC field training, we hop into a bus that roars out beyond the borders of town. The suburbs spread thin and shift into a lush landscape of winding trees. Way out in the middle of who knows where in the heck, we hop off the bus. From a dusty driveway, we march into a field of high grass. Bracing and in single file lines, we await instruction. A fellow whom I haven't seen before leads us.

"Salute your commander," the superior said.

"Sir, yes, sir," we said.

"My name is McDougall, and I will be your field training officer. Each of you night crawlers wants to fly one day. Is that correct? Well, I'm curious, do you have what it takes? They say the academy's cadets are the nation's best, but do you have what it takes?"

"Sir, yes, sir," we said.

He was a curly-haired brunette with a tanned face and a rather large build. Something about him seemed goofy, unlike the austere nature of the corporal that could switch in and out of seriousness.

"You see, I was in your same situation last year, and you gotta push yer troop forward to be the best. But lookie here. No man can push alone."

He lights up a cigarette and takes a long drag. *What the hell is he thinking?* On one hand, he's the highest ranking officer around; but on the other, if someone reports him, this could be a real offense.

"So I'll be working with you to train you maggots. I was put in this position due to my outstanding performance last year. But enough about me. Cadets, at ease. You're going to get to know one another," he finishes.

We break and start shaking hands with one another. None of them seems like a standout. They seem put off by me even, judging me as the only black guy on the squad. These are my comrades. We have a kid with spectacles, which at the academy is a severe disadvantage. Another kid is very tall yet very thin and flimsy looking.

One fellow, Gin, a Japanese American student, walks up to me. "So you're Steven. Your reputation precedes you." His formalities catch me off guard. As he says this, he keeps his head tucked downward, staring somewhere below my ear. I try to keep a cool head as he asks me how I had the strength to challenge Petersson, win the intramural football league, and still hold the highest ranking on our ROTC squadron.

McDougall looks off at the empty field in a fierce gaze. He ashes his cigarette under his foot and turns to face us. "All right, cadets, lets run some exercises," he says.

*****

That Saturday night, knocks ring out on our door. Worried that it's Petersson, my roommates stare as I slowly approach. I open. It's a freshman. "For Steve Wiggins. You are to report immediately to room 312." *That's MacConough's room.* The runner says no more as we both walk in a punctilious manner toward MacConough's room. The runner knocks twice on the door, and Warren answers. Both of the upperclassmen are shuffling through different papers, what I suspect are duties of the officer.

"Wiggins," MacConough announced.

"Sir, yes, sir," I said.

"At ease," MacConough said. "We're finishing up here. Want to join us off campus for some poker?"

Really? He's inviting me to play poker with them? Immediately, Warren's gaze registered, and I thought back to Paxton. Warren was found guilty for causing injury to Paxton, or at least that was what I concluded with the scraps of information I had found out. I gulped, and suddenly, I felt very isolated from the rest of the room. But how could I retreat?

"Wiggins?" MacConough repeated.

I was tempted to think of strategies, but I stopped and remembered what MacConough had already taught me. I accepted. The two corporals gathered their papers. MacConough wrote me a night pass, and the three of us strolled off campus.

The pair lead the way through the dark streets of suburban Charleston. Streetlights illuminate small sections of the city blocks, but the light doesn't manage to get through the trees. The two of them are laughing while I look around for any telltale sign of where we're going. We turn at the arena, and they lead me to a small white house.

"Steve," MacConough said.

"Sir, yes, sir," I responded.

"I said at ease, Steve. I'm calling you by your first name now, so calm down."

"Okay, I will," I said.

"You notice how this year feels different?" MacConough said.

"I've never thought about the years like that, but this year does have a certain feeling to it, sir," I said.

"Last and first year of a decade, they always feel more significant than the mess inside of it," MacConough said. "It's like a punctuation mark. It determines what the next sentence can be."

"Maybe you're unaware," Warren started, "but there's a conflict in Iran right now."

"I read that tensions were rising over break, sir," I said.

"They've reached a boiling point," MacConough said.

"What does that mean, sir?" I said.

When we enter, a couple of other guys are already dealing cards. I snuck in behind the presence of the corporals. The other upperclassmen don't pay notice until something odd happens. Both Warren and MacConough insist on introducing me to everyone. In a formal manner, I say hello, only shaking hands after they reach theirs out. Everyone jokes around. A couple of guys light up cigarettes, and finally, they deal the cards.

The atmosphere is smoky yet cheery and filled with laughter. Several of them sit on chairs around the table and others on the arm of a sunken sofa. Behind the sofa, the TV is on. MacConough offers me some whiskey. I sip slowly, but it's too harsh, and I let out a small cough. The guys burst out laughing. I ween off anxiety and start to loosen up. Over hands, they start sharing stories of their knob year.

"MacConough was always acting up knob year, putting his shirt on inside out during inspections. When corporals—who was that? Oh yeah, Corporal Jones—started racking him for lack of discipline, he pretended to be unaware of what was happening during the whole situation. Like, 'Sorry, sir. Why are you racking me? Why are you picking on lil old me?'"

"The commanders couldn't figure out what was wrong with him."

"Seriously, I wanted to bring some lightheartedness to the whole thing. Knob year can be so glum. The only thing people ever talk about is quitting, how bad the cafeteria food is, and the time of the next rack party," MacConough said.

"Yeah, but you had your crazy streaks too."

"I remember at a hop, you kissed one of the upperclassmen's females. He was livid. Would've beat you to death if he had caught ya."

"If he could catch me. That son of a bitch was like a mule leaving the starting gate."

I looked around at the others' faces. They were full of cheer recollecting knob year. I knew that this was how it was going to be, difficult at the time but fun in memory. *MacConough is incredible at covering himself up,* I thought. *Maybe his tendencies are actually a way of distracting everyone.*

"Well, Warren, you damn near beat a sophomore senseless at the freshman payback event," MacConough said. Warren looked skittish from behind his glasses. I gulped. "You should've seen him, Steve. This man was a projectile in terms of getting revenge. Guns right at 'em," MacConough added.

"Guilty as charged, but I learned my lessons," he said in a cool manner over his hand of cards. He adjusted his glasses and then laid his hand, full house. As I watched him snag the pile of chips, I realized, adjusting his glasses was his tell. It was then that a banner swept across the screen: "Riots intensify in Iran."

"Turn the volume up," Warren said in his soft manner.

"Riots continue in Iran today as the news of the shah's imminent departure spreads." The shah was filmed waving at the camera.

"Ah, fuck," one of the upperclassmen said.

"We're probably going to have to go in there."

"No way," MacConough said. "We aren't going to clean this up. It has nothing to do with the people of the United States."

"It just shows all the glaring weaknesses of Jimmy Carter's good guy act."

"He's making the South look soft, that's for certain."

"We're tougher than his policies."

For a while, the upperclassmen grumbled about the president and his failure in Iran. I couldn't tell if they were actually worried about going to war, if they were eager to, or if they thought the situation would simmer down. According to the newscaster, the shah's departure was imminent. The ayatollah would return, and the power of the Middle East would shift forever.

After a couple of hours of drinking and schmoozing, we returned to campus. It was a little past two in the morning, and with weary eyes and warm stomachs from the whiskey, we crossed campus in the wee hours. When we entered the barracks, I glanced up at the cloisters on the four corners of the barracks. The moon shone vividly on the quadrangle. Once again, it was black and white. Both Warren and MacConough saluted me and said good night.

"Good night, sirs," I replied.

I lay in bed and heard the deep breathing of my roommates. Tonight was somewhere between dodging a bullet and having a great time.

The next Saturday, my ROTC squad meets at dawn, 5:00 a.m. roll time. The cadets dress in gear with packs at their feet, standing at the gates of the academy. Each of the squadrons duck into vans. The commanders swing the doors shut, and we drive out of Charleston.

The vans follow one another like coroners, headlights dimming as the day takes form in a stark gray light. I look out of the window. I haven't been able to tell which direction we are heading, and now the woods engulf us. We turn off a main highway and rumble through a dusty path. Then we park.

There was a clearing up ahead. The only audible sound was the twigs and leaves cracking under our feet. As everyone convened, I spied Clyde. I walked over to him. He had a sunken expression on his face.

"It's too damn early," Clyde said. I snickered.

"Who said that?" A commander approached. We both braced. "Dammit, you will learn the hard way. Drop down, packs on."

Both of us nosedive to the ground. We huff through twenty and then stand up. Puffing, we continue on to a grand opening. A large wooden structure looms in the background. Ropes and rings dangle from its limbs like a mythic Kraken.

On the ground in front of us rest pellet guns. The commander orders us each to take one and strap it to our chest. Through the trees we march and then split off running. I nod farewell to Clyde. We whiz by trees in our measured march. My squad tails me, but Clyde is no longer in my field of vision. He is my first opponent.

A brook trickles downhill, around a bend, and out of sight. We clop past it with our heavy boots, some hopping over the ravine, others trekking through it. The terrain is soft to the touch, moist and unstable. Slim trees reach up toward the sky. Finally, with my adrenaline pounding, we stop, and McDougall turns to face us. This time, he has a toothpick in his mouth, which must've been to mask his smoking addiction.

"All right, squad," McDougall said. "No letting up. We will demolish them." He furiously munched on his toothpick.

"Sir, yes, sir," we said.

"Be serious," he yelled. "This is field training. This exercise will test your ability to follow commands in practice. From now on, the academy is judging your abilities. The guns are filled with pellets, and boys, they do hurt if they hit you. Our goal is to eliminate the other team before they can get to us and capture their base. Each time you get hit, you are to go over to the obstacle course at the entrance and complete it. You got it, maggots?"

"Sir, yes, sir." I look around at a squad of stern faces. Finally, a hoot and hollering good time.

The commander received a message on his walkie-talkie and then yelled, "All right. Let's go, boys."

We split into packs. Gin, two others, and I mushed forward and entered an area of heavy foliage. Peering out, off in the distance, others from their squad were moving forward with a faster pace. They were crouched but at a near run.

"Okay. We should be safe if we stay put," one of them said and sat by the stump of the tree while the other peered beyond its leaves.

"You don't want to be part of the action?" Shots rang out.

"We gotta support them. What are you guys doing?"

"We're good here, Wiggins. You want to go, you go. We'll serve as defense."

I felt Gin's gaze, but when I looked up at him, he turned forward, looking in the direction of the gunfire.

"I'll come with you," he said.

"Thanks, Gin. We got this, man. Any ideas about a plan?"

"Yes. We should stagger. Have one support the other. As it's a head-on assault, there's little room for flanking, so I think as long as we remain calculated, we should be okay."

"That's a good idea. I can lead. You provide support, all right?"

"Cool, cool," he said, and we gave each other some dap.

Looking around, I leave the cover of foliage and mush forward through the sodden soil. When I reach the river, fire goes off again. It rings closer this time. To my left, there is a structure of some sort, possibly remains of a bunker from Civil War times. I give Gin a signal and hedge the brook in the direction of the bunker.

Then off in the distance, I see a dark figure ducking behind a tree. I hit the ground immediately. I hear shots come from Gin's direction and then the other and then silence. The brook runs beside me. Cold air comes off the water. It distorts my hearing, but I realize that also means they can't hear me. I dig into the muck and put it over my body, camouflaging with the wet topsoil.

"Clear," I hear someone yell. *Did they get Gin?* Behind me, someone hops over the ravine where I'm hiding. Another set of footsteps approaches. Instincts kick in. I flip on my back and shoot where they are running from. Tumbling down, the fallen cadet yells out in pain.

I hear footsteps coming back to help, one pair. He holds his breath. There is no escape for him, but I assume they are on the ground, surveying the area.

"Where the hell did that come from?" I overhear.

The other cadet doesn't say anything. Either he's still in pain or he is pointing at me. I only have moments to react. Face first, I slide toward the brook. Taking a mouthful of icy water, I stand up. I can't breathe. Adrenaline pulses, and the cold water slides into my gear.

I see him in a crawling position just like the other. The cadet reacts and shoots. It whizzes by. I make sure not to miss in retaliation. I hit the cadet in the back and then look at the ground where I had hit the other cadet. The cadet is covering his groin. I cringe.

I climb out of the ravine and bullet toward the encampment. Constructed from stone, the walls of the fort tower above me. Water from a recent rain drips onto the floor from the partially enclosed ceiling. There is little light. I sit with my back against one of the walls, exhausted from the last encounter. My sliding maneuver had worked. The cadet missed by inches because of it.

There is no sign of Gin, no sign of anyone. The droplets are peaceful. A handful of dust, I release it into a gust of wind. My gear is muddy and wet. The cavernous fortress grabs my attention. It seems full of a storied hollow, the same as the empty winding hallways of the academy. I take a deep breath and tilt my head to look upward. The ceiling disappears from light.

Then a shot rings out, and pain spreads through me. I look down. A pellet is lodged into the middle of my chest. I turn and see a dark figure emerge, and then I hear a laugh.

"Got you, ya worm." It was Clyde.

"Time to go do the obstacles, Wiggy." He laughed. I gasped for air. After a moment of disbelief, I caught my breath and took the white flag out of my pocket and placed it on my helmet. I stood up and looked at him. *Thwap!* I heard Clyde yell out.

"How long have you been there, Gin?" I said.

"Yes, sorry. I couldn't get a clear shot of him until he stepped out into the open."

"Fucker," Clyde said.

"Good job," I said.

With a newfound smirk, I jog over the empty battlefield past the trees to the obstacle course where others are waiting. A large upperclassman walks up toward me, and I brace. I expect the upperclassman to strike me, but instead, he says, "All right. Get to it, cadet." Somehow, now I am just another cadet.

We wrap up that field training with Gin eventually busting through their defenses and retrieving the opposing squad's flag. He wears a huge smile but quickly pulls me in to celebrate with him and the others. "You made that possible," he says to me. I look to see Clyde sulking in disappointment. He seems like he needed that victory.

The wear and tear from winter nights struck quick. Every other night tugged colder weather along with the gloom. Harry moved through with a smitten motivation, but I would find Clyde silent, either sleeping or scribbling in his notebook. It didn't register that a peppy guy like him had depression, but I wouldn't know what else to call it. The radiators hissed through ESP, janitor duty, taps, and into the darkness.

After this introduction to their poker nights, it wasn't uncommon for MacConough, Warren, and even Nicky to invite me to go out with them. Petersson often shook his head at the decision and attempted to ignore me, but my acceptance was abrupt and difficult to ignore. Several upperclassmen began acknowledging me on campus.

They would shoot me a nod or a "Wiggy." It was beyond my comprehension and beyond my control. I decided not to question the olive branch and just go along with the thought that MacConough wanted to make a friend in me. MacConough seemed like a powerful friend to have. If he could convince Petersson to go along with it, then he could convince anyone.

MacConough shared stories of crazy situations when he was younger and during his prior years at the academy. One summer, he worked on a boat as a deck hand for the mayor, Royce Manning, and the mayor's entourage. The elements took a sudden turn against the crew. A storm was coming. The wind rose, and the ship became near impossible to navigate.

Captain didn't think that these guys were going to make it, so MacConough and a couple other deck hands broke into the bar area and started taking swigs of rum like real seamen. The alcohol settled their stomachs, and they rode it out. The storm passed, and they returned to shore without severe damage done to the boat. The captain reversed his opinion from before and said he knew they were going to make it all along. The lot of them were fired for drinking the alcohol.

Petersson would interject into conversations with brute facts. He was an intelligent man. I couldn't deny this. He and Warren would debate with only one of them losing their cool. Nicky would laugh and goad Petersson into didactic tantrums, quoting Robert E. Lee: "'The education of a man is never complete until he dies.' So you may find yourself taking these teachings that I hand out to ya and altering your viewpoint on things, all right? You'd be better off in life if ya did."

Petersson's speeches were difficult for me to listen to. His verbose seemed directly translated from his excessive rackings and his abusive way of life. He felt the need to dominate. I felt myself clenching my fists and unnerved whenever he voiced an opinion on anything from the Reza Shah to disco music. "It's a four flat, simple chord structure. There's nothing artistic at all about these niggers. It's easy music." I wanted to dig in with him so badly, but that would put a target on my face. What about Sly and the Family Stone, Stevie Wonder, and Marvin Gaye? Petersson swept all these amazing artists under the rug.

The group, however, turned out to be a riot, and after a few weeks of hanging, my stock rose at the academy. Of course, I was different from them, and they treated me appropriately, the little black guy Wiggy, but I relished in this opportunity for some solace and good times.

Days turned to weeks that I hadn't been racked. Instead of being forced to the ground and being spit on, Nicky would hop on my back, yell yeehaw, and wrestle me to the ground. He called it the urban cowboy, but it was done in jest, and that wasn't a terrible trade-off. After each night, I would smile as I clamber back into my room.

I would wake with the same ten minutes to spare before the trash cans. Clyde, Harry, and I descended the stairs with the same punctuality, and things felt normal during PT. In the afternoons, however, the largest differences showed themselves. Freshmen stepped out of my way, and upperclassmen acknowledged me as I marched toward class. Winter was upon us, but I felt like an elegant sun was shining down on me.

"Hey, man, they're taking a liking to you, huh?" Clyde said.

"Yes, definitely," I said.

"Maybe we can use it to our advantage?" Clyde continued.

"What? What do you mean?" I said.

"Use you hanging out with them to our advantage like all the different privileges that they have."

"I don't know if that's a good idea, Clyde," Harry added.

"What? Why not? Steve, I know you can formulate some kind of plan here," Clyde said. "You're good with this kind of stuff. Look, think about how much fun we'd all have if you managed to bring in a twelve-pack beer or something."

This time, I trusted my instincts. I didn't like the situation one bit. "No, Clyde, I'm not going to do that," I said.

"Please, man. This winter is for the fucking birds. I need something to look forward to."

"Maybe we should cut the shit, man. Tell me, what's really the problem?"

"Nothing, Steve."

"Clyde, talk to us, man," Harry said.

"Yeah, you've been acting all funky since you've been back. You killed it with your no. 22 ranking, so what has you in the dregs?" I said.

He stays silent for moment or two, analyzing both of us. Either that or he is searching for a way to phrase his confession without sounding vulnerable. "It was just hard to see my mom, you know?" he starts.

"What do you mean?" Harry says.

"She just hasn't been the same since my dad passed. It's like she's aging fast. Since Christmas, it's been real hard to convince myself that this is the right thing to do. Like, that being here is the right thing to do, I mean," he says. Harry walks over to him and gives a friendly pat on the shoulder. It feels as if Clyde is going to start sobbing.

"Yeah, man. Well, that's a decision you're going to have to commit on," I say coldly.

Harry looks over at me as if to signal, "What the hell is wrong with you?"

"You don't need to hold all of the burden, Clyde," Harry said and paused. "Don't you have some other relatives who can help you out?"

"Yes, potentially. I mean, they have been helping out, but they have their own lives to live, ya know?"

"You two, look at me," I said. I had enough.

"What, Steve?" Clyde said.

I smile at them, and then I slowly lower my hand across my face. When my hand passes, my expression is that of a bull's, that of a soldier's.

"You see that? That's called consistency. Whenever you come to an impasse, you hold on to consistency. It's what makes us soldiers, the ability to fall back on these brutal traits that we've been taught and persevere. You are training right now, Clyde, and so am I, and we need to finish our training, not just for ourselves but also for everyone else.

"There's no backing out, and you've just got to deal with that. Do your best rather than sulking about things that are out of your control. If it's really necessary, pick up the phone, tell her how you feel. Otherwise, put your nose down and keep training. It's only four years of life, and look, you can spend all the time with her this summer," I finish. "C'mon, guys. Let's go to this basketball game."

I look at him, puffing, red-faced. He looks back with a wise-guy smirk on his face. "Wow, quite a speech there, Martin," Clyde says.

I can't read him. Whether he agrees with me or resents me is completely hidden, but I disregard this retort. We grab our gear and head to the arena.

Like football season, the academy requires cadets to shout their lungs out in support of the team. Harry, Clyde, a group of the guys from the floor, and I head there together, all boasting our school's colors and wearing Mardi Gras beads. "Let's go, Bulldogs, let's go," we shout as we go down the halls. Other students open their doors and join the chant. Even Sergeant Edwards peeks out of his room and gives us a half smile.

With the disappointing season that the football team had, I'm not expecting a lot in terms of basketball prowess. We start the season 2–2, and tonight, we are playing Marshall. The gaggle of cadets join the other fourth years in their assigned section where we give one another high fives as we pass through. We all start to sing jodies.

> Marshall ain't got zero chance
> Cadets make their girlfriends dance
> Watch the clock go tick, tick
> Their players shoot bricks, bricks

The game starts as a nail-biter. The academy is up at ten minutes through, but then Marshall ties it at the half. Clyde looks back like his normal self. "I'm going to get them some waters," I say as the screaming makes us all thirsty. I sneak out of the row and out of the arena. Fans of all shapes and sizes—fathers with large bellies and school colors, little kids holding lollipops, upperclassmen in casual wear—are all there. The line to concessions is huge. I scour for some tell of how fast it will move. MacConough and Warren stand near the front. I meander up to them.

"Sir," I say.

"Get in here." MacConough pulls me. "Wiggins, you know better than to engage an upperclassman. Where's your head at?" He slaps me on my forehead.

"Sir, my apologies, sir," I say.

"Now what's this about, Steve? And you better have a pretty urgent reason to talk to us in broad daylight around so many witnesses."

"Sir, the line is long, sir. I was hoping to cut in back of you so that I can get some waters before the second half begins." MacConough and Warren burst out laughing.

"You kill me, Wiggins. What a clown."

"I have an idea," Warren says. "Wiggins, do high knees until we reach the front. Then you'll have a reason for staying in the line."

I begin at the pace of 240 per minute. *Thwap, thwap, thwap.* The line inches forward while my knees shoot to the sky. They sound like a locomotive chugging along. As people walk off with popcorn and soda, they watch me with wary. When we reach the front, I'm sweating, and both of them are laughing. I guess we're friends, but that doesn't make us anywhere near equals.

"Three cans of pop please and two hot dogs, one with ketchup and yellow mustard and the other with spicy mustard and sweet relish," MacConough says.

"Coming right up."

MacConough looks at me. "Oh yeah, and some waters! For having the guts to do that, you're going to stand with us now. C'mon." MacConough takes the soda and hot dogs. Warren grabs me by the back of the neck. It doesn't hurt, but I wince as we walk toward another section.

The view opens up, and we can see the hardwood. We can see the sweat on the home team's benched players and the light reflecting off the ref's whistle.

"All right, Bulldogs!" shouts Petersson.

MacConough does a high-pitched whistle to cheer them on and then distributes the waters. It looks like Petersson has already eaten a couple hot dogs and some fries by himself. Nicky has devoured a plate of nachos. There are empty food containers on the stone ground. They all start yelling, except for me.

"Oh, we gotta train him, Colin," shouted Petersson. "Baby needs a bottle before he learns how to talk." He threw over a flask.

"It's my dad's good stuff, so don't hurt yourself, and don't let them see you," Petersson said.

I take a swig, and like a hiker tasting water for the first time in hours, it's dang near the smoothest whiskey I've ever tasted. "Wow, that's good," I say to MacConough, to which MacConough chuckles.

"I like whiskey. I always have. That's why I don't drink it. I drink scotch," Petersson said and winked at me. "Yahoo!"

The Bulldogs stole the ball, went on a fast break, and scored two—58–57, their lead with one shot clock to go. Marshall passed it in bounds. In anticipation, MacConough had both the collar of Warren and my shirt and said a quick prayer.

Marshall drives it and passes it inside, but an academy player knocks it out of bounds. Five seconds left. They pass it in again and put up a shot. It rims out, and an academy player swipes it and knocks it past half court. The Marshall player dives, but the buzzer goes off. The academy wins.

An uproar spreads through the crowd. Fans are livid, turning and yelling at one another's faces, but like clockwork, I remember Harry and Clyde. *Ah, it's not a big deal,* I assure myself. Petersson and some of the other guys make plans to go out. MacConough urges me to come, so I surrender my plans to join them on their victory lap.

|||||||||||||||||||||||||||||||||||||||||||||||||||||||||||||||||||||

CHAPTER 11

One Night—The Academy Royals

The upperclassmen had an infinitude of perks that rolled along with their class status. They could spend nights off campus. On weekends, they didn't have curfews. Bars gave them discounts on shots—well, drinks and beer—and women showed them an opulence of attention.

Darkness swallows the sun. Before them, each night spreads like a fragrant aroma coating a banquet hall, and they are the guests of honor. They are rowdy guests, tamed beasts but still feral within. Discipline and routine only hamper their hunger for freedom. It doesn't eliminate it.

At this point in the year, a frosty hue had covered Charleston with whiskey and laughter its only remedies. Nights started with hands in pockets, and they only came out for swigs, salutes, and handshakes. After the game, however, our hands were in the air.

We march off campus, back to the small white house. I'm not anxious. I'm excited this time by what the night can bring. Warren opens with a key jingle. Under the lamplight, sitting around the table, MacConough deals cards.

"So, Mr. Wiggins, the Valentine's Day hop is coming up. Are you ready for it?" Nicky said.

"Yes, sir. I've been practicing my ballroom steps."

"Is that so?" Petersson burst out. "Let's see them, Wig!"

"Sir?"

"That's an order, Wiggy. Can Wiggy get down with the piggies?" Petersson said.

The guys laughed, and MacConough gave an apologetic gesture. He flicked on the vinyl player—Blondie, "Heart of Glass."

"Boo," Petersson yelled. "C'mon, put on some good stuff, not this new age, synthesized crap."

"Just give it a try, Petey. Step beyond the boundaries of what you know for a second, huh?" MacConough said. Petersson shot him a look.

I stand and start doing a slow waltz by myself around the table. The laughs and the sounds of beer cans opening fall silent. Only music remains. Smoke rises and circles the overhead lamp. The upperclassmen begin a torrid applause, yelling, hooting, and snapping. But I finish with steely demeanor and sit.

"What's in your head, Wiggins?" Petersson slammed the table.

"Can you deal me in, sir?" I asked.

Petersson took the ignoring of his question as a sign of disrespect. "All right, but why don't we put a wager on it? So if I win this hand, you have to tell us this god-awful thought that gave you that deadpan mug. If you win, well, state your terms."

"Sir, with all due respect, sir," I said.

"C'mon. We each get a small stack of chips, and whoever takes the others wins the bet, all right?"

"I got money on Petey," one of the upperclassmen said.

"I think Steve's got this, actually," MacConough shot out.

"I'm offended, Mid Mac," Petersson scoffed. "Deal up. See, what the knob doesn't know is that I'm a sort of savant in mathematics, so even if they know how to play, they don't know the odds like I do."

"The self-proclaimed savant," Nicky chirped. The others started laughing.

He deals cards between the two of us and taps his cigarette. He takes a drag and leaves it in the tray. He starts a modest bet. *It's best to establish myself.* "I call." After a couple of betting, we flip the five cards, and Petersson shows a higher pair than mine. He smuggles the pile with his cigarette stuffed in a grin. The next hand, Petersson folds immediately, and I take the ante.

"Cards aren't an exact science."

Petersson looks at his next hand and reaches out for the cigarette but pulls back and places a hefty bet. It's over half of my chips. I fold, and Petersson takes the pile. During the next hand, something interesting happens. Petersson picks up the cigarette, butts the ash, and then smokes it. He places a modest bet, and while I have to fold this hand because of an off suit 9 and 5, I place a bigger bet on Petersson's tell.

I am down to a quarter of my pile, but each hand, I place small bets when Petersson reaches out to smoke and doesn't but fold when he butts the ash before playing. From there on out, I win every hand. After each one, the upperclassmen's commotion grows into uproar.

If Petersson lost the hand, he would try to wave it off, saying there was nothing to worry about. But I became relentless. Hand after hand, I kept winning. Petersson looked straight at me and scrunched his face together, searching my soul. I remained unfazed by the commotion, but Petersson ashed the cigarette for good, and just like that, my trump card was out on the table.

After another fifteen minutes, Petersson ends up winning back what I have taken; and after a couple more hands, he takes back all the displaced chips.

"That was an entertaining game, Wiggins. Don't know how you almost beat me, but that was close. I'll cut you some mercy." He reaches out a hand, and I shake it. Petersson's grip nearly breaks my knuckles. "I'm impressed. You showed spine, kid." MacConough puts the music back on and starts imitating me. Everyone breaks out laughing.

"All right, let's get the fuck outta here," Nicky says.

The stereo silences, the lights dim, and Warren locks the front door. We move past the stadium and college houses and all the way to the bars on the north end of King Street before the underpass. Cracks caused by tree roots litter the streets. Large cars rest in driveways of homes. The hubbub of nearby house parties catch our ear every now and again but fall into the shifting night.

The upperclassmen are intent on reaching a bar. Petersson wants some intimate, romantic conversation, or so he claims. But I hear Nicky say that it was "a damn near impossibility." A crowd of people surrounds the dive bar, smoking cigarettes and reeking of cheap liquor. When we arrive, they eye us, fiercely brushing us up and down with looks of resentment.

"Will you get out of the way?" Petersson says, and he careens his large arm, shoving them to the side to cause an entrance. "Punks." This shocks me. I'm unsure of whether to apologize or follow in his footsteps, so I sink to the back of our posse, hoping to remain unnoticed.

We enter the doors one by one with me at the posterior. The loiterers cast a malevolent gaze as I pass. The interior is what one would expect. Dirty, gritty, bluegrass, sloppy people are shooting pool in sloppy form, and rabble-rousers are waving their arms in arguments and emphatic dissonance.

This was a place that I would never come to alone and perhaps would never have come to if I weren't with the upperclassmen. We ordered five mugs of beer. Petersson carried them one-handed, clenching the handles tightly. Nicky slid into an empty booth and slapped the tabletop. "We got a live one!"

"I need some pretty dirty things to talk to quick, or else your boy is going to beeline straight for Vicky's," Petersson said.

"Hound-dogging never worked for you now, did it, Petey?" MacConough said.

"Never stopped me from hound-dogging either, did it, Mid Mac?"

"What's Vicky's?" I asked MacConough.

"It's the strip club on the East Side."

"I have an idea," Nicky said. "Let's have the little guy swoon some women for us."

Quickly, the night sinks into a nightmarish scenario. I can't do that here, especially here. I look from face to face, each of them devilish smiles, perfect examples of what every man should aspire to be.

"I'm going to pass, guys," I said.

"Whoa now," MacConough said. "He speaks!"

Petersson laughed. "C'mon, bub. For us, you gotta do this. Consider this initiation."

"I'd imagine a real initiation being more difficult than this."

"Oh yeah, we could create something off the top of the head."

"Can I have a drink or two first?" I laughed.

This works. Their faces shift. "Let the kid have a drink or two Petey," Nicky says.

"C'mon. Let the boy have a drink or two. You can tell he needs it," MacConough says.

Petersson roars, "Let him drink, then."

We lift the pints, clank them hard, and begin chugging. Seconds before me, Petersson finishes his and begins tipping the bottom of my glass. I burst out laughing as I finish, eyes full of tears.

"And that is the way we do things around here," Petersson says.

Behind the bully, something else exists in Petersson—not a warm person, per say, but truly an altered character from before. People never really change, do they? After an amount of time, however, a new perception of them is revealed depending on what moments in life we judged them from before. My father seemed the same way to me before I started at the academy. He was difficult in the public's eye, but when it came to the confines of his world, he was a venerable source and completely different.

Petersson left the booth to order more from the bartender. The bartender was reticent when Petersson came close, almost as if the sheer force of Gunthar's energy pushed him backward. I much preferred Petersson on my team. When he returned, he returned with seven beers, seven shots, and two women.

"Wiggs, make yourself known," he said.

"Howdy, madams," I said. "My name is Steve Wiggins, and these are my commanders, Corporal MacConough, Corporal Warren, and Corporal Nicky." I had to introduce them in the Guidon's instructional manner.

MacConough whistles while Nicky leans in to shake their hands. Warren raises a glass to them and smiles. A merry old time is forming. We clink our shooters and shoot and wash 'em down with beer. The two girls hold their own with no hesitation or withdrawal. *Impressive,* I think, *but they can't dazzle an audience like my Miranda.*

I think about her soft hair dropping past her shoulders. I think of her warm smile and her sense of badass style with her motorcycle jacket. How she can wear that as easily as an elegant cocktail dress? How she can rebel against her parents and then take their place at New Year's?

A break occurs in the conversation. "Wiggy, what's wrong with you?" Petey says. "Where's your head at?"

"It's right here, sir," I say.

"He's so cute," one of the women say, "dazing off into space like a true romantic. Love must be the only thing that can affect a soldier." She puts her finger to my chin.

"Love and death," Warren says. "Even if we look shut off to it, losing one of your troops, well, there's nothing worse."

"Wow, you're so strong," she says. "But it must be hard to be with one of you too knowing that you're always in danger and that love is the only thing pulling you through the battles. It's a big responsibility to have."

"The troop gives us a lot too," I say.

"This little guy here is one of the leaders of his class."

"How young are you?" she asks.

"Eighteen," I say.

"My, eighteen. When I was your age, I wasn't even thinking about coming to a place like this," she says.

"What's wrong with a place like this?" I say, chuckling on the inside.

"Well, it's just for the type who have seen too much already in life. You come here because all the other places won't have you."

"Looking through my father's eyes, I feel like I already have it all," I say.

The other upperclassmen scanned me. This conversation had become far-fetched. I guessed that the upperclassmen wanted to hear what I had to say.

"Was your father a vet?" Nicky said.

"Vietnam, two tours."

"What the fuck. Two tours?" Nicky said. "You mean he volunteered?"

"Twice," I said.

"Your pops volunteered to go to Saigon twice?"

"To your pops, I guess, huh?" Nicky said.

Each of us glug some more beer. Petersson seems unimpressed but cheers anyway and begins to direct conversation again.

"Live and central, here we go with the Nicky show!" he booms. Nicky looks at him for a moment and then completely changes his persona.

"Welcome, welcome. We're so happy to have ya. Another night, another paycheck for me. So glad we're still on air. Without further ado, let me introduce our guests. Who am I speaking with tonight?"

Petersson holds the mic up toward the females. "I'm Gorf, and she's Worf."

"Gorf and Worf, huh? Those are very, uh, interesting names, and where might those be from?"

"Mine is Klingon," she said.

"Holy cats, we have two Klingons here with us tonight, fellas."

"Wow," MacConough said, imitating a studio audience.

"So we have some callers on the line that are eager to ask you Klingons some questions. Are you ready?"

"Yes!"

"Three, two, one. Caller?"

"The name's Cheese, Cheese O'Ryan," MacConough said.

"What's up, Cheese?"

"I'm wondering how many dates it takes for you Klingons to munch on summa this."

I laugh, and so do the women. "You're cheesy, all right," she says. "No chance, hon."

"Caller," Nicky said.

"Yes?" Mac said.

"Get the hell off the phone." Everyone laughed again. These guys were good.

"*Bring, bring*," Petersson said.

"Caller?" Nicky said.

"The name's Doc Roberts," Petersson said.

"What's up, Doc?" Nicky responded like Bugs Bunny.

"I wanna know and I think everyone out here wants to know"—a dramatic pause—"if you two Klingons know how to dance!" He grabs them by the hands and begins to twirl them about the bar. I don't even notice him slip off, but Warren is over by the jukebox and plays a disco song, to which several disgruntled faces stare at them.

"Get up there, Wiggy!"

"C'mon, boy. That's an order," Petersson says.

I stand and start grooving, thrusting one hand in front of the other, stepping to the beat of the tune. "Wiggs got moves!" MacConough yells. I dance for what seems like my life to try and impress the seniors. Unfortunately, snatching the spotlight is not the right move that night.

All around the bar, I see disgruntled faces turning to anger. I see bodies slowly closing in. "What are you doing, nigger?" I hear. Behind me stands a large man, nostrils flaring, and his ears are pierced by small tusks. Petersson stops dancing as do the women. The man attempts to push me in the chest, and I step back and dodge it, knocking his arm downward. This man takes insult from my move, and a few others stand behind him, boiling, chests out like doves.

"Not in here, boys," the bartender yells, but it is too late. The large man with tusks flings a chair to the ground, and it bounces off the floor with a thud. I stare at this large man, unsure of whether I should fight or flee. Then I feel a large hand on my shoulder. It's Petersson.

"You'd better stand down, motherfucker," he said to the man.

"Er, say that again," he replied.

"Me and these boys are going to beat your ass if you don't slow down on this little guy here. You have no business telling him what he can and can't do, you hear me? That's our fucking prerogative." Before the guy responds, Petersson speaks again. "What's your name?"

"Charles Matthews, but people around these parts call me Ghost. You don't want to know how I got that name," he said. He stood huffing and puffing, ready to swing at me and Petersson.

"I'd ask you, but frankly, I've never cared less about something in my life." MacConough stood up to join us.

"You hear this guy? He thinks because he has a nickname, it makes him a wolf, huh? You a big, bad wolf, Ghost?" Nicky yelled.

These boys were reckless, and continuing to dig into this man, they were seemingly unfettered by the consequences.

"Charlie," Petersson said, "put 'em up, boy."

The bartender sets his glass down. "You need to leave!" he screams, but his warnings instead prove incendiary as others stand to back Ghost Matthews in his affront. There are six of them and four of us. The two women have shifted out of the central location to one of the booths on the side of the bar.

From what I can tell, Ghost and his crew haven't noticed that Warren is with us. They seem fixated on me, but judging by his last swipe, the man is strong but not skilled, not disciplined, ordinary hooligans on an ever-shifting landscape of the Southern underbelly. Ghost, as people called him, can be rotated for any other washed-up ruffian on this side of town.

Suddenly, a crack breaks the disco beat. From behind the gang, Warren hits a man with his glass jug, whipping down on the back of his head like a lightning bolt. The man tumbles to the floor, and then Petersson squares up, and the other upperclassmen start throwing punches.

The ruffians cause a lot of unnecessary movement, flailing their arms, charging for tackles. But each of us is too quick, too embedded with strong reflexes. They tumble to the floor, knocking tables and chairs over. "I'm calling the cops," yells the barman.

Quickly, the ruffians back down, realizing they aren't outmanned but they are outgunned. They surrender. Ghost gives up without much of a fight, both hands in the air like a criminal after being caught in a hot chase. The upperclassmen had defended me from this guy who not only called me a racist epithet but also doesn't think I belong here. The irony of it all, it is a 180 turn in our relationship.

We leave the bar, sure that we'll never be allowed inside again, and mosey down King Street. Huffing without as much as a scratch on our person, Petersson stops us.

"Do you boys even feel like drinking anymore?" he said.

"Wow, my adrenaline is pumping," MacConough said, clapping his hands.

"Maybe we should head to another bar just for one drink to settle down and go back to campus," Nicky said.

"Sirs," I said.

"What is it, Wiggs?"

"Thank you for helping me," I said.

"C'mon, Wiggs, that's what comrades do," MacConough said.

"I would've picked a fight even without all that pretext," Petersson said.

"Does that happen often?"

"Not too much, nah, but everybody at the academy is ready to rough-and-tumble if it comes down to it."

So the five of us stroll through the underpass and make our way to the heavily populated side of King Street. People burst out of bars. Warm lights ensure of local shenanigans. Bodegas full of cigarette packs, fifths of whiskey, and cheap beer cans tossed and stomped litter the side of the road near gutters.

I hear laughter both emanating from the street side and from our own conversation. Nicky is enlivened in a story. I look down across the street, and the lights cut dim. Cadavers like mummies stand on street corners or straddle toward the middle of the road. Market Street in downtown Charleston has become a poor place, one of filth, and is boiling inner city blues.

We fall into a bar called the 7. A neon number 7 lights the window red, and drapes enclose the inside from the street. People dance to some disco, Chic, I believe. A backbeat engulfs us as we enter and barrel straight for the bar. The man has on a porkpie hat with a feather tucked in the brim. We all take a whisky neat and watch the dancing from the bar. None of us at that point is particularly inclined to join in, so we just watch and cackle from the sideline.

After a few songs, we decide it's time to head home. Just then, someone calls out, "Yoo-hoo! Boys." I turn and see a couple of women and some men hanging out in a booth. They wave us over.

Their party looks festive—girls with cocktail dresses and beads, men in dress shirts with slicked back haircuts and bow ties.

"A round for them," Petersson says and points at them.

"Well, how do you do?" Nicky leans in.

"See, here we got some slicks," MacConough says to me. "Bunch of people who went to school up north and now think they're the most cultured men in the seven seas."

"Ah, I see."

"You chaps having a good time?" one said.

"Yes, indeed."

"Why don't you join us for one. Academy boys have always been good spirits."

"Sure, why not?" MacConough said. "What's the occasion?"

"Just finished my doctorate."

"Well, congratulations, *el* doctor," MacConough said with his award-winning smile. The two girls laughed.

"And you two deserve a medal just for the hell of it," Nicky said.

A royal treatment, I guess that's what you'd call the few nights that I spent out with them like this. I couldn't wait to be a senior and be seen as these guys are now. I bubbled with enthusiasm for these slicks to call us over out of respect for where we went to school.

"This little guy is going to be the leader of his class," MacConough said to them.

"Impressive," they said and brought me in to sit with them.

Eventually, we pack up. We tread the black road north and make it to campus around waking time. The blue is there, hovering on the horizon, rising slowly over the surrounding black. They knock on the gates to wake the guard. By now, it's normal that I'm with them. *Since when have we been friends? Are we friends?* This stark question hits me in the eyes as we enter the barracks.

The quadrangle is empty, and the slightest blue hue of the sky segments the castle-like tops from the sky. Petersson, Nicky, and Warren walk ahead, but MacConough stops. He looks at me and slightly shakes his head.

We exchanged this look, not a look of intimacy or of admiration even but a look of sturdy trust, a trust that could've been built out of adamantine. From that moment, he knew that I would go to the grave with his secret, that I had understood his lectures, and that I knew what it was to be a soldier.

He says, "Thanks, Steve," and leaves.

What's left of our soul vanishes. The warmth of friendship, of camaraderie, of being a human, is extinguished, and for now, we must put our masks back on and enter the barracks.

I walk to our floor, open the door, and look at the clock, 5:20 a.m. Perfect. I lie down with my clothes on. The trash cans build from a distant flicker. The beds creak. My roommates awaken. My sight is blurry as I steady my head and thrust on my PT gear. Clyde stands out of his bed.

"What the hell, Steve? Are you really just getting back now?"

CHAPTER 12

One Day—The Pig Push

The process commenced. Either a lack of patience or the numbing sensation of steel persisted to drag me from my room to other corners of the campus. I had had enough of Clyde's attitude. I wanted more of the upperclassmen's attitude. I wanted to seal doubt, worries, and anxieties about breakfast and indulge in supper. This voracious, unstoppable demeanor that the upperclassmen presented toward the world, I strived for it.

That morning, on our jog, I follow MacConough. I spot Simon on the far side of the squad. He seems content. I feel winded, restrained by something that I cannot see. The winds of February swivel past in the morning. Hands lack circulation, and breaths stab deep and exhale smoky resonance. The grass seems damp and seems to have more suction than normal.

As we close PT, I feel exhausted. My hands rest on my knees, and a cold sweat drips down my back. I lumber to the showers and then down to the mess hall. Clyde, Randall, and Harry sit at a table. Harry seems to be going on about something while Clyde and Randall half-heartedly listen. I sneak by. They don't notice me.

I opt for Simon's table, a table that is currently unoccupied except by Simon and his individuality. Simon normally eats by himself or with his roommates. He finds no need to extend a hand or press himself to others and instead gains energy from mornings surrounded by everyone yet alone.

"Morning, Louisiana," I said.

"How ya doing, Steve?"

"Not too bad, not too bad. How about yourself?"

"That's not what I saw. You looked like you had cinder blocks on this morning. I find it hilarious how even when you're obviously in pain, you don't cut yourself slack."

"My dad used to say that I have to work twice—"

"Twice as hard to get half as far, I know. Some boys back home used to tell me that too. Do you think it's true?"

"I don't know. I guess I never really questioned it."

"To me, it looks like you work twice as hard to get twice as far. I hear you're hanging with that lot over there."

"Louisiana, c'mon, man," I said as I shook my head.

"Yeah, you're right. Best to leave that for the simpletons."

"So what's happening with this hop tonight? Are you going?" I said.

"I don't know, Steve. I don't have much interest in all that."

"What? I thought this was your game! What happened to that saying you had? Um, 'when Simon's here, the women all clear'?"

Simon roared, "When Simon's part of the crew—"

"Women accrue. Oh yeah, that's right," I said.

"My roommates keep calling it a pig push, say there ain't much hope in finding a damsel."

"Pig push, what's that?"

"Like a bunch of ugly girls and you just force them to move around and dance, it sounds like."

"Do you believe them? I think that they're probably just covering up that they're insecure."

He laughed again. "Is this senior Steve? Little Wiggs, I like this new side of you, Steve, less reserved."

"So I'll stop by your room tonight? Try to convince the boys."

"Sure will."

"Wiggins!" Nicky yelled. "Get the hell over here."

"Uh-oh," Simon said.

"Sir," I said and walked over to him, Warren, and MacConough.

"Snack time!" I heard Randall yell.

"Shut the hell up, maggot!" Nicky yelled back at him. *That feels good,* I thought.

211

"High knees, go!"

"Sir, yes, sir," I said. MacConough and Warren surrounded me and started tapping me on both cheeks.

"Push-ups, twenty, go," he said. I dropped down and started doing push-ups.

"Hey, you!" I hear Warren yell. He moves in a swift manner out of my periphery. I jump up to my feet after the push-ups.

"Back to high knees, go!"

MacConough leans in. "Sorry about not getting you off campus. This is for later." He drops something in my pocket. It's difficult, but I manage to hold back a smile.

"All right, maggot. Get back to it," Nicky says.

In an urgent manner, I walk off and check my pockets. It is a half pint of whiskey. *Yes.* Valentine's Day doesn't look like it's going to end up too badly after all.

You see, I asked the boys if I could get off campus to see Miranda. It's been about a month and a half since I had seen her, and I thought that they could help. Alas, it was not possible without themselves also in attendance. Then, of course, Nicky joked about being a chaperone.

I guess this bottle is the consolation prize. It's really too bad. About a month and a half has passed, and it's not that I've had much time to think about her, but I'd definitely like some alone time. I figure I'll still give her a call if I have time. I mosey to my knob duties.

That afternoon, our squad suffers the first loss of the semester to Harry's squad. Dirty from ducking for cover and just feeling drained, I watch as the landscape shifts past me, and we enter city limits again. My team has three victories and one loss with Yosh being our leading flag carrier. It's strange. For the moment, I feel disengaged with freshman goings-on. So to me, it's not a big deal.

Before heading out that night, I return back to my room in necessity to grab my uniform. Harry and Clyde are there along with Randall. "Hey, Steve," Harry says.

"Hey, Harry, Clyde, Randall," I say as I begin digging through my belongings.

"Yo, Steve, how has it been going in your ROTC squad? Not too well from what I hear," Randall says.

"Are you asking me? Or do you just want to talk about how successful of a go it's been for you?"

"I've never felt so in my role, you know, like I deserved to run a squad this whole time, and because they finally realize that, a team has never been so successful. I feel like I'm walking into an officer position."

"Yeah, are you guys undefeated?"

"Of course, man. I've never seen the other squad have to do more training exercises than last time. Pretty much when they got in, they went out." He laughs.

"I hear, Harry, your squad is undefeated too, right?"

Harry laughs. "It's true, Steve."

"Oh, don't be so humble, Harry. You're both doing a great job."

"Yeah, well," Randall sputters.

"Don't listen to this asshole, Randall. The man practically wets the bed most nights because of how late he comes home," Clyde says. Randall laughs, and Harry lets out a small chuckle. It is pretty funny.

"If you have a problem, Clyde, you should really say it directly," I say. "Anyway, I expect you boys are going to get some women tonight at the hop?" I say.

Clyde gave me a sour look. If our friendship was on the ropes before, I might have just delivered the knockout blow.

"You know me, Steve," Harry said. "I'm locked down now."

"Are you kidding me, Harry?" boomed Randall.

"What? No, of course not."

"This is the Valentine's Day pig push. You can have whoever you want. These girls see you in that uniform and it's a done deal, man, confirmed."

I move to the corner of the room and get dressed in my full attire. The gray uniform fits snug. The fabric is dense and heavy. Little brass buttons line the middle of the shirt, and on both sides, they lead from my shoulders to my torso. My gray slacks and uniform are separated by a white belt.

"Well, later, huh?"

"See you there, Wiggs."

I trudge down the hall toward the bathroom. Staring in the mirror, I tug my cap on tight and slap myself. The brim shines in the bathroom lights. I leave for Simon's room, one floor up and on the opposite side of the barracks. The long hallways stretch in front of me. *Click, clack, knock, knock,* and I enter. Simon's there, immersed in a philosophical discussion with his roommates.

"Wiggs, pull up a squat," Simon said. "So Carter has two decisions, right? He could let the shah inside the US, which would keep him safe but directly defy Iran and put all of us in danger, or he could condemn him, which puts just the shah and his family in danger. So we all know that he has decided to condemn him. You can see it on every news channel that there is. The shah wants to enter the US, but Jimmy Carter won't let him. He's left him stranded.

"So in this case, it's a huge ethical dilemma. The logical answer would be, of course, to shun the shah, but ethically, what do you do? Do you claim something you're responsible for? Obviously, Carter and his team of advisers have chosen the logical route. So now we have two different instances at the beginning and end of the decade where the US takes on something of a foreign problem, fucks it up, and doesn't take responsibility for it!"

I pull out the bottle of whiskey, swig, and begin to pass it around. "Whoa there, Louisiana. I don't think you can simplify it that much," I say.

"You're really a socialist, huh, Simon?" his roommate says. "I might have to report you."

He takes a swig. "No, sir. I'm just making the logical conclusions, trying to put two and two together about this day and age that we're being raised in. It ain't easy, and it ain't simple. You're right about that, Steve. But goddamn it, it doesn't seem like our country is right—in the right, I mean.

"Sometimes, you have to look at yourself in the mirror and realize that you look too good. You say, 'Damn, I look good,' but do you ask yourself what you've had to do to look so damn good? Only upon reflection do you get this dialogue going. You have to lasso the goat before you wrangle him. Information does no good unless you can find the ethical implementation in it. That's stoicism. That's the way of the soldier." He takes another swig.

"Do you guys always let him go on like this?" I say. They laugh at me.

"I mean, I don't care a damn about it, but what else is there to think about when you're staring at this goddamn ceiling every night."

"I've managed to tune that out of my process. I used to think about random things—family, life before the academy, outside news, and so and so—but I feel cut off now, completely disconnected to what's going on outside. There's nothing other than accomplishing what's in front of me each day." Simon looked at me like I was a suspect in a crime. By now, we had finished the bottle. "How're we going to get rid of this?" I said. "We can't just drop it in the trash can."

"I think we're just going to have to sneak it downstairs."

"I have an idea," Simon said. He took the pint of bottle and shoved it in his pants. "Now if they see it, they have to look, and that's where we get them," he said with a mischievous smile.

"All right. Let's head downstairs."

We check ourselves to make sure our uniforms are adequate and leave. Out on the quad, our footsteps clack. Simon takes the bottle and plops it in the trash. As it clanks, we each pick up our pace to a speed walk. Over to the auditorium we stroll.

Simon makes it apparent that he has no intentions of caring about tonight whatsoever. Remaining indifferent to all that surrounds him, he continues his diatribe about politics, and each of us half listens and half blows off steam to the stars. No one adds a thing. I suppose that seeing the world with the seniors makes his assertions seem juvenile to me. No, they are still original and certainly interesting, but at the moment, I strive for a grounded experience, something I can only get with the seniors.

When we make it to the hop, we stop chatting. The auditorium is festooned in decorative cheer. Streamers and ornaments line the walls, and the room looks somewhere in between a high school dance and a white table cloth restaurant. "Welcome University of Charleston" is draped over the entrance.

"Hope you boys have your steps down," one of Simon's room-mates said.

"Don't have to worry about me. Now show me the women," Simon said.

I laughed. "Where was this five minutes ago?"

"Show me my bride-to-be," he said and clapped his hand.

An officer looks his way at this disruption. Simon pretends to act normal. A hubbub surrounds the opposite doors, and I'm guess-ing it's where the girls are supposed to enter. We are required to brace and act as gentlemen, kindly escorting each of the women to the floor and then commencing a ballroom dance. I remove my cap and place it gently on a table. I see Harry, Clyde, and Randall to my left. Simon and the other guys are to my right. We all brace.

The women enter in all sizes and colors of cocktail dresses. A large ruckus enters along with them. Along with other cadets, I hover over, hardly touching the ground with my steps. It's a mass immer-sion of groups. Our gray uniforms and their colorful cocktail dresses spread out over the gymnasium floor. The quintet plays a soft mel-ody, which drowns out the chatter of introductions.

My first partner is a rather pale woman with a square face and limpid blue eyes, but she wears a look of melancholic disappoint-ment. As we move, I try to analyze her countenance. Is it brought on by me, her own eccentricities, or insecurity?

Her footing is clumsy and lagging and difficult to lead around, but her hands are light and soft, and she twirls. The hem of her light-blue dress brushes my slacks, and the clack of her shoes hits the hardwood. The strings take the form of cambric cloth, heavy, never-ending. I scan around the room. The men seem to be enjoying themselves. Everyone seems to be enjoying themselves, except for my partner. I force a smile, and she reciprocates.

After the dance, we change partners. I don't say goodbye. She doesn't either. It's a tacit agreement. I try again with other girls who didn't complement their partners. This time, I'm matched with a woman with hair like the sun and eyes like clouds. But she also wears an indifferent look as soon as our hands meet. It's strange. Is a dark shadow or is something nebulous following me?

We approach a twirl, and the girl who up until then have been very light on her feet, stumbles offbeat. Couples around us notice the error. Clyde and Randall start laughing. Unashamed, I walk over to help her regain the rhythm, but she's red in the face. This lovely girl with hair like the sun storms away from me to a table.

"You suck, Wiggs," Randall yells. "Somebody tell the man with two left feet that there's a section for him over there."

Several cadets turn my way and burst out laughing, including Clyde. *These guys are best buds now, I guess. The only one keeping that from happening first quarter was me.* Simon breaks off from his dance and brings his partner by the hand over to me. "Don't worry about it, man," he says.

"I'm not worrying about it, but I appreciate your concern."

He looks at me, realizing that I'm not paying attention to anything in the room except for one thing. Alyssa is here.

"Go up and talk to her," he says.

But as he says this, I am already in stride. Alyssa is the same divine woman from the food drive, the one with vibrant skin and a beauty mark on her left cheek and heart-shaped lips. If I hovered across the floor before, well, I float across it now. Past the tables I move, thunking one of them and pretending like nothing happened. Suddenly, she sees me, and her expression brightens up.

"Steve, I can't believe you're here," she said.

"What's so hard to believe about destiny? I told you I went here, didn't I?"

She laughed. "You're smooth."

"I want you to meet my friend Louisiana," I said and turned. He was way back by the dance floor still. "Hey, get over here, man."

Again, she laughed, and then she stood and raised her hand. Simon and his girl moseyed over. "Charmed," Simon said.

"How do you do, Louisiana?" Alyssa said.

"Mighty fine, and how about yourself? Oh, Steve, I didn't get to introduce you, space case, but this here is Lucy."

"Hi, Lucy," I said.

"Hi, Lucy," Alyssa said as if she already knew her.

"What do you say we blow this place and go somewhere a bit more fun?" Simon said.

"Are you sure that we're allowed to do that?" Lucy said.

"That's the spirit," Simon said.

"Why space case by the way?"

"Sometimes, he just stares out there into nothing, just a blank stare. You know things are going on in his head, but he won't let it show."

We sneak behind a curtain, which separates the dance from the rest of the auditorium. The floors shine. We move over to the exit and make a break for the hallways. Footsteps are heard, and Simon puts a finger to his lips, looking at each of the girls. Then he points us in the direction of the restrooms. We enter them, and the lights flicker on.

"What are we—?"

"Shh," Simon said, and he proceeded to check each of the stalls. Then he gave an okay sign.

"Why are we in here?" Lucy asked.

"Because I have this," he said, and then he took out another bottle of whiskey. Alyssa and I gave each other a look.

"So what? Are we going to drink straight outta there?" Lucy said.

"How else goddammit?" Simon said.

"Want me to run to a vending machine?" I said.

"No, Steve, she's fine."

"It's no problem. One sec."

I exit the bathroom and check both ways before going into the hall. The halls seem desolate. It's striking how when a place is off-limits or another is mandatory, the rest of the campus turns barren. Still, with prudence, I walk toward where the vending machines are located, at the end of the hall in a little nook.

Suddenly, as I'm about to turn the corner, a flashback comes to my head. I see myself opening a door, and the door is to MacConough's. He flies backward. Turning the corner, I brace. No one is there. I buy a couple of Cokes and hurry them back to the bathroom. A bead of sweat runs down my back.

"Steve, you're a hero. Thank you," Lucy says.

Simon smiles. "A real hero." He hands me the whiskey bottle.

"Cheers," I say and pass it to Alyssa. She also takes a swig, after which she coughs.

"Uh-oh," Simon says, and she laughs.

"You have just the best laugh," I say and double-take because it may have come off in a flirtatious manner.

"Why, thank you, Steve. So far, I think that you cadets are a pretty funny bunch," she says.

"Oh, you should see us during the day. Show 'em, Steve," Simon says.

I force on my mask, tightening and bracing. My face contorts into one bereft of emotion. My arms flex and straighten to a 180 angle next to my torso. They are perfectly aligned, moving from one angle in swift, precise strokes to the next. I move in robotic fashion, one step after the other, the exact same timing, 120 paces per second.

I see her eyes widen. It must've surprised both of the girls, but at the moment, I don't have a thought floating through my mind. It is all learned instincts. I march from one side of the bathroom to the other.

"All right, that's probably enough, Steve. You're scaring us," Simon says.

"Sir, yes, sir," I say and begin to loosen up.

Lucy passes both bottles my way, and I decline the coke bottle. The two girls begin chatting. Simon looks at them and then turns to me.

"What do you think all this is for?" Simon said.

"All of what is for?" I said.

"All of these formalities, I mean. Why is it that we have to dance a certain way and that men have to act a certain way and that women have to respond a certain way? Haven't we as a society grown out of this?"

"I don't know, man. It's just tradition. This is what comes along with enrolling here."

"But surely some aspects have to change. Tradition is the only thing that's making you fear for your life right now," Simon said.

"But it's the only thing holding me up right now too. I need the people before me to set the example so that I can learn how to do it correctly."

"I guess it's one of those things you can't live with or without," he said.

Once we finished the bottle, Simon said, "All right, who wants to play something even more interesting? Five minutes in the stall. You get to do anything you want. Wahoo!"

He took Lucy's hand and brought her into the stall and slammed the door. The stall door bounced back open, and by the time it opened all the way, they were furiously making out, and he was feeling her up. I looked from them to Alyssa, and I realized that I worked myself into a bad situation. *Miranda, you dolt, Miranda.*

I feel the liquor in my blood. When I need them the most, my words don't surface. I make a dumb face at her, like, "I don't know what I'm doing here."

"Dance? Wanna dance?" I manage to say.

"What, in here?" she says.

My face flushes. "No, um, back on the dance floor. Let's leave them be."

"Thank you, Steve," I hear Simon say.

We slip out of the bathroom, and suddenly, I stop her. The clack of boots registers soft, footsteps coming from down the hall. Damn, we're trapped.

When we head back through the swinging door, Simon and Lucy have halfway transitioned to the nude. "Dammit, Steve! Give us some privacy, man!"

"Someone's coming," I said.

"Shit. No fucking way," Simon said. He hit his head. "Think, dammit. Lucy, we're going to take the fall on this one. Steve, Alyssa, hide in the stalls."

"I can't do that, bud. I can't let you take the blame."

"Better two of us than four. Go ahead. Hurry on up," he said.

We clambered into the stall, and seconds after, an officer walked in. Close call.

"What do you know. Simon?"

"Sir, yes, sir," he said.

"What are you up to, maggot? You in here trying to take advantage of this poor woman? Oh, what's this? A bottle of whiskey. Okay, two new questions. How did you get this bottle, and how did this bottle get empty?"

"Sir, permission to speak, sir."

"Permission denied."

"Sir, no excuse, sir," he said.

"You and your little, um, lady friend having fun?"

"Sir, yes, sir."

"What happened to the dance? Too good for that, are you, Simon?"

"Sir, no, sir."

The officer laughed, and I could hear him pace back and forth a few times. It was an awkward extended silence, one that I could tell was deductive on the officer's end yet terrifying on ours. "Miss, you can go ahead and put your clothes back on."

"Yes, sir," she said. A shuffle. I assumed she put her clothes on.

"All right. Now kindly head back to the auditorium." I heard the door open and close. "Now you, you worthless piece of dog shit. You drop down. You can't keep doing shit like this, you hear me? You're going to learn some discipline," the officer said.

"If you say so, Sarge."

"Do you want to make this worse?"

"Sir, no, sir."

"You better be expecting some visits from General Firos real soon, Simon."

"Firos, huh? Never heard of the lass."

"Dammit, cadet, you are not ease. You cannot just blab about anything you want."

"What are you going to do, hit me?"

Then we hear a loud slap. It echoes off the tiled floor like a gunshot in an empty stadium. Alyssa and I are trembling. This scene has gone on long enough. I'm freaking done with this shit. I can't stand this upperclassman drawing out the situation. On the other hand, if I leave, Simon's sacrifice will be in vain.

Through all this panicking, suddenly, our eyes connect. A warmth enters throughout my body. It flows and spreads and creates a reassuring calm, a contentment maybe, a similar feeling to my mom's cooking. Maybe Alyssa is the woman for me. Maybe she's the one for me and not Miranda.

I joked earlier, but it is starting to feel like felicitous events unfolded to lead us here, pressed together in a time of peril. This is fortune, both from the same neighborhood as children suddenly bumping into each other down the road.

"Now." The officer paused. "How on earth did you two finish a whole bottle of whiskey by yourself? You don't seem that inebriated, do you, cadet?" Beat.

"Hell yeah I am," Simon said. I almost burst out laughing. "Sure, sure. I'm ineb-inebrebated."

"Huh, sure thing," the officer said. Simon was on the ropes. It felt as if he didn't know how to respond to this question. It was a good observation by the officer, one that he potentially held as a trump card.

"So you mean to tell me that you and this woman friend of yours drank an entire bottle of whiskey? Because I saw her put on her clothes and run off, and she didn't seem all that affected by the whiskey. Something here doesn't add up to me, Simon." Shit, it was over.

Then Simon said, "That turn you on, sir?"

"Excuse me?"

"You heard me. You took an awful long time to let her put on her clothes. I saw you pacing around, wide-eyed, looking at her. You want to abuse your power? Go ahead on me. Go ahead on the academy. But a poor girl who doesn't go to school here? I'll stand up for her every time. You can't get away with that kind of shit."

"Simon. Dammit. Dammit, Simon." There was another slap and a loud grunt from Simon. "On whose word, huh? Who will believe you?"

"Maybe no one will believe me, but I think they have different rules at Charleston University. You don't want them changing things because of you."

"You piece of shit. How dare you talk to a superior that way? If you don't see monsters in your future, then you're more naive than you look," he said.

Louisiana had pulled a counterpunch of a lifetime with that one. There was a large silence, and then I heard the door swing open and shut. "Coast is clear, guys. Apparently, I deserve some visits from General Firos and other boogeymen. But other than that, it's A-OK."

"Louisiana, that was quite the ploy," I say. He looks at me and looks down. Suddenly, I realize that I'm holding Alyssa's hand. I whip my hand out of hers.

"Woo-hoo! Boy, what a night," Simon yells.

"Thank you, Simon. That was very heroic of ya," Alyssa says.

"No problem, Alyssa."

We walk toward the auditorium and slip in unnoticed. Alyssa gives me her number for safekeeping and tells me to call over spring break if I want to stop by for some tea or to say hi. Then the girls hop on their buses and leave campus. Simon and I say good night at the gates, and I walk into my room, sober by the time I touch the sheets.

*****

I awaken not by the trash cans or my ten-minutes-prior regimen but by a hand on my shoulder. My eyes are blurry, and it's dark. A flashlight shines on me, and then it reveals MacConough's face.

"Sir," I whisper.

He signals me to come with him. Beyond the darkness, I cross over into the bright hallway. Petersson, Warren, and Nicky are there with MacConough. They wear serious faces. Drunk, I don't think so, but they definitely have an air to them, off-putting and austere in comparison to nights past.

MacConough places his arm over my shoulder and leads me down the hallway. We walk down the stairs to the senior floor where we enter a room, which, after a brief moment, I realize must be Nicky and Petersson's room. The boys surround me.

"Sit down," MacConough said.

"Sir, yes, sir," I said.

"Wiggs," Nicky said, "tonight is very special to us because this is the beginning of your initiation. We're going to show you the ways of the academy. So surrender yourself to what we tell you, okay? Just go along with it. Trust us." Comrades with power also had consequences to their power, which grew as you grew alongside them.

"Wiggs," MacConough said, "you're going to be the one racking tonight."

"Sir," I said, flustered. I took a deep breath. "Sir, yes, sir."

"You're going to release payback on all of these failures of children. Tonight, you are going to be General Firos."

"Sir, what is off-limits, sir?" I said.

Petersson walked up. "Boy, you done cracked the code. There is nothing off-limits. The only thing that you need to know is that we say when it's over, so no pussyfooting."

I remember the pain and isolation of first quarter, the days when I would sneak into the mess hall using the back door, the days of walking through campus, careful to only utilize the shadows, the hidden hallways, the secret routes near the river.

Somehow, through this narrow frame of mind, I hadn't just survived. I prospered. I made it to a point where I could walk on campus just as everyone else did. I sacrificed my body and my freedom to get where I thought I was safe, but now in one moment, the veil was gone.

Enough, I think to myself. I pull my thoughts off this crash course and direct them back into the mask. I conceal them, my prospects of there being another way, my survival instincts. I seal them into a well-trained, disciplined shell that I mold. I look up at the guys. The fear drains out of my face.

"I see," MacConough said. "So here's what's going to happen. We're going to call together a rack party. You just get them together in a little huddle, and then you have free reign."

"Sir, yes, sir," I said.

"Here, we have a list of rooms on our most wanted," Warren said.

Once more, thoughts encroach like the sound of marching. Even the mask can't keep them out. *Could it be possible that Simon made their list?*

"Let's go," MacConough says.

I gear up, putting on a long-sleeved shirt and white gloves to cover my skin. We begin stomping through the hallways. We pass upperclassmen, who salute us on our way. We walk upstairs onto the fourth years and Simon's floor. The upperclassmen wear devilish smiles. I try to separate myself from the experience, but my focus keeps waning and slipping back into the guilt of the situation.

Could it be Simon? The officer had said, "You better be expecting some visits from Firos." *Could they have me rack perhaps my best friend at the academy?* The hallway stretches before me. It balloons into a long row of shame. We approach Simon's room, and then we stop. *Oh no.*

Petersson runs up and knocks on the door opposite to Simon's room. "Knobs, get the hell out here." I slip on the actual mask, a red mask with a huge smile and small slits for eyes, a mask of nightmares. I take a deep breath and transform into Firos.

"Hup, hup, hup, hup," I yell as they exit their room, frightened and in pajamas. In my character, I don't recognize them. "Push-ups, hup, twenty," I say. "Go." They drop to the floor and start push-ups. I smile beneath the mask. It's fun to be in a place of power. In fact, it feels good.

"All right, cadets, General Firos speaking," I say as I mosey around. "Next, duck-walk from one side to the other, go. Transition to burpees, go. Mountain climbers. High knees. Sit-ups."

The power lifted me. The glove fitted. *Commit to the life, right, Pops?* Everything that they had whispered about me when I enrolled here, when I passed them on campus, that they had looked at me in class, walking around the Southern Peninsula, in the yacht club, this was my reprisal. All the critical comments, all the societal prejudices, felt a part of this mask.

I look over at the other upperclassmen, but they don't seem to acknowledge that this is enough. "Back to push-ups, maggots, push-ups!"

Petersson walks over to me. "Kick them," he whispers in my ear.

What? I think. *There's no way I can bring myself to do that.* I can't respond to Petersson because it will break the spell that I have power.

Commit to it, right, Pops? Commit to it. Fueled by the power, the rage, the resentment, I silence all my qualms. This isn't who I am. This is only who I've become, red streaks and the numbing of steel. I lift my foot back and slam the cadet. He cries in agony.

"What was that, cadet? What the fuck did I hear from you?"

"Sir, no excuse, sir," the others say.

I squat down to their level. "Kiss the boots, maggot." Each of them does a push-up and then kisses my boots. I look over to the upperclassmen. Nicky looks to MacConough, who lets out a smirk.

"Get outta here, maggots. Go back to bed."

"Sir, yes, sir."

After they leave and head back to their room, we leave to another room and do it again and again and again. I return to my room that night not tired, not exhausted, but in a state of numb silence, because by the time my head touches the pillow, the mask that I wore is in the far depths of the seniors' possession, but another lies next to me, wrapped in my bedsheets.

CHAPTER 13

One Week—There Are No More Heroes

After ESP, I am to report directly to MacConough's room. The past week has been this way, a small collective talk of about ten minutes between the four seniors. Sometimes we joke. At other points, they are austere. Then we head out to a chosen hallway.

My roommates and I don't speak anymore except in passing. The isolation and moral weight grows each day, and I find myself with supreme fatigue after PT, lumbering from dawn until dusk, surrounded by phantasmagoria, not swiping at it or even acknowledging its sudden presence.

The mask had become essential to my routine. I saw classmates walk hesitantly in passing knowing that at night, Firos might pay them a visit. Most victims were distant, faces that I knew from first semester classes or the mess hall but that I could not put a name to.

The first time I racked someone I knew, it did turn out to be Simon. Petersson yanked him out of his room into the hallway like a man pulling a fish out of water. I stared at him through Firos's eyes and laughed, laughed as loud as I could, to chase away the demons before hurting him, hurting my friend—sit-ups, push-ups, high knees, smack. He was a good sport about it, accepting his punishment for the Valentine's hop offense. He didn't say any quips, and he left in a stoic, sleepy demeanor just as he had arrived.

You have to understand, this was not only in the line of duty but it was also to survive. Each night, no matter how much it could burden someone, it could not burden me. It wasn't optional. The numbing sensation of steel coursed through me now. It was no longer Steve, then a slow progression to Firos. It was a snap of the fingers, a light switch that transformed me.

The numbing brought along a distancing from memories. I imagined guilt slipping off me like rain off a car hood at volatile speeds. But along with this metaphor came the blur of my surroundings. At this point, it was becoming difficult to focus on my studies.

Classes streamed by with note-taking but without a present mind. It was a perpetual cycle without much room for headspace, though I found myself staring in the mirror of the bathroom, convincing my reflection that I didn't need headspace. In fact, privacy and solitude were two things that held me back. I figured that I could let some of my angst go by lashing out at ROTC field training on Saturdays. But still, I felt sluggish.

Trekking through the woods with my pellet gun and my gear, I would hear cracks nearby. I would turn and no one would be there. Then I would hear it on the opposite, and pop, it would be too late. It was a harsh reality to face that my focus was spread too thin. I fell asleep that night exhausted only to be awakened by the seniors. Then I would become a different person.

After hours itself feels different. The light spreads down the empty hallway, trickling down the stairwell. Spirits seem to hover. A sound or a sudden flicker notifies you that someone is there even if there is not. No clacks of footsteps down the tiles. Time and time again, I couldn't properly find my place on the map I had constructed. This night, we approach familiar terrain.

Fear creeps through me that has been numbed by my mask. It falls through my spine like a rock climber slipping and falling into a forested death. Our door. I believe that we are standing outside our door. In an instant, MacConough and Petersson snatch Clyde and Harry and throw them out into the hallway. Blindsided, the two seem disoriented, but then they stand and brace before me.

I lose spatial awareness, sinking into myself. Then another is yanked and pulled into the hallway. I blink, trying to get ahold of reality. It's not them. It's not my room. The illusion dispels, and I realize it is only people who look similar to them—a small brown-haired boy and a lumbering sandy blond with red cheeks.

"Get down! Push-ups, maggots!"

"Sir, yes, sir!" they reply, and so the racking commences.

After a few sets, they begin to slow. From a set of burpees, one stands and stares straight into the mask of Firos, straight at me. It is a different stare than the blank stare of victims. No, it is an inquisitive stare, as if he is trying to solve a problem. Then I realize he could know who is behind Firos's mask, so I quickly walk over to him and put my gloved hand on the back of his neck and shove him to the ground.

"What the hell do you think you're doing?"

"Warren, Petersson, teach these fools a lesson."

Warren and Petersson grab the two of them by the back of their arms. They are far too violent. Clyde-look-alike surprises me. He loses balance and falls to his front quickly. *Clack!* His other hand braces impact and slaps the floor while his nose also thumps the tiles.

"All right, up, cadets."

They slowly rise. The Clyde doppelganger, to my dismay, stands with a crooked, bloody nose, one that looks broken. I see him, fury in his eyes, blood streaming down his face. He's slobbering, hardly conscious, but seething with anger, a primal sort of hatred for me. I know that from this moment, if I continue, I would be found out. When the mask comes off, revenge will be had against me. Not that this boy in particular knew who I am, but karma will find me and exert reprisal for what I have done. A seed has been planted, and it will blossom into an orchid tree.

Firos vanished in the same smoke that he arrived in. Mystery had taken hold of campus. I heard knobs in the mess and passing periods speaking of Firos, wondering who he was and who he was going to attack next. I wanted out. Numb to it I believed I was, but there was a central instability that it had caused throughout the barracks. Rather than looking forward, minding your own business,

Firos had been turning heads, causing people to ask what wasn't warranted to them, to snoop.

*****

It is the beginning of March, and my grades are once again hovering just above a 3.0. The sun slides higher into the sky every day, and flowers begin popping up over campus—first, the azaleas, then the magnolias. Trim green grass reflects the health of a cadet.

My body and mind feel toughened. I feel strong enough to grapple with anyone and anything—no slouching, no dillydallying, no hesitation, no excuse. No longer is there camaraderie in my room between me and my fellow classmates. Firos has become a literal wedge between me and the knobs, and as a result, I have grown more sturdy and further from them each day.

I return to my room from studying in the library. My roommates are studying silently as they normally are. No turn, no wave, as I enter. I put my bag on my bed and take off my shoes. I sit on my tightly folded bed. Turning, I look out of the windows.

Distorted by the stadium lighting, the black sky has a dark shade of blue. Nothing is black and white anymore. It's only shades of blue that form as bruises on the surface of our bodies. Suddenly, Clyde turns. Something is weighing heavily on him.

"Steve," Clyde says.

"Yes," I respond.

"There's something I've been meaning to ask you."

"Me too," I say.

To this, he looks surprised. "What? What are you talking about? What could you possibly have to ask me, Steve?"

"How are things back home? Have you called your mom?" I say in a direct manner. He takes a step back. I mean no harm in the question although it may have come off as steely and cold.

"Um, yeah. You know, I have called, and the situation is complicated—" I shake my head in what I think is a sympathetic manner, but it may, to Clyde, come off as mechanical. "It's definitely complicated. I'm going to be spending the summer there. And yes, yes, it's all going okay. But I don't want to talk about it right now with you, Steve. Okay? Let me ask you something, because I have a serious theory that's been creeping around in my head, and I want to know if it's baseless or not."

"Yes?"

"Where do you go all these nights?"

"What do you mean?" I said, playing dumb.

"I know that you're not here, Steve. You wake up every night and go somewhere and then return back way later. I've seen the way you are in PT and on campus. Something's weighing you down. And I hear them. The demons creep into our room and wake you up. I hear them, Steve. I haven't been able to sleep because of them." Harry looks from me to Clyde. Clyde looks maniacal, like he's fed up.

"It's you, Steve. You're Firos, aren't you? I hear the other boys who back him up are MacConough, Warren, and Petersson. Those are the guys you hang out with, aren't they?"

I stand in silence, neither admitting guilt nor deflecting his assault. In the midst of his tantrum, we suddenly hear a knock on the door. "All in!"

It is Sergeant Edwards. He walks in, and we brace. He sniffs around, looking like a drug hound, snarling at us as he passes our beds, our desks, and our full presses. He looks toward the books. They are all filed from tallest to smallest. He goes through our belongings, socks rolled, underwear folded in quarters. The entire time, I feel nothing. I simply stand there, bracing, bracing, bracing.

The fury of Clyde had slid off me, and I stood with my chin tucked down and my focus on my breath. Edwards moved around the room and then stopped. He had noticed something off-kilter. Our trash can was full. Because of our lack of communication these past weeks, I realized we had neglected this task that required cooperation.

"Demerits for everyone," Edwards said.

"Sir, if I may say something, sir," I said.

"What is it, Wiggins? You may speak," Edwards said.

"It was my turn to take out the trash, and I'd like to take full responsibility for this mishap."

He looked at me from his furrowed eyebrows. "I don't understand. Are you telling me you'd like three tours to yourself?" he said.

"If that is what it takes to redeem my status and uphold my duties."

"Oh, c'mon, Wiggins," Clyde said. "What is with you, man?"

"Did I give you permission to speak, Akron?"

"Sir, no, sir," Clyde said.

"Then tell me, what the hell was that, then?"

"Sir, no excuse, sir,"

"Harold Stevenson, consider this your lucky day. You're off the hook. Wiggins and Akron, I'm assigning you a week of tours each. Meet me after classes for your punishment." Edwards shuts the door, and footsteps clack down the hallway.

"What the hell makes you so righteous, man? Why did you have to step up like that? It's just unnecessary."

"I didn't think about. It was just natural." I took a breath. "Something compelled me, pushed me forward."

"Don't think that this makes you any less of a villain in my eyes, Steve. I know that you are Firos, and oh boy are you in for it."

I stare at him, unaffected by his threat. He's fuming. Harry watches from the sideline, and I can tell he doesn't know which army to join. "Okay, well, good night, boys. Don't let Firos bite."

"Ha ha, Steve, you're a fucking clever guy, aren't you? See you on the quadrangle tomorrow, I guess. We'll see if this masquerade goes away or not with some upperclassmen not putting you under their wing."

It was true that I had escaped most of the scorn of upperclassmen this quarter, but it was also true that I no longer thought about it. In fact, it was time to go to bed, and that was exactly what I intended to do. Everything dissolved as my head touched the pillow, and this time, instead of resting beside me, it felt as if a mask covered my face.

*****

The next day, at 1600, both of us check in at the staff sergeant's office, a small bureau next to the quadrangle. We bring our rifles and uniforms. Clyde and I exchange glances, his full of resentment, mine absent. After a brief period of paperwork, we head out to the Smith Barracks quadrangle.

The March sun pounds on the bright, blank red-and-white quadrangle. In front of us, behind us, and to both sides are dark half-circle openings in the white stone building. The sally ports are open, and the occasional cadet passes through. Punishment such as this is nothing far from normal, though people often glance over to see who is waiting to serve. We begin our tour.

Marching at 120 paces per minute, we turn at the corner and do an about-face. My face is stiff, and my steps are equidistant. We cross the quad again and complete another length. For fifty pounding minutes, the quick clacks of our boots travel across the quad. Even with our training, this task seems strenuous.

The heat funnels downward into the barracks like a desert valley. We cross and turn, cross and turn, marching from red to white square and back to red. After about twenty minutes, something creeps over me. I feel the presence of my father watching from above. An omnipotent gravity presses down. My childhood surfaces, Arthur clapping the pace at my eye level as I march. The clacks of our shoes echo through the skeletal openings of the building. My pulse quickens. I feel faint.

The memory of my father pounding on the door, threatening him to open, yelling "Steve!" and kicking the furniture in my room. His rackings, I can feel his rackings as if they are right now, but I am not that same child. I am no longer him.

"Steve!" I hear from above. "Wiggins is out there." It's Nicky.

"Yeehaw! Walk that walk, Wiggy!" Petersson yells.

At that moment, the muggy heat hones into a spotlight, like an ant underneath a magnifying glass. The punishment grows brutal. Never did I imagine walking to be so difficult, but the psychological aspect of it is overwhelming. With the Charleston heat turned on and the growing crowd overhead, I pray for it to end. I'm chained to this punishment with everything out of my hands. Did I deserve this punishment?

Finally, when it finishes, we mope off the quad and go to return their gear. As I walk back to my room, people are whispering and pointing.

"Wiggy's in trouble."

"Finally, that guy gets some discipline."

Confused and unsure of what I have done to deserve this kind of alienation, I move through the barracks. In the mess hall, it isn't any different. Other cadets are pointing and laughing, telling me that I deserve what is happening after what I have done to everyone. I grab my meal and join Simon. He's sitting with a couple of cadets whom I recognize, and they give me odd looks as I sit down at the end of the table.

"Howdy, Steve," Simon said.

"Hey, Louisiana," I said and started eating in silence.

"You know, Steve, I feel like I know you. I've found that it's rare that you know someone at this place. Everyone holds a false front. But if these rumors are true, I know there has to be some kind of reason behind it."

"Any idea what this chatter is about?"

"Well, I know you don't have an ear for gossip, so I don't blame you for being late to the party," he said. I took a deep breath and turned to my food, planting my fork into each particular pea. After a moment, he said, "This might clear things up for you." He passed me a booklet.

It read, "The Survival Guide to Knob Year Semester 2." There was no author, but I immediately knew the masterminds who created this booklet. It was larger than the last one. Inside the front cover, it had scanned pictures of different corporals along with their character traits.

Colin MacConough, medium danger. Sly, enigmatic, and fair, Corporal Colin MacConough is known first semester for his fierce way of intimidating knobs, but as long as you stay out of his way, he can be fair and even seem kind. A standout student for all three years, his antics haven't held him back from succeeding, though his friends have. He rejected an offer to be a sergeant for a corporal position instead when learning the other three wouldn't receive such honors.

Petersson, high danger. Brutal and aggressive, Corporal Gunthar Petersson gained a reputation after competing in a high level on the varsity wrestling team. In tandem, he scored high on all levels of exams, earning his place atop the general's list for the first two years of his academy career. Last year, he was ensnared as an accomplice to the Theo Waters case, which has since then been buried by the academy. A fiery corporal with mob mentality, don't get in his way.

To see such a blatant accusation out in the open is baffling. Petersson as an accomplice of the Theodore Waters case? How in the hell would these guys know that? Then it had a section on General Firos being listed as Steve Wiggins. This exposure seared into my head like a cattle iron. I want to shut it off, the grinding, numbing steel that I felt flowing through my veins, coating my body with an armor, with a mask. Having this mask and making myself impervious to all surroundings might not be the right answer, but it was the only answer I had.

I wanted to shut it on Firos. However, I continued.

Warren, highest danger. Top suspect in the Theo Waters case.

I stop. I cannot continue. I look over to their table, to my roommates and former friends. They are laughing and joking. As I watch them, an upperclassman nearby tosses a knob's milk. The white liquid spreads down his face and onto his clothing. These former friends of mine gossip. However, they are also exposing a system. They're evening the playing field just a little to give knobs more of a chance of survival. They are like heroes. Thus, I am like a villain.

But I'm not a villain. My choices are made from a dutiful view of what is right, what falls in line with our ideals. MacConough, Petersson, Warren, even Firos all play their roles, although with some degree of difference. They aren't doing anything more than what they are shown to do by those before them. This all stems from tradition, from discipline. So, therefore, they are no villains; and if there are no villains, then there are no more heroes.

*****

Each tour is a salient reminder of the ongoing friction between me and Clyde. Each tour is also a salient reminder of my growing notoriety, my growing legend, as the black kid who plays Firos. The two of us arrive after classes, sign papers, and start marching again for fifty minutes. The large red-and-white tiles invade my thoughts. Blanketed in sunlight, the checkerboard pattern is especially intense.

With the brim of my cap covering my eyes and my polished rifle on the shoulder, I would often find myself spacing out. I would think of my dad, of my mom, and of my sisters and how I felt a growing divide between us. It was agonizing, but behind my soldier's mask, I could withstand the harshest qualms.

I glance at Clyde. He has turned from one of my closest allies, a warm friend with a great sense of humor, to a distant, passive person in my life, a man who takes shots from afar, trying to deter me from my goal. Thinking on it, I have no idea how he feels about this punishment or how he feels about people watching us.

Every once and a while, my train of thought would be broken by a spectator. A hoot from above would snap me into the present. A growing crowd would force me to stay there. The crowd often forms, pointing and laughing. *Clack, clack, clack.* Across the quad we march. Then we end in silence and go our separate ways, pawing through the rowdy upperclassmen and knobs.

The beginning of the day swings around once again. A blue tinge slices the horizon like a gunshot. We dress and run into the sunrise. Daylight opens across Indian Hill, slowly spreading its golden stripes. A lone water tower stands solemn in the middle of the grassy field. We mush past it.

I wear a stoic smile. Each particular PT training, each length, and each stride has brought me to this point in the school year as if suddenly realizing that the repetition, that my reputation, all happened for a reason. The jogs, jodies, and fury of footsteps pacing at 120 beats per minute are all I know. But then as we near the barracks, I fall numb. My face changes.

Today is Thursday, the second to last tour. I notice that Clyde is also there early. It's just us there. It was a silent quadrangle since the officer hasn't shown yet. Clyde hesitates when he sees me coming as if he doesn't want to be confrontational. I walk up to him and look him straight in the eyes.

"Best of luck in these upcoming years. You deserve it, but personally, I'd prefer to terminate our relationship. Don't talk to me on campus. Don't look at me when we're both in the room. I don't want to associate myself with you anymore. A soldier would never sink as low as you did these past few months, writing these silly tabloid articles when you don't know shit. What the fuck do you know about my life, what I've been through to get here, huh?" I shake my head and say, "I want you to know that it's true. I am Firos."

I leave in a stoic calm. He is bewildered. I turn, noticing that today's officer, Sergeant Edwards, has arrived. "All right, boys," he says. I sign papers and walk into the sunlight on the red-and-white quadrangle. Clyde soon follows.

The clacks of footsteps echo through the hallways of the Citadel. Twenty minutes pass this way. *I feel a presence. Is it my father? Is he proud of the soldier I have become?* A crowd gathers overhead.

"Walk that walk, Wiggy." They were hooting and hollering, screaming at me. Sergeant Edwards walked out, and I heard him try to control the crowd, scolding those pestering us. The quadrangle lengths were long, but the clacks from our boots were now drowned out by the echo of the crowd overhead. Suddenly, a flurry of footsteps approached.

I continue, 120 paces per second. Two more paces and then boom, a flash of light. I tumble to the ground. Glare hits my face from behind a large shadow. "You piece of shit." It's Clyde. He punches me and draws back and punches me again. I attempt to cover my face.

"Akron, are you out of your mind?" I hear Edwards say.

"Acorn, get the hell off of Wiggy!"

"This is him. This is fucking Firos right here! A knob has been racking us this entire time!" Clyde, in hysteria, yells, "He did it!"

I try to use this break-in pummeling to scoot away, but Clyde doubles down on the pressure. I'm trapped. After another moment of struggle, I surrender. I close my eyes for a moment, and then I feel something around my neck. He's choking me. I thrash around and try to gasp for air. Clyde hits me again, and I lose track of time.

He hits me again and again. I'm blind. Then suddenly, his weight lifts. Someone pulls Clyde off me. I lie there for a moment in this totality of surrender. Seconds longer and I could've been uncon-scious. I open my eyes but only partially as they are swelling with blood. I see a hand. I take it. Edwards yanks me up over his shoulder to stand me on my feet. At this point, I look around me.

Cadets surround on all balconies. They're watching. They've been watching, viewing my life like a spectator sport. On the far side of the quad, in shade, I see Harry holding Clyde back. Clyde is still fuming, but Harry's larger frame constricts him. I brush myself off and start marching. Once again, I march at 120 paces per minute.

"Wiggins, what are you doing?" Edwards said.

"Sir, finishing, sir," I said.

Edwards gave me a hard glare from beneath his cap. Harry, Clyde, and the rest of the crowd were shocked by the brazen deter-mination. The blood began to dry on my face.

"Dammit, Wiggins, you can stop now," Edwards yelled.

"Sir, no, sir."

"I don't know what you're trying to prove, Wiggins, but you're making an ass out of yourself," Clyde yelled at me.

"Akron, my office," Edwards booms. He speaks in a way I haven't heard him before. Clyde leaves the quad and walks inside. Edwards looks over at me with a stern face and then follows Clyde. I continue marching. Harry, unsure of how to act, enters the barrack.

After the tour, I walk to my room. I look at Clyde's desk in the corner and think back to the first day when he called me a real peace and love type. The past, I shake it off and crawl into bed. Closing my eyes, I imagine a new beginning. Beyond the gates, I picture the unfiltered beauty of Charleston in the spring light: azalea buds opening into vibrant fireworks, spreading from street to street, lining the edge of my memory, and the splash of great waterbirds, such as pelicans, ibises, herons, and storks plunging into the harbor—some-times, I would see one on the water's edge, wayside of the campus—and the springtime scent of morning, fresh dew on flower petals, newly cut grass, the architecture basking in the sun with shadows of steeples covering them in lines at twilight.

On the Friday of that week, the Friday before spring break, it rains. Drizzle pats the quad in the morning, which then picks up into a torrent by midday. Clyde and I hesitantly look out at the slick surface. The reflections of a gray sky and dark barracks shimmer on the surface of the red-and-white quad.

I look at Clyde. Our eyes connect for a second, and then he looks forward again. Something between us, the heat of battle, dissolves with the rain. I can tell that he has thought about what I said, and now with closure, we can move forward. At least, this is my hope.

"C'mon both of you. Let's finish this up."

We skitter across the quadrangle, prudent not to slip. The wet cement is unforgiving, yet the weather is peaceful. No one chants that day, no one yells. The layer of rainwater muffles the clacks of our boots, and I can't hear him, and I couldn't hear the paces, 120 per minute. It is respite. It is peace.

CHAPTER 14
One Month—Sisters

When I arrived home to the tree-lined suburban street of West Ashley, I found myself once again bruised and battered but, this time, unfettered by these battle scars. With an unflinching straight face, I knocked on the door. It took a moment. The door slowly opened. My sister Lorna answered. She smiled, and I smiled back. I dropped my bag. I hugged her and noticed Maisy standing behind her.

Walking up, I hug her too, pulling her off the ground. I set her down, and she traces my face with her fingers. I have a scar on my forehead, swelling on the other side of my face, and bruising underneath the eye. She doesn't say a word, just gazes up with her large brown eyes.

The two of them are amazing, bright, shining trophies of the neighborhood on a warm spring day in Charleston. Throughout my time at the academy, I feel as if I've earned an atlas of experience. However, since I've been gone, they've grown a lot too.

Lorna stands tall, completely out of the awkward teenage years. With this new posture comes confidence, a distinguished stance of intelligence and cultivation. Maisy seems more composed, less focused on stealing the show. No utterance about her accomplishments or her current whims fill my ears, just a cicadaless silence throughout the foyer.

There's no sign of Loretta—I had been dropped by MacConough—even if her car is in the driveway. It's possible that she's cooking, preparing a meal for my return, per ritual. However, I hear no running water, no clanking of cookware.

A champion's glow surrounds me. It's as if I'm a hero returning back to a sanctified place after my most difficult battle. Mentally as well as physically, the last few months have been excruciating. Turning from the victim to the victimizer is a heavy burden, especially considering that the victimized are those with whom I once laughed and learned. Pulling over the mask to conceal my emotions, to not focus on each particular incidence of pain I caused, but instead focus on the larger, emboldened principles, is a process. I feel, however, that I'm on the other side now.

I step upstairs. Our hallway quivers with the feeling of time passed, yet the hallway itself is unchanged, full of vibrant yellow tones of sunshine spilling from windows of different bedrooms. A row of doors are ajar, mine still being the same, first on the right.

I envision the same bedroom like an empty throne before I open the door—the bed faces the drawers, my desk next to my closet, my tennis balls, my football gear, the picture of me and my prom date in our powder-blue attire, and that attire buried somewhere in my closet.

Opening the door, immediately, I'm taken aback. The room has canvases strewn about. A white tarp scrolls across the floor. The desk is still there, but my bed, my desk, and—I open the closet—all my personal items are gone. I rush out of the room.

Downstairs, I find my sisters. "What's going on?" I say.

"Oh, I forgot to tell you," Lorna said. "Mom and Dad moved your things downstairs so that Mom could have a room for her paintings. You're in the guest bedroom now."

"Oh, okay," I said and moved my duffle bag through the dining room and kitchen, then I stopped. "Where are they, by the way?"

"Mom and Dad are out back," Lorna said.

I slowly open the door to the guest room and see the bed and my desk. The room is dark with a small window showing a slight amount of daylight behind slanted shades. The ceiling of the room has the angle of the stairs. If moving to college is the beginning of some process, returning to see your room displaced and being shoved into the far corners of the house must be the end.

Out back, I follow my sisters. What a sight! What a landscape. The grass grows in long blades the color of lime peel, already on their way to dehydration. Bushels of deep-green leaves plus pink and red fireworks wait to be trimmed, plucked, tied in sweetgrass, and placed in vases. To my surprise, Loretta and Arthur are both in the grass.

My father has his military uniform on and is in a stance reminiscent of Sergeant Edwards that first day, the ubiquitous stare of a commander as if he is staring at you no matter where you are positioned in the line. My mother paints, a canvas placed in front of her. She is painting a portrait of him!

It was a strange sight. First, I had no idea that she focused so much on her painting now. Second, I had never seen Arthur engaged with this passion. They weren't like this when I lived here.

"Sir, ma'am, just wanted to let you know that I'm home."

"Steve, you're back? Spring break?" Arthur said.

"Yes, sir."

"Hey, Steve. Why don't you make yourself comfortable? We'll come in when we're done here and figure out what to do for dinner."

"Yes, ma'am." She hadn't reacted to my bruises, though she hardly reacted to my presence at all.

I leave and walk inside. There are no dinner plans and no special meal to celebrate my return. I brush these negative thoughts aside and head to my room to unpack.

*****

Over the week, I don't speak with my parents much. This is my normal relationship with Arthur, but with Loretta, I'm still not used to it. I feel no need to tell of my academics, but in reciprocity, she doesn't ask. She keeps her promise of distancing from me as I continue to distance myself from emotion, from nostalgia, and from sentiment.

Each of us has our own methods of protecting ourselves, I realize. My father as well. And while his resilience through the most difficult war of our era is a bunkered strength, one of protocol and teeth clenching, she's just as strong for bringing him back from this place.

At dinner, they seem happier than ever before. After dinner, they both sit on the same couch, reading different books or watching the same programs. My youngest sister, Maisy, does she understand yet? She carries through the day without any qualms and with a whimsical enjoyment, buzzing from one subject to the next, almost lighting the room. It is a similar warmth to my mother's. However, my mother would flip this switch only when she wants. I suppose this makes the ability to shelter our emotions something we learn as we age, not something we inherently know.

To take it one step further, my father's stems from the sights and experiences he had over in Vietnam. My mother's comes from his and, I guess, my emotional distance. But my precaution comes from my father's outbursts on me and the rackings at the academy, so it's not something we learn as we age but something we learn out of the necessity of aging, of maturing.

My elder sister, Lorna, she also had a reticent approach to life, taking a calculated approach like myself. One night, while I read in the darkness of my room, I heard a light knock. Surprised, I put my book down and sat up. "Come in." Slowly opening the door, Lorna came in and shut it lightly.

"Hey, Steve," she said. "I need advice on something."

"What is it?" I said harshly, and then I saw a look of shame cross her face, like she shouldn't have come to me. I chuckled and artificially lighten up. "Sorry. Excuse me. That was academy Steve. Back to big bro Steve. What's up? What can I help you with?"

"So as you know, I got into both USC and University of Charleston, but I also got into Yale and Princeton."

"Yeah, I recall. Dad wants you to stay in-state, so you had to reject Ivy Leagues because of him. That's a tough situation."

"Well, what if I told you that I didn't reject them?"

"No way. Really?"

"Yes, I accepted Yale. That's where I'm going to be headed. I'm going to be at Yale fall of 1980. But I haven't told anyone yet."

"Lorna! Good for you." I clenched my fist tightly.

She laughed and blushed. "I couldn't tell if it was the right thing to do or not, you know. It took a lot of thought. My friends, my counselors, everyone told me that it wasn't the right thing to do, well, except mom and you. I'm still ambivalent, but my heart said that I needed to leave Charleston and start something else, to go up North, maybe visit New York, DC, and see other parts of the country."

My eyes widen as I listen to her. "Mom's going to be happy."

"I'm worried about Dad."

"Don't worry about him. I don't think anything pierces his armor." I pause. "He's more worried about the tuition. You could move to Australia for all it matters. Now that I think about it, it'll be harder on Mom, but she'll be happy in the long run. She wants this for you."

"I agree with you, Steve. I just feel bad because I feel like I'm leaving her behind."

"You just gotta do you."

"I know that's what you did. No, actually, it feels like you're doing what Dad did."

"That's because it was important to me to follow his steps. I felt like that was the only way I'd eventually be able to step out of his shadow."

"Steve, but we don't talk at dinner anymore. Are you ever going to make up with Mom? It's been weirder every time you come back now. Mom's not even cooking when you come back. I think that she thinks that you don't like eating as a family or something."

"That couldn't be further from the truth. Mom's cooking is the only thing that makes me feel like I'm home. Look, now I live down here in this cave, tucked away from everybody. I swore as a cadet that I wouldn't speak in any type of way about my path of discipline. It has been hard keeping it to myself, but that's part of duty.

"Mom and I made a pact when I started that I'd think of you and her and Maisy before I make each decision at the academy, and if I failed to do so, well, I think neither I nor Mom understood that the pact was destined to fail when we made it. All I know is, when you start something in life, you have to finish it no matter the cost or how bleak it looks while you're doing it."

"Is that Dad speaking, or is that you? You haven't even been there a year, Steve," she said.

"Yes, well." I paused and looked around the room. "You haven't even been there a year"—these words pounded on my skull, echoing on the inside of my armor. "We'll see how things are when I've finished this year. In the meantime, your secret is safe with me."

"Thanks, but I wasn't asking you to keep it a secret. I was hoping for advice in telling Mom and Dad. I want to tell them, but I don't know how yet."

"That's true. Let's see, how about in song?"

"What? Like I sing it to them?"

"Yeah. It's always something you've liked."

"That's ridiculous, Steve. Can you imagine that? I gather them in the backyard and start belting out a chorus about how I chose Yale? Dad would leave before the second verse."

"What's predictable about them is that you can't predict what they're going to do. I learned that the hard way. You just have to bring up the thought and follow through with words. Just go with your gut," I said. She began laughing. "I'm serious. It's good to be calculated with some things, but this isn't one of them. It's a matter of delivering it in a genuine, earnest way, and always tell the truth." I paused. "One more thing. Can you ask Mom that we'll sit down for dinner when I return this summer?"

"Yeah, of course," she said. As she closed the door, I added that I was proud of her.

*****

Good mornings and good nights fall over the household like patterns of the sun. I maintain my routine of waking at 5:20 a.m., rising at 5:30 a.m., running until 6:15 a.m., showering, eating, and studying notes. It is as though instead of living, my body is a vessel to live through. I would smile as I see a family member. The closeness of the household never comes into the open, but at this point, it certainly isn't there.

The alone time, however, was convalescence. I would look at the insides of my hands and notice how the blisters scabbed and faded away. The bruises on my face healed as well. I was able to regain my focus on each subject in school and engaged with them, creating different taxonomies of psychological theories or math formulas. The cave on the ground floor, my room, felt as if it was a cocoon.

One day, when my mother is away, I decide to walk into my old room. I creep up the steps, making sure not to allow a sound. On the door hinge, markings for measuring my height during my childhood are still written. I smile as I see this. I click on the lights, and the room comes to life as if without lighting the paintings are in a deep slumber. My mother has been hard at work. There must be at least ten to fifteen completed pieces in here, paintings like the ones I had seen at the Thanksgiving food drive.

I look at the half-finished portrait of my father. It's done with acrylic, yet it still holds his same demeanor from the picture downstairs. The look of confirmation changes to one of understanding. A mutual code is to be upheld between us. I shut the door.

At dinner, the table is set in a way reminiscent of days before I enrolled at the academy. On Thursday, we finally sit down as a family. Forks and knives clank on the porcelain plates, and the ice in the sweet tea rattles around the pitcher. Pleasantries are exchanged, but other than that, silence.

I look from my mother to Lorna, who reciprocates my glance. She seems preoccupied with her reveal but hesitant as to whether it's the right time. My mother and my father look rosy and exchange playful glances from one end of the table to the other. Maisy, the poor girl, looks lost.

The family dynamic is forever shifting, moving on as the older children move out. This process happens in a way that a child at my age can understand but never expects. Someone my sister Maisy's age, however, could have difficulty understanding this change. For me, childhood is seen with nostalgia, and I know that the past, while it holds fortified imprint in our mind, is one-dimensional, capturing less truth than even a painting or a photograph. For her, however, being at such a tender age, she holds no distinction between childhood and now.

Later that night, overwhelmed by the rush of emotions, I want to call Miranda. I'm still reeling about my experience with Alyssa, and I have been debating what to do for a while now. I think it may only be the proper thing to do to break up with her and ask Alyssa on a date.

As the phone rings, I prepare myself with what I'm going to say, but nothing comes to mind. *Go with your gut,* I think. *Beep. Beep.*

"Hello? Who is it?" an older woman answered.

"Hello, ma'am. It's Steven Wiggins calling for Miranda," I said.

"Steve, I've heard so much about you. You accompanied our girl to the New Year's bash. Why, you've made a tasteful impression with near everyone who's met you," she said.

"Why, thank you, ma'am. It was really a great event. You must be madam…um," I said.

"Yes, so why are you calling? Are you on spring break?" she said.

"Yes, ma'am, I am," I said.

"Well, that's great to hear," she said. There was a pause in our conversation, a strange pause, awkward even.

"So, um, can I speak to Miranda please?"

"Oh, this has put me in an awkward position. Miranda has actually taken a semester abroad in England. She left in January and won't return until, let's see, mid-June."

"I'm well aware of what a semester abroad is, ma'am. Where in England?"

"She's at Cambridge. Do you know it?"

"Yes, I've heard it's a great school. Well, anyway, thank you, ma'am. I hope you have a lovely evening."

"Thank you, Steve. Toodaloo."

"Bye now." I hung up the phone. "Okay," I said to myself with the receiver in my hand. My thoughts moved backward until I dived into the scene from New Year's. She had been crying, but maybe that was what it all was about. We only had a few dates, but I could admit they had been interesting, like a swathe of newness exchanged between us, the passing of candles, stories, from two sides of the same river.

"Now what?" I said to myself, receiver still in hand. I couldn't end our relationship over a postcard. For now, I was stuck. Alyssa would have to wait for me. *Yeah. Right.*

*****

I return to campus with the wind at my back. Entering through the gates, I feel as if I can already see the finish line. As I enter the room, neither of my roommates is there. I unpack my things. In a precise order, I move my pressed white T-shirts, joggers, and underwear back into the drawer. Before I can finish, however, I'm called to the door by a knock.

A runner. I'm to report to MacConough. I'm already back at it. I follow him down the stretching hallways and toward the staircase and walk downstairs. We exit the stairs and head toward MacConough's room. I walk in, and he stands as well as Warren and Nicky. Petersson isn't there at the moment.

"Sirs," I said.

"How was your break, Wiggy?" Nicky said.

"Sir, uneventful, sir," I said.

MacConough laughed. "No partying? No drinking?"

"I'm shocked, Wiggs. I thought you were going to represent us well while we were gone."

"We went camping by the beach," MacConough said. "Anyway, I'm aware that it must've been nice having a little break from all of this Firos drama."

"Sir, I must admit, sir," I said.

"Yeah, we put you through a lot, but it happens to all the classes. It's a tradition. You know, consider it like stepping into a path toward success. Each company has a chosen one, and I don't know if it means a lot to ya, but you're the first black Firos."

"Kilo's a real progressive company," Nicky joked.

"As long as it pairs well with your other scores, like your grades, your ROTC field training, such and such."

"Sir, yes, sir," I said. "Sir, were any of you Firos?"

"Not allowed to disclose that information, cadet," MacConough said. "But yeah, we were." He laughed.

"It's how we met sophomore year," Nicky said, "though the way that guy leveled you on the quadrangle, I've seen some knobs go berserk, but not quite to that extent. Did you know him?"

"Sir, he is my roommate, sir."

"Whoa, that's buck wild," Nicky said.

"Another thing." Warren suddenly stood up. "I've seen the pamphlets going around the mess, how to survive knob year. Any idea who wrote these?"

Randall and Clyde, why, of course. "Sir, no, sir," I said.

A silence descended over the room. "Sir, is what they wrote true?" I asked Warren. He immediately shifted his glasses. That was his tell in cards. In the same way that Petersson ashed his cigarette, Warren shifted his glasses when hiding something.

"Wiggins, you are out of line with that question!" MacConough said. "I guess you've seen 'em? They have you suspected as Firos too. They have him suspected on some horseshit. Luckily, the bastards who wrote them don't have any idea of what they're really talking about—no clout, no evidence."

"Sir, what do you mean, sir?"

"Well, they're poor man's observations. It's someone guessing about a lot of things. Either it's a freaking knob who was busy in the library compiling these notes or it's a pathetic upperclassman who doesn't know us and has some sort vendetta against the system. Either way, it doesn't bother us too much. We just have to do our duty and uphold these traditions. Ain't that right, Wiggy?"

"Sir, yes, sir," I said, and in an instant, I understood. I had been chosen, and this mask, the mask of Firos, was like an exam to validate that I had been chosen correctly. The entirety of this thing, my relationship with these four corporals, of me being called to their room, wasn't a friendship or some big brother bond. It was more like having four proctors watching my every move, and somehow, by acting on instinct, I had done everything in the correct manner. They could trust me.

Though with MacConough, it was something else. By accidentally walking in on him that November day, I had stumbled into some strange echelon in the academy, some hidden room or hallway. The labyrinth of rooms in the barrack's underground came to mind, like finding a chest that held old family secrets, except doing what I had felt was the right thing, acted as the key.

Without this occurrence, would the upperclassman still have given me this right of passage? Would MacConough still have me underneath his wing? As Firos, I found it is not important to ask these questions but, rather, to figure out what comes next.

I lie on my bed, listening to eerie taps fade out into the sounds of my roommates' heavy breathing. Warren's secret is another level of murky weather. He has shown his tell when I asked him. This mean he's guilty. Theodore Waters, death by suicide in the Ashley River, there must be a reason Warren shifted his glasses. He was involved, but there's no telling how or why.

*****

The next few days passed in a flurry. I found myself at random times—shining my boots, organizing papers, brushing my teeth—thinking about Warren, MacConough, and Firos, about how for those few weeks I had slowly transformed and became him. And now even though I was free of the mask, my relationship to everything had changed. I was branded, watched by upperclassmen, scoured by knobs in my grade. The mess hall would part as I walk through with my peas, mashed potatoes, and noodles with red sauce. No longer was I part of the food chain or part of the bottom feeders called knobs.

That Saturday, I felt a swelling in my chest as we took the bus out to the woods for ROTC. I sat staring out of the window as the surroundings grew darker and more forested. Off the main road the van went and down a small gravel path until we stopped in a dirt lot.

After the first ROTC session where I had covered him and led him to victory, Gin, the knob who once enthusiastically greeted me, now led the team. He had shown his true potential through the semester. He was very skilled in terms of marksmanship and stealth and prevented the other team from scoring more times than one. As we stepped off the bus, I nodded to him. He treaded over to me.

"Wiggins, is everything all right?"

"Yeah. I have a good feeling about today. I'm at your disposal. Just tell me where you want me."

He nodded. "The team we're going up against is undefeated, so it's good to hear that you're feeling it, Wiggs."

"Yo, Wiggs," I heard. I turned, and it was none other than Randall. "How's it going, Firos? Steal any kid's lunch money lately?"

"Undefeated, oh yeah," I said, remembering his track record.

I look at Randall as he turns around, surrounded by his comrades, augmented as the pseudo leader of his platoon. Unfazed, I begin to walk away. I have two weeks left to show what I'm capable of—we mush out to our starting points—to show the entire class what the four corporals see in me. An official blows the horn in the distance.

I stay back, watching Gin and my other comrades swarm around him, and then depart in different directions. Three take the lead, mushing through the woods at a much faster pace, and two trail them, providing cover. He motions for me to come over. "Steve, flank them, okay? Take a wide route outside. You're going to be solo, okay?"

With the brush crunching underneath me, I take off toward the outside of the perimeter. As I'm running, I remember the fortress where Clyde had shot me and head in this direction. White flags mark the out-of-bounds. I turn there, barely inbound. Leaping across the river, I stay low, hearing the clack of pellet fire in the distance. The body of the fortress becomes visible. I close in, walk inside, and stand in the center.

Suddenly, a surge of serenity covers me. The last time I was here, it marked my defeat. Clyde had shot me while I was resting and looking up toward the empty black of the top of the cave. Now I sense something else. I clench my fist and take off, barreling through the woods. I must be on the opposing side by now, I think. So my route changes, and I circle back toward the center.

Clack. I hit one, a dark figure in the distance, and consecutively dive to the ground. Moments pass, and I lurch back up and take off as fast as I can run. *Clack.* Another falls down. *Where are all of my teammates?* I hear someone to my left. I turn and shoot. *I have to be nearing their flag now. This is my first time coming so close.*

Wait, where is it? There it is. There it is. In the clearing ahead, perched on a fallen tree, crooked, ripe for picking, is the flag of the opposing team. I bottle toward it, my heavy boots noisy on the soil.

Then I have an idea. I would be heard anyway. I might as well lure them in. I shoot several shots into the air, signifying that I'm by their base. My hope is that they'll retreat and fall onto the defensive.

I snag the flag and turn. There's one. *Clack.* He's down. I keep falling back, deeper into their territory, deeper into the darkness of the woods. And then without thought, I turn and start flanking once again, straightening out and heading straight for our base.

After about fifteen seconds of sprinting, I'm once again parallel with their base. A cluster of four cadets, who must've retreated after my shots, look around. *Wap. Wap.* I hit two of them. The other two turn and point at me. I run for cover, careening past through the brush and toward the stream. Only what's in front of me, my sole focus is what's in front of me. A figure waves, and as my vision clears, I see that it's Gin.

"Attaboy, Steve. You got it. I'll cover your back," he yells as I pass. My heartbeat throbs louder than his yells. My steady pant becomes stressed and irregular as I hop the stream. I'm closing in on our base. Another figure. I don't think. I shoot. *Whap.* The man stops. He's hit. It's Randall. I hit Randall, who has our flag in his grasp, and according to rules, he must relinquish it.

I pass him with their flag in my hands and lay it safely at our base. We win. In the midst of fifteen, maybe twenty, minutes, I took out six cadets on the opposing team and returned their flag. I had blinked and defeated my rival. I won the exercise. My team surrounds me, patting me on the back, throwing fists into the air, but I'm not joyous about the victory. The steely sensation from Firos has taken hold. I feel nothing. It is just a part of what I have to do.

Both teams join together at the end, and we complete cooldown exercises in unison. Hands in the dirt, we crank out push-ups and complete the obstacle course several times before grabbing sandwiches and calling it a day. Randall glances at me in passing, serious in demeanor this time. We load the bus and leave.

Word of my performance spreads throughout the barracks. As I walk in the sally port on a sunny day in April, through the white columns and around the red-and-black quadrangle, "He's a freak, a monster, a beast" is what I hear. These labels pass in both negative and positive regards and slide off me.

I had gotten used to this role—being pointed at, whispered about—and for once, it was nice to see this turned around, to be labeled for something I had done rather than for how I looked. This training didn't showcase my potential. I had simply been feeling good that day, feeling in the moment.

From an outsider's perspective, one could say that my legend continued to grow. The knob who stood up to Petersson, who ravaged others as Firos, and who finished his tour after a severe beating now had one of the single greatest ROTC performances. The old me would have wanted to bump into Randall, to shove his face into it, but now I walk by my accomplishment unaltered and onto the next stage of life. Taps covered the campus, and the lights dim.

A blue line cracks over the horizon, and thus starts a new day. Trash cans echo through the halls, and my roommates and I rise without words. We gear up and head down to the quadrangle. In PT, I warm up, keep to myself, and jog behind MacConough. My roommates and I stay out of one another's way in the mess, in the halls, and in our room. There's no animosity, just silence.

I walk through the campus without much thought except what I'm currently doing and what I'm doing next. I walk down the glimmering halls with uniform doors placed equidistant throughout them. I walk through the campus, and I walk down those halls, the same ones that I have been all year.

The night before Recognition Day, MacConough and the crew invite me for a game of poker. I brace as I enter their domain. There is no sign of the mask, Firos, or of any shenanigan. Like the beginning, we exit campus with permission granted from them. Down the black streets of Charleston we go. Tree branches sink over the streets like large cobwebs. We head to the white house, just one block to the right of the academy's football stadium.

CHAPTER 15
One Night and One Day—Recognition

One could consider the entire year preparatory for Recognition Day, but for us, the process becomes official days after spring break. This is one of the rare instances the entire campus cohere with one another, one of the rare instances that I witness Lieutenant Dorchester give a pep talk.

He had the same Napoleonic vigor as on Hell Night, his veins popping out of his short, thick neck as he stressed the importance of this day to the academy, the evolution of the fourth-class cadet and so forth, showcasing how they are no longer knobs but are now on the path to becoming leaders.

No longer would we have to square corners, brace, or trudge through the gutters. This was a recognition we received from a year of racking, of enduring the discipline, and of experiencing the same tribulations as those the years before. This was a reciprocal glance across the vast war zone of experience between upperclassmen and us, the first time we would amount to more than a pile of dirt.

After Dorchester finished his speech, a dress rehearsal took place. This, however, was only reserved for the upperclassmen. MacConough explained the night before.

A haunted aura swallows the dimly lit street of Charleston. The air is still, yet tree branches dangle and writhe without reason. The statue of the bulldog on the southwest corner of the football stadium glares into the black holes of night. Staring up at its fearsome presence, I feel overcome by some sort of sensation. We arrive at their house.

"Yeah, when we were knobs, you get your hopes up. They treat Recognition like it's the day that everything gets leveled, perk ya up with all types of promises—'After today, you'll be a man'—like you're one of the pack now. Then all of a sudden, they clamp down on you."

"What do you mean by that, sir?" I asked.

"Notice how your compadres are feeling. Watch the fire in their eyes vanish from the announcement toward the actual day."

MacConough sips some beer and looks around at the other upperclassmen. They are all getting a kick out of these stories. I, however, don't bite.

When the upperclassmen left the gymnasium where Dorchester had given his speech, the knobs were exuberant. I recalled Harry coming up to me. Actually, it was the first time he had spoken to me in a while, though I had forgotten what he had said.

Instead, I remember staring at him and noting that his face was different. His cheekbones emerged much more defined than when I had first met him. He no longer had fat red cheeks, and now his face's shape was a rigid square. Through the pressure of knob year, he had transformed as much as anyone else, if not more.

Direct and active, his squadron ended up tying with ours for first. And even though our team had beaten both of the other top teams, their record spoke volumes. Now he kept up during training and only became winded during those long training sessions when the officers pushed us and the dang heat pushed us even further.

*****

"Recognition Day, what does it truly mean?" MacConough continued. "You're going to hear that all day. Generals will say, 'What does this day mean, cadet?' When you're doing push-ups, sergeants will yell, 'What the hell does this day mean to you?' The janitor will ask you in the am.

"No, but seriously, they're not going to just announce it and then give it to you. It's like everything else at the academy—right when you think it's over, it comes right back to get you. They want you to work for it to the last second.

"I guess you could say, with all this pent up animus from upper-classmen to lower-class men, there's nowhere else for it to go, so it's released with one final day. The upperclassmen take one last roll call." MacConough took a sip of beer and looked across the table at Nicky.

"Picture yourself in a marching line in a large field, which you will have to do on Recognition Day, by the way. But this marching line is one by one, and those who you're marching with disappear. When everyone's disappeared, you're alone," MacConough said. Nicky laughed. "Look at him. Big Wiggs ain't scared."

I wore an earnest look of determination—eyes wide, mouth clenched—and each word navigated past, clear as a battleship in broad day.

"It doesn't matter if you're scared or not. Being scared is never the right answer," MacConough said.

"I think he already knows that, Mid Mac," Nicky said. "C'mon, you'll be just fine."

"So it's not that bad, sir?" I said to Nicky.

The night after Dorchester gave his speech, I came back to my room late at night and walked past an upperclassman with a smirk on and his brim low. Whimpering came from beyond the door. It was Harry. He was sitting on the corner of his bed and looked up at me. Immediately, he stopped.

"Where the hell do you go anyway?" Harry said, turning red in an instant. "How come every time that you aren't here, there's another fucking rack session? You're hanging out with them, aren't you? I can't believe you're betraying us like that." Harry trailed off.

"Harry, calm yourself," I said in a level tone. "I can see that Clyde and maybe even Randall got to you. They utilize rumors and stories when the soldier's way says that we shouldn't speak. I know you've gotten tougher. I mean, shoot, you have the nerve to confront me like that. But you might want to think about formulating your own truths."

"But you are Firos, aren't you?"

"A cadet must never lie, cheat, or steal" flashed through my head. "Yes, I was," I said.

"Steve, what the hell!"

"Quiet," I said, putting my grip on his shoulder, looking downward at him like a brash older sibling. "Do you remember my good friend Louisiana, K Company, different floor and wing?"

"Sure," he said.

"He said to me once, 'If you are Firos, I'm sure you have a reason. And for that, I can forgive you,'" I said. "Because of the way he thinks, I admire him as a friend. You, Harry, the way that you saved me from Clyde, giving me brain damage, the way you've matured and beaten a lot of your demons, your body, your temerity, I've grown to admire you as well. But this. This. Remember to be stoic, Harry. Remember who we are as soldiers. I'll let you come to your own conclusions and hope that you don't let fear and cynicism corrode these conclusions."

His look changed. What was once a frumpy face resembling the Harry from Hell Night, the Harry who wanted to give up, turned back into this new man. He nodded at me, and I left him and exited the room with my toothbrush.

*****

"I think he just means it catches you off guard," Nicky said. "Even us, who would goof around during basically all the training, were really forced to be serious during this day, and that was horseshit. Like, imagine us, pretty much the coolest cadets—"

"Extremely modest, Nicky," Warren said from the far corner.

"Wiseguy. Anyway," Nicky continued, "imagine you've got me and MacConough, like the two rebels who don't take shit from no one, and you got the star athlete and two top students in Petersson and Warren. Of course, we're going to have hotheads, and during most of the school year, yeah, we'd get racked, but we got away with our shit clean.

"We were chosen as Firos respectively in our companies and suffered through it. Nothing could be harder. Then Recognition Day starts coming up, and the upperclassmen come down on all the others around us. You wonder when they're going to get you, if they're going to get you. When you think you've mastered mental toughness, a fear creeps in again. Boom. Suddenly, they decide that they have to show the higher-ups that we've been trained proper, so they start making up ground for lost time."

"Sir, Recognition Day is tomorrow, and no one has racked me yet," I said.

"Really?" Warren said.

I stare straight. Warren seems as if he doesn't understand why this hasn't happened to me. A bead of sweat forms on my forehead.

"Steve," Nicky said, "you ain't the chosen one. They'll get you."

In an uncomfortable flurry of thoughts, I look to MacConough, who prudently looks away. He pretend to have no link to my fate even though he holds all the cards. I glance away quickly. Warren is staring through his glasses. Does he know? Or did MacConough just dodge a bullet?

*****

At five thirty on Recognition Day, I head downstairs to the quadrangle. Focusing on each step, trying to awaken, my body feels numb and heavy. The overhead lights still cover the red-and-white squares in an artificial color. A dark blue paints on the sky, a line shredding through the edge of the horizon. My roommates are already there and don't acknowledge me as I walk onto the quad. Well, for a moment, Harry looks my way, though Clyde stares straight.

The air at dawn seethes with the warmth of the upcoming day, but the stone quadrangle is icy. My hands press against that cold ground during our morning push-ups. It centers me. Sergeant Edwards, the silent giant, is leading drills today. He walks back and forth with his commanding, precise manner, not exhibiting any superfluous movement.

After PT exercises, we arrange ourselves in squads, or large blocks of cadets. The regimental commander gathers everyone's attention, and we leave the barracks for phase one: the Regimental Run.

As we exit through the sally port, I can see other companies in the distance starting from their particular barracks. They jog around the center field and then swing to the outskirts of campus, beyond the classrooms. Our company makes a big turn around the back of the halls, and we pass the field once again. Huffing and sweating, I realize how fatigued I am from the night before.

The rest of my squad keeps pace as we swing around the far side of the center field. *I must persevere.* Then we aim toward the Ashley River marina where Clyde, Randall, and I had snuck off campus for Halloween. Each area we cover reminds me of a different memory of the year. The path my roommates and I took, cheering to the football field, is still imprinted.

Where I had spoken with Paxton about his scar, scrambling to class after Petersson and Nicky's rackings, and an assortment of difficult exams and lectures resurface as we passed the corresponding halls. My late winter nights clung to me when we passed the library. Memories that I had forgotten marched past in my stoic determination in the same speed uncover themselves as we move in a solid unit around campus.

After the marina, we run up Indian Hill, and I remember ROTC trainings, obstacle courses, and morning runs at dawn. The blue crack crosses the horizon once again. I did it. I had made it. Finally, we end up back at the central field, circling it once more and entering our respective barracks. Then we await the next phase.

Rumors had been floating around about the general making an appearance today. It had been since the hazing pamphlets that I had seen him, the ones that promised to crack down on hazing. To be frank, his policies had accomplished nothing. Pieces of paper cannot change a tradition so meshed in the fabric of our school, a forgotten shadow cast by the leader over campus.

From Paxton to my treatment, the general was not doing a good job implementing his new agenda, so this speech was highly anticipated. I had escaped hazing this second semester to become the one who hazed and harmed. This tacit agreement with MacConough shaped my first year.

MacConough, while we hadn't spoken of our agreement since first semester, seemed fully content by how it had worked out. He said some candid words that night: "Steve, you've grown into one of my comrades here," he had said. "You aren't just an idiot freshman like the rest of them. I hope you know that. I wonder if down the road we'll meet again at some point."

"Sir, thank you, sir. I feel the same, sir," I respond.

"Well, I guess I should be back and visit at some point next year," he said.

"Where are you headed?"

"Up North. Grad school," he said.

"You guys better fucking visit, man! Don't leave me hanging in this town for too long by myself," Petersson said. "You too, Nicky."

"You'll be fine, Petey," Mac said.

"Where are you going, sir?" I asked Nicky.

"Out West, baby, the Golden Coast."

"For what, sir?"

"What do you think? Do you know me at all, Wiggs? Acting! You're going to see me on posters before the next time we actually see each other," he said to them.

"I'm envious," Warren brooded. "I'd like my life plan to commence as well."

"Sir?"

"Because of my absence, the academy is requiring me to do another semester," he said and shuffled in his chair, catching everyone's attention in the room. "Sorry, but there's something I need to say. I think your class is going to be in a lot of trouble."

"Why is that?" I said.

"This oughta be good," Petersson quipped.

"Well, let me take a stab at it," Warren said, adjusting his watch. "Back when we were first years, the upperclassmen came at us with the same intensity as we did to you. They told us, 'Do it this way.' They didn't reward us. It was just the way to do it. And even if you two hate to admit it," he said, referring to Nicky and MacConough, "we were overwhelmed. But we kept going at the upperclassmen.

"You see, the rules have changed dramatically in our tenure here. We found each other and stuck together because we all excelled at stressing the upperclassmen out, at pissing them off in new ways. It was easy for each of us, and we reveled in the success at going at them. Then the media started stabbing the academy. I went home on breaks to a series of articles illuminating the world how things happen here.

"The general has been taking a lot of flack for not updating the academy with the shift in society, so he eased up. And, Steve, look at your class. You have students writing bulletins, spreading slander. You have the general frightened for his career and issuing all types of restrictive agendas. The natural order is shifting. The eighties, when you all become the ones in charge, is going to be something of a wake-up call. You have a bunch of cadets trying to change the rules with cowardice and by going around them rather than by challenging them." Warren shook his head. This was the most I had ever heard him say.

"It's personal. They ruined my reputation. They ruined my four-year plan. At the bottom of the food chain, there are serpents, and they managed to jump up and bite me. I was courteous, safe this year, but if any of them try that next year, they will pay," Warren said. He shifted his glasses. "Of course, Steve, I don't consider you like them. You're different. MacConough advocated for you, and I can see why."

"Boy, when you stood up to me," Petersson said, "I wanted to wring your neck. I still could too." He laughed. "But even then, I wouldn't be convinced that'd keep you down." For a moment, I couldn't breathe. My eyes darted across the table to MacConough, who severed the tension with a comedic wink.

"Maybe it's a shift in society. Look at this matchup coming to fruition." Warren pointed at the screen. Two promising basketball players, Magic Johnson and Larry Bird, respectively led their teams to the finals of the NCAA tournament this year.

"What's your point?" MacConough said.

"Both of these boys are Steve's age, and they aren't playing the same game that we knew. The game has changed now." We watched a highlight of Magic throwing a no-look pass to his teammate.

*****

After a quiet and steady breakfast, my fellow cadets were racked by upperclassmen while I ate Cheerios. We split back into squads and entered a classroom labeled "Phase 2: The Leadership Experience. As I walked toward the class, my thoughts continued to trail back to the night before.

I walk into a classroom and scan for familiar faces. Randall is up front with a couple of others, and Simon sits over toward the side. They sit me in the first open seat. I fiddle with my pen to try and stay in the moment. The guest speaker is introduced as a former cadet and sergeant of the academy. He smiles as he and the current sergeants exchange small talk at the front of the classroom.

His eyebrows slope inward as if he is always directing other people's attention toward an important fact. This is a step above Warren and Petersson and Nicky. Only MacConough has the offer to become like him. I watch his sharp movements, perfect posture, and refined nature just during the course of a mundane activity. We sit in silence.

The former squad sergeant had broad shoulders and a commanding smile that spread throughout the classroom. He looked as if he had continued a rigorous exercise program after the academy as his thick neck and forearms extended a hello.

"What does Recognition Day truly signify? What does it embody?" He paused. "Recognition Day is the verification of your work, period. Today, we will be grappling with some higher concepts. But in this space specifically, we'll be talking about leadership. Leadership, as you know, is one of the guiding principles of the academy. You've been raised under the supervision of such future leaders as these men here. At your age, some of their actions can seem harsh. But I assure you, there's a reason.

"They've instructed you with the foundation. Now that you've done the grunt work, we can show you the rest. Understood?" He paused. "Positive feedback, loyalty, optimism, setting a good example—these are all qualities of leading with which you will exit the academy. So we're going to have a little discussion about your next steps. How do you apply this foundation to whatever you want to accomplish in life?"

*****

"They discuss the exact same thing that they've been saying all year," MacConough started up again, "the things that we're told to get fired up at you about. But how does this make you become a leader, you know? The words don't correspond with what the cadets have been experiencing. Knobs get beaten up, then we tell 'em, 'All right, son, lead now,'" he said. "Apparently, it was even worse in the beginning of the seventies. You thought what we did was bad? Well, I heard of kids getting cut up and missing parts of toes, things like that."

Warren shakes his head in agreement. I look around. MacConough enters his brooding state where the depth of his eyes increase. "Sir, did any of that happen to you all?" I ask.

"Like I told you earlier, we were all Firos."

"So," I pause, "you did that to others," I say in a steely manner. The upperclassmen scan me to gauge how I feel, but I keep my brow low and my face unreadable.

"Being stoic gives you the capability to become a great leader," MacConough says, "the ability to accomplish and not speak out, to persevere without letting outside voices get to you. We do what we're told, and when it's over, then we can say, 'All right, this is how we're going to do it better.' You won't get anywhere unless you see it through. Do you get that, Steve?"

"Mid Mac, enough of this kind of talk. Are we going to get a game of cards in before we head out or what? Seriously, you guys need to cut all this melodramatic shit out," Petersson burst. The tension diffuses. Everyone starts laughing.

"Fine. Just trying to give our little Wiggs here some advice seeing as this is the last time we might all see him."

"You want some advice, Wiggins? The education of a man is never complete until he dies. Meaning, don't expect anyone to know more than you do, because tomorrow, we might all learn the same lesson."

Petersson shuffled cards while Nicky divvied chips, and finally, we began playing poker.

*****

The academy graduate's speech impressed our room. He seemed prepared, natural, and exuded an aura of success. The way he flowed from one talking point to another dwarfed any doubt if the academy graduates were the best in the country. After the leadership class, we switched back into our T-shirts and camouflage pants and returned outside for Phase 3: The Gauntlet.

An attack from above, the midmorning heat strikes us as we march outside. It is muggy with gusts that signal that a storm will come. In addition to the densely layered heat, the gauntlet is a tumultuous test of thirteen trials within an hour and a half. Each station has a teamwork building exercise with random members of our company. I take deep breaths as I jog toward my group, a group of cadets whom I may have seen around but don't know.

Around the periphery of the field, I see Corporals MacConough and Nicky goofing off, of course, and kicking a soccer ball. Immediately, I forget my worries and smile and carry this smile to the beginning of the first station. Tractor tires sink into the light-green grass. My squad is to pair up and flip the massive tires from one marker to another. This course uses a communal focus and effort, each cadet coming together in coordination to accomplish one thing. After a whistle, we are off.

The tire flip is an explosive exercise focusing on our legs, back, and shoulders to complete the flips. We huff and puff for each flip. The tires sound in a damp thud after a success. Foot by foot, we gain the lengths. My wrists and neck tighten. My forehead throbs. Then we finish. Relief but only for a moment, then the next exercise.

The second station was a crawl, which had us clamber on our backs for a quick yet cumbersome length. Our team stood, having each completed this individual exercise, and dashed toward the next station. The third station was similar to the first, combining team strength to accomplish one goal rather than explosiveness. This one focused on endurance and tenacity.

A large log lies on the grass as we line up. On a signal, we lift it. Oof. Then a fifty-meter shuffle, hup, hup, hup. My forearm and fingers throb through the exercise. Finally, we reach the end, let go, and are allowed to grab water. My heart speeds wildly as I look out over the field.

A hot gust of wind knocks the hat off an officer in the distance. I try to breath, put my hands on my head, but I am gassed. I give my teammates high fives to try and reangle my focus. Sweat rolls off my face toward the dried grass.

*****

"All right, everyone, I think it's time we head out," Petersson said after collecting from a winning hand. He took the deck of cards, tapped it on the table, and sat up.

"Yeah, you might be right," MacConough said as he checked his watch. A clock ticked, and the TV gave off a small amount of static, but MacConough silenced it with the remote.

"Uh-oh. Don't be scared, knob. You'll do fine," Nicky said.

But what is he referring to? Recognition Day? Gathering the chips, we put everything away and head back toward campus. As we leave the house, however, I notice we take a detour. In Charleston, the sidewalks stretch at night. The light on street corners gives the illusion that they are far more distant and difficult to reach.

We aren't headed toward the academy, I realize. I notice this as I walk in the front with Nicky. He blabs about when who-knows-what happened to him, how he is nervous too, how it's like losing your virginity because it isn't something you can practice for, though not that his first time didn't go well. It went great, and he digressed into his rambling.

"Sirs," I asked, "where are we going?"

A vast silence spread down the sunken street. Shrubbery and foliage in shade made the streets seem as if they had walls. No place to run. Now in my position, I could've freaked out. The remnants of Theodore Waters's story hung low in the air.

I trusted the upperclassmen, but walking through the silent darkness of Charleston backstreets along with the supposed murderers of Theo Waters could leave one prone to worries. But I wore my mask. It was completely on with no holes for air. It was the ultimate success that I didn't think of Theodore Waters, and instead, I marched along with my commanders.

"Just take a deep breath, Steve. It's all going to be all right," MacConough said.

I pay attention to my breath, then everything goes black, and I start hyperventilating.

*****

There was no comparable feeling to Recognition Day. It was a unified triumph in our abilities, the look of cadets bowed over in exhaustion, slapping one another on the backs, picking someone up if they had fallen. It was a unified exasperation on a muggy ninety-degree day. After each exercise, my hands grabbed for the back of my hip bones as sweat continued to slide off my face. "Water, water," the field team chirped across the field as we switched stations.

The next one was an interlocked exercise where we all linked arms and completed a set number of lunges. Nicky led this station. When I reached Nicky, he looked at me with his playful smirk. "C'mon, Wiggins. Not too tired now, are you? Ya punk. Get your ass interlocked."

I laugh, or I sort of cough, laugh, and gasp for air at the same time. It's an accident, but this turns into a gap in concentration. My group stumbles to the ground with me at the helm. My face turns toward the grass. I hear a whistle and heavy footsteps. A hulking sergeant paces over and grabs me by the neck of my shirt and pulls me up. I nearly choke.

"What's the matter? Are you okay, knob?" he asked as he scanned me for signs of heat exhaustion. "You feeling dizzy?"

"Sir, no, sir. Sorry, sir," I said.

He blew his whistle in my face, and I nodded to the rest of my squad. *I'm sorry.* The team went back to their interlocked position, this time for a length in an interlocked crawl. Our legs thrust over one another in push-up stance. We create a crab-like block and crawl toward the other side.

From my position, Nicky and I exchange glances. His palm covers his face in embarrassment, but he peeks through his fingers. I smile again. We make it halfway across. The palmetto ferns dance and along comes winds gusting across the field. With a renewed determination, altogether, we cross the finish line.

The sixth station has us complete super sets—push-ups, burpees, squats, mountain climbers, anything to punctuate the fact that we can never be fit enough for this day. Finishing the last one, I'm completely out of breath. I sit on the grass for a moment. A squad member bends over to help me up. As I stand, I feel light-headed, off balanced, weak.

We are halfway through the stations. Another water break and another batch of towels fly in our direction. *I can't catch it.* The towel lands on top of my face, and it takes me a few seconds to move my arms to wipe the sweat off my forehead and neck. I catch myself staring at my roommates from across the watering area. Harry and Clyde are laughing and joking about something, patting each other on the back. Then I feel a hand on my shoulder.

"Fuck, Wiggins. We going to make it outta this alive?" Simon said. I smiled and nodded but couldn't respond. "Damn, boy, they took the life outta you." He laughed. "C'mon, Wiggs, suck it up."

I leaned over, unequivocally out of breath. "I can't lie. This is hard," I managed to say.

He laughed. "I love it. You know what they say about the mighty."

To this, I change my face into a serious one. My breath evens. I look him in the eyes. "You want some of this, Louisiana?"

"There he is! Hang in there, bub. Save your dance moves for the summer." I wilt once more. I can't do it. "Here, Wiggs, don't think you're in this alone. That's the hardest weight to carry."

He hands me a cup full of water. We both start chugging. Dark clouds shift overhead like large jellyfish. A flash of lightning whips over the Charleston horizon. The grass changes from green to black, back to green, and then all of a sudden, it goes black permanently.

"Uh-oh. Look at that!"

A drop taps my nose, then a deluge commences. Something stirs within me.

*****

After about ten minutes of walking in silence, we must have arrived because we stopped, and I heard MacConough murmuring to a voice whom I can't place.

"Steps," Nicky warned.

We climb up a flight of stairs, and our boots begin to clack on whatever new domain we enter. They echo throughout the chamber of the room. The atmosphere is different, damp, cooler than outside. *This is just a normal, average day at the academy,* I think. It must've been at least ten minutes that we walk slowly through this cave or tavern. We stop, and Nicky rotates my shoulders to face someone.

"Welcome, Firos," a large voice echoed through the chamber. An unfriendly silence coated the space. It must've been a final test, or worse, we were repenting for our sins committed this year. A nerve sparked on the back of my neck and fell to my feet.

"Remove," he said.

I brace. Someone slips their hands underneath whatever was covering my face. It's tugged off, and something hard and all-encompassing slips underneath. It covers my face from chin to forehead: a mask. It is a mask, and I can only guess that it is the mask of Firos.

"Open your eyes and look around at your peers."

It was a shadow-filled chamber. Light emanated through stained glass windows above the ceiling, slanting into a half dome, which rose into darkness. One could only guess that the building was a church, or at least that it once was a church of the Holy City. Now it was empty, abandoned. Its original structure had been utilized for this piece of dramatics, though.

As the leader, whoever he was, he stood at the top of the steps, augmenting himself like the body of Christ. The setup reminded me a bit of Hell Night when the upperclassmen surrounded us and Dorchester stood above in a light, seemingly separated from us.

The Firoses stood in a large circle. There were about fourteen, fifteen, or sixteen of us, and we all had unique masks on. One was a court jester with white skin and red cheeks while another was a jack-o'-lantern, and one looked strangely similar to President Nixon. I could only imagine that mine was the blood-red Chinese mask that I had racked cadets in earlier this year.

"You have been chosen as the next representatives of our cadre." This was recognition. "Forty-one, forty-two, forty-three," a voice chanted. "Throughout the next three years, you will receive gifts. These gifts are rewards for enforcing our way." Forty-nine, fifty, fifty-one.

*****

The quadrangle is flooded. Our hands, our hair, and our uniforms are soaked. We complete push-ups, but I can't seem to stay focused on this exercise. Had this night just been a dream? That's definitely what it feels like. I don't enjoy being dragged out of the moment, but the events that unfolded yesterday were too much, starting with each of the different masks and the christening ceremony inducting us into the association.

"Come on, cadets! Keep the pace. This is the last push!"

A final class set, okay, time to stay in the present. We were to complete this final class set to demonstrate to the rest of the academy that we made it, that we had arrived. I needed to be here and now.

*****

"Sixty-six, sixty-seven, sixty-eight."

With the ceremony completed, I now represented Firos. "Eighty, eighty-one, eighty-two!"

*****

When we finish the push-ups, instead of collapsing as we did on Parent's Day, we stood, and we saluted our officer, Lieutenant Dorchester. I heard a salute from Dorchester himself, and then, "Class of '82, the fourth class system is now over!"

Suddenly, it was as if the entire campus was at ease. Various upperclassmen—some who had mocked me, others whom I had seen in passing, and several who had racked me earlier in the year—walked up and shook my hand. Everyone smiled, laughed, and patted us on the back of our sweat-soaked uniforms.

The odor of grilled ground beef and sweat rose from the barracks. The heat persisted, and large water jugs were dragged out to the quad. This was the first time that I had seen smiles on the quad. These red-and-white squares that had encapsulated pain and discipline had turned into the grounds for a barbecue. High-ranked officers with their brims tucked low, with their uniforms emblazoned with badges, stomp through the sally port, and in the center of them all comes the general.

The general walked toward the center, and everyone silenced. He began. "Class of 1982, it has been a privilege to accompany you through your knob year, especially as this marks a pivotal year in my life." He paused. "President Carter has called me to his office. Thus, I will be stepping down as general of the academy. I wanted to have a chance to speak to you on this because, in earnest, it was a pleasure serving all of you fine students."

A sudden fervor broke out among the cadets. I couldn't believe it. While the terrain of the academy had shifted this year, America's footing in the world had shifted more. Either Theodore Waters's death, the suspected murder of yet another black man, had finally caught hold or it just was a sign of the eighties. The academy, the last bastion of continuity, had been slipping and now would fall into an abrupt change.

"So I'd like to announce that at the academy, each year, we like to recognize students for exceptional work ethic and discipline. This list is comprised of your peers who took the extra steps during training and who demonstrated unwavering attitude in the face of adversity. Without further ado..."

*****

After the Firos ceremony, the upperclassmen and I walk back to campus together. My anxieties have lifted, and the dark backstreets of Charleston finally feel comfortable. Churning with jet-black thoughts, night walks down alleys always feel as if something is lurking around the corner, out of sight.

I never knew what was in the minds of the upperclassmen and what the night could bring along with it. Now it felt as if a mystery had run its course, and I had grown into someone affected by that mystery. MacConough put his arm around my shoulder and brazenly said, "Glad you poke your nose where you're not supposed to."

No one else knew what he meant by this, of course. Throughout our interactions, I had been the utmost formal and deliberate, because I had accidentally gone down the wrong hall and unknowingly knocked on the wrong door that this voyage set sail.

"Let's see, it's about 2:00 a.m.," MacConough said.

"Don't forget to watch the final march when we graduate," Nicky said.

I nodded. "C'mon, let's head back to that bar, the one where we got into the fight."

Nicky and MacConough gave me inquisitive looks, and I saw that Warren was surprised by my caprice.

"There he is," Petersson said.

*****

"Steven Wiggins!"

I blink rapidly, attempting to grasp my surroundings. Glare bounces off the ashen-colored barracks. I'm on the quadrangle again.

271

Several cadets turn toward me and applaud. Simon's hollering at the top of his lungs, and even Harry looks happy for me, and Clyde claps, though Randall doesn't turn.

"Zachary Williams."

I knew that I would receive honors. I had done well, admitted to the dean's list, and, well, there was MacConough. He had influenced this placement. Having my name called meant that I was to report to the barracks early next year and attend a special course. We would be paired as roommates and put on a fast track to leadership positions.

The general stepped down for the last time that day. He shook many hands. The knobs clapped and saluted. An era was over. And then the cookout began.

At the end of the day, becoming in my white uniform, alongside my schoolmates, we march down a vibrant proud parents-lined King Street. Each cadet wears a white cap and white boots and a rifle strapped across his white suit. This is the pinnacle of our knob year, and we dress as such.

Church steeples cast long shadows as the sun set over the Ashley. There had been glory in this day. Shop owners and families line the streets to watch. Each year, as a child, I had watched this scene from atop Arthur's shoulders before he went off to Vietnam that second time and alone while he was gone.

It's an awful thing to say that the act of war is what brings us together, but somehow, it's better to say that we're connected by the act of duty even if in duty we wage wars.

We reach Marion Square. Standing on the northwest corner, in the position where we had stood when I was a child, stands my father, Arthur, his bald head above the rest of the crowd. He sees me. He sees that I see him and, to my surprise, lifts Maisy into the air. She shoots a huge smile and waves emphatically. I turn back to the lines. We turn and enter the square, and I have one more chance to pass them. I see that Lorna is also there with the two, but my mom is absent.

CHAPTER 16

One Week—The Past Is Smaller than It Seems

Dead Week settles over campus, and I find myself deep in the library, buried in stacks of books. In the philosophy section, an isolated area where no one goes, I sit with a pile of papers, notes collected from the past semester. I sort my files and memorize different terms for finals, writing, underlining, and circling. Scanning my taxonomies, I procedurally move from one bullet to the next.

After an hour, I would stand up, mosey around, and look out the window for five minutes. Sometimes, my eyes would connect with other cadets, or I would see cadets with their face buried in their arms. I would look at the stacks of books, read the flap, and get a snack, anything to get a small break from studies.

The library fills with cadets working on group assignments, clacking out theses on typewriters, or napping. Some move in brisk manners through the lobby, engulfed in discussion, while others munch on chips, slurp soda, and chat. Last semester, when I worked with all my floor mates, talking shit and throwing questions at one another's way, was too much fun. This time around, it's a task, but I'm more efficient, getting in and out the front doors in just hours and at a decent hour for sleep.

One night during Dead Week, a particular book, a red leather-bound book, stands out on the shelf. The label reads *Stoicism, the Forgotten Ideals.* I nab it, slowly trace the spine, and open it. The book is about becoming a stoic, the philosophy behind our military training. I crease pages to start the text.

The canon of stoicism stems back to Greece. It began and came about at around the same epoch as Epicureanism. While the two philosophies search for the same answers, they come to very different conclusions. In the beginning of the book, there is a definition of the stoic's true goal: apatheia, or freedom from passion. Apatheia does not refer to passion in the sense of an affinity to art or culture like we colloquially know it in the United States but in the sense of an intense judgment when subject to stimulus.

They define freedom from fear not as what I would think but perhaps as what I used to do, "the overbearing sense that an event will be worse than rationally possible." At the beginning of the year, I overstrategized and thought of several solutions in order to escape a large, unending fear. In the eyes of a stoic, this is a falsehood.

Stoics can still feel fear, but it is defined in a rational sense or as a caution. A cadet's practice of bracing is a caution because you prepare for just the unseen and not the worst. The mask of the soldier can be seen as the ultimate triumph for the stoic because it prepares you for the unseen as it will for all circumstances even if they are circumstances full of gravitas and brutality.

I take this thought along with me into finals. I prepare in a rational sense, unfazed by the possibilities of tricks or obscure questions, and instead, I divulge my full attention to the topics that we have covered. As soon as finals begin, in a whirlwind, they pass. One after another, I stay up late, prepare, fall asleep exhausted, and wake up to complete the final.

My anxiety disappears. Whether I'm successful or not isn't a thought. It's just an outcome from the adequate preparation. A smile forms on my face that Friday as I turn in the last final. I run through the halls, unable to contain it, exit the doors, and lie down in the grass.

The light-blue sky is immense. The wind whistles through the blades. The heat presses you to the grass. At this time, no officer yells or upperclassman spits on me. They are gone, focusing on their upcoming graduation. I am no longer a knob, and they, the seniors, are no longer at the academy.

> Oh, —— we sing thy fame
> For all the world to hear,
> And in the paths our fathers showed us follow without fear.
> Peace and Honor, God and Country, We will fight for thee. Oh, —— we praise thee now, And in Eternity.
> Oh, —— though strife surrounds us, We will ever be, Full conscious of the benefits that we derive from thee.
> Stand forever, yielding never, To the tyrant's Hell
> We'll never cease our struggles for Our mighty ——.

The final weekend is a notorious event for all remaining students of the academy. On the Atlantic coast, the upperclassmen rent a large beach house in Folly Beach where they host a bit of a year-end morale boost for the knobs. The upperclassmen set up kegs of beer, barbecue, sports, and the knob's favorite event, sophomore payback. It is a one-on-one wrestling match in the sand where a freshman singles out a sophomore to challenge them to a beatdown.

To my surprise, our ROTC leader, McDougall, separates himself from the crowd to referee the match. "All right, boys," he says with a toothpick in his mouth and sleeves rolled up to his elbows. "Who's gonna deliver some payback today, huh? Let's make this thing count. Of course, anyone's fair game, even me. Wrestle until someone submits by saying, 'I give.' Winner grabs a beer for the loser so as no hard feelings. Up first, who do we have?"

Simon walks into the circle. He mimics a cowboy with a lasso jumping around as cadets chuckle at his display. "Gimme this guy here. Yeah, you, the one who threw the rack party for my birthday. Don't be scared now, boy. I see you."

"Get him, Louisiana!" I yell.

"Calm these guys down," the sophomore said.

Several cadets look my way and wait for the sophomore to step into the circle. Finally, he does. The sophomore, buzz cut with a pretty boy demeanor, steps up to Simon. He must be a half foot taller because Simon's head barely reaches the guy's nose. They center their gravity. Simon hops from one foot to another like he is square dancing, and to this, the sophomore thumps his chest. I'm worried for Simon. He, however, doesn't show this same feeling. This guy not only is bigger but looks much stronger than Simon, but Louisiana wears his same smirk.

"Ready? Go!"

Simon strikes first and leaps toward him like a madman, attempting to use his opponent's height as a weakness. He sweeps at the legs. The other cadet is quicker than that. He sidesteps the strike and thrusts an arm bar back into Simon's chest. It slides up, locking under his chin. For a moment, they struggle, but then Simon steps back to reangle his attack. He puts his hands on his knees as if he was tired. I know him better than that.

This time, the sophomore strikes. He manages to plant both hands on Simon, digging him into the dirt. Several knobs look worried. This is not a good way to start the event. The pressure causes Simon's feet to dig in the sand, being pushed backward, but Simon uses the cadet's pressure against him.

In one move, he slips from the upperclassman's hands and circles to dive toward his legs. He wraps them with both arms. In a huge feat of strength, he flings the guy to the ground like tackling a goat. The upperclassman flails his arms, attempting to stand, but it's too late. Simon has him in submission.

"Right, right," McDougall said. "That's enough."

Simon stood, chugging like a freighter. "Got him," he said.

"Attaboy. I'll get a beer with ya," I said.

"Yeah," he said, panting. "Gimme a minute."

I watched Louisiana leave the circle and sit on a log. From what I had heard from him, he hadn't done exceptionally in his ROTC squadron and really hadn't kept his head above water in academics, so this would leave my buddy Louisiana in the middle of the class in terms of scores.

This surprised me, but at the same time, it didn't seem like the guy attended the same school as the rest of us. He always formulated his own agenda, walked his own path, which only he knew, and somehow got away with. He never complained about racks being too difficult or the upperclassmen. Louisiana hadn't found his audience yet, but I knew he would.

A couple of rounds of wrestling played out. A knob from a different company had a high school state championship for wrestling in his past. He was a small, stocky guy with agile movements and a ridiculous flexibility. The sophomore he called out talked big, thrashed around, kicked sand in our faces, and ended up with his own face full of sand. The knob swept his leg and knocked him off his feet once more and then pounced and put him into submission. The sophomore admitted defeat as he huffed and left the circle with cuts and bruises.

I decided to grab a beer and a hot dog. Walking toward the BBQ, I heard, "Can we challenge a fellow freshman?"

"Oh, now that's an interesting proposition," McDougall said.

"I want to challenge Firos," I heard, and I turned. Randall stood on the inside of the circle, looking toward me. He had a huge smirk and said, "You just gave yourself up, Wiggs."

I'm not in the mood to participate, but I suppose now I have no choice. I walk toward the circle like a pariah. Clyde and Harry look at me as I pass the mob to the middle of the circle. "Sir, do you endorse this challenge, sir?" I say to McDougall in a serious, unbreakable glance, completely disregarding Randall.

"Wiggs, I guess that's up to you," he says.

I turn and look at Randall. His smirk disappears. His confidence falters. "I accept, Randall," I say, and as I say this, I recall my comrades—MacConough, Nicky, Warren, and Petersson, especially Petey. "Let's have some fun with this. How about we put a wager on it?" I say. Then I wind my arm around and stretch my legs as if mimicking Petersson.

"Like what?"

"Loser shotguns both beers?" I said.

"Fuck that. Drop the act, Steve," Randall yelled.

"Look at the boy. He's scared, shaking in his flip-flops," I said, mimicking Nicky. *This is fun.* "I mean, c'mon, Randall, what act? What act? You're the one with the tough guy act calling out Firos.

Yeah, right, big man. Takes a lot to jump to conclusions. Takes a big man to jump to conclusions," I said and started chuckling.

"Sir," Randall said.

"Go ahead, boys. I ain't stopping you," he said.

Randall grunts as if trying to regain focus. "C'mon, let me hear something!" he yells, and the knobs erupt in a chant surrounding him. He gets into a more centered stance. I look around the circle. Almost everyone is chanting, "Randall! Randall!" Then I see Gin and others from my ROTC squad watching with curiosity.

I squat down and dig a small hole in the sand. This perturbs Randall. "What the hell are you doing, Steve?" he yells.

"Attaboy, Steve. That beer you wanted is waiting for ya," I hear Simon yell.

"Beat that nigger up!" I hear.

I finish my hole and stand up. Secretly, I'm imitating Warren, though only those who know him well know of his enigmatic nature. Suddenly, Randall leaps at me. I move out of his way, two side steps, and shift my position so that I'm facing him like a boxer. He keeps going and circles around.

Closing in, he manages to get a hand on my arm, but I whisk it free. He's strong, I think, as it takes a bit to break my arm free. One of the qualities I admire in Randall even from the beginning is, even though he has shortcuts, he still works as hard as anyone else.

The chanting dies down, and it seems the other cadets are as invested in this face-off as we are. This time, Randall manages to grab my right arm with both hands, putting it into a locked position. His move is textbook. After submitting my arm, he'll toss me to the ground. For a normal person, being off balance like this would be devastating. It would be considered a win. I know better than that.

He throws me to the ground, and I hit the sand with my back. *Thud.* Instantly, I use my left leg to propel myself into a roll and back to a push-up position. He quickly realizes that I'm escaping his move and dives at me, trying to finish the job. I roll again and grab him as he bullets toward me. Tangled up, I manage to put his head into a headlock. For a moment, we struggle.

It's tense. My arms become fatigued as his legs thrash against the sand. He throws a dull elbow, which catches me in the face, as we rock a bit. Then shifting my weight, I roll once more, this time with him wrapped up, and I stand. I win.

Randall's face lies in the hole that I originally dug. He does a push-up. "Fucking asshole," I hear him murmur. I reach out a hand to him. He takes it, and I pull him up, the signature MacConough mercy. We look each other in the eyes for a moment.

"Beer coming your way," I tell him and walk out of the circle. Gin gives me a nod as I walk off. I grab Simon to get a couple of beers.

"Thanks, man," I say to him.

After handing Randall a beer, the moment finds me by the shore. Critters buzz, spinning around my head and leaving my proximity. My feet dig into the damp off-white sand. The shore is a bit breezy, and midsized waves swell and crash onto the coastline.

A bite of my hot dog—extra ketchup and extra char-grilled—reminds me of family barbecues and how the hot dogs were always a little overdone. I look down the shimmering coast. I could walk all the way down the peninsula, all the way to the edge of everything.

Someone plops down next to me. I turn. It's Harry. "Steve," he says.

"Hey, man," I respond.

"I want to apologize for how we… I don't know. I feel like we alienated you toward the end there." I look at him, say nothing, and look back at the coast. "When you told me that I should consider there being a reason you were Firos, it changed the way I saw it. It just felt like betrayal, and that's what I saw it as at first.

"But it's true that you'd have no reason to betray us out of thin air like that, especially considering how much you helped me and Clyde out the first semester. All of these nights, I've been thinking about that, how the academy pushes you together and pulls you apart. It's brutal, but in the end, we're all the same.

"Even though we may have had different results on our exams or ROTC or, shit, raised differently, we're all similar in that we made it through this fucking year. I hope that we can put it past us and keep in touch over the summer. Maybe you can visit my lake house."

For a moment, there was silence, and then I spoke. "How's Claire? You still together?"

He chuckled. "Yeah, Steve, we are. I even convinced her to come up for the Fourth of July. My mom is going to freak out when I tell her."

"That's good. Good to hear that." I nodded.

"How about you? Anything with Miranda?"

"Actually, she's studying abroad this semester."

"What? Really?"

"Yeah, and that reminds me."

"Of what?"

"She should be getting back. I need to contact her when I get home." I look back toward the camp. Wrestling matches are still taking place.

"You beat the hell out of Randall." Harry laughs.

"He got a good move in on me," I say and look toward him. "Look at you, man. Did you challenge anyone? I'm sure you could take anyone."

"Ah, I'm not really feeling like it."

"After all the rackings and shit throughout the year?"

He laughed. "I've learned to live with that."

"Learn to live with it, Harry, or learn from it," I said and then winked. "I think JFK said that. Show the sophomores you made it and that now you guys are equals," I said. "I'm going to go take a walk, all right? I'll be back in a few."

"By all means," Harry responded as I stood.

The sea breeze and surf brushes over me in a turbulent spray. Seabirds hop from one location to the next as the wake scours across the sand, leaving it crystalline in the sun. I pass families on vacation, who lie under beach umbrellas or sprawled out among vibrant blue and orange blankets. A few eye me as if I'm up to no good, but nothing is on my mind except the sensation of it all. Lo, how inviting, the sensation of warm air and cold water, the two contrasting, damp sand and an endless sandbar for one to walk.

To Charleston natives, the peninsula is called the End of America. It's a twelve-and-a-half-mile stretch of sand that extends upward into summer houses and outward into the sea. This drag of coast defies anything of the rational world and rather embodies the mythic size of the past.

The point at which I had started was beyond visibility. The farthest I could see ahead was a bend where a lighthouse stretched into the water, its beacon turned toward the Atlantic. Dragging my feet in the sand, I head toward it. Its robust stature grew before my eyes, towering over the ocean.

The white lighthouse, with its stone cloister reaching from the sand to the sea, has a narrow inlet of metal stairs. Without a thought, I find myself making my way to the bottom of them, looking up, then ascending. One by one, I climb as the wind increases.

The narrow spiral clings to the body of the lighthouse and leads to a viewpoint where I assume you can see across the ocean. As I reach the top, instead, I see a deep blue with white caps. I hear something amid the winds, churning, calling me, pulling me forward. My eyes widen.

The winds rise. Off in the distance, a huge wave forms, and it's not too distant now. Seconds pass, and it nears the lighthouse. I brace for impact. The crest of the wave crashes upward, engulfing the landing with water. The wave slams me into the body of the white lighthouse. My arms tremble. My shirt and face are wet from sea spray.

I breathe deeply. *What am I doing up here?* Fear for my life isn't how I would describe this situation with my back against the mast of the lighthouse, but I do feel a rush that I haven't felt in a long time. Something washes over me, something new.

I look toward the stairs, but they are slick and covered in residual surf. I see another wave form on the near horizon. The sun's glare coats the first step, luring me forward. In a swift movement, I skip down each stair—hup, hup, hup, hup, like in ROTC training—and dive across the last few steps and onto solid ground. When I reach the tract of land where sand turns to grass, I stop and grasp at the blades.

The cadets weren't here. If the wave had been a few feet taller and I were swept out to sea, hours would pass before someone notices. As grand and encompassing as the academy was these past months, there was always something immediately larger, more sturdy, and more vital to this world. The academy is only the academy.

I turned to see a man walking up. He was raggedy with a huge beard, his shirt sea-worn and unbuttoned. "What the hell were you doing up there? I saw the whole scene. Didn't you hear me yelling at you to come down? There are a lot of waves at this time of the year."

"I don't know what I was thinking, sir. I apologize for worrying you," I replied.

"Well, you best get back to where you came from. These things ain't no joke. You can't be fooling around like that by yourself."

"Sorry, sir. Yes, I'll make my way back. I don't know what I was thinking."

On the walk back, I thought about what had just happened. It felt like I was touched by the divine. As I approached the beach house, I noticed all the ruckus that they were making. McDougall was leading the cadets in jodies, and they were singing like a bunch of drunk shipmates lost at sea.

"Okay! Okay, cadets! And the winner for the most valuable teammate of the ROTC scrimmage goes to Gin, you Asian son of a bitch you. Come here!" I see Gin mope toward the center of the circle in his reticent manner. The cadets clap and hoot.

"This squadron that I led with Gin at the helm won the most matchups, so I declare that each of you get to fill two beers, one that you give to someone to chug and the other to pour down their knickers without any reciprocation," McDougall yelled. He was clearly drunk too.

"Sir, can we drink our own beers too?" Gin asked.

"Chug along, good sir," he said.

Gin looked over to me, and I gave him a look. Then I found my other comrades, and we headed toward the keg to pour beers. I took both of mine and walked up to a person who needed one. It was Clyde.

"Here you go," I said.

"Steve," he said, nodded, and took his cup. We stood in an awkward silence while the other cadets yelled and cheered and chugged their beers.

"Well, cheers, Clyde," I said. He nodded again. "How are things? You looking forward to getting back?"

"Yeah, of course I am, Steve."

I looked him square in the eyes. "How's your mom?"

He looks at me. His eyes soften. I remember my breath, and in consequence, I am reminded of the rest of the beautiful wooded scenery that surrounds my once friend's face. It's not just us. We exchange a glance, the same as that rainy day at the end of our tours. Resentment no longer exists between us, but he doesn't respect me, and he doesn't trust me. And despite all that happened, I've forgiven him.

"She'll be all right," he says. "Anyway, thanks."

With that, he walks off. Simon walks up and passes me a cup of something that surely isn't beer. I take a swig and immediately feel it. We start singing jodies at the top of our lungs. I motion for Gin to come over, and I throw my arm over him. We light a raging fire. It burns through the night as we sing jodies, play games, and exchange stories until the faint blue line crosses the Atlantic and awakens us to the last burning embers in the wee hours of the morning.

*****

Horns float across campus. A distant tune, one of accomplishment and valor, swells as the knobs complete their final cleanup duties. Much like the janitorial duty, we are in charge of closing campus for the year. We replace all trash bags, mop the bathroom floors, and make sure our rooms are devoid of any outside material. We complete this task in silence, perhaps in thought or a tacit respect for the graduation ceremony as it proceeds.

When the horns finish, a muffled voice speaks over a loudspeaker. An applause, then it's the loudspeaker again. It is a beautiful day outside, mideighties and rising. The sun emboldens the freshly cleaned floors. A vibrant blue sweeps over the skies. Looking out for a moment, I see a plane pass, breaking the limpid blue, either landing here in the water or heading down to Florida.

The seniors must be in full uniform. I can picture MacConough and Petersson patting each other on the back when accepting achievements or, even worse, goofing off during graduation. Something else is audible. The guitar riff of "Sweet Home Alabama" reverberates down the empty hallways. Radios aren't allowed, so a fourth year must've struck up the nerve because of we're no longer watched over.

As we continue cleaning, the shadows of the room shift. Sun pours in, and it was a bright, hot day in Charleston. "Damn near feels like the devil's ballroom," I recall someone saying of the quad in the middle months. "If it weren't for the sea and the steeples blocking us from the sun, we'd have a real problem in Charleston."

I hear a distant gunshot rumbling in the distance and then another closely followed from a different origin. Glancing out of the windows, I see parents emptying the arena and walking over toward the main campus. The ceremony is over.

I peer out of his room into the hallway, and cadets are descending the stairs to watch the seniors stride off into the abyss. With the rumbling of footsteps, we run over the quad and through the sally port to the center field. Parents line the borders of the vast field to watch.

MacConough, Petersson, Nicky, and Warren—wait, Corporal Warren isn't graduating. He must be here on the outside like the rest of us. Isolated, standing on the side of the barracks, is the medium-build Warren in civilian clothes. He has on a classic white polo, khaki pants, and a woven belt. Adjusting his glasses, he smiles and watches quietly.

"Sir, have you seen any of 'em?"

"Hey, Steve. Yeah, they're there, ten from the left, three rows back. Squint because the sun is doing a number right now."

I squint and make out Petersson, the tallest of the bunch, then the two others. Their faces are devoid of their character as they march across the field. It takes resistance to hold back my emotions. I feel a clenching in my chest, something hot rising like water funneling through an espresso machine. They pass beyond the borders of the field. Then the grass is empty, quivering in the wind.

"That was something, sir," I say.

He looks at me with a smile. The glare strikes the frames of his glasses. A setting sun is visible in place of his eyes. "Yes, it is, Steve."

"That'll be you next year," I said.

Suddenly, his smile vanishes. "Yes. Hey, Steve. I know what you did for MacConough. I know what secrets you kept for him," he says. My smile shifts. I give him an austere face. "Next fall, I'm going to graduate. There will be no discussions and no further investigations about Theodore Waters anymore, Steve. Do I make myself clear? You are not to say anything."

I took a deep breath and stared beyond his glasses into his limpid, lifeless eyes. "Sir, with the departure of the general, that discussion next year is imminent. I'm afraid it's not up to me."

He shifted his eyeglasses. "I suppose that's true, but we can all play our part to keep this place the way it's supposed to be."

"Well, for now, what do we do?"

"Wait. Just wait until next year. Have a good summer, Steve."

We part ways with a looming silence between us. He is right, there is nothing I can do except wait until next year. It never ends. Next year, I will have to stomp out wildfires; but for now, summer spreads before me.

I walk back into the barracks, and we complete a final survey. The shuffling of steps in the halls, the shutting of doors, each of the cadets grabs his backpacks, boxes, or duffle bags and brings them down to the entrance. Many say farewells. Others run to freedom. And when the last cadet takes a sentimental glance at the barracks and leaves, the halls are silent once again.

Epilogue
One Hour

The drone of cicadas greet me. I step out of the car that Friday afternoon in West Ashley. Yelling goodbye, I snag my belongings and turn toward my house. Summer have already extended its full reach over Southern United States in a way where every aspect of life tells you of the season. The trees dress differently with Spanish moss draped from the long magnolia branches. The air smells unique. An aroma of barbecues carries as you bike down the dry, sunken streets.

Restaurants switch to their summer menus, and the streets look different with outdoor seating areas covered by colorful large umbrellas. I've never been to New York, nor have I been San Francisco, but I would be surprised if there is another city dressed as well as Charleston in the summer.

The door is already open. "I'm home." Three months—I have three long months of summer break ahead of me and three months at home. On my final return from the academy, the glare from the sun illuminates my little sister Lorna's face in a way that makes her look angelic, and sunshine spills behind her into the hallway like God herself parting the pearly gates.

Standing with my clothes, my uniform, and my gear in a massive duffle bag in my right hand and my essentials in a small pack slung over my left shoulder, I stepped into the house. It was a sweltering day in May. Sweat gathered on my brow and also where the strap lay across my shoulder, but the inside of my childhood home felt cool. The blue tones that composed the interior of our house had never seemed as essential.

Stepping into the foyer, I embrace both sisters and then walk toward the guest room to drop my bags and unpack. Neither my father nor my mother is present. I pass the kitchen and notice its stillness. *What could they be doing?* Opening the door, a small plume of light shines through the side window. I open the curtain, but still, it doesn't light the room, so I'm forced to turn the light on to see what I'm doing. I put that thought to the side to focus on my folding. I roll my socks, quarter my boxers, and square my shirts.

When I finish removing each item and hanging them in the small closet or placing them in my bureau, I flip off the light, sit on the bed, and ponder what to do next. I wonder what my mother and father are doing. My mother, Loretta, was absent from the ceremony at Recognition Day. I hadn't thought about its significance then, but it had mattered. It does matter. It cuts deep that my own mother wasn't present. And once again, on my return, she's not here. I had looked past it at the time, but now I cannot. She's not here.

I lie in bed not embraced in the arms of my mother, who raised us singlehandedly for many years, but tangled in the midst of her obstinate promise, of her silent distance and disapproval. Maybe that's not the truth. Maybe it is my failure to keep a promise, my responsibility.

Childhood has gone. A child can be forgiven, but adults have consequences to their actions. Suddenly, a question dawns on me, and it does so with such intense gravitas that I have to say it out loud. "Can I fix this?" I gasp.

And what of my father, Sergeant Arthur Wiggins? I thought he would be here on my return. This again shows the magnitude of difference in our experience. His return from duty had been massive to the family and the community, but my return feels as if its importance doesn't reach further than myself. It's deflating.

Like MacConough had said, "Recognition Day is a glance across a vast battlefield of experience." However, the vast battlefield is still there, and I must still mush across it. The shadow of my father is still upon me, and it covers me like the dense darkness of this room and the silent stillness of this house. I want to relax, to unwind, but life doesn't pause just because it's summer.

Has Lorna asked them to have a family dinner like old times? I wonder. Has she told them about Yale? It's as if someone uncorked a pungent bottle of alcohol, and now its dank smell engulfs the room. It's inescapable and all-encompassing. Has Miranda returned from studying abroad? I suppose I should call her and confess how I feel— how I feel about us and how I feel for someone else. But how do I feel? It's impossible to quantify. At the academy, I neglected these thoughts. No, either I neglected them, I was too preoccupied, or they didn't exist.

What are MacConough and the boys doing after graduation? I miss them. I miss MacConough and wish I can have some guidance right now. I can picture Sergeant Edwards's moon-shaped face, Lieutenant Dorchester's vein, the general's slick salt-and-pepper haircut, McDougall's toothpick, Nicky, Petersson, Warren, and most of all, MacConough. The upperclassmen are probably on a boat somewhere, partying. Either that or they are already on a plane to their next lives. I feel that I need them. Without them, I have no superpower. I am fraudulent and certainly no hero.

My last time home, this had happened too. Absent are the rigors of training and the scruples of surveillance. My mind is wandering uncontrollably. It's fluttering around porch light. I try to catch it, and once again, I breathe deeply. I exhale. Everything becomes quiet again. It is pitch-black, a blackness of a South Carolinian night or the depth of the violent leagues under the ocean. Then in the stark silence, I hear a voice.

"I'm going to tell you something that I've never told anyone before," I hear MacConough say.

"Sir," I say as my eyes open. "What is it, sir?" Through the curtains of the dark room, slim slits of light shine. I had been sleeping, napping, something I hadn't done all year. *Thump, thump, thump.* I hear one of my sisters run down the steps just above my head. *One hundred twenty paces per minute,* I think. As I lie there thinking this while staring up at the black ceiling, I realize it has only been a year.

"Steven?" I hear my mother say. I lurch forward, dig around in my bag, and pull something out. Standing up, I put on a mask.

About the Author

James Wigfall is currently the chief executive officer for Sound Generations, a nonprofit organization providing food security, transportation, health and wellness, and assistance services to older adults and adults with disabilities. He graduated in 1982 with a degree in Mathematics from The Citadel, a military college located in Charleston, South Carolina. After college, he served for four years in the US Army and was honorably discharged in 1986 as captain in the Signal Corps in Augusta, Georgia.

After leaving the military, James joined The Boeing Company in June 1986. He started out as a computer programmer, then progressed through various levels of management. He retired in December 2017 as the vice president of business support to Boeing Commercial Airplanes.

Outside of work, James serves on the boards of King County Library System Foundation and on the advisory boards for the Baker School of Business and The Citadel Foundation. He lives in the Puget Sound area of Washington.

CPSIA information can be obtained
at www.ICGtesting.com
Printed in the USA
LVHW050455031121
702295LV00001B/15